CENSORETTES

Stonehouse Publishing Inc. is an independent
publishing house, incorporated in 2014.

Cover design and layout by Anne Brown.
Printed in Canada

Stonehouse Publishing would like to thank and acknowledge
the support of the Alberta Government funding for the arts,
through the Alberta Media Fund.

Government

National Library of Canada Cataloguing in Publication Data
Elizabeth Bales Frank
Censorettes
Novel, Second Edition
ISBN 978-1-988754-32-1

CENSORETTES

A novel by ELIZABETH BALES FRANK

PART ONE
CENSORETTES

01.

Bermuda, 1941

Lucy Barrett did not intend to spend the war in paradise. After her mother was killed in the Blitz, her father sent Lucy out of England, all the way to Bermuda, deaf to her pleas that there was no place of safety in this ever-growing war.

But Bermuda seemed determined to prove her wrong, this cossetted island of keen colours: coral beaches, sunsets, pastel-painted limestone houses bearing up rain-scrubbed white roofs. Lucy walked under a placid sky unburdened by barrage balloons, bomber planes, or even the soot of industry or the exhaust of motor cars. The morning dew breezed away the brine as though the air, like Lucy, relied on a restorative wash to cleanse bad dreams and brave the new day. She departed from the resort hotel where the Censorettes were lodged, the Bermudiana, and walked a lonely slope with her roommate, Rebecca Lark, called Lark, to the resort hotel where they worked, the Princess Hotel. Hamilton was the only city on the island, and Princess, named for Louise, a daughter of Queen Victoria, had popularized Bermuda as a vacation spot when it had until then not been known for much except pirates and onions, smuggling and shipbuilding.

Now it was clip-clopped by one-horse carriages called *gharries*, or traversed by bicycles bearing pleasant clerks to their offices in downtown Hamilton: *good morning, good day*. Lucy's task, as a member of the Imperial Censorship Detachment, was to read letters in the Reading Room, a basement in the Princess Hotel. She had arrived in grey January. It was now March. Among the hundreds of letters she had read, she remembered only one clearly, written by a Joe in Brooklyn to an address in Bremerhaven, Germany. It had made an obscure reference to Shakespeare.

This March morning, Lucy read another letter from Joe. She pulled her blouse collar away from her sticky neck and re-read the letter:

The store caught the fire and burned down, but fortunately most of the goods were still in the wear house in Red Hook. The waiting is hard, but we must have the patience. The days are long and full of wonder. But remember the words of Romeo, 'Do nothing until you hear from me.'

Sincerely, Joe.

Another reference to Shakespeare. But this second letter was pocked with tiny bumps.

Lucy traced her fingers along the bumps. Was it Braille? Did it mean something? Did any of her work with the Detachment mean *anything*? The men of the Detachment boarded the ocean liners traveling between warring Europe and the neutral United States. They knocked down cabin walls, ripped open luggage, and seized contraband: funds, bonds, stolen artwork. They interrogated, threatened. They clapped potential saboteurs in handcuffs and hauled them into custody. The men of the Detachment did not read letters in a basement.

She raised the letter to her reading lamp to study the letter's indentations. The letter bowed toward her like a weak wave cresting. *"But remember the words of Romeo 'Do nothing until you hear from me.'"*

Someone's words, mayhap, Lucy thought, but not poor Romeo's. In Brooklyn Joe's first letter, he had referred to Shakespeare as the 'Swan of Avon,' rather than the 'Bard of Avon.' Although no one asked her to, Lucy had investigated the 'Swan' reference. It was a mystery she could try to solve, unlike the question of why her father had decided that this remote colonial outpost was the best use of the skills she had acquired after years of rigorous schooling. *Swan of Avon. Romeo. Wear house.*

On her Saturday half-days, she bicycled through the narrow lanes of Bermuda, past palmetto trees and hibiscus shrubs. First, she stopped at the Bermuda Library, a grand name for a large cottage with a small yard, enclosed by a stone wall. The full-time librarian had devoted a fruitless hour to the 'Swan of Avon' question before suggesting that Lucy interview the island's schoolteachers. Each teacher met her with civility, services of tea, and no insight beyond a suggestion of another resource. They sketched rough maps to guide her to her next destination, until Lucy knew the parishes of the fishhook-shaped islands better than the back of her hand. The back of her hand, actually, had tanned into a stranger's, despite the many pairs of white gloves Granny Barrett packed for her when it became manifest that Lucy could not escape her exile to Bermuda.

Lucy pedalled the island unenlightened, unimpressed. Bermuda's greatest casualty of war was the absence of tourists enjoying her slim beaches, rolling golf courses and discreet hotels.

Finally, Lucy returned to the Bermuda Library on the last Saturday of the month when, the librarian had told her, the cataloguer, Clara, came in to log the collection's new arrivals.

"Excuse me," Lucy had said to the back of a head of curls bent over a book, *The Constellations as Seen From the North Atlantic.*

"I'm told you might know, has Shakespeare ever been described as the 'swan of Avon'?"

"Funny you should ask." Clara was the first to find it amusing. Her curls framed a tawny face. "Ben Jonson called Shakespeare the 'sweet swan of Avon' in a eulogy published in the First Folio. There's a bit about the constellations later on in the eulogy." She gestured at her book.

"Why 'swan'?" The question had nothing to do with the case, but it seemed ages since anyone had taken Lucy seriously.

"The Greeks believed that the souls of poets set up house in swans after they died. You sound like you're from London. Have you ever seen one?"

"A Greek?"

"A First Folio," Clara said. "They've a few at the British Library. I used to dream of getting a job there. Small chance of it now, though."

"Yes. So, the *First Folio*? I suppose they're quite valuable."

"The last ones went for seven to ten thousand American dollars. I was at Smith at the time. Smith College," she explained, in response to Lucy's inquiring look. "One of the Seven Sisters."

"Seven Sisters." Lucy glanced at Clara's book. Constellations. *The Pleiades*?

"No, it's a nickname," Clara smiled. "For a group of women's colleges in the States. Anyhow. The First Folio. Only a hundred-odd copies still around."

Fewer still if the Luftwaffe hit the British Library. Was Brooklyn Joe a rare book dealer, flogging a First Folio to raise funds for the Nazis? Valuables were smuggled out of Europe all the time. The August before Lucy arrived in Hamilton, men from the Detachment had found a small art gallery behind a panel in a stateroom on the *SS Excalibur* of the American Export Line: canvases by Renoir, Cezanne, and Manet, confiscated by the Nazis from Jewish owners, headed to New York for sale.

Paintings were solid proof. 'Swan of Avon' was an errant phrase. When Lucy brought the first letter in to her supervisor, Colonel McKay, he had dismissed it. But now she had a second letter. And it had bumps.

She walked to McKay's office at the end of the reading room. McKay, the supervisor for Lucy's division, Encrypted in Plain, had lost a piece of his right leg and some movement on the left side of his face in the Great War. His workaday expression was one of bemusement, as though he wondered daily how his valour in the first apocalypse had brought him to a post shepherding a flock of women in the second one.

At her knock, he looked up. "Yes? Barrett? What's that?"

"Another letter from this man Joe from Brooklyn." When McKay responded with a palms-up shrug, Lucy elaborated, "I've flagged him before."

"One of the ten thousand letters which've passed through, you mean? Very well. Set it down and return to work. I'll call for you."

Lucy returned to her seat and continued reading. The letters from Europe: *Please send funds for our passage. They favour those with an essential trade. We must leave here, but no one will take us. So many countries have closed their borders. I am a welder. I am a carpenter. We have had no word of him since his arrest. We hope to make it to Lisbon.*

And the letters from the States: weddings, babies, christenings, although not always in that order. *What can you do? The young will be young.* Two months of reading felt like twenty generations, like a chapter from the Old Testament. *The Book of Tedium.* The naughty characters were more compelling than the good. But all of these escapades, however engaging, had to be quickly scanned if they did not involve Nazis or Nazi sympathizers.

And of the few useful responses from New York, none reached Europe if they came through the hands of the Detachment. Items destined for a country in the hands of the Germans—Poland, Holland, Belgium, Denmark, Norway, France, any place turned dark on the map—were confiscated. And it was out of the question to pass along funds. The Censorettes turned over funds immediately: a roll of dollar bills whose grubbiness testified to the toil spent accumulating them, a thin gold bracelet heavily wrapped in protective paper, a wedding ring. Of all of this, sent off to be pawned into a glutted market by desperate sellers, none would reach its destination.

Lucy watched Rebecca Gwynne, called Gwynne, sashay through the Reading Room with a tea tray and a file. McKay's secretary, Gwynne was a buxom Cockney resentful of the Censorettes and their university degrees. She was a teenaged widow, her boy husband killed in France. From this tragedy, she had forged a steely cloak which she donned when delivering telegrams bearing news of death back home. It was Gwynne who would deliver the bad news about Lucy's brother Matty, if bad news were to come. He was an RAF pilot who had not returned from Dunkirk. When she left McKay's office, though, Gwynne paused by Lucy's table only to say, "Colonel will see you now."

McKay was sipping tea and reading her personnel file when Lucy entered his office.

"I remember now." McKay drained his tea and nibbled a biscuit. "Our Brooklyn Shakespeare scholar. 'Wear house,' is that what troubles you?" He wiped crumbs from his chin.

"'Do nothing until you hear from me,'" Lucy said. "That troubles me. It's not the ordinary sort of wrong, like 'wherefor art thou, Romeo?' Everyone thinks it means where is Romeo, instead of 'why are you Romeo?' 'Wherefor' like the French '*pourquoi*' or the Italian '*perque?*' Anyway," Lucy added, as McKay's attention had drifted toward her uneaten biscuit. "Romeo never says that."

"You've memorized the play?" McKay reached for Lucy's biscuit.

"My family performed Shakespeare often after dinner."

"I see. How nice."

Lucy might have been a small granddaughter displaying a grubby embroidery project.

In her father's study, there were often as many as a dozen copies of one play, so each player could hold a volume. Chuckling dinner guests lured into the study with the promise of brandy were pressed into service *(No, no, Barrett, I'm rubbish at this sort of thing!)* only to become so caught up in the drama that their shouting roused the dozing cats.

"My mother wished to improve her English."

"Ah yes." He glanced at her file. "Your mother's an *Italian*."

"Yes. She was." It still happened, that clogged throat that prefaced her correction of the verb tense, the tight twist in her gut, like a contraction. Well, what was a contraction but the indication of loss, an apostrophe where a letter had been, *won't* for *will not*, as in *we won't ever see her again. Maria Theresa Gheldini Barrett. Tessa.* Lucy's eyes filled. She blinked rapidly, but a tear fell to her chin before she could stop it. "She was killed. In a Luftwaffe bombing."

"Yes. Frightful business." McKay failed to indicate whether it was Tessa's death or the Blitz which was "frightful." "Your degree," he went on. "French, German. But not Italian?"

"I'm cradle-fluent in Italian." Lucy dabbed her eyes with her wrists, claimed her cup of tea. "My father chose German. In German, you decline nouns, adjectives. Learning to decline would teach me to decline men, he said. His favourite joke."

"Never had daughters." McKay rubbed his hands together as though cleansing them of the threat of female offspring. He peered at the file of this man who had withstood two daughters, mitigated by the one son, Matteo. Paul Nicholas de Guise Barrett, Royal Naval Intelligence. "There was a de Guise when I was at Dartmouth. Sebastian."

"My great uncle."

"Indeed? A de Guise married an *Italian*. So," he went on as the tips of Lucy's ears burned at this second spitting out of *Italian*, "What does your Joe mean by 'do nothing until you hear from me'?"

"Just that. No action is to be taken. What the goods are, where they are going—that's still unknown. And then there's this."

Lucy held the letter to the light. The page had been used as a cushion to protect the platen of a typewriter. She remembered all too well from the painstaking term papers on Dante and Goethe she had typed at Girton, manually adding accents and umlauts. "This paper was used as second sheet on a typewriter. Whatever was typed here might be useful as well."

McKay stood, leaned on his office door, bawled "Smith!" and sat again. He took the letter back from Lucy. "'The days are long and full of wonder,'" he read. "He has a point, your Joe."

A freckled young woman with abundant unruly red hair arrived at the doorway. She flinched when she saw Lucy and shaded her eyes with the back of her hand, as though caught in the beams of a searchlight. McKay put his hand on her shoulder. "This is Miss Barrett, Smith. She's in the Languages Division."

McKay nodded at Lucy with impatient encouragement, as Granny Barrett had when Lucy as a child became tongue-tied meeting visitors at tea.

"How do you do, Miss Smith," Lucy said with the formality she had learned in her grandmother's parlour. "It is a pleasure to make your acquaintance."

Her words sounded unnatural to her own ears, as though she were trying the phrases in a new language (Arabic was her latest), but they seemed to do the trick. The woman lowered her arm, blinking rapidly, appraising Lucy. Then she said, "You've been crying. Is someone dead?"

She asked as though unaware that all of them were there, in a basement on an island, because thousands of someones were dead with each new day. When Lucy shook her head, McKay handed Miss Smith the letter.

"What do you make of this?"

As she studied it, her eyes moved up, down, left, right, the way one takes in a painting, not left, right, the way one reads. As she read, she rocked gently, as mothers rock infants. She pulled a tendril of her wild hair and twisted it around her finger.

"The 'Swan of Avon' man," she stated.

"You're certain?"

"The same T's. D's. Dots his i's with a semi-crescent." She held the paper to the light. "This is second sheet. These marks—"

"Yes. Can you read them?" McKay asked.

"'In reference to your shipment of 12 February, the condition of the goods received was'—I can't make that out. 'We are therefore return them with this post. Please to redeliver to Red Hook location when goods are complete. Regards, Joe Karte, Warehouse Manager.'"

"Warehouse," Lucy repeated. "Spelled correctly?"

"Yes." The woman plucked a pencil off McKay's desk and was rubbing it against the paper before he could rise from his chair and remove the pencil from her grip. He said in a tone Lucy found surprisingly mild, "You're not to alter the documents, Smith. Remember? Be a good girl and go copy it out for me. Exactly. Then bring it back."

She walked out without a nod or a further word.

"Who on earth was that?" Lucy blurted. "What division is she in?"

"Ruth Smith? I thought you knew. Bit notorious. Rather her own division," McKay said. "Needs a bit of handling, that one. Oh, and Barrett? She's to be your new roommate."

02.

Lucy already had a roommate, a fine and pleasant one, thank you very much. Rebecca Lark was the daughter of a Presbyterian minister from Ontario, Canada, and had been embraced by the congregation of the big pink St. Andrew's Church downtown next to the Parliamentary buildings. It was also next to the Bermuda Cathedral, which was Anglican and whose services Lucy should have attended had she any denominational loyalty. But her loyalty, for the comfort she received in her early days as a stranger in a strange land, was to Lark.

On Sundays, Lucy accompanied Lark to church in the mornings and in the afternoons, served as her caddy, cycling behind her as she pedalled to the golf course, lugging her golf bag up and down the damp slopes. She wiped the clubs dry before she handed them to Lark, paced the distance to the hole. As a caddy, she was meant to determine wind direction. But on Bermuda, the wind blew in all directions: it keened; it slapped sheets of brine into Lucy's face like a ghost enraged by her meagre mourning. It wept in pity for Lucy's banishment.

Lark returned from church duties to read volumes of a medical journal called *The Lancet*, which were as well-worn as her Bible. She ministered to Lucy's grief, never complaining when Lucy's nightmares woke her. When Lucy wrenched awake from visions of her mother, the Blitz, her brother, she found provisions from Lark resting on her bedside table: a cup of tea, a peach-coloured rose, a freshly ironed pillowcase to replace her tear-dampened one. Lark sat on Lucy's bed, content to chat, hand in hand, and listen to tales of old Barrett life. Brother Matteo was in the RAF? Matteo for Matthew? And Lucia for Luke? And the young sister was Marcia, for Mark? After the apostles? That was nice! On some nights, Lucy fell back to sleep with her head in the soap-and-violet-scent of Lark's lap.

The assignment of additional roommates, in a new hotel, so much further from St. Andrew's, was *so* inconvenient. Lark was not one for complaining, but—

"Lucy, I'm not one for complaining, but our meals are served here, and it's so close to the church. And what of your crying? I don't reproach. My father counsels that grief is a river and we must make navigate its tributaries, detour us how they might. But do you think you're *ready* for new people and a new room? *Four* of us in a room!"

It turned out to be two enormous rooms, a sitting room and a bedroom, each larger than any bedroom Lucy had ever seen, let alone occupied. Lucy, Lark, and Hector, the Princess Hotel porter, stepped off the elevator with their suitcases and foot lockers, but before they could knock, the door was swept open.

"Welcome!" cried a blonde so glamorous she could have pranced off a cinema screen. She wore tennis whites and bore on her wrist three "bracelets" of keys looped through pieces of string. "I'm Georgina Taylor. Call me Georgie. I'm your roommate. Rebecca Lark,

Lucy Barrett," she bestowed a key on each of them, identifying them before they could introduce themselves. "Ruth Smith is our fourth. She was already here at the Princess, so it's only a matter of hauling her things up. Speaking of, have you more things than these?"

"My books," Lark said. "Two boxes. They're still back at the Bermudiana."

"*Books*. Very well. We'll send for them." Georgie's tone was bemused, as though Lark had included a beehive in her luggage. Lucy thought of a beehive because Lark often returned from church carrying sticky jars of honey, which she ate happily from the jar with a spoon, like Winnie-the-Pooh. Georgie, Lucy noted, had traveled here with three tennis racquets, pressed into their wooden frames, leaning against the sofa in the sitting room.

The sitting room was sequestered from the foyer by a door, and from the bedroom by a pair of windowed French doors. The sitting room held a wet bar on the immediate right, and an upright piano on the far left. There was also a long white couch, coffee table, chairs, two wardrobes, and a desk. The bedroom held a large four poster bed, two bureaus and a wardrobe. Another pair of French doors opened onto a balcony which faced inland. Lark strode to the balcony and opened the doors. She then opened all the windows. The room was on a corner; windows faced both south and east. On the left wall, a bathroom abutted a spacious walk-in closet.

"The honeymoon suite, in happier times," Georgie told them. "Newlyweds of the upper crust, film stars, bits and bobs of minor royalty. And now, us! I say, Hector, could you ask someone to find Ruth Smith? She's on the third floor, and she has red —"

"Yes, ma'am. I know who she is."

But when Hector opened the door, Ruth Smith walked in, staring at her fingers, which she knitted together and apart in a rapid version of the finger game Lucy had taught her sister Marcia: *here is the church and here is the steeple/open the door and see all the people.*

"I am not late," she informed them without looking up. "You are early. You are Lucy Barrett, Rebecca Lark, and Georgina Taylor. It is exactly noon. I'm to sleep here? I see one bed."

"I'll set up camp in the sitting room," Georgie told her. "The couch pulls out. I won't be here all the time, so that will suit me. We'll have that large bed removed and replaced with three single beds. Ruth?"

Ruth had wandered in to the walk-in closet. She pulled a string, igniting an overhead light in a frosted glass shade. They gathered in the closet door to watch her. She said, "I want this room."

"My dear," said Lark. "This isn't a room. It's a closet."

"I want it." Ruth emerged, holding her hand against the glare of sunlight streaming from the windows.

"Will you have enough space?" Lark asked.

"I don't mind about space," Ruth said. "I mind about *quiet*. I like a piano." She nodded at it. "I like the idea of one. But with all these people," she shook her head at Lucy and Lark, as though they were a clamouring mob, "I need time alone. I was told," she addressed this last to Georgie, "to tell you what I need."

She pulled from a pocket of her dress a folded piece of paper. Georgie opened it, and immediately closed it again.

"We'll manage something," Georgie said, with an air of quelling competence that reminded Lucy of Granny, although Granny accommodating a guest's aversion to strawberries did not seem akin to obliging a Censorette's demand to live in a closet. "If you don't mind a cot. A single bed won't fit. So we'll need two singles to replace—" She waved at the four-poster. "If you two can bunk in together for a few nights before I get that sorted."

"We can bunk in every night!" Lark sat on the mattress, patting it. "Such a firm mattress, must you send it away? Come, Lucy. I only thought, with your bad dreams …We've grown quite cozy, Lucy and me," she said to others, who, occupied with their own luggage, paid no attention. "Although, she's a bit untidy. In fact, Lucy, why don't you let me unpack for you."

As Lark dragged Lucy's suitcases toward the bed, she added, "Georgie, you're keen on tennis? So is Lucy. Golf's my game. Maybe you two could partner? But not this afternoon, if you don't mind, Lucy. You said you'd help me about the lilies."

It was the Saturday before Palm Sunday. Lark wanted to ask some of the lily farmers in Bermuda to donate lilies for the Sunday service at St. Andrew's. Lucy knew many of the farms, from her bicycling in aid of the "Brooklyn Joe" mission.

Then Lark removed Lucy's framed photo of Matty in his RAF uniform, and placed it on the bedside table farthest from the eastern light. Lark pressed her fingers against the top of the frame, as though blessing it.

Georgie hummed in appreciation. "*Dishy*. Your beau?"

"Her brother," Lark told her. "Matty."

"Available?" Georgie asked.

"He's not available even to his family," Lucy said. "He's on active duty. And wherever he is—" Lucy yanked open the top drawer in the desk of the sitting room and pulled out pre-war embossed stationery, *The Princess Hotel, Hamilton, Bermuda*. "—He's not in a honeymoon suite in a fancy hotel in the middle of *nowhere*."

Lucy's face twitched with frustration. Lark hummed happily, hands full of knickers and brassieres. "I'll place my smaller garments in the second drawer, and yours in the top?"

"Whatever you like. Lark, can you see about the lilies by yourself?"

"I suppose I could. But won't you come with me? I don't know where to go."

"South Road and then turn left. Away from the golf courses. Smith Parish is good. Here." She hastily drew a map on one of the sheets of stationery. "I'm sorry, I must write to my father before the next post goes out. I could just make it."

The Pan Am flying boat left Darrell's Island at two-thirty on Saturdays, having stopped en route from New York for a refuelling. It then proceeded to Portugal. The Censorettes were not encouraged to add their letters to its haul. But then, the Censorettes were not encouraged to do very much at all.

***

Hector the porter informed her that hotel policy dictated that unaccompanied ladies were not permitted in the Gazebo Bar, yes, ma'am, even during wartime when there were no guests in the hotel to presume the lady was in a bar for immoral purposes and even when the lady was being quartered in the hotel and needed to write a letter. Orders of the Censorship. He offered her the patio by the hotel's saltwater pool. Lucy set up at a glass-topped table with the stationery from her room and wrote.

April 5, 1941

Dear Father,

You and I are a world apart and both living in grand hotels. We were so recently a family of five at 5 Mowbray Crescent. It seems ages ago.

03.

London, 1940

"I believe they speak English in Bermuda, as it's a territory," Lucy says. "They've no need of my language skills."

Her father's standing floor globe, a wedding present to her parents, displays countries whose borders and names have changed too often since 1919. Lucy and Maddy played with it, studied it, drew maps from it on so many rainy Saturday afternoons. Lucy gazed at it when performing Shakespeare in the study, when the men had chosen a war play, one of the Henrys, and she waited through hours of arcane blather to deliver a single impassioned speech: *O yet, for God's sake, go not to these wars!*

She shivers in her father's study, lit only by the fire in the fireplace. It is chilly, but still light out. The darkness is his preference.

The windows, shrouded with blackout curtains, face the kitchen garden, never good for much except for the cook's tiny plot of herbs and shallots and turnips, a place to shoo the cats when they became too unruly. Now the garden is untended, and the cook and the maids gone for war work. Matty is lost in France, Tessa a month buried. Marcia has been sent off to Knoll House for the duration, with the cats—Lucy's tabby Horatio among the thoroughbreds— apart from Charmian, Paul's smug charcoal Persian who stretches along the length of his thigh, deigning to accept his strokes. Paul is as ferocious about not parting from this ungrateful animal as he is cold about dispatching Lucy across an ocean.

"So why on earth should I go there?"

Matty counselled that Lucy should call Paul "Dad," and not "Daddy" if she wanted him to heed her. But since her mother's death, she could call him Prime Minister and still be no more heeded than a voice calling in the wilderness. Between Matty and Lucy, they call him "Paul," because he has always been more a figure than a father, one who funds their talents and decrees their fates. He has always been a dictator. It is only recently that he has become a despot.

"The Censorship Detachment is moving there," Paul says. "They've been in Liverpool, but that's being bombed to bits as well. So, Bermuda. They need clever girls. You'll be of use, Lucia. I fail to see why you're making such a fuss."

"We agreed on diplomacy. I was grateful for it, that I could even have a career, sss—"

The half-formed word catches in her throat: *since. Since Tessa hadn't*, since she met you as soon as she peeked outside her convent school. "A teacher, perhaps," Tessa would tell Lucy as she braided her hair before bedtime. "A teacher of mathematics. *La matematica.* So musical, the word. And feminine. The mother of rules. *La matematica* commands music, the stars, the design of the world. Some people do not approve of the education of women, but I was lucky in my father. Luckier than you, *mia cara.* My dear papa was not so ambitious as yours."

Paul cradles a snifter of brandy. Brandy was traditionally presented only on Sundays, the supply depleted further when there were dinner guests who would later read the kings and thanes and soldiers of Shakespeare. Now Paul drinks brandy every night that he is home, alone in the chilly study, Charmian the cat his lap warmer. He won't light a fire but is still sufficiently civilized to decant the brandy, allowing Lucy to calculate how much he drinks from the number of empty bottles. When she mentions it one night, he sighs, "The strain I'm under, Tess."

At first Lucy hears it as "the strain I'm under—Tess." Then she understands that he has mistaken her for her mother. Either way, this is the real cause, she suspects, of her exile.

"I've always done everything you wanted—"

"Then do this, Lucia. Just do this! It's little enough to ask."

She drags her finger along the spines of the volumes—the dozens of *Hamlets*, the *Lears*, the *Romeo and Juliets*. This argument between them has grown as familiar as these texts. She cannot remember a life before study. She began at four. At sixteen, she went up to Girton to read modern languages at the same time that Matty, at seventeen, headed to King's College to read classics. But it was already 1936 and they were no sooner out of the sight of Tessa weeping on the station platform than Matty handed Lucy his stack of books, as though she was meant to do his reading as well as her own. He would spend his time with the Cambridge University Air Squadron, he told her, and she, too, should think about how to make her education best serve the war, because the dogs of war were already slipping.

She was finding housing for refugees when Tessa was killed. She was planning to surprise her father with the news that she had interviewed and was accepted into the Women's Royal Naval Service when he surprised her with the news that he had already enlisted her in the Censorship Detachment. They have quarreled ever since, night after night. Paul will turn the house over to the Admiralty as soon as Lucy leaves it.

She spins the globe to look at Bermuda, a small pink dot in the

Atlantic, lacking even the sisterhood of fellow islands, like the ones in the Caribbean.

"I hear Churchill is organizing something," she says. "Girls with good French. The Special Operations something or other —"

"Bermuda." Paul stands so abruptly that Charmian plops to the carpet. Paul snatches her from the floor and slings her over his shoulder like a dropped kit bag, murmuring apologies, scratching her neck to soothe her.

To soothe *her!* Lucy is enfeebled with outrage furthered by shame at her jealousy of a cat. Paul is saying, "Take what you want from the house. You must be out of it by the end of the week. The Admiralty will take it over then. You leave for Knoll House. I'll see you there at Christmas. Tessa's things. Her jewelry and her—her clothes and—personal … I'd be grateful if you could deal with them."

When he is gone, Lucy pulls volume after volume of *Romeo and Juliet* from the shelves until she finds Tessa's copy, with its penciled annotations on the pronunciation of antiquated English words. She takes it, leaves the others where they fell. Let the *Admiralty* tidy them. Her father's desk bears the photo of Matty in his RAF uniform, sporting the cocksure grin of the king of infinite space. She stacks it with the *Romeo and Juliet*.

Does a photo of you exist where you don't look insufferably smug? she asked him when he presented it to Tessa.

Ma, sorella bella! He had kissed both cheeks and her forehead. *I have so much to be smug about!*

She will return from Bermuda with much to be smug about. She will return as soon as she reaches her majority, before a year is out.

04.

Bermuda, 1941

Lucy read what she had written so far:

You said you had a plan for me. A career in diplomacy. I understand that war is a failure of diplomacy. Or, as von Clausewitz said, 'The continuation of politics by other means.' Diplomacy failed, but why am I punished for it? I have my languages, and they could be put to better use closer to where they are spoken. I have said all this befor. Please let me come home. I want to come home.

No. She would not beg any further. Perhaps she should not write just now. She should wait until she could appeal to his reason, since he was indifferent to emotion. She could write other letters. A letter from Granny related that she had been required to take in more evacuee children: "filthy East End boys" and their "constantly weeping" sister Hannah. (Granny did not flourish in the company of children.) Half the flower garden and the entire sloping west lawn, all the way to the service road, would be turned to raising vegetables. Lucy and Matty had sledded that slope on Christmas holidays, rolled down it in the summertime, until, abruptly, Lucy's frolicking on the slope was deemed too "wild" and she was brought into the house to spend her afternoons in gracious rooms of ticking clocks. Now the lawn itself was too wild and would be cultivated for the duration of the war. The tennis court might have faced the same fate, had it remained grass. But Matty had engineered its transformation into a clay court, one of his last acts before he signed up to be bridegroom to the skies. Clay'll keep better than grass, Granny! he had told her cheerily, and then called to Lucy, "Work on that backhand, mia bella sorella, if you want to keep your county crown!"

As tears brined her eyes, Lucy leaned her head back, well-trained by then to leave no trace of herself on a letter, even her own. That world was so lost that Lucy had never considered packing her tennis racquet when she was sent to Bermuda …

And yet Georgina Taylor, her new roommate, had packed three, as though Bermuda held its own Wimbledon tournament. Three tennis racquets in their frames, three girls in a room, Georgie in charge of them all … why?

"Beg pardon. Are you Miss Barrett? The boy inside said I could find you here."

A tall young man stood between her and the sun. His silhouette blinded his face. She inventoried the rest of him: a pink-dusted Lacoste shirt and Bermuda shorts revealing long, well-shaped but pale legs and rather nice knees. A recent arrival to the island, then (Bermudian men wore full trousers until May), and, from his accent, a Yank.

She gestured to him to step out of the sun. "I'm Barrett. What is it?"

"Your friend. Miss Lark. There's been an accident."

She jumped to her feet so quickly that she toppled the glass table she'd been writing on. He caught the table with his foot, inches from impact, and righted it, then flashed her a grin meant either to celebrate his dexterity, calm her concern, or both.

"She's okay," he said. "Be right as rain. They wanna keep 'er overnight, so she sent me to here to ask you to bring her some things at the hospital. My jeep's in front to drive you back."

"Your what? Your *jeep*?" She looked again at the pink dust he had raised on his clothes. "Dear Lord. *Yanks*. You're here."

"Yes, ma'am. U.S. Army Corps of Engineers. Just posted to your pretty little island."

Eight months earlier, in September 1940, the United States had given the British Royal Fleet fifty U.S. Naval destroyers of a quality which had not pleased Paul Barrett or his friends at the Admiralty, in exchange for ninety-nine year leases on Britain's colonial islands, on which the Americans would build military bases. This "gift" occurred only because of a clever parlay on Churchill's part. Since Joseph Kennedy, the U.S. Ambassador to the Court of St. James's, had departed England, declaring its defeat "inevitable," Churchill had pointed out to Roosevelt that if England went, so went her territories close to the States: Newfoundland. Jamaica. The Bahamas. Bermuda.

"Hardly *my* island," Lucy strode into the hotel lobby. "And this *jeep*. Is that what caused the accident?"

The Yank hurried after her: "Well, yes, ma'am. Miss Lark, she was bicycling up this long hill and we came 'round a bend and I guess y'all aren't used to jeeps—"

"We are not." Lucy waved across the lobby at Hector. She didn't relish the thought of climbing six flights with the Yank behind her, attempting to charm her backside. Hector opened the lift door as the Yank caught up with her.

"Yours is the first *jeep* here." Lucy spat *jeep* as McKay had spat *Italian*. She nodded at the Yank's clothes. "Raising that dust would require some speed. The roads here are coral. Do slow down. The island is quite small. End to end, it's two dozen miles."

"Twenty-two," the Yank said, earning interest from Hector as they stepped off the lift.

Lucy told him, "Please wait outside."

Men were discouraged from the women's floors. But once she had unlocked and pushed open the door, the Yank strolled in behind her with the air of one to whom rooms were never barred, hands in his pockets, wide-eyed as though he had ventured from sepia Kansas into technicolour Oz. A cedar-scented breeze billowed the curtains away from the open windows.

He released a low whistle. "Hol-eee cow! This is how the Brits billet secretaries?"

Lucy glanced up from her packing. "There are four of us here, Mister—"

"Lieutenant William Inman." He extended his hand. "Call me Bill."

Loo-tenant. She knew from the cinema that the Americans said it that way, yet still found it strange to hear it pronounced "loo" and not "lef"-tenant. People in the southern United States were said to have an accent most like the English, which was why English actress

Vivien Leigh had been such an enchanting Scarlett O'Hara in *Gone With the Wind*. "Better an English girl than a Yankee," the book's author had told a magazine, which had puzzled the girls at Girton College: weren't they *all* Yankees? Vivien Leigh and their own dear Leslie Howard, who played Scarlett's adored Ashley Wilkes, had sunk happily into the honey-slow accent. There was much that was honeylike about Loo-tenant Inman, Lucy noticed, now that she paid attention: his hazel eyes, his dark blond hair, his sticky sense of his own charm. He smiled at her appraisal of him.

Lucy had never met an American. He was smaller than she'd imagined, the way that actors encountered on the street in the West End (Leslie Howard, for one!) were slighter-statured in real life. Paul encountered, in the course of his work, more Americans than he cared to. The highest praise he bestowed on one was "reasonably informed. For an *American*." When Tessa encountered them at embassy dinners, she spent the following mornings writing Polonius-like letters to Matty at Harrow. He received, bewildered, a list of admonishments for social gaffes he hadn't committed. *Do not say "If you ask me," if no one has. Do not discuss money: that is vulgar. Do not swear in front of ladies and then apologize for doing it—that is a twice insult.*

"Miss Barrett? I was saying, I promised Miss Lark I'd make myself entirely at y'all's disposal. She said she's got a mess of errands, with the holiday tomorrow."

"Palm Sunday!" Lucy snapped, as though the Easter season were a personal affront. "The bloody *holiday*." She yanked Lark's knapsack closed. Her previous Palm Sunday had unfolded in chilly London. She and Matty shared a hymnal; so had Paul and Tessa. Marcia sang in the loft with the children's choir. This one would take place on warm cedar pews, with the thin harmonizing of the makeshift Censorette choir. "Come along, Mr. Inman, you can tell me what happened on the way."

She led him out of the room and began running down the stairs.

"We drove out to see the golf courses. Thought we'd have our own Army-Navy game tournament." Bill trotted behind her and took her knapsack. "The Navy's posted here, too."

"Yes, yes, part of the Destroyers for Bases Act."

"You follow politics?"

"They're why I'm here."

"Not the war?"

"War is the continuation of politics by other means."

"Yes, I've heard that," he chuckled.

"And you find it funny?" Her glare punctured and deflated his smile.

"No, I just don't recall seeing any girls, let alone one so pretty, up at West Point."

He stepped backward up a stair. *Some fool will pat you on the head and tell you you're a bright little thing,* Paul used to tell her. *But you must learn to be diplomatic.*

She pivoted and resumed down the stairs. "If you're with the Corps, you're here to build an airfield."

"We are." Bill loped after her cautiously. "Over on St. David's Island."

"Yes, there was something in the *Royal-Gazette*. Families being moved, their homes destroyed, to make way. What's your role, lootenant? Are you a pilot?"

"I'm an engineer. A topographical engineer. I adjust the land to — "

"Yes, yes. A landing strip must be flat. This island is mostly rock, so you'll have to blast to level out the land."

They stood at the front entrance. Her swift description of his job left Bill Inman momentarily lost.

"You still haven't told me," Lucy added. "What happened to Lark."

He led Lucy to the jeep, opened the door and helped her in. "Hit her head, might be a concussion. Scraped herself up. Arm looked broken. Dodd scooped her up and brought her to the jeep. We drove her to the hospital. She sent me here. And here I am."

Jumping into the driver's seat, he yanked one gear forward and another back, then turned to her with a grin that demonstrated why smiles were sometimes called "disarming."

05.

Lark was awake, sitting up in bed. She greeted Lucy with a pert expression and glassy eyes. The stitched-up gash on her forehead was the most immediate proof of her fall, until Lucy realized that what she had at first believed to be a little red shawl draped over Lark's arm was in fact her skin. The area between her shoulder and her elbow was tender pulp. Lucy sat on the bed and placed her hands on Lark's shoulders, fearful of grazing a wound. At her touch, Lark began to tremble, so Lucy pulled her in tighter. Her sister Marcia had trembled that way when Lucy held her after their mother died.

"I'm fine," Lark said through chattering teeth. "Careful about the arm, if you would. I'm *injured*. That man Alan Dodd was so kind, Lucy. He's a Presbyterian."

"What?" Lucy had given only a glance and a nod to the tall man with thick dark eyebrows slumped in the white enamel chair outside of Lark's room when she strode into Lark's room and firmly motioned Bill not to follow. "How on earth did that come up?"

"He sang a bit of a hymn on the way here," Lark told her, and then sang, "'In the beauty of the lilies/Christ was born across the sea.'" She asked, "Does that mean 'born,' do you think, or carried? The way we were borne here? I was borne here by shame."

Lucy pressed her palm to Lark's cheek. How severe *was* her head injury? She was practically performing Ophelia's mad scene, *they say the owl was a baker's daughter*—if Ophelia had been confined to a hospital bed in a colonial outpost.

"Morphine," a nurse explained as she entered carrying a tray bearing rolls of gauze and a pair of scissors with long thin blades to the bed. She motioned Lucy away, as Lark kicked the bedclothes over, exposing her thigh.

"The leg, too, look!" She peered at it with a young boy's fascination of wounds garnered from rough play. The broad river of the scrape on her leg was augmented by tributaries of scratches, and clotting ponds of purple bruises. "And my *hip!*" She twisted to show the dark continent of the contusion forming where her body had taken the impact of the fall. Lucy tugged the sheet back over her. "I was *injured* but I am not *damaged goods!*"

"A small sip of water only. Shock brings thirst, but she'll be out soon, and we don't want her wetting the bed." The nurse, wielding a hypodermic needle, spoke with the forbidding vigour of the hospital sisters who had cared for Tessa, the ones so bloody strict about visiting hours. Perhaps they were trained to be forbidding. Lucy held Lark's hand as she listed tasks: see to the lilies, arrange for someone to rehearse the children's choir and find a Mr. Furbert, lived in a house on a lane near the sea.

"Lark, that describes many Bermudians."

"*In Smith Parish!*" Lark's tone was peevish, as thought it were as obvious as King George living in Buckingham Palace. "He's the source of the roses. And the honey. The minister knows him. Don't tell him what happened to me."

"*What?* Whyever not?"

"I was only hurt," Lark whispered.

Once Lark fell asleep, Lucy launched the American military into action.

At Girton, Lucy had organized the public lecture series, an administrative role rather than a performing one. She was a dutiful, not talented, pianist. Music was a mere continuation of language by other means. She refused theatre, shy of performing outside of the haven of her father's library. Her refusals brought her a reputation for being aloof, just as she was thought stuck-up in Bermuda for declining to join any of the Censorette societies, although she had no more talent for singing, sewing or folk dancing than she'd had at Girton.

But she was adept at giving orders.

After questioning the minister at St. Andrew's, Lucy learned

Furbert's address and sent Ensign Dodd—("Call me Alan")—there. Alan returned to the Princess Hotel with an abundance of Furbertian provisions: peach roses, jars of honey, a satin pillowcase. Then she located the backup choir instructor for the children and asked her to take the final rehearsal. After he had jeeped the roses and honey back to the hospital and sorted the rehearsal of the children's choir, Alan returned to the command post Lucy and Inman had fashioned from a table and a telephone in the bar area of the ground floor. Inman purchased the respect of the barman with a large tip for the order of two rounds of Dark and Stormies, a local drink made from ginger beer and Gosling rum. Lucy sipped at hers. *I was injured but I am not damaged goods.* What on earth could that mean? When Alan stood before her and asked, "Anything else, Miss Barrett?" his expression was so chastened that she pushed her Dark and Stormy toward him when he said, "I am awfully sorry about this."

"*I* was the one driving, Doddy." Bill sucked at his second Dark and Stormy, as Alan sipped cautiously at the one Lucy had bequeathed him. Bill flung his arm across the back of Lucy's chair, like a boy in a cinema advancing intimacy by pretending to stretch. Censorettes barged through the front door in a Sunday evening mood, boisterous yet resigned to the sun setting on their day of leisure. Lucy tilted Bill's wrist to check his watch and saw that she had missed dinner. Several girls regarded them curiously before they turned to mount the stairs, but Gwynne sauntered over to be introduced. Lucy obliged her with the whole tale. It would save her from having to repeat it, as Gwynne spread news more effectively than a British Pathé newsreel.

"We hold dances here sometimes on a Saturday," Gwynne said. "Perhaps you gents could join us. Where are you posted? Is it far? Well, how *could* it be far? Jolly clever of Lark to run into you."

Lucy stood and held her pose. Granny had spent hours teaching her this stance, aided by Tessa, who referred to it as *la freddezza*: chin up, shoulders down, eyes distant, no smile, a dismissal which transcended words, a position required by ladies and beauties, but particularly by ladies of beauty.

Bill said, "That's mighty kind of you, Miss Gwynne. I'm sure when I tell the boys of my good fortune, they'll want to share it. Lucy'll tell you how to get word to me."

He placed his hand on Lucy's shoulder, as though they were already a unit, he the man of business, she the wife arranging social events. He pranced his fingers on her shoulder, awaiting some acceptance from her, a cock of the head, a leaning back. Instead, Lucy smiled a dismissal at Gwynne, who drank it all in—she never missed a trick—returned a smile to Bill, squinted at Lucy, and hurried toward the herd of Censorettes waiting for her news.

Alan said, "I need to get back. I wonder, did you pack Miss Lark's Bible?"

"A hospital's gotta have heaps of Bibles," Bill said. "Like hotels?"

"You'd know more about that. I'm never in hotels." Alan set down the Dark and Stormy. "Well, I guess I'm in one now." He surveyed his surroundings with an arch eyebrow lift that reminded Lucy of Tessa. Her smile almost hurt; she'd been grinding her teeth all day. "I thought Miss Lark'd like her own Bible. Passages she's marked, ribbons and bookmarks. The heft and smell of it. She struck me as that sort."

"You're very thoughtful, Ensign," Lucy said. "Lark said you sang her a hymn. She was awfully struck by it. Something about lilies?"

"'In the beauty of the lilies, Christ was borne across the sea,'" Alan sang in a tenor so resonant that Hector and several Censorettes turned. "'Battle Hymn of the Republic.' Five years in the Navy choir. Now, if you want to go up for that Bible ..."

"And you can get changed while you're up there," Inman added. He gestured to the girls coming in. "I made you miss your mess. I'd like to make up for it."

What on earth did that mean? Inman had told her that he was the middle son in "a mess of kids," and had gone on to name them ... Benedict, Georgia, Carlton, Virginia, Evelyn ... no, one of those was where he'd grown up. She'd only half-listened, absorbed by Lark's injuries and her list of Easter chores. She tested the term: *A mess of Censorettes streamed into the Princess Hotel.*

06.

Knollborough, 1928

On Easter Sunday, the Barretts held a lawn party and Easter egg hunt on the grounds of Knoll house to celebrate the christening of Marcia Mary Celestina Barrett, which took place at the Anglican church in the village of Knoll so that the local gentry and villagers alike could see for themselves that although Paul Barrett had married an Italian, his children were consecrated as proper English Christians. Lucy, seven, wore a white dress so fine she feared to move in it while Matty, eight, shed his formal suit as soon as they returned to Knoll House.

Lucy suspected he intended to play a prank on the Jenner children from the neighboring estate, which Granny called "the estate" (compared to Knoll House, which was a working farm), Paul called "the Jenner place," Matty and Lucy called "next door" (despite the fact that it was acres away), and Tessa painstakingly termed "the nay —bores," as though "neighbour" was a new word to her in English. These particular English were not neighbourly, although they were bores (to Matty and Lucy) as well as boors (to Paul and Tessa).

The Jenner children were the son and daughters of George Jenner. George's sister Veronica was unmarried. It had been understood (although who exactly understood it baffled Lucy, once she grew old enough to understand) that Veronica would marry one of the Barrett boys. But Verdun took John and the Somme took William. Paul, who spent the war at sea, not free from danger but at least free from the fatal mud of France, refused to be taken as a consolation prize, by Veronica Jenner or anyone else, particularly after that fateful lecture at Cambridge on celestial navigation where he met Maria Theresa Gheldini.

Lucy was collecting coloured eggs from the croquet lawn and putting them into the basket carried by little Harriet Jenner when they heard a commotion from Granny's rose garden, screams from Lydia and Guy Jenner, followed by scolding from Veronica.

Lucy ran, heedless of Harriet toddling behind her. She knew what had happened.

Back in London, Matty and Lucy had been taken to the opera. Two couples had been meant to go: Paul and Tessa, and some Admiralty colleague and his wife. Tessa had excused herself due to her pregnancy, and Paul's colleague had immediately bowed out, so Paul had taken his children.

The opera was "Don Giovanni," a favourite of Tessa's. Matty was captivated —no, *electrified* — by the character Il Commendatore, the man Don Giovanni kills, whom Giovanni later encounters as a statue. As a joke, Giovanni theatrically invites the statue to dinner. Tessa explained the entire libretto to Matty and Lucy before they went, using children's language — "bad man" and "unfortunate woman" — but primarily playing on the piano important musical passages. The role of Il Commendatore, Tessa told them, was played by a *basso profondo*, the lowest of the vocal ranges in opera. She thrummed the lowest keys on the piano.

In the opera, the statue of Il Commendatore crashes through Don Giovanni's door, a ghostly marble white figure, thundering, "*Don Giovanni! A cenar teco m'invitasti e son venuto!*" (I have accepted your invitation to dinner!) When this occurred, Matty jumped to his feet, clutched the railing and stared at the action on the stage. Don Giovanni and Il Commendatore roared in argument: "Repent!" "No!" "Repent, you old devil!" "No, no, never!" Then "aaaaargh!" down to Hell, indicated by stage smoke and red lighting, although to Matty it was real enough. Riveted, he gazed on the scene as his grip on the railing turned his knuckles white. When the audience rose to applaud as the curtains closed, Paul ruffled Matty's hair. His hair stood up where it had been ruffled, as though he had emerged from the laboratory of the mad Dr. Frankenstein.

And so, Basso Profondo was born. He first appeared at the foot of Lucy's bed, in the middle of the night, rendered ghostly by talcum powder, wielding the wooden sword from his King Arthur costume at Halloween. Lucy, finding him at her bedside, shrieked. Matty was so gratified by this reaction that he embarked on a career. He honed an ability to still himself and concentrate, during his Basso Profondo days, which served him throughout boarding school and flying lessons. His success in these realms was down to Basso Profondo and the hours he spent at the foot of beds—Lucy's and nannies and Italian aunts—waiting for their shock at the small powdered figure standing silent and stern at the foot of their bed. *Repent!*

At Easter, Matty covered himself in the ash and lime the gardener kept in his shed to shore up the crumbling brick walls. He stood still in the rosebed for nearly half an hour while the Jenner children hunted for eggs and treats in the lawn outside, until they at last entered the rose garden. When Guy Jenner reached for a chocolate rabbit wrapped in colourful foil, Matty shouted *"Repent, you old devil!"*

Guy screamed and fell back, toppling Lydia to the bricks. Lydia screamed (more from surprise and for attention, Lucy surmised as she arrived on the scene) and Veronica—"Auntie" Veronica—seized Matty's arm, then dropped it swiftly when the lime burned her hand. (Matty wore long underwear under the lime.) Auntie Veronica slapped the back of Matty's talc-covered head so hard that he stumbled and fell. She had previously felt free to "box" his ears, drag him by his ear out of the room, smack Lucy's knuckles when she reached for a second cake at tea, yank Lucy's shoulders back when her posture slumped.

Lucy, sensing that the blood was up in Auntie Veronica, screamed *"Daddy!"* and then *"Papa!"* and then whispered to Guy Jenner, *"Baby!"*

Lucy stayed with the Jenners long enough for Paul, dashing across the lawn, to arrive panting in the rose garden.

"Ah." Paul's cheerful calm maddened Auntie Veronica further. "Basso Profondo strikes again, eh son?"

He approached Matty with a handkerchief.

"Papa," Lucy said. "Basso Profondo is in a *paste*. You must use the garden hose. Douse him, like a rose bush."

Basso Profondo was Italian, so Lucy spoke of him in Italian.

"*Ah. Un cespuglio di rose.*" Paul headed for the garden shed. "Guy," he added as he passed him, "run to the kitchen and fetch some towels, will you?"

"Paul! I understand that the children must speak Italian with their mother as a matter of necessity," Veronica said. "But oughtn't they to speak *English* among English people?"

"It's not, in fact, a matter of necessity with Tessa." Paul's tone was polite but Lucy had learned, even then, to recognize the muscle in his cheek that twitched when he controlled his temper. "Tessa started English when she was Lucia's age. Step back, if you would," he added a fraction too late so that a bit of the hose water misted Veronica's dress. "Tessa speaks several languages fluently, and so will Lucia. It's a gift to know another language so well. Lucia learns Italian from her mother, French from her nanny. She loves poems and stories of all sorts. Don't you, *cherie*? *Merci*, Guy."

Paul accepted the kitchen towels Guy brought, turned off the hose and handed it to him. Guy raised his chin at Lucia as he coiled the hose, to prove that he was capable of doing a man's work, even if he had screamed when Matty startled him.

After Paul wiped at Matty with the towels, he ordered, "Straight upstairs. Bathe and change. Quick as you can. Children, it's too wet to hunt in the garden any further, so go back out to the lawn. Veronica, give them lemonade and cake. Lucia, a word."

After everyone had obeyed his commands (it was times like these that reminded Lucy and Matty that though Paul was now earthbound in Naval Intelligence, he had spent his war years at sea), Paul put his hand on Lucy's shoulder and knelt beside her.

"Lucia, darling. Your mother doesn't need to hear of any of this. Matty played a prank, no harm done. Veronica Jenner is a bitter woman. She has no right to speak of your mama that way. Mama is foreign. It would only hurt her to hear this."

"I understand, Papa."

"Good girl." He kissed the top of her head. "I'm proud of you."

Her father's esteem, she realized that day, was something she needed to earn, while her mother's was something she needed to protect.

07.

Bermuda, 1941

After Lark's accident, Saturday half-days were no longer Lucy's to command. The very next day, Palm Sunday, as they walked a tender but determined Lark home to the Princess Hotel from the service at St. Andrew's, Georgie said, "I hear you're in need of a worthy opponent, Lucy? Tennis?"

"I'm awfully used to winning," Lucy said.

"The spirit that built the Empire," Georgie said.

"I'm used to playing men."

"Aren't we all? And speaking of, I hear things are moving along at a nice clip with that dishy lieutenant?"

"I beg your pardon?"

"The one who ran Lark over yesterday," Georgie clarified, as though the question were which dishy lieutenant and not how she had heard. But that raised the question, Lucy thought: How many dishy lieutenants were there? How many engineers in the corps of them? How many of U.S. Navy stationed here? The American military had little enough to occupy them, God knew, aside from building bases on borrowed islands.

"Strange, isn't it," Georgie added, with that slightly theatrical manner she sometimes had, as though she were was rehearsing a play and her roommates were merely stagehands, arranging the set around her. "We're in a hotel full of empty rooms. Yet there's so little space for intimacy. You might want to go up on the roof next time."

"We're allowed on the roof?" Lucy asked.

"What intimacy?" Lark, turning, winced from the brush of the sleeve of her dress across her scraped upper arm.

"Well, since everyone knows, apparently—a kiss," Lucy said.

"A good kiss?"

"*Lark!*"

"Call me old-fashioned, but —"

"Everyone does, dear," Georgie interrupted.

"—I hope he's a better kisser than he is a driver."

"It was—American." It was a kiss confident of its welcome, no preamble, no head-duck and cheek-peck testing of a Cambridge undergraduate. It was a full dive in, a fuller, longer kiss which had liberated the tension in Lucy's spine like a marionette collapsing upon release from her puppetmaster. Comfort, touch, and attraction, instead of terror, exile, and blame. It had been ages since she'd experienced a kiss so lacking in farewell, a kiss that was a beginning; he had after all concluded by stroking her chin with his thumb and whispering, "What time tomorrow?" assured of both his welcome and his tomorrows.

"So we'll put this little one to bed," Georgie continued, nodding at Lark who was the tallest of the three. "With some aspirin and a nice snifter of brandy. And then I'll beat you at tennis and you'll have time to bathe before you meet your lieutenant for—dinner, will it be?"

"A walk along the harbour."

"Best make it dinner. You won't feel much like walking by the time I'm done with you. Get him to take you to dinner. Find out what he knows."

"What he knows?"

"Well, he's out of West Point, and they have to know someone to get in to there. And I hear he looks like money and protecting their money is what Yanks care about. Did you pack tennis whites?"

Lucy had not packed anything for tennis apart from a misguided faith in her own abilities. Telling Georgie that she was skilled at tennis was akin to telling Hitler that she was persuasive at German rhetoric.

She never won a game. For the next three Saturday and Sunday afternoons, and Wednesday evenings, Georgina Taylor, sporting a series of tennis whites in which she could have modelled for *Vogue*, broke down every strategy that Lucy mastered. Her groundstrokes were punishing. Her high serve might have shattered clay pigeons: *Pull!* She might have stepped out of a Nazi propaganda film: muscled arms and calves, fair hair, fervent pale eyes focused skyward toward the calling.

She administered defeats slowly. Rather than responding to a weak return of service from Lucy with a swift point, *Ace!* Georgie ran Lucy to rags, high front court, low back court. Lucy had never been aware of, let alone felt such ache in, certain parts of her body. On that first Sunday when she found Lucy curled like a shrimp on the floor by their bed, Lark suggested that Lucy call Hector for an ice pack. The following Saturday, when Lucy pressed Lark's hand on her thigh to share the sensation of her twitching muscles (much as Tessa had shared the livening of Marcia with Matty and Lucy by pressing their hands to her womb), Lark suggested a hot bath. On the third Saturday, Lark suggested that Lucy seek a gentler opponent. Lucy hugged her knees and shook her head. *Did her people back home have the option of seeking a gentler opponent?*

On the fourth Saturday, they played under a sky of clouds pregnant with rain. A ship stopping to refuel on its way to Lisbon had been boarded, her mailbags seized, and her bags dragged to the basement of the Princess. The Censorettes had been urged to extra haste; the captain of the ship wished to outrace the storm. Lucy had discovered another letter from Brooklyn Joe, another bit of puzzling iambic pentameter, but Colonel McKay had had even less time for her speculation. Ruth was busy elsewhere. There were no indentations on the page. She was told that the Shakespeare was nothing more than a feeble attempt at poetry by a homesick German: she should be looking for evidence of *weapons, espionage,* support for the *Bund,* the *American Nazi Party,* for heaven's sake. If she wanted to waste time dwelling over pretty phrases, she ought to have stayed in Cambridge.

Returning to the room, she had barely had time to study the notes she had scribbled regarding Brooklyn Joe's latest letter, the foray into Shakespeare she could not quite place—*thus I turn me from my country's light*—before Georgie bounded in from wherever she went when a ship came in.

"Don your whites, chop chop!" Georgie clapped twice at her before flinging open her wardrobe. "We need to hurry if we're to get a match in before the rain comes!"

Either Georgie allowed Lucy to take three games or she actually won them, smacking the tip of her racquet against the meat of her hand in iambic pentameter *thus I turn me from my country's light*, as she shifted her weight from foot to foot awaiting Georgie's homicidal serve. She seethed from the condescension of her superiors. The women of the Censorship were put through absurd *time-and-tide-wait-for-no-man* haste, like steeplechase horses. She successfully broke Georgie's service twice and won three games before she felt a drop of rain on her hand. Then, with an *oh-dear-look-at-the-time* glance at the darkening sky, Georgie dispensed with Lucy's flush of pride, and the next game, then the following five games and thus the set, as easily as one would swat gorged flies at a windowsill: *Ace! Ace! Ace!*

"*Ouch!*" called Bill from the sidelines. "Game, set, and match Taylor!"

Lucy clutched her thighs and dripped sweat onto her knees, sucking in air as one near-drowned. *Horses sweat,* Granny Barrett always said. *Men perspire. And ladies glow.* She was not glowing. The sky released more drops. Merely to move through the air courted perspiration. Why was Bill here?

Panting, she glanced up to see Georgie waving him onto the court, but at least he arrived with a canteen of water, a tin of aspirin, and a towel. He took her elbow and guided her to the sideline bench, where Georgie patted herself with a towel wearing her smug *Wot larks!* smile, while batting like a cat at the ribbon adorning a large wrapped box Bill had brought.

"Brought you a present," Bill said unnecessarily.

"Oh, Bill."

He had given her so much already: the lilies for the Easter which had come and gone, roses afterwards, and bottles of bourbon, brandy, rum and gin (*"I noticed y'all's wet bar didn't have anything wet in it."*) from the Corps' PX. These Lucy had accepted: one could not unpick a flower, and liquor had medicinal purposes.

Now he was here with a large box on the sideline bench. She drained the entire canteen before she found the stamina to ask, "How did you get here?"

"That's a fine hello." Bill kissed her sweat-soaked hair. The men of the Corps worked until four on Saturdays—no point in wasting daylight, and on Sunday mornings, officers were required to attend religious services on base, as an example to the men, so Lucy at least knew (or thought she had known) when she might encounter Bill, since she would, all else being equal, prefer not to do it when looking like a plough horse at the end of a scorching harvest day.

"I took a *gharry*. I ordered this for you when I saw what lickings you keep taking. Too late for today's. Thought you might be helped by a better Excalibur. Supply ship just came in," he told them as Lucy pulled the ribbon and unwrapped the box. "We let the men knock off a little early. Read their mail, open their care packages."

"A *Cortland*!" Georgie exclaimed as Lucy pulled a tennis racquet from the box. "Look at that wood! What a beauty! May I?"

It was inappropriate to accept such a lavish gift and her granny would not approve but the racquet was, as Georgie said, a thing of beauty. Lucy bounced her hand against the taut strings until Georgie commandeered the racquet, as she had all things tennis. It was a handsome racquet, the best to be had, no doubt, and Georgie backhanded with it, while Lucy, mindful of her odor, gave Bill a brief gingerly kiss of thanks.

"Was there any news, Bill?" Georgie asked. "In your post?"

"My sister Caroline's getting married in June and—oh, you'll like this, Lucy. My baby sister Evie has received permission to apply to a girls' college in Atlanta. She'd be the first girl in the family to go to college. It's my doing, if I can brag. I told Mother that I'd met girls like y'all who've been to college and it hadn't spoiled their looks one little—"

"No news of new appropriations toward the war effort?" Georgie mimed a serve with the Cortland. "Nothing about aid? Nothing from that senator uncle of yours?"

"He's not—y'all ask the funniest questions."

"One hopes to amuse." Georgie handed Lucy the racquet.

"Y'all's personal mail," Bill asked. "Is it full of politics?"

Lucy's annoyance at her own grubbiness was eclipsed by her annoyance at Bill's question. For one thing, her personal post was quite erratic. The Yanks' mail arrived efficiently from a port in Virginia, 640 miles west of Bermuda, not across a sea stalked by U-boats. Further, *all* the mail she read was full of politics: *no one will take us. Please help, we are desperate* from Lisbon. From America: *we are trying to secure a visa for you* and *Check every week at the American Express office.*

Thus I turn me from my country's light, Brooklyn Joe had written. *To dwell in solemn shades of endless night.*

"If you'd call my childhood home being reduced to rubble, then yes, politics," Georgie answered, looping her arm through Lucy's to quell her surprise. "I'm afraid we must get back ahead of the rain. Mustn't spoil Lucy's new racquet. Will we see you tonight?"

"Wouldn't miss it," Bill strode toward the stack of bicycles leaning against the Bermudiana. All the hotels, despite the lack of tourists, still provided a fleet of bicycles.

"You'll meet our fourth roommate!" Georgie called after him.

"Will he?" Lucy struggled to keep up Georgie's pace, but her legs wobbled as though she'd just stepped off the trawler that brought her here. "I doubt Ruth will go to the dance. She never does."

"She will tonight." Georgie glanced again at the ominous sky and smiled, satisfied that even the clouds obeyed her commands. "You'll make sure she does."

08.

"This rose looks like a peach." Ruth painted a watercolour of a vase of peach-coloured roses which stood on the coffee table. These roses were not bouquets sent from Bill, but a bowl of short-stems from the garden of Lark's mysterious Mr. Furbert.

"It was bred to look like a peach," Ruth informed them. "Notice the blush. Peach, rose, then a bit of orange. An orange is orange. A peach is peach. But a rose is not always rose. People say 'rosy cheeks.' They mean pink. They say 'you've lost the roses in your cheeks' but they mean 'you're pale.' Why don't they say that? If a rose is a rose, why is this one peach?"

"Ruth." Lucy looked up from lotioning her legs. The others had granted her the lion's share of the hot water, and she had soaked in a bath for a quarter of an hour until the muscles in her legs ceased twitching. "Enough about roses."

"People say 'flesh-coloured.'" Ruth continued after a slight pause. "People say 'flesh-coloured tights.' But 'flesh' is not a colour. If Hector's sister wears flesh-coloured stockings, they're not the colour of *her* flesh. I wouldn't wear stockings called 'flesh' if they were not the colour of *my* flesh. It is rude to talk to people about things they don't have in common with you. So it is rude to say to Hector 'rosy cheeks' or 'flesh-coloured stockings?' I asked him if his sister minded having to buy 'flesh-coloured stockings.'"

They all turned, Lark from adjusting the shoulders of a white satin dress onto a dressmaker's dummy, Georgie from studying hand-drawn maps she would soon lock into her desk. Once she'd grown accustomed to their presence and understood that they would not ridicule her, Ruth talked, and talked, and talked, voicing every thought. It did no good to ask her to stop; the request would only inspire talking about talking. They grew to regard her as a radio drama playing in another room, although if they'd had an actual radio drama on, Ruth would find it distracting. She was always talking, even if most of her conversations were solo. Her lips moved, and sometimes she nodded in agreement with herself.

"Hector? Hector *downstairs*?" Georgie asked, as though Ruth might have summoned a figure from the Trojan War.

"The coloured man in the lobby. Very polite. Runs the elevator. Takes messages. Carries luggage and— "

"Why are you talking to him about *stockings*? And cheeks?" Georgie snapped. "How do you know he has a sister?"

"I asked him," Ruth said. "I asked if he had sisters, and if they wore stockings. I asked him just this morning, when Lucy sent me to get the watercolours and this drawing pad. I tore a stocking on the way back. I didn't want to wear stockings just to walk into town, but Lucy said I had to. I asked him if his sister minded wearing stockings labeled 'flesh-coloured' when they weren't the colour of *her* flesh, and there were no stockings for sale that were."

As the only one among them with a sister, Lucy had been elected to advise Ruth on the things which flummoxed her. Ruth received each piece of counseling with an earnest nod and repetition: "'Good night, Vienna' doesn't mean Austria. It means 'that's the end.' 'That's all she wrote' doesn't mean that a woman has finished writing something. That also means 'that's the end.' I think people might *say* 'that's the end,' if that's what they mean. I'm being tiresome." Only that last apologetic comment, made so often, gave Lucy any indication that Ruth had had actual parents charged with the duty of integrating her into society, which they had evidently found too "tiresome" to do.

So off into Bermudian exile went Ruth Smith and it was now down to Lucy to explain things, all things, every sodding thing. Although Georgie had revealed to Lucy and Lark that they'd been housed into the suite to help Ruth overcome her shyness, they soon found themselves wistful for the days in their suite when Ruth sat alone in her windowless room. Georgie tried to jolly her into taking part in the Censorette group activities: the sewing society, the dramatic society. Lark advised periods of prayer and meditation. Neither appeal had worked and slowly, they'd instead tacked in to Ruth's quirks. She combed her food but not her hair. She so disliked figures of speech that she even disliked the phrase "figure of speech."

"Speech is not a figure," she informed them. "A figure is a geometric form."

Sudden noises frightened her. She shrank into herself at the sound of a group laughing. Girls who had themselves been considered too bookish in their own countries mocked her in this new one, oddly jubilant to see the shoe on the other foot.

"Ruth," Lucy said. She counted out her pause: *And Ruth-andtwo-andthree-andfour*. "You mustn't talk to coloured people about being coloured."

"Why? Coloured people know they're coloured. And *all* people are coloured. But why is only one colour called 'flesh'? When flesh can be so many colours. Like roses."

Lucy turned to her roommates for assistance, but Lark had returned to her stitching and Georgie to rustling her maps. *Damn them.*

"Well, Ruth," Lucy said. "Yes, we are all different, but we should try to muddle along. And it isn't nice to point to people how they don't fit in. My mother was Italian, for example—a bit of colour! —and I took a great deal of guff for it at school. I'm sure you had similar experiences."

"They said I was an odd duck. Mental. Loony."

"They make you feel inferior. A lot of people say things to make the coloured feel inferior. Because they're coloured."

A fool of an official welcoming the boatload of Censorettes Lucy came in with had lectured them on how to comport themselves. They must not consort with sailors, or inflame the "inherently weak sensibilities" of the local coloured men by wearing provocative attire. The official had addressed them in a stateroom at the Bermudiana Hotel, before at least half a dozen coloured waiters pouring pitchers of water and iced tea for the welcome luncheon. The news of their inherently weak sensibilities transmitted like a fever among the *gharry* drivers, busboys and janitors, who the next day greeted the women with a haughty contempt woven through their compulsory deference. Lucy wondered that Hector gave any of them the time of day.

"But people say—"

"Back to your roses. But no more talk about them."

"The roses that are peach."

"The roses that are not always rose," Lucy agreed firmly. "I need to practice piano now."

Ruth frowned at the door, as though to make a run for it.

"Are you going to play that jazz that you're not good at?"

"No," Lucy said. "Just Bach. He's mathematical. You'll like him."

She had promised Lark she would play at her church. Four weeks past Easter, they were now in what the church called "Ordinary Time" and a sameness shaped their days. Lucy selected the 10th movement of the Bach cantata "*Herz und Mund und Tat und Leiben*," the popular chorale "*Jesu, bleibet meine Freude*." Or, as it was known in English, "Jesu, Joy of Man's Desiring."

"Listen. Relax," she said, and Ruth obediently crumpled, releasing herself like a slackened marionette, resting her chin on the top of the upright. Lucy closed her eyes. It was Myra Hess's transcription of the "Jesu," and she knew it by heart. Shortly after the bombing began in London, pianist Myra Hess organized lunchtime concerts at the National Gallery. Lucy had attended with her parents as often as they could manage. Tessa had always favored Italian composers, but began to appreciate, after she grew ill, the steady, reassuring order of Bach. In the Barry Room at the Gallery, she had already begun to display the weakness that would send her to doctors and later to the hospital. Paul pressed her hands between both of his, and her worried eyes closed as she smiled and leaned against him.

Pulled from that reverie, Lucy found Ruth sitting next to her, her head leaning on Lucy's shoulder, such a rare physical demonstration that Lucy didn't dare move. Ruth picked up the sheet music.

Lucy winced and then relaxed, since if anyone could be trusted to handle a precious document, it was a Censorette.

"It's so *natural*. The way it balances. Like algebra. It can only go where it does go." She pointed to a notation in Tessa's handwriting, "*lente, lente, luc.*"

"That's my mother's note reminding me not to rush," Lucy explained.

"'*Lente*' is Latin for slow," she stated. "What is 'luc?'"

"Lucia," Lucy said. "My name."

Ruth set the sheet music down on top of the piano, on top of the handkerchief Lucy had placed there to keep the music from sticking to the piano from the damp. She touched the keys and pressed out the first two measures. She closed her eyes, shook her head, opened her eyes, and nodded. Lucy started from the beginning. As Ruth's hands imitated Lucy's in the air, Lucy realized that Ruth couldn't read music, didn't have what one would call an "ear" for music, but had rather, the eye for it. She was memorizing the movements of Lucy's fingers, as a dancer learns a dance from observation and imitation. Lucy guided Ruth's hands to the correct position on the keyboard for the opening notes. When she hesitated, Lucy demonstrated with her own hands in the air. In this way, she picked out the whole of the first section of the piece, then looked directly at Lucy, with the air of a pupil expecting praise.

Lucy obliged. "Good! Now, *da capo*."

"Head," Ruth translated.

"*Take it from the top.*"

She played it a second time. When she began it a third time, Georgie put away her maps and Lark stripped the dress from the dummy. They'd been frozen in place, observing the strange piano lesson. Lark beckoned Lucy to try on the dress, white satin with a softly pleated skirt, satin waistband, and plunging V's at neck and back.

"It's for *me?*"

"Of course. I made it from Mr. Furbert's daughter's wedding dress. I *told* you." She flicked stray threads from the bodice. "I've been measuring you these past few days, what did you think that was for?"

It was true she had cornered Lucy with a tape measure a few times, but Lucy thought she was being measured for a uniform. Whether the employees of the Detachment should wear a uniform had been proposed at several of their meetings and shot down for various reasons: they were not supposed to be conspicuous, cloth was scarce, and the reading room baked already, without adding a required suit. Lark favored a standard appearance, but the Censorettes were already a varied group, and only becoming more so. Danes and Norwegians arrived on each boat, with a variety of skills and ideas of "proper" behavior. Thwarted, Lark turned to sewing exceptional dresses from the donated jumble at St. Andrew's.

Lucy slipped the dress over her head. Lark buttoned. Lucy spun.

"Bosom." Lark pulled up the straps and seized a hand full of pins from her pincushion. Georgie jumped to act as tailor's apprentice, but they both tilted their heads toward the piano and bulged their eyes at Lucy. Ruth was still playing the "Jesu." Georgie held the straps. Lark snipped. Lucy said, "Ruth! Could you stop playing?"

She halted. "My playing is irritating. You don't like it."

"No, I do! You learnt it so quickly! You play very well. Perhaps you could learn some of those hymns I was trying out, for church."

"I want to get some of the girls more involved," Lark said, through the pins in her mouth. "And to liven up the music."

Lark stitched the strap, then patted Lucy's shoulder and turned her around. Georgie opened the door to one of the walk-in closets, which had a full-length mirror, so that Lucy could see herself in the dress. Lark, pleased, spun her sewing shears like a gunslinger in an American western film.

"We have a pair of Belgian sisters who do a beautiful close-harmony," Lark added. Lucy twirled so that the skirt flared, looked over her shoulder at her exposed back, then twirled again. "They'll do 'Swiftly Pass the Clouds of Glory' in a few Sundays. I'd like them to do 'In the Bleak Midwinter' come Christmas."

Lucy froze. Her skirt swung and settled at her legs. "Christmas?

You expect to be here at *Christmas*? Not me. When I turn twenty-one, when I can sign my own papers, I'm going back to the fight."

"We're in the fight in our own way," Georgie said. "But tonight, we dance. You never know what a besotted soldier in the arms of a pretty girl might let slip about U.S. foreign policy."

"I think their policy is pretty clear: America First."

In just four weeks, Saturday dances at the Princess had grown from quiet tea-sipping and two-step affairs to music on the wireless into dances worthy of attendance by the American military, who divided the music between phonographs and a band cobbled together from their musicians, with Alan Dodd on trumpet, and occasional vocals provided by the Censorettes. Lucy had never been more grateful that Barrett singing talent had been pooled into her sister Marcia.

"Now Ruth." Georgie rummaged through a drawer of scarves and necklaces, held them up for inspection. "What about you?

"I would like allies in the war as well. But I understand the Americans think that this is a European war."

"I meant, what are you going to wear?"

Ruth stroked her skirt and shook her head. Georgie nodded at Lucy.

"To the *dance*, Ruth," Lucy said. "You're going to the dance. I want you to."

Ruth glanced at her closet bedroom, then to Lucy, first the bolt-hole, then the ally.

"I—I haven't—haven't clothes—"

"You can borrow something of mine," Georgie said. A hard knocking on the door made them all jump. Georgie went to the door. "I have a—"

When Georgie opened the door, a young man, tanned, sandy-haired, dressed in beige which matched his colouring and furthered his intention to make no impression at all, stepped into the room, as he had many times before. Usually, he had a note for Georgie, which she read and returned to him. He had never been introduced and had never said a word. This time he merely stood in the doorway. After a glance down at his noteless hand, Georgie raised her head and they looked into one another's eyes with a peculiarly intimate stillness, before Georgie inhaled audibly. She hurried to her wardrobe and took only a cardigan and her handbag, locking the wardrobe after her. In the hearty voice she used when she meant to tell them nothing, she said, "What a bore. I won't make the dance! Lucy—see if the Vionnet will fit her."

"You just locked your wardrobe."

"Oh." Georgie tossed her the key. "Here. Not the Schiaparelli. Too much for her, I think. The Vionnet."

The door slammed, which, combined with the brassy cheer of her performance, would have prompted the fall of the curtain and happy applause at a comedy in the West End. But the three of them stood silent, left to wonder which country had just been invaded by, or had surrendered to, the Nazis.

09.

It was no keen feat of espionage to unlock a door to which she had been given the key, but Lucy could not suppress a triumphant tingle as she fitted the key into Georgie's guarded wardrobe. Ruth asked, "The V&A? She has a dress from the Victoria and Albert Museum? It must be a costume. Is this a costume dance?"

Lucy laughed and half-embraced her. "Oh, you are an odd duck, but you're *my* odd duck. We'll turn you into a swan yet. No, duckling, a *Vionnet. Et voila.*"

She flung open the doors of Georgie's wardrobe: blouses, skirts, shorts and slacks, but also, on the right, a thin stripe of scarlet and white glamour. There was a red Vionnet tea gown, which Lucy quickly flung to Lark and Ruth to get them started, while she inspected the other items in the collection. The Schiaparelli was a red satin evening gown.

"That would be too much," Georgie had declared. *You don't say.* It was not only too much for a canteen dance, but for almost any occasion Lucy could imagine might take place in Bermuda, including a visit from the Duke and Duchess of Windsor, who had in fact stopped by the previous August on their way to the Bahamas. Had Georgina been invited to *that*? And here was another Vionnet, this time white: an evening gown with a patterned tulle overskirt. Lucy plucked it from the wardrobe and held it against herself. The sight of it was an actual thrill.

As a bribe for spending her sixteenth summer at Knoll House with only her sister Marcia for company, Lucy had been allowed to choose a fine dress. After much research in magazines and shops, she had chosen a Chanel: a black day dress with big red flowers. While elegant, the dress was practical, could be worn to graduations and weddings. This Vionnet was a fever dream. Had she seen it during her research it might have altered the course of her life. Just to wear this dress, she might have agreed to marry Guy Jenner, become a country housewife—*pull yourself together, girl! It's a dress!*

But what a dress. What else did she have? Evening bags? Beneath the rack of clothes, there was a set of drawers; atop them, shoes, sensible and athletic, a rucksack, an ordinary handbag. Perhaps a necklace, in this drawer? She slid the drawer open. It contained two passports with the cover issued by the U.K. The Vionnet rustled when she knelt and picked one up.

"I'm sure Georgie didn't give us her key so we could pry," Lark said behind her.

"I'm sure it's not prying if she gave us her key."

She opened the passport. It was issued to Annegret Maria Lincoln, born in Berlin in 1914, with a photograph of a younger, more wide-eyed version of Georgie. Confounded, Lucy could only stare. This must be how Ruth felt all the time, confronted by things that appeared to say one thing but could mean a multitude of others.

"*Lucy!*"

Lark snatched the passport out of Lucy's hand, tossed it back into the drawer with the others and slammed the drawer.

"Lark—that *passport*—it says—"

"Lucia Victoria Gheldini *Barrett*! Snoops get exactly what they deserve."

Lark then took the white Vionnet from Lucy and held it aloft, glancing between the designer's work and the dress Lucy wore, then returned the Vionnet to the wardrobe with a resigned shrug and shake of the head which shamed Lucy with the flush of ingratitude she'd sometimes felt at Christmas when she unwrapped a grammar book instead of a hoped-for game and saw her parents' disappointment in her reaction.

"You did a lovely job, Lark," Lucy told her. "Very neat stitching. I could never do such neat stitching."

"Neat stitching is my business," Lark said. She locked the wardrobe and turned to Ruth. The red Vionnet had not quite transformed Ruth from a flower girl into a duchess, but she looked markedly different. Lark had brushed and then plaited Ruth's hair, and then gathered the plaits into a chignon. It was a style, Lucy noted, that Ruth would have quite a job tearing apart. Her hair usually looked like a wig of bracken because she pulled and twisted her tendrils as though trying to extract a demented thought from the confines of her mind.

"I'll only embarrass you and you'll be cross," Ruth said. "Why do I have to go?"

"Just for one dance. Have you ever been to a dance?"

"No."

"That's why you have to go, I expect," Lark said, holding open the door.

***

"You're late," Bill said, his back to her, when they came into the canteen. He hadn't turned to see her but had registered her entrance by the reaction of the women surrounding him: the sudden droop in their smiles, the dulling of their animation, the half-octave dip of the drone of their buzzing. Whenever she left Inman alone, she returned to find him surrounded by chattering women. He neither encouraged nor discouraged this popularity but accepted it as the natural order, like the heir to a titled estate. Perhaps he was one. Perhaps that's what "*We're tobacco growers*," delivered as such a casual boast, meant in the States. He spun around and took her hand with Astaire-like grace, the eyes of all the girls still on him. At their chorus of sighs, Lucy realized that she could hear them. The rain had finally stopped.

Alan was plucking the strings of a bass cello in tonight's makeshift band, while Lark's Belgian sisters, with the long sallow faces found in Renaissance paintings, sang a close-harmonied "I Can't Get Started" in Flemish-tinged English, then stepped back as Alan lifted his trumpet to conclude the song. Lucy offered Bill her cheek to kiss but kept her eyes on the stage, noting the largesse of the U.S. military: how the drum kit had increased in size since the last week, how the upright piano was keenly in tune. There were three microphones where there had been one. The phonograph had been replaced with a larger one, and the tea urn with two vats containing bottles of beer and Coca-Cola in melting ice.

"The band is better every week," Lucy said. "Bill, this is my roommate, Ruth Smith."

"This is my first dance," Ruth said. "I had to come because I've never been. But now I've been and I'd like to go back to the room."

Bill turned to Lucy, awaiting a translation. When none came, Bill said, "Nice to meet you, Miss Smith. Pretty dress."

"I shouldn't think it is nice to meet me," Ruth said. "Since I don't want to be here. I don't understand a 'dance.' You don't invite people to a 'sing.'"

Ruth managed to add, "This isn't my dress and I didn't want to wear it," before Lark nearly dragged her away to meet the two newcomers, "those Belgian sisters I was talking about."

Someone put "Moonglow" on the phonograph and Bill pulled Lucy into his arms.

"Alone at last! I assume that *is* your dress and you *did* want to wear it. You look like a princess. The princess of the Princess. Have you recovered?"

Lark danced with Alan. The Belgian sisters laughed at something Ruth was saying. Or perhaps, *at* Ruth. *A language barrier?* They seemed puzzled; Ruth seemed earnest. Then they seemed earnest, and Ruth seemed puzzled. The sisters giggled. Ruth looked at her feet and a protective instinct surged so strongly in Lucy that Bill felt it too. He squeezed her fingers in his own and steered her out of the sightline.

"Hey. Over here. *Honey.* Where are you tonight?"

"I'm worried about Ruth."

"No girl in my arms should ever worry. You should've left her home. Wallflowers're happier at home. Take my sister Evie. Me and the cousins dance with her and then she's allowed to go home with a headache. Back to her books."

Across the room, Alan guided Ruth onto the dance floor.

Bill asked, "Where's Georgie tonight?"

"She was called away. I say, Bill, have you heard anything?" At his raised eyebrow, she added, "You lot have short-wave radios."

"Don't y'all? Rumor has it you got a full intelligence set-up here."

"We just do routine clerical work," Lucy said. This had been drilled into her, like German adjectives and verbs: *When you speak of this, and you must never speak of this, you must say 'routine clerical work,' although you must never speak of this.*

"Well, maybe that's true. But maybe it ain't. Know what I heard? Heard you girls were chosen by how good your legs look."

"There is that rumor."

There was indeed that rumor. Some official's wife had suggested that girls with "finely turned-out ankles" might be best suited for censorship work.

"Moonglow" ended and a small group gathered around the jukebox, the women pointing at titles, the men digging for pocket change. Bill leaned in to kiss her, and she responded with the kiss she gave him when they were alone. Georgie's mention of kissing on the roof had referred to the practice of the few Censorettes who had boyfriends sneaking them onto the roof—they called it "stargazing"— in order to spend some time alone without having to resort to petting on a bench by the harbour.

The clarinet and saxophone-soaked opening of "Moonlight Serenade" began. The man selecting the records seemed in a lunar frame of mind. Then she stepped back, her hands still entwined behind his neck. He looked pleased and pliable. "Will you do me a small favor, Bill?"

"Whatever you want, honey."

"Will you ask Ruth to dance?" As Bill rolled his eyes, she waved Alan over.

"Yes, ma'am?" Alan arrived, his fingers perched on the back of Ruth's hand like a lord on his lady's. Ruth looked flushed but calm.

"Bill would like a turn with Ruth."

"He wants to dance with *me*?" Ruth's face was such a mask of disbelief that even Bill softened. "*All* the girls want to dance with him."

"She's a great dancer, now I've taught her," Alan assured them.

"But he hasn't asked me," Ruth said. Lucy stepped just in front of Bill so that she could kick his shin with her heel.

"Would you care to dance, Ruth?" Bill asked in the tone he would use to repeat an order to a daydreaming private. Lucy took Alan's hand and led him away.

"That was a lovely performance, Ensign." She adjusted her frame to Alan's. Bill was an easy fit, but Alan was taller and broader than most of the other men. Wearing a trench coat, he could have held his arms above them and provided a tent in a storm.

"Well, thanks, Lucia. But don't call jazz 'lovely' and don't call me 'Ensign' since you're not my C.O. It's Alan. Lark tells me you play piano."

"Only what's written down for me. I've no talent for improvisation."

"Improvisation is thinking about how something could go another way."

So what does your Joe mean by 'Do nothing until you hear from me'?

"Alan. What do you know about the New York City harbour?"

"The Statue of Liberty lives there?"

"Do you know Red Hook?" At his shrug, she prompted, "It's in an area called Brooklyn?"

Alan laughed, "What're you asking me for if you already know?"

"Is Red Hook near the harbour?"

"It's near the Navy Yard."

"There's a naval yard in Brooklyn?"

"Lemme think." He squinted. "This is a tough one. Oh, yeah. It's called the Brooklyn Navy Yard."

Lucy blushed. *When had she last been teased to a blush*? Not since Matty. She relaxed her twitching mouth into a smile.

Alan moved his hand from her waist to a spot between her shoulder blades, his hand warm against her bare back as he pulled her closer. That hand, and his hand which held hers, pulsed into her, and then ebbed. She exhaled slowly. "Moonlight Serenade" ended. Lucy clenched both her hands against Alan, her hand in his, her hand at his shoulder, signaling him not to release her. *Not yet.*

Someone put on the record "Mood Indigo."

"Ah, 'tis my lord the Duke of Ellington." When Lucy pulled back so he could see the shake of her head at his weak joke, Alan winked at her. "Stick with me, kid. We'll make you a jazz hound yet."

"Jazz hound."

"Maybe a jazz puppy."

"Jazz is so *American*."

"Oh yeah?"

"Bold. Forward. Doesn't follow the rules."

"I suspect you mean rude."

"Perhaps rude. Perhaps I'm rude to say it. Flirting is something else I've no talent at."

"Are you flirting?"

"We should change the subject."

"Have you met the Belgian sisters?" Alan asked obediently. "Ruth told me. They're called Fleur and Roos. Flower and Rose. 'Flower' and 'rose' are both nouns and verbs. Both verbs indicate the transformation from one state to another."

"Ruth can be a bit … focused in her conversation. You were kind to ask her."

"What about asking you? Was I kind to do that?"

"As I recall, you didn't ask. As I recall, you haven't asked still."

***

Lark was so shocked when Lucy told her this, later that night as they readied themselves for bed, that she paused in brushing her hair and straightened her spine as though called to *attention!* Lucy may as well have confessed to placing Alan's hand on her bare breast.

"You said *what?* That is so *flirtatious!*" Lark whispered.

"I like him."

"You hardly *know* him. If anything, I know him better than you do. He carried me in his *arms* to that stupid jeep."

Lucy shrugged. "And did you feel safe? He makes me feel safe."

"You *hate* feeling safe."

"No. I hate being sent away to safety. That's a different thing entirely."

"You'll be glad of it tonight," Georgie said. They were accustomed by now to her silent comings and goings, to calling out a question from their room to hers, then walking in to hers to find her vanished in mid-conversation. "London's taking a heavy hit tonight. Very heavy. The worst yet. Parliament. St. James. The whole city's on fire."

When she said "fire," Lucy felt the heat leave her body. She asked, "The Admiralty? How do you know? Do you have the BBC?"

In good weather, they could sometimes get the BBC. More often, they received the Canadian Broadcasting System, which, unless repeating information from Britain or the United States, was consistently dreary to those who lacked an interest in farm commodities. Regardless of the reception, news from the wireless was only news, not truth. They would never be told how bad it really was.

"Georgie!"

"I don't know any more than you do!"

"And if you did, you wouldn't tell us!"

Their raised voices brought Ruth out of her closet. Georgie walked to the wet bar. Lark led Lucy to the couch and made her sit down. Georgie handed them each a glass of whisky and returned to the wet bar.

"Whisky, Ruth?"

"I prefer Mother's ruin, thank you."

They glanced at her in surprise, then Georgie poured. "Mother's ruin" was a nickname for gin, but how did Ruth know that, and since when did she drink it? Lucy pulled her down to the couch next to her, and when they toasted, "*Absent friends,*" Lucy could barely stifle a sob. She was stupid. The Luftwaffe had bombed London every night since the bombing that had killed her mother. It bombed London on the nights she fell asleep in her cool sheets and the cedar breeze, puzzling over a letter she had read. It bombed London on the nights she tossed in the bed next to the tranquil Lark, kept awake by her leg spasms from the tennis. It bombed London under the same full moon—*bomber's moon*—under which she "stargazed" with Bill on the roof of the Princess. So why did it seem worse tonight? The fear in Georgie's eyes. The fact that she had said "Parliament." The fact that she had poured them all drinks. The fact that she had poured Ruth Mother's ruin.

"Worry won't help anything. 'Which of you by taking thought can add one cubit unto his stature?'" Lark quoted.

"I can't help taking thought."

"Take my hand instead."

Lark, on her right, took Lucy's hand, kissed it, held it. Ruth, on her left, plucked at one of Lucy's fingers, and then another, as though she wanted to take her hand but feared that the hand might turn on her, like a baby forest animal, a hedgehog or a badger, and nip her.

"And what the bloody hell is a cubit?" Lucy finished her whisky. "The last thing that I said to my father … not even to him, to that WREN of his … he wouldn't come to the phone. The pips were going. At the dock at Liverpool. I was about to get into that stupid boat that brought me here. I told her 'Tell him' *Pip! Pip! Pip!* 'tell him I will never forgive him.' That might be the last thing he ever hears from me."

"I think good fathers are like the good Father," Lark said. "They see more than their children do. Children are brats and fathers forgive them. That's how it'd go if I were in charge of this world. I told my father I'd never forgive him. I haven't yet. But never is a long time."

"Forgive him for what?" Lucy asked.

"I'm glad that my father sent me away," Ruth said before Lucy could probe Lark further. "I don't embarrass him here. I can walk the whole island in one day, and draw whatever I like. Hector doesn't laugh at me. I do things Aunt Verity said I would never do. I can wear red. I can go to a dance. I can have friends. I've never had a friend. What? Have I said something wrong?"

"No, my duckling." Lucy set her glass on the coffee table and stretched her arm around Ruth's shoulders. "You have said exactly the right thing."

Ruth reached her right arm above her head and tapped, with her index finger, the tip of Lucy's middle finger. Then she traced her index finger down Lucy's arm. Lucy quivered at the surprise of it. Ruth stopped her finger at Lucy's elbow.

"That is the length," Ruth said. "Of a cubit."

10.

London, 1940

The hospital room smells almost like home, or perhaps it is more correct to say her mother smells like herself again, instead of like a patient. Now that she has been permitted to sit up, Tessa's first concern is for her toilette. Her hair must be washed. She cannot walk to the bathroom, so Lucy washes her hair at the bed, painstakingly wetting, shampooing, rinsing, one pitcher at a time, emptying the basin again and again, then toweling and combing Tessa's hair, then smoothing the ends of it with olive oil. She waits to do this until the ward sisters are well out of sight; they would disapprove of this Dago practice. She overheard one sister tell another, "The Dago in bed twelve needs a bedpan." They scowl when they hear Lucy and Tessa speaking Italian to one another.

"*Ratta tatta tatta*," mimics one sister as she changes Tessa's linen. "Can't you lot speak English?"

It is October 1940. Mussolini declared war on the United Kingdom in June, just after Dunkirk. Shortly thereafter, more than 4,000 men born in Italy but living now in England were rounded up and sent to internment camps. "*Collar the lot!*" Churchill had ordered, and so the authorities had, down to the pastry chef who made Tessa's *Torta Pasqualina*, the barber who had tended to Matty since he was seven years old, and the grocer who sold the olive oil.

Tessa is sufficiently distressed, with her son missing, her native country at war with her adopted country, and now her womb removed, without being taxed to speak English. Groggy, in pain, drifting in and out of her sedatives, she finds her native language easier. Lucy obliges. To hell with the nursing sisters. It had taken most of the spring and summer for the combined forces of doctors, Paul and Lucy to convince Tessa to submit to the surgery. Tessa wants to keep her womb, her ovaries. She has reached the last age for children, and there was hope of one, she thought, but then she bled and bled. The doctor discovered tumors. There might be cancer. The mission of cancer is to spread, and so these cancerous organs in her must be removed. Even so, Tessa can barely forgive Lucy for siding with the enemy.

"When you have trouble and you are a woman, they will always say the trouble is that you are a woman," she told Lucy. "You will see. You have been blessed with excellent health, but you will see."

Tessa's excellent health had been a part of her, like her radiance: four healthy births: three living children and the baby, Marco, who lived only a month. She bid goodbye to maternity, as all women must, and now withstands the indignity of the loss of her womb. But after weeks in this bed, her radiance has begun to return, along with her impatience for home.

Lucy dabs her fingertip with olive oil and rubs her finger along her mother's dry lips. Olive oil is Tessa's cure for chapped lips. Tessa kisses Lucy's fingertip. Lucy kisses her mother's cheek and then her forehead, the goodnight benediction of her childhood. Then she rises, walk to the sink and washes the oil from her hands and towels them dry. She finds a linen closet she is certain is off-limits to her and brings fresh towels to the room. She places one around Tessa's neck and arranges it over her wet hair. She pulls out a bottle of Drewe's hand lotion and lotions Tessa's hands. Both women inhale its vanilla-almond scent. For the first time in weeks, Tessa's smile is genuine.

Is she vain to think her mother beautiful? She must be, because everyone says Lucy is her mother's very image, even Granny Barrett, who was overheard to sniff that of course, Tessa's *beauty* was never in question, but were there not beautiful English girls about? There were, but their beauty was not like Tessa's, whose face to the world was no mere felicity of features, but an exuberance which Matty inherited and Lucy did not. Tessa loves music and Matty loves flying and each, when they speak of their love, sparkle with gratitude for the gift of this love. When at school Lucy reads the line from Browning *She had a heart too soon made glad*, she thinks of both her mother and her brother.

"You must tell me, Lucia, is Matteo dead?" Tessa asks. "If my son is dead, there are arrangements I must make in my prayers. Her Son died before her also. She will understand."

Tessa has all these years attended Anglican services both in London and at Knollborough, an obedient wife, but perhaps all the time, her prayers have been beholden to Rome, like a Catholic in Tudor England, showing one face to the vulgar world but her true devotion, exercised in secret closets, to her true faith.

"Would you tell me if you *did* know?" Tessa insists. "Do not nod," she adds, when Lucy does, "Tell me, how long have you been lying to me?"

"Mama!"

Lucy has been lying to her since she was old enough to set foot outside the house. Lucy and Matty kept things from her to save her pain, remarks made in the playground, comments overhead at birthday parties. *That Dago! The last of the Barrett boys! Thrown away on that foreigner.* They had joshed her away from the reasons why certain people would not come to their house, why Paul focused on Lucy's education over her social status. *No distressa Tessa,* Matty dubbed it. They built their world around her, and if it was a smaller world than it would have been otherwise, it was their world and they loved it.

"*Mama!*" Tessa mocks. She displays her hands. "You lied to me about this very hand cream."

Che seccatura! Lucy hoped Tessa had forgotten. On a summer day in 1939, after the annexation of Czechoslovakia but before the invasion of Poland, Tessa and Lucy spent an afternoon on an aimless stroll in Kensington Gardens, a habit of theirs since Lucy's childhood, an Italian custom, the *dolce far niente*, the sweetness of doing nothing, of observing: that tree, the pretty dress on that little girl, the formation of that cloud: *Very like a whale.* They returned to find Matty hauling from the boot of Paul's car a crate of Drewe's hand lotion and a crate of Drewe's cold cream. Tessa entered the black-and-white-tiled foyer behind Matty, removed her hat and held at bay Paul's welcoming kiss.

"Apparently, my skin is too *rough* to kiss, since it requires so much lotion."

"Nonsense." Paul stroked her cheek. How her parents endlessly cooed at one another! So *unEnglish*, all this petting. *Carezza Tessa,* Matty dubbed their public displays. Paul said, "Drewe's might be going out of business. I wanted to make sure you had enough."

"Drewe's! *Ma è così benuolute!* Going out of business?"

"Or shifting its business," Matty said, carrying a crate up the stairs.

"That will do," Paul said, with a sharpness that snapped Lucy into the realization Paul had received intelligence on this very thing, Drewe's shifting its production. Lucy met Matty's eyes. *To what? They produced lubricants.* From greasing women's skin to greasing the wheels of the war machine. Matty gave her just a small nod, but not before Tessa saw it, looked at Paul, then looked at Lucy, with a frown at her betrayal.

"I don't know where Matty is," Lucy says.

"*I leali* strike again."

"Your sedative, Mrs. Barrett." A nurse comes in with a glass of water and a pill in her outstretched hand. "Time for you to go, Miss. Visiting hours are over."

"I'd like to stay with her until she falls asleep."

"Visiting hours are over."

"Yes, but it's a private room, and I only want to stay with my mother until she falls asleep. We'll be quiet."

"Rules are rules, Miss. I can't think why you lot think you're an exception. You lot especially. Can't you understand the King's English?"

"Goodnight, Mama." Lucy speaks in an English far closer to the King's than the nurse's. She kisses her mother's forehead. "I'll see you tomorrow."

Outside the evening air is cool and sulfurous, though the fog lifts as she walks. She should take the bus or the Tube to make it home to the empty house to take shelter in the cellar when the Luftwaffe comes. They have not missed a night for weeks, and it is a full moon tonight, a "bomber's moon." But she needs to walk off Tessa's hurt, her belief that Paul and Lucy would conspire to conceal such important knowledge as Matty's whereabouts. Paul might, but Lucy wouldn't. She has missed an entire day's work with Karolina Diehl's refugee organization in order to bathe and tend to her mother. She has been rewarded with a parfait of affection and reproach. She wishes Matty were here.

The air raid sirens wail. The nearest Tube station is far, and she has no provisions with her. She ducks instead into a pub whose sign in the window promises a cellar. The bartender, a chubby-faced man with thick dark hair, thick brows and pale eyes (she will remember these details forever), pours her a pint to take downstairs. She waits out the bombing with the crowd.

When the all-clear sounds, she leaves the pub. She hears one of the ambulance drivers call out that the hospital has been hit. She runs through the crowd, down streets that seem to go on forever, past arms that hold her back.

She sees her father on his knees, diminished to a howling thing in the rubble of the streets, lit by the flames of the burning hospital, with a keening that sounds like an air raid siren. She feels that this must be what Hell is like, a burning landscape of grief endured by thousands, a private anguish exposed to a public too consumed with the common suffering to offer comfort to one individual. Her father's loss does not evoke even a pause among the rescue workers. The loss is one among multitudes, their devastation a spark in an inferno.

"I thought you were with her," he shouts. "I thought you were *with* her!

"They made me go," Lucy says. "The ward sisters."

"'ere, miss, get him off the street, can you? We got to pull the hoses through."

The fire warden and two older men from the night watch help her carry him off the street, each taking a limb. His screaming abates to an athletic sobbing. The Red Cross worker who comes along knows better than to offer him the Blitz cure-all of a "nice cup of tea." After a few slaps to Paul's face brings no reaction other than gasps for breath akin to a man drowning, the volunteer pulls him to his feet and asks Lucy, "Neighbour of yours, is he, love? We need to see to the others. Can you help him?"

"Yes, of course. He's my father."

"Your *father*?"

"My mother—the hospital." Lucy gestured at the flames and rubble behind her. The ambulance driver took both her hands and raised her up. "I'll see to him. Thank you."

He touches her shoulder before he moves on, with an expression combining compassion and contempt. Compassion for Lucy, having to try to piece back together a man who would display such weakness. And contempt for Paul for displaying it, especially before his child. He had all but said, "Pull yourself together, man!"

11.

Bermuda, 1941

The next day, their small wet bar had grown into a gleaming Manhattan of tall liquor bottles provided by the Yanks. Lark shook Lucy awake for church. Only the fact that Lark had, the night before, confessed that she had not yet forgiven her father (although she had not revealed his transgression) compelled Lucy to pull on Sunday clothes that morning, ignore her whisky-aching head, and trudge down the hill to St. Andrew's. Ruth, after a few more glasses of "Mother's ruin," had fallen asleep across Lucy's lap, and it had taken the combined forces of Lucy, Lark and Georgie, to compel her into her closet and strip her of the red Vionnet (but not her handsome coiffure).

When Lucy and Lark returned from church, they heard the noise of the visitors as they climbed the stairs. They opened the door to their rooms to find a party in progress. Bill and his friends had come with three bottles of whisky, a bottle of gin, two bottles of tonic water, a bottle of the local Gosling rum, a box of saltine crackers, a chunk of cheese and a jar of pickles. Everything apart from the rum was courtesy of the personal stashes of the men, whom Bill had bullied into donations. Alan had brought some off the Navy. News of the presence of men rippled through the hotel, and a few women pushed past Lucy and Lark as they stood in the doorway to their rooms, still in their church hats and white gloves.

Lucy started to back out of the room but Lark cuffed her with her hand. "Oh no, you don't. You're not leaving me here with all these men, and Ruth."

"But who asked them here?"

"Honey, you look so tired." Bill crossed the room in three long steps and gathered her in his arms. "You get any sleep at all? Me and the boys, we brought some things to cheer you up. We heard it on the radio. The palace, the parliament ... poor old London. We all thought you wouldn't want to be alone."

"It's very kind of you," Lucy said, somewhat mechanically, since she felt no gratitude, only a weariness and a yearning for the company only of those for whom this was not a distant, foreign drama.

Over his shoulder, Lucy surveyed the room. The men sat on the sofa, the chairs or the floor, reserving the bed for the women. Ruth sat on the piano bench, facing the room, twirling a strand of hair pulled from her chignon. Georgie, at the French windows, watched the entry to the hotel. Georgie could have invoked the "no men on the floors," rule an hour ago or clapped her hands twice in that way she had: *Chop! Chop!* and cleared the room. Since she hadn't, she must have had a reason for allowing them to stay, although she seemed to have drawn the line at entertaining them. Since none of the actual occupants of the suite indicated enthusiasm for the role, Gwynne embraced the role of hostess, distributing tumblers of whisky poured over ice, the way the Yanks drank it.

"Well, now you lot'll have to come in," Gwynne said, made more Cockney by the whiskey. "You can't let Hitler take over all of Europe."

"He hasn't got England," Georgie said without turning around.

"Y'all say 'come in' like you're invitin' us to a barbecue," Bill complained, releasing Lucy and striding toward his whisky, which he snatched and downed. He held out his glass for a refill. "It's a goddamn war, started from a bad treaty after the last war. And if you ask me, that war started because of some goddamn Kraut lunatic and a bunch of grudges between a bunch of kings and queens who're all goddamn cousins to begin with. Why's it our fault if y'all can't sort out your borders?"

"Military history must be a rather simple course at West Point." Georgie picked up the ice bucket and distributed the last of the ice cubes with a pair of silver tongs.

"Sorry, Georgie, but that's a hell of a lot more history than the average Yank understands at all," Bill said. "These dumb goddamn Yanks you're asking to 'come in' and spill blood for you. We sent money. We sent guns."

"Lark doesn't like swearing," Ruth said. "You've said 'goddamn' four times."

Lark made her way across the room, stepping around men as gingerly as a cat skirting puddles after a downpour. When she reached her own living area, she pulled off her gloves, unpinned her hat and nodded at Fleur and Roos, sitting on her bed.

"I apologize for my language," Bill said. "I don't usually discuss politics with ladies."

Then why didn't he go somewhere else and discuss politics with men? Why didn't they decamp to a bar on Front Street, where their manners and their language would be more welcome? Why were they drinking whisky at half-past two? If it was half-past two in Bermuda, it was half-past seven in England. By now, the glass and debris in the streets would have been swept, the hoses wound up, the filthy-faced wardens and ambulance drivers collapsing onto cots. People would be on the move, always on the move, carrying things: buckets, blankets, babies, bodies. Some would be heading for the shelters already, with darkness creeping back over the City, the same bright moon set to appear, the Luftwaffe refueling for return.

She could only imagine. Imagination was worse than knowledge. She hadn't been this clutched by a girdle of dread, when she had been in the thick of it. It was worse to hear about it than to be in it, and it was much worse to wonder than to hear.

"It's not just politics to these girls, Inman," Alan reminded him. "I guess they've got a right to talk about it."

"With foreigners, then."

"I guess in America you can be a member of America First," Alan smiled. "But I'm not sure what the rules are in Bermuda. We're all of us foreigners here."

"Hector is Bermudian," Ruth offered. "Hector in the lobby."

"With foreigners who don't understand American politics." Bill's smile grew strained.

"Can't say I understand American politics myself," Alan said.

"I suppose you want us in the war," Bill snapped. "I suppose you're chomping at the bit to go get killed overseas for a bunch of foreigners."

"What I want hasn't mattered since I set foot in Annapolis." Alan stood up and a few of the women scooted back, as though expecting blows between the men. "I navigate ships. I follow orders. I play the piano. Ruth, mind if I have a look at that one?"

"Lucy is teaching me a song, Alan." Ruth surrendered the piano bench to him and showed him the sheet music to the "Jesu." "Do you want to play this?"

"I thought …" Alan placed the sheet music on top of the piano. Then he tested the action of the keys and played a few rapid scales. Lucy, trying to blink away the sand crusting in her sleep-deprived eyes, felt a pulse of a smile at his nimble ease. He played several chord progressions. "Something jazzier. Need help on vocals, though. I'm better on the trumpet."

"Yeah, buddy, we're all better on the trumpet!" said one of the Navy, inspiring a cackle among the men.

Bill snapped, "Ladies present!" while Alan launched into an arpeggio introduction.

"Alan, ve vould like to ree-hearse de song from last night," Fleur or Roos said. They joined him at the piano. The rustling room settled, taking a communal sip of their whisky. Then he began to play "I Can't Get Started." *I've been around the world in a plane …*

Lark tugged the bed into shape. Georgie strode across the room. The men leaned out of her way. She walked around Lucy and opened the door, with Ruth in her wake.

"Lucy." Ruth rocked like an actress impersonating someone on a storm-tossed ship. "I don't like all these people in here. The singing. I'm sorry I'm so tedious."

"You're not tedious, duckling." Lucy took her hands. "I don't like it either."

"I'd like to go to my room and sketch. May I?"

Lucy kissed her on the forehead. Across the room, Inman, watching, finished his drink, poured another and started towards her.

Ladies present. Well, quite so: ladies were present in this gathering because the gathering had descended upon the ladies' residence. The men were respectful enough, keeping their elbows in and their hands off of things but it was obvious that they were content to be in the presence the civilization provided by ladies—the starch-pressed curtains rustled by cedar-scented breeze, the bowl of peach roses, Ruth's watercolours, Lark's sewing basket, the fragrance of Drewe's lotion and lavender talcum powder.

Yet the female sensibility that brought about these domestic pleasures was the one that must be appeased, with no reference to politics. They had been roused to comfort the ladies ("*I brought some things to cheer you up*") by the very thing that they were reluctant to discuss in front of them. Abruptly, Lucy desired the presence only of *ladies*: no men.

Alan led the Belgians into further verses of the song, stating the lyrics to them before each line. Georgie returned, with the man who had fetched her last night. He paused in the doorway, disconcerted to find a party in progress. Georgie handed Lucy a slip of paper.

A transcription of a telegraph message read: "SAFE. ALL MY LOYAL CHILDREN SAFE. STAY WHERE YOU ARE SO I DON'T WORRY. DAD."

So *you* won't worry. The *cheek* of it! She'd rather be drinking in fumes from the fires, dispensing tea and blankets, than tucked away in this tranquility, dispensing whisky, nibbling on the bitter bread of banishment. *Bitter bread of banishment*, that was Shakespeare, that was what someone said in what play ... *focus*, Lucy, there's something else in this message.

Lucy read the message again, holding each word in her mind as though writing it on a chalkboard, holding her breath, so that when she remembered to breathe she had to gasp for breath, as though surfacing from the sea. *All my loyal children safe. I leali strike again.*

Bill stood before her.

"Everything OK, honey?"

"Yes, Bill." Lucy turned to Georgie's friend, he of the beige clothes that were neither too formal (short trousers, as the Bermuda constabulary wore) nor too casual (coupled with a white shirt, and beige tie and jacket), he of the watery eyes which protruded too far while his chin receded too much, leaving only a thin lower lip, his mouth like a precarious footpath on a cliff that has crumbled. His eyes appraised her, judging her reaction. She donned *la freddezza*, and kept her expression cool.

"Yes, of course," Lucy said to the man. "I'll come at once."

She took her gloves from the window ledge, kissed Bill swiftly, then swept out as the man, who had betrayed only a flicker of confusion before falling into her ruse, held the door for her. She ran down the first flight of stairs, and then the second, without glancing back, and only paused on the third landing to allow her messenger to catch up.

"There's no need for you, Barrett," the man said. "I delivered a message. Now I must get back."

"Of course. I shan't keep you." She descended the next flight down. "I see you know my name, I don't — ?"

A Granny gesture: the wave of a gloved hand, the incomplete question: *the protocol of the colonials? Do enlighten me.*

"Reginald Teck."

"Thank you, Mr. Teck. I did need to get out of that room." Teck shuffled alongside her, eyes ahead. "The telegram read 'All my loyal children are safe.' *I leali.* The loyal ones. Matty's been missing since he flew off with the RAF at Dunkirk. You know all this already."

"I don't see what you mean." Teck gazed over her head. She watched him drift away and then oar himself back in to the moment with an *ahem.* "Why would I know the pet names within your family? Now I must get back—"

"Not yet. I'm sure he's watching. Don't look. Walk with me toward town."

Teck raised a sandy eyebrow but obeyed. They turned onto Front Street and started down the gentle slope.

"How did you receive this message from my father?"

"The way we receive most messages."

"Morse code, was it? Sent from the Admiralty, transmitted ship to ship, across the Atlantic. Crawling with U-boats. You must think me awfully selfish."

"No more so than the recipient of most messages." At Lucy's anxious glance, he clarified, with a raise of one corner of his mouth, "Which is to say, not. I say, Barrett, do you *know* Morse code?"

She shook her head.

"Might do well to learn it." They had reached the small building by the harbour where passengers bought tickets for the ferry.

"I'll learn anything you like if you tell me where my brother is."

"As you told *me*, your brother's with the RAF. If he was missing and is now safe, one must presume he is back with the RAF."

"But where's he *been*? He's been missing nearly a year!"

"I couldn't say. As I'm sure you appreciate, even if I knew, I couldn't say. And as we're out of the eyes of jealous boyfriends, I must press on. Good day."

Teck walked back the way they had come. Lucy yearned to do the same. She was exhausted. Now that this long-awaited relief had been delivered, she felt a chemical release of her fear, as though her mother had come in the middle of the night to embrace her and return her to bed: *only a bad dream, tesoro mia.* She craved sleep. She wanted her bed, but couldn't return to her room of singing sailors and harmonizing Censorettes, a Bill full of questions, a Lark full of indignation. She hadn't brought a handbag so couldn't go to a tea room. Anyway, she wanted sleep, not tea.

She looked at the note again, as though it were written in her father's own hand. SAFE. ALL MY LOYAL CHILDREN SAFE. STAY WHERE YOU ARE SO I DON'T WORRY. DAD. But where *was* Matty? Why hadn't he written to her? Was he actually in the RAF, or in Intelligence? Perhaps both? Were Paul and Matty conspiring to treat her as they had Tessa?

If she could find a place to sit and think. There were benches, she remembered, in front of the Bermuda Library. She walked up the slight hill and saw that the gate to the yard of the library was open, which seemed a small miracle on a Sunday. She found a cedar bench under a tree.

The scent of cedar had once invoked anxiety and the stomach clench of failure. There was a cedar chest in a bedroom at Knoll House in which Lucy stored the linen she was made to embroider for her marriage. Her embroidery was abysmal and she always hoped, as she added another botched *serviette* to the pile at the conclusion of a long, nagged-at afternoon, that the husband imposed on her would not be bothered about fine stitching. In Bermuda, cedar was an industry, the communal pulse of the island, the breath of the breeze. It was the underlying scent of exile. *The bitter bread of banishment.*

She had that diet in common with Brooklyn Joe, the bitter bread, but she was stuck here. If Joe was that homesick, why did he not go back? *Do nothing till you hear from me* meant something would be done, at some time in the future, and that Joe would be the one to tell them when. Was he merely drumming up support for the Nazis among the people of New York City? Then why mention *goods* in a *warehouse*? And why did she keep thinking of harbours and ports?

"Lucy? Hello. So sorry to wake you, only—"

Clara Frith, the librarian who had supplied the answer to the 'Swan of Avon' mystery, shook her awake. She had to leave the library and lock up the gate, she said, and if that should happen, Lucy would be locked in the yard until the following day. Lucy had been found asleep on a public bench, with both dried and fresh drool forming trails to her chin. What would Granny say to *that.*

***

"The Reverend telephoned last night." Clara settled them in a tea room on Reid Street, after insisting that Lucy allow Clara to treat her. "In the wee hours. He wanted to re-write his sermon after listening to the wireless last night. They say the Jerries hit *Big Ben*. The weeks after Easter are usually a bit of a free-for-all for the reverend. So the sermon he had was just ordinary. He wanted to buck us up. He wanted that speech from *Richard II*. You know, 'This blessed plot, this earth, this realm, this England.' The bit that goes 'This fortress built by Nature for herself/Against infection and the hand of war.' I *do* like that. The pages of my copy were glued together from the damp. So I went to the library to find it this morning before church and then I returned it. And then I found you."

"'*The bitter bread of banishment*,'" Lucy said. It was from the same play. It had been Matty's line. He had minced it, as he disliked alliteration, earning a frown from Paul. Paul had declaimed the 'this earth, this realm, this England' speech. It was an old man's speech and he'd been the oldest man in the room. She'd had no lines. There were wives at the dinner party that night, and so few women in *Richard II*, so why had it been chosen? Lucy had busied herself refilling drinks, clearing ashtrays, redistributing cats, and avoiding the winks and smiles of Paul's younger, bored colleagues from the Admiralty.

"Bolingbroke." Clara nodded. "The 'blessed isle' is John of Gaunt."

Lucy held up her hand, the way Ruth sometimes did, when other people's wanton speech interfered with the noise of her own thoughts.

"'*Thus I turn me from my country's light*,'" she quoted. "'*to dwell in solemn shades of endless night*.'"

"Mowbray, when he's banished," Clara said. "Mowbray, the Duke of Norfolk."

"*Norfolk*!" Lucy said. That was the name of the naval base in Virginia, she remembered, which sent the Yanks their mail. "So. Clara. You have keys to the library."

"If you want an insider's look, I'm afraid the collection isn't impressive."

"Might it have maps of the United States?" Lucy asked. "I'm particularly interested in the naval bases and the shipyards."

***

When she returned to the room, eager to study her maps, she found the other three tidying the flotsam left by the men. Georgie emptied ashtrays. Ruth carried glasses to the bathroom sink to pour out their remains. Lark looked at her gravely and led her to the piano.

Men had set down their drinks on the sheet music of her "Jesu, Joy of Man's Desiring." As the afternoon wore on, the ice in their drinks melted, so that when, during cleanup, Lark lifted the glasses, chunks of the paper came away with them. The sheet music was ruined. It was partly the fault of Bermuda—everything must always be kept dry and kept moving—and it was partly Lucy's fault, she realized, for not keeping a better eye on things, for having left with Teck. Lark sorted the pieces of what remained of the score onto the table, dampened and torn away so that they resembled an archipelago. Lucy gathered them together, and made for the rubbish bin, but Ruth took them from her, and carried them away into her small room.

PART TWO
MAIL

12.

The following Saturday opened in ferocious rain. Rain always held up the men, both the Navy building the port and the Army building the airfield. Rather than risk mayhem and mud trooped into the hotel, the Princess dance was cancelled. The residents of the honeymoon suite pored over the newspaper in search of cinematic offerings. Lark pointed to Charlie Chaplin's The Great Dictator, which Lucy and Georgie immediately nixed with swift head shakes. They would not put themselves in the position of explaining satire to Ruth. A romantic comedy was deemed too silly, a film about the war, too dark. Then Georgie turned the page of the Royal-Gazette, grew still, and then abruptly stood.

"We're going to see To Sin for Love. Hurry, now. It starts quite soon."

"How can you sin for love? If you act out of love, is it a sin?" Ruth asked.

Lark said, "This is Hollywood, Ruth, not doctrine. But I suppose we'll see."

When she saw the film starred Leslie Howard, Lucy agreed. Georgie twice-clapped and barked, "Umbrellas! Hurry!" and they all trooped into the late afternoon rain.

Lucy knew from the film magazines Gwynne collected, and left in the Reading Room, that *To Sin for Love* was to have launched into prominence the film career of Howard's young co-star, Patience Cobb, who had until then played the kid sister or the best friend. But Cobb died of cancer before the film's debut. Lucy remembered the photo of Leslie Howard and the film's tall blond writer and director outside the cinema house at the film's debut, a space between them to honour the absence of their ill-fated ingénue, the black rose each wore in his lapel. Neither man, the gossip columnist wrote, had been able to hold back his tears.

Lucy found the real Hollywood tragedy far more compelling than the one on the screen. Howard plays a man falsely accused of murder while on his honeymoon with the impossibly radiant Cobb. The investigating detective offers to drop the charges against Howard in exchange for the sexual favors of Cobb. Cobb gives in to spare her husband, but once spared, he abandons her, proclaiming her "forever tarnished."

Afterwards, the roommates decamped to the tea shop where Lucy and Clara had discussed *Richard II* to debate the somewhat lesser merits of *To Sin for Love*.

"Idiotic prig," Lucy pronounced. "Better off without him, I say."

"She gave in willingly," Lark said. "Nobody forced her."

"He forced her hand."

"When?" Ruth asked. "I never saw him touch her hand."

"That means he gave her no choice," Lucy said. "But the whole thing's ridiculous. For one thing, it's *Measure for Measure*, only stupid."

"What is *Measure for Measure*?" Georgie asked.

"Shakespeare?" Lark asked. "It's about a nun?"

"A novice. 'Some rise by sin, and some by virtue fall.' Maybe that's where the writer took his inspiration."

"I am almost certain that is not so," Georgie said. "Honestly, Lucy, are your friends at home able to follow you? The way your mind leaps about?"

"But what kind of love is that," Lucy went on, "if he leaves her for saving his life?"

"He didn't love *her*," Lark said. "He loved his idea of her."

"Well, isn't that what men do?" Lucy asked. "Women love romance and men love some vision in their head. If they're lucky, by the time it all fades, they've grown used to one another."

"How cynical you sound," Georgie said.

"My experience, anyway." Lucy sipped her tea, thinking of Guy Jenner and the young men at Cambridge, and Bill with his bounty and his courtly manners.

"Your vast experience," Georgie teased.

"It's ridiculous," Ruth agreed, startling them. "A detective doesn't have the power to press or drop charges. That's down to the prosecution and the judge. All the detective does is find the evidence and make the arrest."

"That's not the point, Ruth," Lark said.

"I don't see why it isn't. If you apply logic, the story falls apart. Anyway, that detective wasn't so bad-looking. He wanted to spend time with her alone, he said? What's wrong with that?"

Georgie and Lark looked to Lucy to supply an explanation. She responded with one strong shake of the head.

"If it'd been that judge," Ruth said, "that would've been a harder time. Judges are awful. My father's a judge."

Lucy, dazed with the understanding that Ruth had made a logical point, turned to Georgie and found her wiping away tears.

"Patience Cobb," Georgie said quietly. "Was so very beautiful."

She spoke in the wistful tone of a defeated rival. Lark, sipping her tea, raised a curious eyebrow, as Lucy, puzzled, took Georgie's hand.

"Did you know her, George?"

Ruth said, "She was lit to look beautiful. Real beauty is in the bones." Ruth surveyed the quadrants of Georgie's face as a traveler did a map: northwest, northeast, southeast, southwest. "Jawbone. High cheekbones." She rustled in Lucy's bag (she never carried her own bag) for a pencil, found one, and sketched on the folded copy of the *Royal-Gazette* on the table. She displayed her sketch up, a series of arcs within an oval: eyelids, cheekbones, lips, jaws. "Like yours, Georgie. If we're talking about beauty, then you are beautiful, by actual parameters. You and Lucy. Lark is pretty. I am not."

Ruth looked at that photo of Patience Cobb in the ad in the *Royal-Gazette* for *To Sin for Love*. "I'm glad I'm not named Patience. My cousins are Charity and Faith. It seems like a burden." She reached for a sandwich and added, "I don't think about people being named Lincoln. I think of the American president. Or the town Lincoln. In Lincolnshire. Or Lincoln's Inn, if your father is a judge. My father is a judge."

Lucy reached for her handbag to settle the bill.

"Oh Ruth, what are you on about?"

"'Written and directed by Nick Lincoln.'" Ruth tapped the ad.

"Oh, yes?" Lucy pulled out her wallet, dislodging her National Identity Card, which fell to the table. Lucia Victoria Gheldini *Barrett*! Lark had snapped at her, because she looked into one of the passports in Georgie's locked wardrobe. The passport issued to Annegret Maria Lincoln.

13.

June 14, 1941

Miss Lucia Barrett
Princess Louise Hamilton Hotel
Hamilton, Bermuda

Dear Lucia,

This letter of apology is long overdue to you, but my mother says that an apology means nothing without an amend. I hope you and your roommates will accept these gifts as a token of my regret for the destruction of your property. I know that just having a replacement score of your Bach piece is hardly enough. Ruth told me that it was filled with notes made by your late mother, and was precious to you for that reason. I am sick when I think about it. I meant to be careful by having the men set their drinks on paper rather than on top of the piano, where it would leave rings.

I asked my mother to pick up the libretto of the opera Don Giovanni since Ruth says it is your favorite. She says you are always humming it. My mom picked up some other things she thought ladies on rations might want. She writes that she was happy to shop for girls for a change. Our family is all boys.

Finally, I'd like to apologize for the remarks my friends and I made that Sunday when you girls had us over. I am sorry the language got a little "blue."

Yours truly,
Alan Dodd

"Jam, chocolate …" Lark unpacked the hamper, setting the items out on the communal table. "Lipstick, stockings. Whisky! *Canadian* whisky!"

Lucy had returned from swimming laps at the pool to find this bounty being unloaded. Her hair hung in wet braids. An ocean liner had docked the night before and the Censorettes had spent the evening and all of the morning in the Reading Room. Happily, a naval supply ship had docked at the same time on the other side of the island and delivered the mail to the men of the U.S. Navy, including Mrs. Dodd's boxes to her son.

"Jam." Lark took over the unpacking as Georgie opened each tube of lipstick and drew little lines of red on the inside of her wrist. "More jam. Cherry."

Lucy read the libretto of *Don Giovanni*. It was her parents' favorite more than it was hers, although they had dragged Lucy and Matty, and later Marcia, to enough performances. She was unaware that she hummed it in the room. She considered Lark the hummer, sampling hymns for services. Georgie tattooed the inside of Lark's wrist with the four different shades of red of Max Factor Tru-Colour.

"This one, I think." She tapped a crimson line. "Hold still. Let me see." She painted Lark's mouth.

Ruth came into the room and cautiously handed papers to Lucy.

It was the sheet music to the new "Jesu, Joy of Man's Desiring." Ruth had re-created all of Tessa's notations, the "*lente, lente, luc*," the "*devoto*," the "*insistendo*," and of course, the "*profondo*." All of her markings were there, even the row of x's over a direction she had given and then rescinded where they'd had a slight disagreement of whether, in the bridge, Lucy's playing grew a bit too plaintive "*piangevole ma non troppo*," Tessa had written in the original, so firmly that the letters were raised on the other side of the page. Then Tessa had decided to let Lucy have her own interpretation and crossed out her preference.

Ruth had inscribed everything where it had been on the original, with a forger's accuracy.

Lucy dropped the sheets onto the table quickly, so that her tears would not cause another disaster of smeared ink, and pulled Ruth to her. She kissed the top of her head. Ruth stayed in her embrace and allowed herself to be pulled closer. She brought her fingertips over Lucy's shoulder blades.

"Thank you." Lucy stroked Ruth's hair from forehead to the nape of her neck and kept on doing so because the stroking seemed to please her. "Duckling, *grazie mille*."

"This feels good," Ruth declared. "I don't like hugs. But I don't mind this. Alright, I am finished now."

Lucy patted her shoulder as she stepped away from Ruth. "Why don't we write a thank you note to Alan? That is was nice of him to send us all these things."

"He didn't send them, he brought them," Ruth said. "Just now.

When he brought the package. He asked if I wanted to go up on the roof."

Lucy scrambled to find her sandals, pulled a dressing gown over her bathing suit and ran up the stairs to the roof. She arrived panting on the rooftop, ready to warn Alan off the notion of trifling with Ruth. But he was, in fact, stargazing. That is, he would have been, had it been night. He had set up a state-of-the-art telescope and was peering at the houses of Hamilton through the lens.

"We're all so grateful for the gifts," Lucy said. "I wanted to tell you. Oh, what a handsome telescope!"

"Isn't she a beaut? She came in with the mail. Thought I'd try her out here. It's the highest point on the island I can get to, besides the lighthouse, and there's no room for her there. Want a look?"

She bent over, and peered at the houses of the island, their steep white limestone roofs designed to catch rainwater and store it in cisterns, their candy-floss colours: pink, peach, pale blue, lemon yellow. Local legend had it that the colour of a house was specific to one of the forty founding families, the Outerbridges, the Goslings, the Tuckers. Only households set up among them could claim the colour. She turned the telescope outwards, to the sea.

"If you need to change the focus, you— "

"Yes. My nonno is an astronomer. I mean, my grandfather." She adjusted the focus and steadied her breathing, as Nonno taught her. Squinting one eye caused some to hold their breath, he had told her, and the key to seeing through the small lens of a telescope is to breathe in a rhythm and to surrender to the limited view. She had finally mastered how to look, but had never been able to see the patterns in the stars.

"Not much to see in the daytime," Alan said.

"Oh, no, there's so much! Blue! So many shades. *Il cielo celeste, il oceano azzuro, l'onda acquamarina ...!*" Lucy turned the telescope toward the ocean, then paused when she saw the yacht club. "Marina. Alan?"

"Ma'am."

"If you were going to invade Bermuda, how would you do it?"

"Why would anyone invade Bermuda?"

"Get closer to the States? Why are you building a naval base here? It's strategically important. It always has been. Suppose you Yanks hadn't come as part of Destroyers for Bases. Suppose you'd just taken it. How would you do it?"

"Nothing here but lumber and flowers and boats. Take out the boats?"

"Quite." Lucy straightened up from the telescope. "The Luftwaffe's bombed the dickens out of the Royal Dockyards."

"You know, Lucy." Alan put his hand on the telescope, a casual but proprietary gesture, just as his voice grew from casual to cautious. "I don't mean to sound vain, but if you were a flirty kind of girl, I'd think that the reason you always talk to me about ports and harbours is because I'm in the Navy and you're trying to flatter me. Like, maybe you were told to talk to a man about his job, or what he's interested in. Like, I guess you talk to Inman about blowing up the ground with dynamite."

"No." Lucy patted the telescope and turned away. She could kick herself for being so transparent. "Actually, I don't need to flatter Bill at all. He's so flattered with himself. I'm sorry if I've led you astray. My father served in the Royal Navy, and now he's in the Admiralty. I suppose I talk about ports because I'm homesick." *Good*, she soothed herself, *good*. "He raised me as a bluestocking. Everyone was shocked. Do you have that expression?" She summoned a scrim of tears—it was easy enough to do—and turned her face to him. When he shrugged, puzzled, she said, "A woman with too much education. Which for some, means any education beyond, how did you put it, knowing enough to make conversation to flatter a man. Before I was sent here, I'd hoped to be a WREN. Women's Royal Navy Service."

"A WREN with a Lark. Your room's an aviary!"

She smiled at the vision of the residents of the honeymoon suite chirping and fluttering about the room which was, she supposed, what men thought they did together. "In wartime, women take on the non-combat positions—I would have been an electrician, or a clerk— "

"Clerk?"

Surely the Americans had clerks in their armed forces? "Someone who does office work?"

"Oh, a *clerk.*" He pronounced it to rhyme with "Turk," whereas she rhymed it with "Lark." He said lightly, "Now I *am* going to sound like a vain man. I did think you were flirting. Don't get me wrong, I'm flattered. But Inman staked his claim and— " He held up his hand against her squawk of protest. "—and he'd knock my block off. And I wouldn't let that stop me except that I've got my eye on a different bird."

"I'm so sorry if I've made you feel — " Lucy felt such an eddy of emotions — relief that she had diverted the conversation from her too-obvious questions about ports, irritation that Bill was considered to have claimed her, embarrassment at Alan's embarrassment about her flirting — that it was a moment before she understood. "Oh, it's *Lark,* isn't it? You like Lark. '*In the beauty of the lilies …* How *lovely.*"

"So far we've only talked about hymns and harmony and the apostles. If there's anything you could do to, you know, move things along … It's ladies' choice tonight, they tell me. Though if you ask me, it always is."

Lucy hummed a chuckle. "I'm sure it seems so, from your vantage. But we're so often made to do what's expected. I was near-engaged to the boy next door. You must ask her, Alan. She will never ask you, however much she wants to. Lark is no Lucia."

⋇⋇⋇

At the dance, Fleur or Roos addressed her when Bill saw Lucy and tried to slip out of her hands. "This night is ladies' choice, Lucia, and I hath not finished viss heem yet."

Lucy nodded with a be-my-guest gesture, which Bill answered with a look of mock (she hoped) indignation. But it would take sterner stuff than Lucy possessed to try to wrench him away from the Belgian flower sisters, and besides, the change might do him good.

"Does he sveeng?"

"You'll have to find out," Lucy told her, and saw Alan by the phonograph. She sauntered to him, fell into an exaggerated curtsy, and asked if he would honour her.

The tune changed then, from the peppy "A Train," to a ballad with a coy, sultry horn. He locked his fingers through hers and placed his other hand on her hip, pulled her in closer.

"Cootie," he said. "This is called 'Concerto for Cootie.' Cootie Williams. He was Duke Ellington's trumpet player. I've seen him up in Harlem."

He hummed along with Cootie Williams's trumpet.

"Alan," Lucy said. "When you said you were better on the trumpet and one of the men said—"

"Oh no no no, Lucia, don't ask me that," Alan said, although his blush revealed the answer.

Bill tapped Alan's shoulder. "Say, Doddy, mind if I — "

"In a minute." Alan guided Lucy away from the intrusion before Bill could protest. He was claimed by Gwynne.

"*Trumpet*," Lucy said. "That *is* a new one for me. Mind you, I've led a rather cloistered life. But I think I grasp the concept. *Trumpet*. For a man's — "

"I was thinking I might ask Miss Lark to rehearse a duet with me," Alan said. "For trumpet and organ. There's a certain piece by Bach."

"To play in church."

"Yes. Church."

Across the room, Georgie cut in on Gwynne and danced with Bill with the too-bright smile that signaled her banter bordered on interrogation. She wore a blue dress—blue was her best colour— nicely cut, flattering, but not a Schiaparelli, which she carried from country to country for what reason? Bill usually loved nothing more than answering questions about himself but Lucy saw the tension in his spine. He saw Lucy and waved eagerly.

Cootie Williams hit a crescendo, then it faded. Alan kissed her cheek, high near her ear, and whispered, "Thank you."

Alan sought Lark as Bill strode towards Lucy, parting the dance floor the way his jeep had ripped through the soft coral roads of Bermuda, leaving a wound in his wake. The queue of women who had formed to be his next Sadie turned their heads as he walked by, the resolute blondes and redheads of the British Isles, the imperious Danes. They betrayed no delicate pining, no shy hope, but rather the kind of demented determination that led the Maenads to tear the poet Orpheus to pieces with their bare hands. It was obvious that Lucy would not be excluded from their wrath, as she was his destination. Bill took her hand and kissed it.

He bowed to the crestfallen queue behind him. "Goodnight, ladies. And thank you. Lucy, come outside to say goodnight, won't you?"

Bill led her into the front lawn and sat with her on a white wrought-iron bench.

"I have to leave after the next song. My captain's giving me a ride in his jeep. I caught a ride on a freighter. It leaves at first light. My sister's getting married, I think I told you. I'm on leave for her wedding."

"How nice for you to be able to see your family so easily."

"Yeah, I was hoping … well, I was thinking, 'cause I know I'll be thinking, at the service, how nice it'd be to let on to my folks that they may see another wedding soon. As it is, well, the other boys got married long ago. Benedict, Carlton. Now it'll be just me and Evie. And like I told you, she's just a kid and wants to go to college."

He cupped her left hand in the palm of his right, stroked her ring finger between the knuckles.

"Lucy, I—"

A noise startled both of them and they saw Gwynne, one of the Rebeccas, and several other Censorettes watching them for the porch. Bill returned his attention to her hand and traced his finger over the rises and falls of her knuckles, the tributaries of her veins. She had always hated the prominence of the blue veins in the back of her hand, having seen their ultimate maturity in the hands of

Granny, whose veins protruded like swollen rivers on a topographical map, with brown spots indicating large towns or cities, bulging knuckles like a mountain range separating the penisula of fingers from the mainland of the hands.

Bill raised his eyes to hers and she took a strong breath, hoping not to clench her fingers, not to betray her fear that he would ask for her hand, now that he held both of them.

"I'd like to bring something back for you, Lucy, if you'd let me."

"Oh, would you? So kind! If you have the time, a sketch pad?"

"Sketch pad?" Bill looked at her hand, as though it had displayed a bizarre trait, not just a talent to sketch but an alien finger.

"For Ruth," Lucy said. "Her pad's filling up and her watercolours calm her so. And paper's rationed for us."

"Rationed for us," Bill repeated blankly.

"Us." Lucy retrieved her hand and raised it to circle the air in a royal wave to indicate the Censorettes, Bermuda, the United Kingdom, the greater world at war. "So much is rationed."

At the sound of approaching footsteps, Bill jumped to his feet and saluted at a silhouette.

"Captain Jackson, may I introduce Miss Lucy Barrett. Lucy, I'd like you to meet the man in charge of our endeavors here on your little island."

Although Lucy could barely see him in the dim light, she could discern, from the heartiness of his voice and the fluid bow he made over her outstretched hand, that he was not much older than Bill. His American accent was equally soft and southern. "Well, at last! The princess of the Princess! Now I see why Lieutenant Inman tries so hard to get away from his duties."

"I hope that's not true," Lucy said. "But you're very kind."

"I will have to take him from you. We leave in five minutes, lieutenant."

As the captain and the other men walked away to the jeep, Bill returned to tracing Lucy's hand. "I'll be back in two weeks."

"Have a lovely journey." She tried to give his hand a comradely squeeze but he was still holding it as though it were a delicate artifact. She kissed his cheek. "Best wishes to your sister."

He kissed the back of her left hand, the back of her right. Then he stood, and kissed her gently on the mouth.

When he got to the jeep, she heard Captain Jackson say, "You didn't have to be such a gentleman, Inman. I wasn't watching."

And as the jeep drove away, she heard Bill say, "If you weren't watching, how d'you know I was a gentleman?"

To the sound of their retreating laughter, Lucy turned and saw Gwynne and the girls fanning their faces with their hands, giggling at the moonlight-and-magnolia drama. She hurried into the lobby and covered her face in frustration. Hector walked to her, rang for the elevator and patted her shoulder.

"He'll be back, Miss Lucy," said Hector. "Don't you worry."

"*Hector*?" Lark, a few minutes later, interrupted Lucy's angry recounting of the scene. The hand caressing! Gwynne! The misplaced sympathy of Hector! "First Ruth, and now you? Should we invite him to move in with us? So, what is it, Lucy? You say your farewells in public, but what do they say, all's fair in love and war. My mother complained that she had to kiss my father on the train platform in the first war. She spoke of it often, strangely enough. Until my little brother thought a platform was a place on the face, like a cheek or a forehead."

Lucy sighed, "It was a *performance*."

"He likes to display you. You must be used to that."

"Yes, I like nice dresses. Dancing. But I'm here to do a job. The way he *looked* at me, Lark. He thinks I'm something I'm not. He loves a girl who isn't there."

Lark stilled. Lucy had been prepared to go on, to further illustrate her incompatibility with Bill, but she was halted by her Lark's sudden slack expression. Eventually, Lark collected herself and lowered her hands to her lap.

"I understand." Lark set her sewing aside. "I was a girl who wasn't there. When I saw that look from Gavin, I released him from our engagement."

"Release," implied liberation. "Engagement" meant both a

promise to be bonded and a clash between troops. Lucy had forgotten that Lark's former fiancé was called Gavin. One of the few times she had heard Lark utter his name was when Lark had ticked off the names of the merry skaters on the frozen pond in the photograph she kept on her bedside table: brother, brother, and Gavin, with a beaming Lark in the center. The brothers were bent double in laughter, but Gavin was focused on Lark, smiling at her smile.

"Looked at you." Lucy sat cautiously on the bed beside her. "How?"

"Damaged goods." Lark picked up her sewing.

"What! What on *earth* could you have done? He must be— "

Lucy glared at the photo. *Lark*, damaged goods! Raised by a mother so modest that the scar she nursed from the Great War was having to kiss her husband goodbye in public on a railway platform. How high was this prig's pedestal!

"Did you dance with Alan tonight?" Lucy asked.

"Yes." Flushed, blinking rapidly, Lark stabbed her finger hard with her sewing needle, raised the finger to her mouth to suck the blood. "He's quite a good dancer and quite musical. There's a Bach duet for organ and trumpet, did you know? We might rehearse it together."

"Organ and trumpet," Lucy repeated. "That sounds like a nice combination."

June 29, 1941

Miss Lucy Barrett
Princess Hamilton Hotel
Hamilton, Bermuda

My beautiful Lucy,

No doubt I will get back before this letter does, but I'm thinking of you and I wanted to write and to get away for a minute from all the noise.

I don't understand why one wedding requires a dozen parties. Last night was the men-only party, so at least I wasn't forced to dance and make small talk with a mess of silly girls. You have spoiled me. I now expect a girl to be beautiful and smart as a whip. But even the prettiest ones here don't hold a candle to you. And they only talk about weddings. I sure wish I could give them another wedding to talk about.

Last night, I was speaking to a friend of my father's who's in the House of Representatives here. We have frozen the American bank assets of Germany and Italy. He thinks that means we're one step closer to joining the war. "Doing everything but the fighting now," he said.

Public sentiment is strongly against our joining in. "All aid short of engagement" is how people think. Most folks at the bachelor party are members of America First. We haven't even got an army ready! There's a rumor that the men over at Fort Bragg are using sticks to train with because we don't have enough guns to supply an Army.

Do you know I don't even have a photo of you? I keep telling everyone how beautiful you are and they want proof! I miss you. I'll see you soon.

Love,
Bill

Fleur or Roos handed Lucy a letter in the Reading Room: "They say you wish to see the letters of this man?"

30 June, 1941

Joe Karte, Warehouse Manager
Buttermilk Channel Warehouse and Storage
3 River Street
Brooklyn, NY
USA

Dear Mr. Karte!

Kindly advise status of goods. Please confirm that the new staff we sent are suitable for employment. The days are long. We hope you have found brotherly friends with who you spend the hours and times.

With great respect,
J.

Unlike the letters she had seen which had gone from Joe to Germany, the letter from Germany to Joe was typed, so there was no point in handwriting analysis.

"We could test the paper," Lucy argued to McKay. "We could still send it to Inks and Papers."

"And risk delay, or staining it? Best to record it and send it on its way."

"*Something* is going on. Why would Germans conduct business in faulty English rather than in *German*? What does 'the day is long' mean? They keep mentioning friends. The Bund? I think they're growing. Their organization is growing. I can't shake the feeling that it's something to do with shipyards. And there's the Shakespeare."

"Shakespeare?" McKay reread the letter. "Sorry, Cambridge, I'm not seeing it."

Being your slave what should I do but tend
Upon the hours, and times of your desire?

"Hours and times," Lucy said. "It's from a sonnet. I think there's a pattern. The letters with Shakespearean references are special. They're the ones with hidden messages."

"I doubt the Nazis are so keen on Shakespeare," McKay said. "If that were the case, they might not be bombing England so vigourously."

"But you have to admit— " *Why couldn't it be code? What if every reference led to an agreed-upon code book, a copy of* Romeo and Juliet, *a volume of sonnets, some anthology?*

"I *have* admitted. I've told you how to handle it. I know you're quite eager to do your bit, Barrett. But let's not let your need to matter make a matter where none exists, eh?" He looked pleased with his turn of phrase. "Now, if there's nothing else …"

There was much else. On the wall behind McKay's desk was a map of Bermuda in relation to the United States. North Carolina was due west of the island. Below that, South Carolina. Above the Carolinas, Virginia and Maryland, below them, Georgia. All named for queens and kings of England when they were loyal colonialists, now so vehement in their lack of allegiance. *Public sentiment is firmly against us joining the war in Europe.* But he'd written something else.

"I hear that the Yanks have frozen the American bank assets of Germany and Italy."

"Have you indeed? How have you heard that?"

"It's in the American newspapers." It most likely was. The Yanks could still afford to print their business.

McKay sat back, clicking his tongue. She had succeeded in annoying him.

"German. Italian. I'm fluent in both."

"Do you know how to read a bank statement?"

"Is it terribly difficult?"

"It's a bit beyond managing your pocket money. Do you have accounting experience?"

He looked triumphant, knowing that she couldn't make such a claim. He turned his attention to a ledger on his desk. Lucy had taught herself to read upside down. The ledger was a chart of the Censorettes: names, countries of origin, languages, skills, assigned duties. He was no doubt searching for a Censorette with experience with the paperwork of banks. He'd find one, but would he find one fluent in German and Italian?

Lucy didn't tell him that even managing her pocket money had been beyond her. She'd been so careless that, when she was at St. Paul's, Tessa had made her carry a small notebook in which to track her expenditures. She wasn't a spendthrift, but a soft touch. The richer girls at St. Paul's never carried cash. The scholarship girls had none to begin with. Lucy, in the middle of the spectrum, paid for cream teas, or sweets, or taxis, anything for any girl short of change.

As for the Barrett household account, that was Tessa's domain. She was fond of numbers. Nonno was an astronomer, and astronomy was numbers. She worshipped music, and music was numbers. In her convent education, numbers were not subject to theology, while all other subjects were. Paul was happy to leave the bookkeeping to her. Tessa managed the domestic account-book, planned the meals and budgets with the cook, and managed the household staff.

The family budget, then, was just another casualty of her loss. By the time she died, there was no staff left to supervise, nor their salaries to budget. With food and fuel rationed, households struggled more with what could be bought than how to pay for it.

McKay cocked an eyebrow.

"Your ambition is …" His expression said "exasperating," but the word he selected was "commendable. But we don't have the resources, and you've proved yourself quite capable at doing other things. You're coming along quite nicely. And now, I need to find someone with bank experience, so I'd be obliged if you'd run along now."

14.

Knoll House, Knollborough and London, 1936

'Run along now' is one of her least favorite phrases, and her father says it often. He says it as she gallops into the parlor at Knoll House in search of Horatio, while he is deep in discussion with Professor Diehl, a German-Jewish emigré who was fired from his university job in Bonn for being a Jew, and then appeared in their living room at Mowbray Crescent, with a trunk and his teenaged daughter Karolina. They stayed at Mowbray Crescent for only a few days. Matty was at Harrow, and Marcia bunked in with Lucy to leave Karolina a room of her own, although Karolina seemed less inclined to complain about her lodgings than anyone Lucy had ever met. She accepts the bed, Lucy's donated clothes, the *sauerbraten* and *latkes* the Knoll House cook labours over to give the Diehls a "taste of home," with an indifference worn like a shroud. The Diehls were gone inside a week, when accommodations were found for them, but Karolina still comes by, to help Marcia with her *lieder* and to assist Lucy with her German grammar and pronunciation. Professor Diehl, intrigued by the notion that Lucy is considered "gifted" with languages when she speaks only four, drops by from time to time to test her "gift" with lessons in modern Greek.

But that spring, during the long vacation, Cambridge is months away. Lucy has been graduated by St. Paul's, passed her exams, been admitted to Girton College. Paul is proud of her, except when she behaves like the sixteen-year-old girl that she is, tromping through his conversation with an émigré mathematician, in search of her wayward kitten.

She healed Horatio perhaps too well. At the last Easter term, Matty returned from the nearby Ripple farm where he had gone to help with the lambing. He brought back a skeletal kitten, a damp mewling comma that fit inside his palm. Matty had stayed the hand of Farmer Ripple on the verge of dropping the ill-favoured creature into a bucket of water to drown it. It was the runt of the litter and unable to latch. "Act of mercy, Barrett," Ripple told him. "Farm has no place for the weak." But his sister does, Matty suggests. A kitten might be a welcome distraction in the life of a schoolgirl driven nearly mad by study.

Paul disapproves. Barrett cats are pedigreed Persians named for Shakespearean attendants, not farm tabbies. The local vet prescribes feedings from an eye-dropper every two hours. The Persians hiss at Horatio; Marcia pets him too hard, and Paul deplores Lucy's practice of bringing him to the table in a sling around her neck to feed him from a saucer. In this, he is overruled by Tessa and, surprisingly, by Granny. Both believe that Lucy may as well learn now rather than later how to feed a hungry infant. "Her life will be more than study, Paul," Tessa says. "It will be good practice for her."

But it is June. Horatio, long-liberated from the sling, gallops from the fields into the house, deposits slaughtered voles at the kitchen door, on Lucy's pillow. It is Paul and Tessa's wedding anniversary. The house is full of guests, both overnight and dinner-only. In the music room, the dolorous Karolina Diehl drills Marcia through her program for the evening's performance, *Batti, batti, o bel Massetto* from *Don Giovanni*. The backyard tennis court pocks with a game. Ladies play bridge in the sitting room. The Jenners from the neighbouring estate have organized a ride. Knoll House abandoned its stables during the Great War, when the horses were commandeered.

But the blankets, currycombs and troughs remain, so the Jenners use the Barrett stable to let their horses cool and drink before trotting them gently home. The Jenners cherish their horses. Lucy has overheard Guy singing to his mare, "*Snow was falling, snow on snow, snow on snow,*" soothing her as he picked a pebble from her hoof. The cat Horatio is fond of the ghost horse smell of the stable. Living horses frighten him. Lucy seeks to lock him in her room to keep him safe.

"Fine stable in its day," she hears the Honourable George Jenner tell his son Guy when she reaches the stable. "Sound building. Fireplace. Fine stock the old pater had."

"Pity Lucy doesn't ride," Guy responds.

"I thought you'd outgrown that particular crush."

"Oh, I wouldn't call it a *crush*," Guy says so casually that even the horses must discern that there is nothing else to call it. "But you must admit she's charming, Pa."

"That's as may be. But she'd make you unhappy."

Lucy creeps away from the door and crouches beneath a window to hear more of her capacity to inspire unhappiness in Guy, who had eschewed university in favor of "managing the estate." Lucy had begun to fidget and blush when the Jenners come to call. He may not be clever, but Guy is undeniably handsome and effortlessly courteous. He brings baskets of pears from the Jenner orchard. But his conversation is so stilted he might be learning English (his only language) from a phrase book: *Are you well? You look well. The garden is lovely, Mrs. Barrett.*

"They're sending her to *Cambridge*. No, son. No. A wife should take her husband's ideas. And that young woman has far too many notions."

"They're an old family, though, Pa. One of the oldest in the county. You said you always wanted to join the lands. And she's pretty but not vain."

Leaping from a stable window, Horatio trills and pads toward Lucy. Panting up the hill from the tennis court, Matty catches her crouching by the stable window and has the sense not to call her name as her trots over to join her, while Lucy awaits further elaboration of her beauty and her modesty.

"I'll give you that. And from looking at the mother, I'd say that that won't fade any time soon. But I'm afraid she's already ruined."

"Ruined!"

"Oh, not in that way. Full of herself, as I said. Sending a slip of a girl to Cambridge! What *for*?"

Lucy kisses Horatio's hay-dusty head. Matty pulls her to her feet and leads her up the hill to the house, whispering, "Never marry anyone, *sorella*. Become an ambassador. Run an embassy and throw great parties."

"Oh, where?"

"Somewhere chic, of course. Monaco?"

"I say, Lucy!" Guy Jenner shouts. He runs to them. "Once I help get the horses back, clean up a bit, do you fancy of game of tennis before dinner?"

She beats him six—two, six—one.

At dinner, Matty announces, "I say, Lucia trounced Guy at tennis."

As Granny frowns, Guy commands a smirk he had not earlier, on the court, been able to summon. "Well, as they say, 'If you can look on victory and defeat with equal grace, you'll be a man, my son!'"

He lifts his glass. The table follows: the Jenners, the Diehls, Paul and Tessa, a dozen other gentry. Lucy enlightens them, "What *Kipling* says, is 'If you can meet with Triumph and Disaster/And treat those two impostors just the same/If you can bear to hear the truth you've—'"

"To our English poet!" Granny quavers. After everyone echoes her toast, and drinks, she adds, "You must excuse Lucia. She is *awfully* fond of poetry."

Granny's lecture at breakfast the next day is blunt: Lucy is too wild. She behaves boyishly rather than in a manner attractive to boys. If she is not to be finished (and there is no question of a finishing school with Cambridge achieved), she will at the very least be instructed, as Paul's sisters had been instructed.

As a result, Lucy is separated from her family for the summer holidays. While Paul and Tessa will visit the Gheldini cousins in Florence, and Matty spend a term in Paris perfecting his French and his violin, Lucy will summer with Marcia at Knoll House, following Granny's fiendish schedule of social engagements: teas, luncheons, horse shows, and dances, with mornings spent writing notes thanking her boring hosts for the tedium of the previous day.

"I get deported and you get deportment." Matty pets Horatio in her bedroom on the day of her departure. "I'd rather stay here and put in the flying hours."

"And look, Lucia, this dress!" Tessa scurries in with boxes. A new wardrobe to suit Lucy's summer engagements and to mollify her outrage. "A complement to your Chanel. You may borrow my garnet necklace. And lipstick, but only at night."

The dress is solid red, with a draped neckline, bracelet sleeves and a flared skirt, undeniably lovely and generous but … *no*! Lucy snatches the dress from her mother's hands and throws it to the ground.

Paul stands in the doorway in his Saturday outfit of grey trousers and blue pullover.

"Lucia! With me," he orders in what Matty calls his "keelhaul" voice.

Paul's discipline is not physical, but cruelly creative, particularly when he discusses beforehand with the convent-tortured Tessa "how best to address this." As children, Matty and Lucy are deprived of sweets and treats, made to read and report on dusty philosophical tracts (*when St. Augustine in his youth stole pears*), or forced to write out phrases a hundred times ("*it is better to be kind than clever.*") As they creep toward adulthood, they face a repertory of lectures: "Privilege and Duty" and "Your Public Behavior is a Reflection of Your Mother."

Lucy will not be deterred—what punishment could be worse than spending the summer of her 16th year with *Granny*, while Matty gets up to who-would-ever-know-what in Paris. She stomps behind Paul all the way to his study.

"I never thought I would say this," he begins. "But you have proven my mother correct. You do need to soothe your manners."

"If you make me go, I'll make you sorry. Because I quoted a *poem at the dinner table?* I'll *show* you bad behavior. I'll marry the first sheep farmer who says hello."

"Will you? I know little of sheep, but I daresay they're more complicated to mind than a kitten."

"I'll disgrace you. I'll ruin your name. I'll become the town whore."

"For God's sake, Lucia! That *word*. Don't let your mother hear you."

No distressa Tessa.

"*Whore whore bloody whore!*" she shouts. "What do you think you're training me for? All this *time,* the future perfect, the pluperfect, the imperfect, the perfect perfect! To end up trimming roses, paying calls?"

"I've made it clear to Mother that you're to be given time every day to study."

"Oh, *grazie mille!*" Lucy stomps her foot. "If you're only going to marry me off, I'll take Guy Jenner! He's handsome at least! And they've always wanted to join the land!"

"*Lucia!*"

"Matty does whatever he wants! And don't tell me 'Matty is a *boy*.'"

"*No*," Paul says so firmly that for a moment she thinks he is going to tell her that Matty is not a boy. "He doesn't do whatever he wants. None of us do. Particularly now. I have reasons for doing what I do. You must trust me."

She glares at a corner of the ceiling, the way she has seen Tessa do in an argument.

"Don't be a fool, Lucia. I'd rather see you *with* a shepherd than the Jenner boy. But you'll be encountering Guy Jenners for the rest of your life. Bores will pat you on the head and tell you you're a bright little thing. You must learn to endure it. Think what your mother's endured from these damned English snobs. In the future, you should be able to say to a *fascista*, should you find yourself at a state dinner with one, 'Forgive me, *signore*, I cannot agree.' Or 'I wonder if you have considered an alternative.' Rely on your talents. Your upbringing. Rather than your temper. Look," he placates, because her glare is unyielding. "I will give you a reward for this. What would you like?"

"I would like to see Nonno."

"You know that's impossible. All the plans have been —"

"I don't mean with *you*," Lucy spits, as though her father is the most oppressive travel companion she can imagine. "I mean by myself." She brightens at the thought. "Next summer. If I do well at Girton? I can go see Nonno and the cousins."

"Send my daughter alone into Mussolini's Italy?" Paul is so dumbfounded by this notion that he addresses it to the cat Charmian sleeping on the windowsill. "I never heard of anything so ridiculous. Half your cousins are conscripted."

"It's Nonno I want."

"And so does poor Tessa. That's why we need to get this trip in before—"

"Before what?"

"Before it's no longer possible."

"You think there might be a war."

"I think I want you safe in England." Paul pets and wakes Charmian, then cradles her in his arms. "With my mother. As long as you're under my charge."

15.

Bermuda, 1941

Having been told by McKay to "run along now," Lucy felt no urgency to return to her chair at the long table of women reading other people's mail. She returned the Joe Karte letter to Fleur or Roos and proceeded to the Inks and Papers room. When she opened the door, she reeled, as she always did, from the heat of the Bunsen burners and the sting of the chemical smell. Flinching, she waved to Lark, who handed her beaker to another gloved Censorette and hurried over. Lark pulled down her surgical mask and pushed Lucy into the corridor, closing the door behind.

"What's happened?"

"Nothing." The mere appearance of any one of them out of context had become a portent of tragic news. "Do you know any bankers?"

"Bankers."

"I need to learn how to read a bank statement."

"Mr. Furbert, from St. Andrew's. He works at the Bank of Bermuda. He's a manager there."

"Do you think he'd help me?"

"We'll go after church. He'd be delighted. He's all bees and banking and boating. He's a dear. Bit of a stick now he's alone. I'm sure he'd like the company."

"A stick." Lucy wondered to what depth of dullness Mr. Furbert had sunk in order to earn the label from Lark, who could find an afternoon's entertainment in a spool of thread. "Thank you, Lark."

She pressed her hand against Lark's cheek, cupping her chin in her hand, saw Lark startle at this gesture in an almost Ruth-like way, and then turned back to her own work, and left Lark to hers.

After church the following Sunday, Ruth, Lark and Lucy walked with Furbert to his house in Pembroke Parish, about a mile west of the Princess Hotel. His bungalow was buttermilk yellow. The garden, thick with peach-coloured roses, amaryllis, and birds of paradise, was so dense with flowers that the silence in the yard was tempered by a steady low drone of bees, a Bermuda version of an RAF flyover.

Lark and Ruth prepared tea as Furbert walked down the hall to his study, adorned with nautical maps and a framed photograph of a small handsome yacht. Furbert explained balance sheets (a statement of assets, liabilities and equity of a certain entity at a specific point in time), a "frozen" account (one where a bank or brokerage has prevented any transactions occurring in the account), and bearer bonds (an unregistered debt security).

"Unregistered?" she repeated. "What does that mean, exactly?"

"No records are kept of it," Furbert said. "Not of the owner, or the transactions. Whoever holds the bond, owns the bond."

"Holds?" She picked up a folder from his desk. "You mean physically holds?"

"Yes, they are pieces of paper you present to the company to cash out."

"Why not just use cash?"

"Bonds are an investment vehicle. They earn interest. They're quite useful if you'd like to hide funds. Evade taxes. They were very popular in years past with the more sophisticated of the American gangsters."

"Are bearer bonds frozen when assets are frozen?"

"Excellent question. The certificates, as we've said, do not hold the personal information of the bearer, so bonds could escape a freeze. I assume you're referring to the Americans' freeze on the assets of Germany and Italy in the United States?"

The bonds were identified by specific numbers. What if Brooklyn Joe's Shakespeare letters concealed numbers instead of … instead of what? Maybe it was, after all, nothing. A homesick German in the Red Hook neighborhood of Brooklyn storing goods (bonds?) in a warehouse? Squirreling funds away in a Swiss bank account? Funds funneled from where and to what end? Perhaps Tessa had been correct to focus on numbers, and Lark on chemistry. There was less ambiguity, less nuance. Perhaps Lucy should focus on what Brooklyn Joe said about numbers.

***

Monday morning, she was presenting newfound knowledge to Colonel McKay when Gwynne interrupted them, poking her head around the door.

"Danville says turn on the wireless. The American CBS is coming through most clearly. Hitler's invaded Russia."

Even from McKay's office, Lucy heard a quiet cough across the Reading Room. Some of the men of the censorship joined Gwynne in the doorway, the men wondering how Hitler could be so foolish as to repeat Napoleon's mistake of invading that unforgiving country, Gwynne wondering whether this meant Jerry would leave "us" alone now. Lucy wondered that they wondered. Hitler had said he would invade the Soviet Union. He had written it in *Mein Kampf*, which Lucy had read in the original German at the behest of Karolina Diehl. Karolina had wanted to expand Lucy's reading from the exhaltation of Schiller, Goethe and Rilke to the grievance of tyrants.

She rose and left McKay's office without sharing these musings with anyone, having learned from too many episodes that they were not welcome.

16.

On Saturdays when a ship was in, Gwynne strode the halls, clanging a handbell. When it was only a Pan Am Flying Boat landed at Darrell's Island to refuel, she chimed a triangle. Fewer Censorettes needed to respond to the summons of a triangle, but Lucy always did. The next Saturday, responding to a triangle, Lucy was intercepted on her way to the Reading Room by Reginald Teck.

"Let's go back up to your room, Barrett. We'll talk on the stairs. Rather urgent. Any of your delightful roommates in?"

"Ruth is. What is it?"

They rounded the bannister of the first flight of stairs.

"You need to come out to Darrell's Island. I've a motor launch waiting at the hotel dock. Won't take a minute."

"Twenty, I believe." The intercepted mail on the flying boats took forty minutes to be transported to the basement room at the Hamilton and then back. The Censorettes were expected to process it in less than that time, still leaving the flying boat passengers waiting close to two hours.

"Not much post on the Clipper this go-round. Good morning, good morning." On the second floor, a few Censorettes passed, surprised to see a man on the floor. "The men can go through it easily enough on the island. There is, however, a Madame Foulques on board. Wife of a Vichy diplomat. Says she's returning from a shopping trip to New York. Thing is, we'd like to have a look inside her pouch."

Would you, now? At her raised eyebrow, and mindful of the Censorettes streaming by (including an interested Gwynne), Teck switched to French. "She's carrying a *valise diplomatique*. But she was never actually seen going to the embassy while in New York. She stayed at the Pierre Hotel. Went sightseeing. Shopped. No embassy trip."

"Even so," Lucy replied in French. "If she's traveling on a Vichy passport, we can't open her *valise diplomatique*. We have no right. The Yanks've recognized Vichy. Unless that's changed. Things do change so rapidly, and we mere girls are told so very little."

"Oh yes, you *will* do." She had apparently passed an audition. "Yes, indeed. Quite right. Technicality, really, but the address on the pouch still says Paris. I suppose they have a supply of the pouches laying about the offices at the embassy, and whoever packed it forgot to cross off 'Paris' and write in 'Vichy.' So, as Paris is now in German hands and we are at war with Germany, we can, in fact, open it. Madame is none too happy. We've put in a trunk call to New York to get it straightened out but those things can take hours and in the meantime, there Madame sits. In an office at the terminal on dull little Darrell's Island. We hoped you'd come out and keep her company."

"*Me*? We have actual French girls."

"You have certain other qualities. I say, please don't think me rude, but could you make yourself look as nice as you can in as short a time as possible? When you see Madame, you'll understand."

Teck waited in the hallway while Lucy dressed. She chose the Chanel, but there was nothing to be done about her hair. She had swum laps in the saltwater pool last night, and rinsed out the salt, but had spent the rest of the night in a towel-turban, teaching Ruth piano.

Ruth tried to brush Lucy's hair out now, following Lucy about the room while she slipped into her dress, found her white gloves and added white sandals. Lipstick, powder, what else could she do?

"Ruth, can you braid this? I've got to get to Darrell's Island and the *wind*—tie a ribbon at the end?"

In response, Ruth pressed her shoulder to make her sit.

"This will hurt a bit.'

It hurt more than a bit. Ruth tugged and pulled her hair and shoved Lucy's head into place.

"I always did Charity and Faith's hair for formal occasions. They said I had no charity or faith with their hair, but they always came back to have me do it. They're plain dressers, but I'm sure you've already guessed that."

"No, how would I—" *How would Lucy know how Ruth's cousins dressed? Ow.*

"My father married out of the faith. He was wayward before that, according to my Aunt Verity. He had to be, to advance in his career. Then he married a red-haired Presbyterian and look what happened." Ruth pulled Lucy's hair.

"What—*ow.*" *Bloody ow.* "What did happen, Ruth?"

"As you see."

Lucy cautiously turned her head—previous turns of her head had been rewarded with hairbrush raps. Ruth brandished a fistful of her own wild red hair as evidence of *what happened*, as a gameskeeper might display a dead lamb to expose a wolf.

"*Miss Barrett!*" Reginald Teck knocked on the door. "Time and tide!"

"That should hold." Ruth swung open the door to the public wardrobe (not Georgie's locked one) and showed Lucy her tight French braid. She tossed the flimsy scarf to Lucy. "Wear that over your head to keep it in place."

"What will you do while I'm gone?"

"Take a walk. Take my watercolours. Fresh air and exercise. Georgie says," Ruth imitated Georgie's double-clap, "'the body responds to routine.'"

Lucy laughed. Ruth smiled. Lucy could not recall having seen her smile before. She kissed her on the forehead and ran to join Reginald Teck, who was by then pounding on the door.

***

Madame Delphine Foulques' own coiffure was as severe as Lucy's: a lacquered, marcelled blonde helmet confined by a snood and two diamond clips. Lucy would have marveled that Madame Foulques wore diamonds in her hair as part of her traveling clothes, but the rest of her clothes were equally marvelous. Like Lucy, she wore Chanel—a black suit with a cinched waist. Her eyes swept up and down Lucy's figure, noticing, Lucy noticed, Lucy's own Chanel. Lucy introduced herself, in French, adding, "They have asked me to keep you company."

"They said you were *une angliche*. But your French, it is …"

Matty had been told during his Paris summer that he spoke French with a slight Italian accent and no English accent at all. This must have been true for Lucy as well, confusing Madame Foulques. Lucy smiled rather than explain.

Madame Foulques rolled her eyes and folded her arms and gazed out at the dock, to the plane which had brought her here. The flying-boat station at Darrell's Island, which received and replenished the Pan American Clippers, was designed for function rather than luxury. There was one long, narrow building which held engine parts and fuel hoses, a room for the crew to relax in while the sea plane refueled, a barren room where the passengers waited—the clippers could transport just over thirty at a time —and a few offices. Madame Foulques and Lucy were in an inner office, while Teck and other functionaries sat in the receiving area, processing the mail. They handled the correspondence much more roughly—flapping open letters, waving them in the air to request a second opinion—than the Censorettes. The Censors murmured to one another, watched the women through the open door and pretended each glance was happenstance. Madame Foulques attempted English.

"*Alors, Mademoiselle*, it may be your people regard this as an error. The silly mistake of a clerk. But if you persist, it will be *un incident diplomatique. Il fera du tapage.*"

"*Fera du tapage.*" Lucy shrugged Gallicly, pursuing her lips for good measure. "*Je m'excuse, Madame. Les idiomes, je regrette de dire—*"

"*Il y aura une fureur internationale!*"

They might be treating this as a diplomatic incident, but the Frenchwoman intended to make a lot of noise about it. Lucy pretended not to understand that "make a lot of noise," was an idiomatic phrase, so Madame Foulques went further to indicate that the actions of the Detachment would result in an international furor. Lucy doubted that a peek inside the *valise diplomatique* of the wife of a minor Vichy official would arouse much uproar. But she understood that Madame Foulques also knew this. She was hiding something, but it was not, Lucy suspected, in the *valise diplomatique*, which sat on the desk occupied by Reginald Teck and at which Madame Foulques had not so much as glanced.

"*Une fureur?*" Lucy shook her head as though she were accustomed to not understanding things. "*Je ne comprends pas. Der Führer* will be angry— you say Herr *Hitler* will be angry if we look into your pouch? *Je n'avais pas compris que vous fussiez une femme aussi importante.*" *I didn't realize you were a woman of such importance.* "Mr. Teck!" she called. She turned back to her companion, "I am calling my superiors, Madame. We must avoid *une fureur mit dem Führer*. Oh, I beg your pardon. I seem to have confused my French with my German. But of course, that is something you would understand well."

"You wish to be humorous, mademoiselle. It is not feminine."

"Ladies?" Teck stood at the door. "Some refreshment? Tea?"

"I do not wish your *tea!*"

"I would love tea, thank you. With sugar! I'll wager there's sugar on the Clipper. I've heard there's everything on the Clipper."

The Pan-American Clipper was as big as a ship, and yet it flew. It held a formal dining area which served four-course meals, a recreation area in which to play games and piece together jigsaw puzzles, curtained sleeping berths, and even a honeymoon suite. It sat in the bay like some fantastic invention only Jules Verne could have imagined. Matty would love it. The Boeing 314 flew slowly (for an airplane), and at great expense, but it made Bermuda from New York in just five hours, and then to the Azores in seventeen more. From there, it would go to Portugal, and then Madame Foulques would journey on to Occupied France with whatever she was hiding.

They waited. On the table to her left were Madame Foulques's hat, gloves, handbag, and a portfolio. Was she an artist: pencils, pastels? Unlikely. Her only interest in art was in the presentation of herself. The portfolio was bound in a rough black fabric: raw silk? Linen? The handbag was an Hermès Lucy had seen advertised in a

French fashion magazine.

Madame Foulques did not ask about Lucy's business in Bermuda, how temperate was the weather, or how she had come to speak French as she did. In turn, Lucy did not ask what it was like to travel on the Boeing 314, or whether there were children in the Foulques household. She rather hoped there weren't.

Teck entered the room bearing a tray as though he'd been a household servant all his life: a tea service and a plate of tiny sandwiches and slices of cake. Lucy nodded and averted her eyes, as though such food made up her daily meals. The tea sandwiches, the lemon-frosted cake, the raisin-filled scones, did not excite her as much as the hill of sugar cubes in the bowl. She wondered how many of them she could smuggle home to Lark.

Lucy removed her gloves very slowly, pulling out the cap of each fingertip before she released each hand slowly from its sheath. She set the gloves by the plate of cakes. She dropped two lumps of sugar into her cup, picked up the Pan Am-branded teaspoon, and stirred. The spoon circumnavigating the cup produced a skating sound, which, as she continued to stir, seemed to grow in volume, like turning up the sound on a phonograph, until it dominated the room, over the breeze that rattled the windows in their swollen wooden frames, over the shouts of the men on the dock, over the murmur of the Censors in the anteroom. She studied her tea as if the dissolution of sugar in a hot beverage required the keen focus of an engraver. Madame Foulques cleared her throat. Lucy understood the thrill of hunting dogs on the scent.

As she waited for the tea to cool, she laid her hands across each other in the shape of a cross, as she had done so many times during that tedious Knoll House summer. Madame Foulques exhaled a puff of impatience and reached for her handbag.

"That is lovely." Lucy nodded at the bag.

Madame Foulques shrugged: of course; why would she own ugly things?

From her lovely handbag, she removed a silver cigarette case, monogrammed "DMF." from this, she removed a cigarette, which she lit with a silver lighter, also monogrammed. She blew the smoke, returned her silver articles to her Hermès bag, and returned the purse to its position atop the portfolio.

"What is that?" Lucy pointed at the portfolio. "Do you draw?"

"They are photos of my visit to New York."

"You have it at your side?"

"They are searching my luggage. I do not know where they will put my things—on some open dock? In the damp? In the circumstances …"

"You are wise, Madame. Things can get sticky."

Lucy stood, reached over and picked up the album. "I've never been to New York. Did you like it? I always think of that film, *King Kong*. Where the great ape takes the girl to the top of the Empire State Building. Did you go there? Oh, yes, here you are, practically in the sky!"

"It is gauche, that building." She looked about for an ashtray and chose a saucer from the tea tray. "I prefer the Chrysler. That is the more chic."

The album was almost the size of the tea tray. Lucy could still not determine the fabric of the cover, only that it was some thick industrial material, not silk, linen, or leather. It was hand-stitched, with black pages, better to set off the representations of Madame Foulques in her stern poses before the monuments of Manhattan.

The pages were unusually thick, thicker than the stock of paper would warrant. After opening thousands of pieces of mail, she knew the intent behind the choice of paper: the onion-skin sheets of the voluble thrifty, the linen-plump paper of the reticent rich. Holding a page between her thumb and forefinger, she squeezed. She gazed at a photograph of Madame Foulques before a statue of Atlas shouldering the world. The pages were folded over each other. They appeared to be two pages thick. Each page appeared to represent two sheets. But when she turned the pages, they didn't buckle in the middle from the weight of the photos, as they would have with a mount of two sheets of paper. They remained stiff, stiffer than they would with the support of just two sheets.

The photos. Madame at: the Empire State Building, the Rocke-feller Center, the lobby of the Woolworth Building, a park by a harbour with the Statue of Liberty in the background.

"*Mais alors*, it all seems so exciting, Madame! I would love to go to America!" Lucy sipped her sugar-sweetened tea, and turned the pages. "How long were you in New York City?"

"For ten days."

In each photo, Madame wore the same black suit. In each photo, the diamond clip in her fair hair was in the same place. Her hat was the same, consistently angled on her head. The sunlight changed as the day wore on, but all of the photos had been taken on one day. She was always the only one in the photo. The photographer had apparently never switched places with her. *Alors*. Lucy had before her a photo album meant to record a ten-day visit but which was in fact a record of just one day, with pages of remarkable thickness, in an album expensively hand-stitched but with a plain, thick cover, from a woman whose bag was Hermès and whose cigarette lighter was engraved.

"Thank you." Lucy stood, and smoothed the skirt of her dress. "Mr. Teck!"

When he appeared, ready to accept an order for tea, she asked, "Would you have a pen knife? Or a pair of scissors?"

When he returned with the scissors, she tilted her chin behind him, at a Censor. "What's that? The call to Madame's embassy has gone through?"

"Finally!" Madame Foulques stood, mashed her cigarette into a saucer, and hurried toward the anteroom.

Lucy clipped a corner of a page of the photo album, dug in with one blade of the scissor, and dragged the blade across the width of the page. She pushed her finger between the pages and encountered, as she expected, a stiff sheet of paper in the middle. From the black page displaying the photos, she extracted the hidden document, a thick paper adorned with ornate engraving. It was a bearer bond worth a hundred thousand dollars.

***

There were ten of them in all—a million dollars. A million dollars that would not reach the coffers of the Nazis. Madame became so hysterical that she had to be restrained. Diplomat's wife notwithstanding, she endured the infamy of having her hands cuffed before she was moved into the motor launch and taken across the bay to Hamilton to be arrested. And although Lucy had uncovered, rather than committed, a crime, she was subjected to repeated questioning and paperwork. How did she know what to look for? (She didn't.) How did she know where to look? (Madame was indifferent to the pouch, but barely took her hand off the album.) How did she know what a *bearer bond* was? (A girl should have a hobby.)

At last she was released into the custody of Teck. He tucked the paperwork into his rucksack and piloted the launch across the bay back to the dock of the Princess Hamilton. She had claimed, as her reward for exemplary service, the bowl of sugar cubes from the Pan Am Clipper. Teck held them while, with his other hand, he guided her out of the launch. Then he led her to the front door of the hotel.

The Censorettes spilled across the lawn like dandelions. The Folk Dance Society followed Fleur and Roos through a Belgian dance which involved endless spins. Someone played accordion to encourage their stomps and twirls. *When*, Lucy wondered, *had an* accordionist *arrived, and how had the Censorette had the foresight to bring her instrument?* Had she somehow known that this assignment was a kind of prolonged garden party?

The Censorette Sewing Society sat in chairs on the porch, or cross-legged on the lawn, basking in the rosy light of the late afternoon as they peered at their stitching. The sunlight here was as pink as it was golden and buttery in England. It was the rock of the islands, the yellow limestone of England and the coral of Bermuda. The rock created particles of dust which scrimmed the daylight and perhaps even predestined their respective islands to a geological temperament.

"I say, Barrett." Teck ruffled through his paperwork and handed Lucy a plump envelope large enough to accommodate a fashion magazine. "You might be so good as to deliver this to Taylor."

It was addressed to Georgina Taylor, care of the Princess Hotel, Hamilton, Bermuda. And that was all.

"No postage," Lucy said. "No return address. Curiouser and curiouser."

"Yes, questions," Teck said. "We all have them. 'A girl should have a hobby,' you said about the bearer bonds. Bit frivolous, no?"

Lucy looked pointedly at her folk-dancing and sewing colleagues. "You find *me* frivolous? When I asked to look at financial statements of Germans and Italians, both languages in which I am fluent, I was told to 'run along.' I found that dismissal, as you say, *frivolous*. I didn't know how to read a financial statement. So I found a tutor. I wouldn't say I'm fluent now. Let's say 'working knowledge.'"

The Censorship's taxonomy for knowing a language was: reading knowledge, speaking knowledge, working knowledge, translation knowledge, simultaneous translation knowledge (a strange category, since the Censorettes only read letters and were never put into a position to translate active conversations), fluent, fluent with slang, and mother tongue.

"What tutor?" Teck asked.

"A banker here on the island. And you have your result. A million dollars denied the Nazis. 'An ill-favoured thing, but mine own.' Mr. Teck. I've said this and I'll say it again. *This cannot be my war. I can do so much more.*"

Lucy waved her hand at the dancers, the seamstresses. Was there actually a world at war out there, or was she lost in some abandoned Jane Austen story, reading letters, coveting gowns?

"And what is this?" Lucy shook Georgie's package at him. "No return address?"

"She'll be pleased," Teck said.

"*Will* she!"

"Very much, I'm led to believe." Teck turned to leave, then pivoted back. "I say, Barrett, don't be disconsolate. It was *very* well done. You certainly lived up to your billing!"

"My billing."

"Haughty as a duchess, persistent as a badger." He whinnied a laugh. "*Une fureur mit dem Führer*.' I could kiss you for that." When Lucy tilted her head in assent, they kissed cheeks, one-two-three, like the French, as suddenly out of breath as though they'd swum back from Darrell's Island. "Still, triumph and disaster, treat those two imposters just the same, and so on."

"Yes, I've heard that," Lucy said. "So what now?"

"What do you mean?"

"A note in my file, a word in someone's ear, more significant work? What *now*?"

"Well, *just* now I'd say you had better attend to that man on the porch waving so frantically at you. With your roommates."

Lucy followed his look. Bill stood on the porch between Lark, sewing, and Ruth, sketching, and he was, in fact, waving urgently.

Teck held out the sugar bowl from the Pan American Airways Clipper, with its "PAA" logo showing a map of the world adorned with wings. He bowed his head. "'Sweets to the sweet, farewell.'"

Since he turned and walked away, Lucy had no choice but to do so as well. She walked down the path with her parcel and sugar bowl, passing the dancers, climbing the three stairs to the porch, where Lark and Ruth sat at a table.

"Lucy, honey, *where have you been?* Who was that man?"

"Hello, Bill."

Lucy kissed his cheek and set the bowl of sugar cubes on the table. At the sight of the sugar, Lark dropped her needle and immediately popped two cubes into her mouth. Ruth did not complain; she never did when her subjects moved. Lucy suspected that Ruth's sketches were finished, in her mind's eye, from the first stroke of her pencil, and every moment after was mere recording. She moved behind Ruth to see her rough portrait of Lark as a series of small reversed smiles: the eyebrows, her long eyelids, her cheekbones, the half-smile she wore when absorbed in a task.

"Lovely!" Lark mumbled over the sugar cubes. "Where did they come from?"

"The Clipper. I was at Darrell's Island."

Bill said, "Lucy, I've been here *two hours.*"

"Why were you here? I never said to come. I had work."

"*You* had work, but none of these girls did?"

"As I said."

"Didn't look like work. Looked like you kissing another man."

"Kissing?" Lark paused with a sugar cube halfway to her mouth.

"We weren't *kissing,*"

"I *saw* you, Lucy!" Bill cried.

"Who were you kissing?" Lark asked.

"Lucy likes kissing." Ruth explained. "She kissed me this morning." Still sketching, she stretched her head toward them like a horse seeking a proffered apple, to display the stain on her forehead from Lucy's red lipstick, which she bore with honour, as a Catholic carries the smudge of Ash Wednesday. Lucy's lipstick stain had faded some, but not so much. Lucy wondered that Lark had not corrected it.

"Darling, you—" Lucy licked her thumb and rubbed at Ruth's forehead. "Lark, whyever didn't you—her *face*—"

"Lark is busy," Ruth nodded toward Lark's sewing basket, which contained a meringue-like heap of white linen. "Blouses from bed linen for the Belgians. That's alliteration."

"Will you stay out of this, you *retard!*" Inman snapped.

The other sewing Censorettes raised their heads. Lark set her sewing down. Lucy felt a paralyzing heat of anger.

"I'm not a *retard.*" Ruth was more puzzled than hurt.

"Of course you're not, duckling." Lucy stroked Ruth's hair.

"It would've been easier if I'd been a *retard.* They could have sent me somewhere." Ruth set down her sketch pad. "'Over and done and no fuss about it,' Aunt Verity said."

"If you'd like your conversation to be private, Lieutenant, conduct it in private." Lark gathered her linen into her fist. "You can't come to our quarters and behave this way."

"Bill," Lucy said. "With me?"

All those lectures in Paul's study had not been in vain. Silence was one of her father's favourite gambits, with "*Well*! I hardly know where to begin!" a close second. Lucy led Bill into the Gazebo Bar and folded her arms.

"You will apologize to Ruth."

"Kissing her! '*Darling*' her! You've never called *me* darling!" Inman paced. "You keep me waiting hours. I don't even get a proper hello—"

"Bill, we are at war."

"What can a bunch of girls do about that?" He gestured toward the front lawn. "Maybe the guys're right about y'all. Unnatural. You like each other more than you'd like a man …"

"We're here to do a *job*." She kept her voice low but she could not keep it from shaking. "We're not here for you."

"Honey, don't talk like that." Bill tried to take her hand. "Look, I like a chase as much as the next man, but you can only push a fellow so far."

Georgie burst in from the porch. "Lucy! I heard about *la triomphe francaise!* The post came—oh, hello, Bill. I suppose the same ship that brought you in brought this for Lucy. The diplomatic pouch from Washington. Look!"

"And I have this for you." Lucy handed her the thick parcel from the Clipper. "No postage." She ripped open the envelope Georgie had handed her; it was addressed to her, so why take especial care? "No postmark, no—"

"*Mia cara bella sorella,*" the letter began, and a long high whine deafened her to the world around her, as though she were caught in an air raid.

17.

Cara sorella bella,

I write to you from Knoll House. I am alive and well, safe and sound, and all the other reassuring phrases. A bit of an eyesore, according to Granny, who said "pulled backwards through a hedge doesn't begin to cover" the state of me, just before she burned the clothes I stood up in. Which was rash, as clothes are rationed, and now I am wearing a pipe-smelling jumper of Grandad's. I have been through some bramble, truth be told, but it was forward, across the Pyrenees.

So, as brevity is the soul of wit: I was shot down at Dunkirk. I landed in the drink. Some French fishermen fished me out and hid me. I banged up my shoulder and some ribs, and wasted precious time convalescing. Then I joined their operation. There are networks, known as "lines," that get people out of France, farmhouse to barn to church. Forged papers, clothes, food, train tickets, carts, bicycles, until we reach the Spanish border. The danger is indescribable. The long and short of it is, I decided I could do more good by sticking with them for a bit, helping others get out. I wasn't the only flier to come down, that day or the many days after. There were other RAF men, but also civilians. Anyone who needed to get out of France.

Because of trying to compete with you, I had better French than almost all of the downed pilots, and because of all that time in Dad's study, I could draw better maps. Because of my flight experience, I could calculate the trajectory of planes that were hit. I could predict where the pilot would try to steer a plane on fire, and when he would jump, if he were able to jump. Sometimes we were able to get to the crew before the bloody Gestapo did. As part of the line, I helped get more than a dozen people out. One of them was supposed to deliver a letter to you, but you it seems you were not at home. More on that later.

Eventually, someone on the line was arrested. Once that happens, the jig is up. We broke it up and went into hiding. I hightailed it into Spain, and then to Portugal, and then home via KLM.

It is not becoming for an officer to make his own decisions when downed behind enemy lines. In peacetime, I'd get a proper bollocksing for it, but the men I saved seemed disinclined to take time off from protecting the Realm against the Luftwaffe to testify against me in a martial court, so the powers in charge gave me a medal instead, and tossed me back up into the air. Where, frankly, I would rather be than in another beastly meeting with those men, who think they know better than the people who have been there. They think a stiff upper lip would get them through Gestapo torture. They think their thinking doesn't cost lives.

Now. Before you hear it from Marcia, know that I did not compare Paul to Caligula. I compared him to Augustus Caesar, who banished his daughter Julia to that barren rock island. Of course, he did that because Julia had had it off with every plebe in Rome. Your only sin is in looking so like Mama.

(And in not saving her, Matty, Lucy thought. And in not being with her.)

You can imagine it was a bit of a blow to hitch my way back to London to find our home occupied by Admiralty toffs. They were at least decent enough to let me sleep in my own bed, and let me have their hot water rations. Because I was a hero, and because of Mama.

Then I spent no small effort getting to Knoll House only to find out that you were in Bermuda. Bermuda! Why not Shangri-La? Why not Cloud Cuckoo-Land? I was absolutely furious with Paul. I can only imagine how anguished you felt. To be sent away so soon after Mama. My mother and my sisters were my first thought every morning and my last thought at night. This is true of every fighting man I have met.

So we had a blazing row. Screamed the plaster off the walls. Every woman in the house was driven to tears, even that evacuee girl Hannah, who has nothing to do with the case. But I did _not_ compare him to Caligula.

I know you'll find a way home. Know that once you do, you will be approached. A girl of your abilities will prove irresistible to the intelligence services. Do nothing until you hear from me. Above all, do not go to France to set up radios. Those girls are caught instantly. When *they are caught, it is not like in the movies, with a clean firing squad. What the Gestapo does to those girls is horrific. Do not go to France.*

God only knows when we will meet again. In the meantime, I would not beteem the winds of heaven visit your face too roughly. (Although I know you are not in the tropics, no matter how often Granny says it.)

I'm told I have to wrap up. We are all writing letters. Paul said he would pull strings to get our Barrett bundle into the diplomat pouch headed for Washington. That's why I've been able to write so frankly.

At least I know you are safe. At least I know you won't be distracted by suitors. I can't think the Detachment is staffed by the cream of the crop but even if you should fancy one, know that he can never love you more than,

Your loyal brother,
Matteo

P.S. Your chum Horatio is here at Knoll House. Like all of us, he has a war job. Field vole patrol. Earning his stripes, you might say!

Tides of emotion shifted within her at every paragraph, sometimes in a single sentence. Relief, gratitude. Homesickness, *the bitter bread of banishment.* "Do not go to France, do not go to France," had an incantatory, Shakespearean rhythm to it—might it be a reference, a sibling code as they used to do? One of the Henry plays? But the Henrys were always charging *into* France, claiming kingdoms and princesses. Perhaps he meant merely "do not go to France." As though she had an option, as though she had any option of where to go other than down to the basement of the Princess and back up the stairs to the honeymoon suite.

She read the letter again, not with an eye to code, but imagining herself at Knoll House—the flowers on the rows of root vegetables dotting the sloping lawn, the peaty, chalky scent of Granny's rose garden wafting into the sitting room, where the ticking clock competed with the clicking of the metronome as Marcia thundered through "The Minute Waltz," even little Horatio snuggling in Lucy's lap while she scratched his head. Always warm and redolent of the recent baking, the kitchen, with its sturdy scarred table, was where Matty preferred to write his letters, despite Granny's repeated and repeatedly ignored offers of the use of their grandfather's "perfectly good study," the screaming match between Matty and Paul, which she conjectured was rivalled only by the many she had had with Paul when he delivered his Bermuda decree. Matty was outraged at her exile. Matty was a war hero. But she, Lucy, "a girl of irresistible abilities," was, notwithstanding, not to go to France without seeking the counsel of another male relative. They were still protecting her. She was Tessa in the incident of the Drewe's hand cream.

The sounds of Bermuda filtered into her subsequent readings: the evening birds alerting one another of the sunset, the hearty joshing of the Yanks outside, arriving for the dance, Lark, splashing in the bathroom, crooning "*In the beauty of the lilies/Christ was borne across the sea,*" Ruth practicing only the right hand part of the "Jesu."

Lucy opened the French doors which led to Georgie's portion of the suite. Georgie, on the couch, had covered herself with the many pages of her own letter, a page on each breast, on each thigh, on her stomach, one hand roaming to caress the pages, as though she could press the words inside her body. With her other hand, she clutched the remaining pages, stroking them with her thumb as she would a lover's hair. She met Lucy's eyes with a sated smile.

"My ally has returned," Lucy told her.

"So—has—*mine!*" Georgie shouted, raising both her arms on her last word. She tenderly gathered the pages together, like a mother cat nudging her kittens. She kissed the stack of pages and set it carefully on the couch. Then she stood and embraced Lucy in a hug that crushed her ribs.

"Good news, then?" Lark strolled in and Georgie hugged her as well, but more gently. Lark wore her pale green Easter dress. Her pale hair had been cajoled into soft waves.

"Better than good. Better than I'd hoped for!"

"Well. 'Ask and it shall be given to you.'" Lark bestowed a kiss on

Georgie's forehead. Lucy bent to look at the pages. They were illustrated in coloured pencil, like an illuminated manuscript, as though the sender felt that words could not convey his meaning, although there were thousands of words as well, adorned by small drawings: a faceless blonde's bridal-veiled head, a woman in tennis whites, the Brandenburg Gate, a palm tree in a shaft of sunlight.

Georgie said, "You look fetching, Lark. Fetching someone tonight?"

"It's the dance." Blushing, Lark scanned Georgie, who wore slacks and a blouse. "Aren't you coming?"

She looked hopefully at Lucy, still in her Chanel dress, which she had donned just eight hours ago, although it seemed eight days, before she foiled a Vichy smuggling plot. *Do not go to France.* To leave the grassy breezes of Knoll House for the clammy dance hall, Bill's reproaches, Gwynne's glowering—

"No," Lucy said.

"I don't have to go if Lucy doesn't!" Ruth shouted immediately from the other room, over the repetition of the "Jesu," which inspired the three of them to shout, "*Stop playing!*"

"I don't want to be proper. I don't want to be polite. I don't want to put everyone at ease. I want to run and run and roll down the big slope at Knoll House. Like I did when I was a child."

"Right-o," Georgie said. "Let's go, then. I can't give you Knoll House, but I'm sure one of the golf courses can provide a suitable slope. I expect you'll want to change." Georgie nodded at Lucy's dress. "And Lark, do try to have a bit of a lark."

18.

When Lucy awoke Sunday morning, she wondered if it had been a dream, until she was reassured by the sight of Matty's letter and the grass stains on her shorts, crumpled on the floor. She had stripped

off her clothes and fallen into bed. The morning began with recrim-
inations from Lark, plucking her clothes from the floor, "I suppose
some of us grew up with a maid!" Then church, at which Alan appeared, trying to subdue his usual cheer into a sober piety, and then
Ruth's *dolce far niente*, for which she packed the watercolours and a
sketch pad, to sketch her favorite tree, an old banyan in the agricultural station. And then at last, time alone to write her letters home.

Bermuda lived in a permanent embrace of moist air, but you
could not milk the air for water, so the Bermudians harvested the
rain. The tiled limestone roofs of the houses collected rainwater and
diverted it into cisterns built beneath their homes, which posed the
danger of overflow during hurricanes. That was Clara Frith's phrase:
"the danger of overflow." Lucy remembered it when she was finally
liberated from roommate duties and left, in the late afternoon, to
address her own correspondence. In addition to Matty's letter, there
had been one from Marcia, with her merry approach to spelling.
She did not, as Matty had warned, relate that Matty had compared
Paul to Caligula. But she did describe their quarrel as "like something out of Wagner!" Granny's letter knitted her relief at Matty's return into her usual skein of fretting: such an *awful* row, and in front
of the *evacuees*! And was Lucia being really *vigilant* about minding
her skin in the tropical sun? *Nothing* ages a woman more quickly.
Had she yet been invited to any affair which might also include the
Duke and Duchess of Windsor? Did she require additional gloves?

There was no letter from Paul.

Her heart was too full. There was the danger of overflow. She
decided to tackle the simple first. She would sort out, once and for
all, this business of Bermuda, the Bahamas, the Duke and Duchess
of Windsor, and the "tropical sun."

July 13, 1941

Dear Granny,

I must disabuse you of your notion that Bermuda is in the tropics. She is not. I enclose maps I have drawn. The first shows Bermuda as she relates to America. The second is of the island itself, with an X marking where I live and work. The third is Bermuda as she relates to America and the Bahamas. The Duke and Duchess of Windsor are in the Bahamas. I am not. You see how the Bahamas are south-south-east of Florida, while Bermuda is due east of the Carolina states."

Drawing the maps took no small amount of time. There was no atlas in the room, but Lucy remembered the map on the wall in McKay's office, and when she had finished her sketches, she showed the maps to Ruth. She allowed Ruth, who never wrote letters of her own, to watercolour the sea blue, and the relevant states green and peach, while Lucy painted the Bahamas tan, and Bermuda pink.

The following Monday, Lucy breakfasted at the Bermudiana, as usual, but ran upstairs when she arrived back at the Princess to fetch the letter and maps to put them in the next post. They were not where she had left them. She scanned the top of the piano, where all the residents of the honeymoon suite were still foolish enough to leave the occasional paper despite the episode of the lost "Jesu." They were not there either. There weren't that many places for things to go astray. Ruth was rigidly systematic in how she kept her things. Lark held to the Presbyterian credo that things should be kept "decently and in good order." Georgie kept everything locked. Lucy was the slattern of the group, leaving where they fell her hairpins, knickers, gloves and handkerchiefs.

The letter and maps were gone. And now she was late for work.

When she arrived at her desk, there were no letters waiting for her. Fleur or Roos had barely finished saying, "The Colonel wants to see you," before his hand tapped her shoulder, "A word, if you please, Barrett. With me. If you could." His hand remained on her shoulder until she understood, and offered him her arm. A few heads looked up, before the rustle rustle cough of the room resumed.

They walked out of the basement, through the lobby, up the stairs—slowly—to the third floor, through a locked door, and down a corridor of rooms which, from the sounds of conversations and typewriters, seemed to be used as offices. McKay deposited her in an office that held a drafting table, a wall lined with bookcases, a phone and a desk. Georgie leaned against a desk, arms folded, gazing, like a cat, at an invisible fascination. Behind the desk stood a sinewy man, staring out the window at the saltwater pool. He wore Bermuda shorts and a grey Lacoste shirt.

He nodded when McKay introduced him as Archibald Danville, started, as though snapped from a hypnotic trance: *Danville. Yes, that's me.*

Lucy's letter sat opened on a desk with the maps she had drawn fanned out like a hand of cards. As the colonel limped out, Danville sat behind the desk.

"Do sit down, Barrett. Your maps. How did you come to draw them?"

"I was demonstrating to my grandmother, Colonel—captain?" Danville waved away his rank. He had grey eyes, round spectacles, greying fair hair and skin which had seen so much sun that she couldn't determine whether he was closer to forty or to sixty. She stumbled on, "She thinks Bermuda is in the tropics—"

"Taylor says you drew these maps straight out without the aid of an atlas. The southeast coast of the United States. The surrounding islands. All quite accurate."

"I recently saw a map in Colonel McKay's office."

"And your beau," Danville said, as he pulled from beneath the maps and letters a brown folder. He read, "Inman, U.S. Army Corps of Engineers. Perhaps you draw maps together."

It was illegal to carry a map in England, lest the Germans use them after a successful invasion, but did that law apply in Bermuda? Who would invade Bermuda and who, if they did, would need a map? They could traverse the whole island place between breakfast and lunch. She looked to Georgie but Georgie focused on a faraway horizon she seemed determined to conquer, as though posing for a recruiting poster. *Join the WRENS and free a man for the fleet!*

"Your mother was Italian," Danville added.

This seemed to be her true north, the point on the compass which set the conversation: *your mother was Italian*. She wondered if Ruth's manner of speaking was the result of the same kind of thing; perhaps Ruth merely laid out the rules at introduction as an attempt to address her shortcomings only once. *My name is Lucia Barrett. My mother is Italian.*

"I do hope my loyalty is not being brought into question." Gran ny would have approved her delivery.

"Have you been to Italy?" Danville went on, as though she hadn't spoken.

"Of course I have. I have family. My aunts, my uncles, my cousins …" She added, "Not for a long time, though. Not since I was a child."

"But you've seen maps."

"Of course. Geography is quite a passion of my father's. There was a globe in his study. My brother and I were expected—"

"Where in Italy? Where was your mother from?"

"Firenze. Florence. The summer we spent there, we stayed at my uncle's villa near Cecina."

"And where is that? Show me."

Georgie skipped over to a table and laid out a large piece of drafting paper and a jar of pencils and gestured at Lucy to sit. "Care for a coffee, Lucy?" Georgie asked brightly.

"No, thank you."

She drew a line to indicate the west coast of Italy, then sketched in the regions along the coast: Piemonte, Liguria, Toscana, Lazio, Compania, Calabria, the islands of Sardegna, Sicilia, Capri. Cecina was in Toscana. The villa had been seventy-two stone steps above the beach where her cousin Santo had kept a sailboat. He had taken Lucy out to show her the dolphins. The dolphins leapt around the boat, an aquatic *corps de ballet*, trilling. Santo told her they rushed to welcome him every time he went out. He took just her, no Matty, and none of his sisters. He had a soft spot for his *cuginetta inglese*. "Does the sea sparkle like this in England, Lucia?"

Danville touched her shoulder. She leapt in surprise.

"All of Italy, please. The Adriatic side. A sense of North Africa. Certain about that coffee? It's the real thing, not the swill we give you girls. Sometimes a bag or two does get left behind by the ships from Brazil. Ah. Milk and sugar?"

Coffee appeared, with fresh milk. When she finished, the cup was whisked away. A tray appeared with more coffee and a plate of soggy oatmeal biscuits. She coaxed Italy from the drafting paper. She and Matty had always drawn maps—real and imaginary, the grounds at Knoll House and the Hundred Acre Wood of Winnie-the-Pooh. When Matty was sent to Harrow, he sent home maps of the routes of his days. When she passed her exams and was admitted to Girton, he mapped out the colleges of Cambridge for her.

She was shading in the Dolomites when they took the map away. Apparently, she was not under arrest. She would not be thrown in with the local internees, a sad collection of about thirty women and children unfortunate enough to have been married to or sired by a German or an Italian. They were kept in the Military Hospital in St. George's Parish, unresisting and bored. She shuddered at the thought of joining them. Life on the island was dull enough, and St. George's was the remotest part of Bermuda.

Danville gave her another sheet of drafting paper.

"Less Leonardo this time, Barrett," he said. "You've five minutes and the man who reads this has only a torch in the dark."

"And let's say, Lucy," Georgie chimed in, having shed her *freddezza* and been recalled to life as a Girl Guide keen on a leadership badge, "that a group of men are on foot. They need to get to the south coast. One of the beaches. Horseshoe Beach."

"Horseshoe Beach is too obvious," Lucy said. "Although they could huddle in those Stonehenge rocks. Wait there for a signal from a boat."

"Get them there," Georgie said. "Say Harbour Road's off limits.

All the main roads are off limits—Middle Road, South Road. Full of enemy convoys. Get them from here to there."

"And it's too dangerous to go straight over to the south beach, say to Hungry Bay, and then along the beach?"

Danville nodded, pleased. "Yee-esss. The beaches are patrolled."

Lucy sketched a course. She avoided the marsh, took them across a golf course, through the park and down a steep hill.

"And here, they could hide in the rocks and wait for a signal."

"Yes." Danville stood and studied the saltwater pool through his window. "You have a talent or two. The great Matteo told you you'd be approached. We're approaching."

"Matty—my correspondence is read." Lucy tried to recall what she had written. "But the diplomatic pouch?"

"Bit naïve to believe in the sanctity of the post." Georgie, in front of Danville's desk, placed her palms on the desk and hoisted herself onto it. She crossed her legs, the *chanteuse* perched atop an upright piano. This morning she was an entire theatrical production, performing every role. "Considering how we spend our days."

"So what are you asking?"

"Your pedigree, though impressive," Georgie folded her arms. "Was not enough. Your dogged pursuit of Brooklyn Joe? Eh. Snaring Delphine Foulques and her bearer bonds? Pooh pooh. But what ho! The girl *can draw a map.*"

"Now, Taylor," Danville said.

"Now, *Archie.*"

"What are you approaching me for?" Lucy thought of the many times her parents had debated her future in front of her without as much as a glance in her direction.

"For the time being," Danville said. "You'll train. With Taylor. She says you're fit enough, but a little rigor in the regimen never hurts. She also says you speak German like a Cambridge bluestocking. So we'll work on that. You'll leave what you do now, once you're through with the proper training. Do you understand what we're asking?"

"Toward what end?"

"Well, not France, obviously. Heaven forfend the great Matteo's sister goes into France," Danville said. "We thought … Italy. When the time comes. And you'll have to dispense with that young man of yours, that Yank, what's his name?"

"Bill Inman," Georgie said.

Their smiles faded and they both looked at her, lips pressed together.

Danville said. "Not an ally. You'll have to break it off."

"I've tried," Lucy said. "But I will for certain."

"Best to limit attachments," Georgie said. "Cuts down on the fear and pain."

Lucy suppressed a shiver at the way Georgie said "fear and pain," much the way Danville had said "milk and sugar." And perhaps it was at the end just a preference, how she "took" a war, like her coffee. But of course, it was no choice at all. She knew what she would do. She had known as soon as Danville said "the great Matteo," in that half-mocking tone. But she'd known before that. She'd known when he said "five minutes," and "torch," that finally, her talents had found a use.

"You won't have much time for courting anyway, not in the next few weeks. I'm handing your training over to Taylor. You'll sign the Official Act here. Though there never *was* a here. You didn't draw maps. We didn't give you good coffee."

"*Especially* the coffee," Danville mock-shuddered, as Lucy took the papers and began to read. "They get so shirty about confiscation."

19.

Because she spoke German "like a Cambridge bluestocking," Lucy was set up to have breakfast and tea with Georgie, who had both a native accent and an alarming palette of colloquial terms for sexual parts and activities. To improve her running, she was set to running, across the golf courses which had been commandeered for such use, across the beaches, and through the residential streets of the parishes, with Georgie pedaling alongside her. Because she needed to build up the strength in her arms, she did push-ups and pull-ups on a climbing frame in a local schoolyard. The last, she found agonizing.

"And yet it's the most useful set of muscles you can cultivate," Georgie said with her enraging mildness. It was the third Saturday of the regimen. Georgie studied a pocket watch, then the horizon, as though foreign troops might that minute rise over the hill.

"Is this to make me used to pain?" Lucy hung from the bar, unable to lift her chin over it one more time.

"Builds strength in your arms. They don't expect that in women. When you parachute, strength helps. True, the belt holds you, but it helps if you feel in control, when you're holding onto the ropes. Start bicycling your legs in the air and try to hit the ground running when you land. And if you can't do that, at least land on your bum and keep rolling. Alright, if that's the best you can give me, come down."

"I'm to parachute?"

"You're versatile. A tomboy, but of course, as you know, a beauty." Georgie took Lucy's hands in her own and leaned back, pulling Lucy's arms into a stretch. Georgie added, "We may put you in an evening gown instead of a parachute."

"A *Schiaparelli* evening gown?"

"I'm afraid Schiaparellis are thin on the ground these days. And do you think you could, erm, do that? Flirt in a ball gown with a *fascista?* Even … be intimate with a man you didn't love?"

"Wouldn't be the first time." Doing it with a man she loved would be a first time, although she had fond memories of her rewarding tumble with Guy Jenner in London. *Eat, drink and make merry,* her Girton friends had said. *For tomorrow we may die.*

Georgie released Lucy abruptly, sending her staggering. Then she picked up her knapsack, hooked her arm through Lucy's and led her out of the schoolyard, onto Woodlands Road, down the hill towards the harbour.

"It probably won't come to that. Cloak and dagger. Midnight assignations. Whatever notion you have from the cinema. You'll most likely be in an office, translating. Much like now. On the other hand, it'd be a shame to waste your Italian. And you have family there. We just won't know. Archie believes they may do a landing there. In Italy. Europe's soft underbelly. Before they try to open a second front. He hasn't quite worked it out and of course, he's in no position. But as for that Mata Hari stuff —it was alright for me. I was an athlete. Sleep with a man for a cause. Fling yourself around a pair of uneven bars. Same thing. A means to an end. It'll be different for you."

"What? Sorry, I'm a bit lost."

"I'm saying, you may have to do things … things your Daddy wouldn't like."

"Yes?"

"Like in *To Sin for Love*," Georgie said. Lucy stopped in the road to study her.

The afternoon was surrendering to evening. The pink sky coaxed in the approaching indigo. The evening buzzed with insects released from the close heat of day. Moths fluttered toward the streetlight. Fireflies pulsed light from within themselves. Georgie and Lark pulsed from within, Lucy thought, each glowing with purpose. Gwynne was a moth. Ruth kept her light to herself. Lucy's own light seemed to her a weak bulb on a buoy when she yearned for it to be as strong as the beacon of a lighthouse. But instead she merely bobbed, offering dim warning of shoals, doing her small bit in the vast ocean of the war, of life itself. Yet she believed that somewhere else, with someone else, she would find her incandescence.

Lucy and Georgie's arms were linked. Now Georgie joined their hands. "The film," Georgie added. "*To Sin for Love*."

"What, that silly Leslie Howard movie? It would never come to that."

"It did come to that. For me. My husband made that movie."

They were behind the wrought-iron gate which shielded the garden behind the Bermuda Library. There were benches and bushes in the back garden, as there were in the front one, where Clara had found Lucy sleeping that May morning. The library was open or, at least, the librarians were still there. The lights burned inside, illuminating stacks of books, so many lives and stories waiting to be opened.

"Your husband," Lucy repeated.

"Taylor's not my name. Neither is Georgina."

"Your name." Lucy recalled the Schiaparelli dress, the passports. "Is Annegret Lincoln."

"My mother named me Annegret."

"A German name.

"A German mother." Georgie gestured at Lucy. "An Italian mother. My husband made me Lincoln. Nick brought me in to the service. As I brought you in. He was a cameraman. A damn good one. We'd just been married when we went to Berlin to film the Olympics. I was barely older than you are now. Then … we parted ways. I had to do … perform a task. The Mata Hari stuff, if you will. The seductive spy. Do I need to spell it out?"

Lucy shook her head.

Georgie continued, "With an Untersturmfuhrer from the Gestapo. My friend, my German friend, my German *Jewish* friend, was under arrest. It wasn't so straightforward as you might think. As … *transactional.* He didn't demand, Tomas. The Gestapo man. I flirted with him. 'Oh, I thought you were more influential. I had that impression because of the strong way you carry yourself.' And when Dorchen, my friend, was released, and safely out of Germany, I realized I could … I could save others. But imagine proposing that to your husband. Married in June, Olympics in August."

Lucy could barely imagine that she was hearing this.

"He couldn't forgive me, Nicky. And I couldn't forgive him. He'd brought me in, he'd *trained* me. Have you any idea what Berlin was like when the cameras were turned off? Those films were bad enough, the marching, the idolatry. Nicky went off to Hollywood. When I saw that silly Leslie Howard movie, when I saw what a terrible prig he'd made that character, I thought there might be a chance he realized what an *idiot* he'd been. I wrote to him. Lark helped me write the letter. And Archie helped me make sure it reached him."

Lucy stared at her in wonder so long she had to remember to breathe. "Golly, George."

And she'd thought her *parents* had set an impossible standard for romance.

"That kind of *love*," she said to Georgie. "Spanning half the world. Half a *decade*. An apology by cinema. It's … it's an *epic*. So romantic!"

"Don't be soft." Georgie plunged her fists onto her hips. Lucy envisioned her in the gymnasium, flinging herself into the air, landing on the lower bar, swinging to the higher one, falling to the mat, leaping back to the bars, falling, glaring. Bruised, sore, determined. The furthest thing from soft.

"It's not at all like the cinema. Music up, curtain down. We'd been so crazy about each other. We were so in love it made people sick. And he left me. And he left me to do the telling. Then I learned I was pregnant."

"Oh, George."

"I called her Rebecca. After an aunt."

Lucy took her hand and Georgie let it be held, but didn't allow her own hand to respond. She hummed a sigh which Lucy understood was a method she had used to control her voice when she continued to say, "She only lived three weeks, my Rebecca. She was so frail. Just never right. She wouldn't take my breast. Wouldn't stop fretting. Until she did. She stopped. She just stopped. Nick never knew about her. He was gone by then and I didn't know how to reach him. I wasn't good for much after that. The service let me teach German. I worked in a tailor's shop. So I took the name Taylor. Georgina, in honour of the new king. I found safe houses. Then the war brewed up. The branch was afraid I'd crack up if they sent me back to the field. So they sent me here. To fish for recruits. Ruth could be doing so much back home, we all thought. But her father sent her here. So did Lark's."

"*Lark's*? Why?"

"That's her story to tell. But the thinking was, if we put you together, you might do something. You might bring Ruth out, so she's comfortable with others. You've done well so far, but you need to do more. There's a place back home where she could do so much. It's entirely dedicated to code-breaking. If you can just get her to be more at ease around people. You do." Georgie took Lucy's hands in hers. "You do put people at ease."

20.

Despite the fact that she wore a floppy floral frock that had seen better days, and that Lucy wore athletic shorts and a blouse grimed by her sweat, Georgie led them from the back of the library to a pub on Front Street where, by the same alchemy with which she had brought Lucy into the intelligence branch, she conjured, with a few words to the maître d', a dish of lamb chops, peas and potatoes. Lucy ate like a feral cat. She gulped down, as well, the wine Georgie produced with a wave of her hand, so that by the time they climbed the slope that led to the Princess, Lucy was sleepy and stupid. The six flights of stairs sneered at her. The floors were clamorous. Censorettes ran the corridors, as though summoned to battle stations, in their dressing gowns, curlers in their hair, calling for loans of belts and earrings. Floor three, floor four, and then on floor five, they encountered Gwynne, wearing a mask of face cream and a snood over her curlers, striding down the hall. Gwynne snared Lucy's elbow.

"'allo, Barrett! I say, you *will* lend us your boy tonight? Share the wealth, eh?"

"Goodness, the *dance!*"

"Yeah, and you're not 'alf ready." Gwynne swept her eyes up and down Lucy, her limp hair, her grimy blouse.

"Would you tell Bill I won't be coming tonight?"

"I'm sure he'll ask others to dance in that case," Georgie added brightly.

"I need to stay in and look after Ruth," Lucy said. "She's not well."

"Not *well*? I saw 'er at Horseshoe Bay, splashing about. Crowing about how she mucked up the nerve to put 'er 'ead under water. She's a duck, she says, like Lucy wanted. And you say she's ill?"

"She's ill." Georgie guided Lucy up the final flight of stairs. "So the wealth's all yours, Gwynne."

"First rule of interrogation," Georgie whispered to Lucy as they ascended. "Stick to your story. 'That's what I saw, that's what happened.' It's the nasty little nobodies who want a leg up, like our dear Gwynne. Don't outsmart them. They hate smarts. Be as dumb as you can. Ah. Home again, jiggery-jog."

Home meant an available bathroom, at last. Lark, a light dressing gown thrown over her ensemble, painted her mouth carefully with one of Mrs. Dodd's Max Factor lipsticks. Ruth sat plopped on Lucy's bed, also in a dressing gown, her wet hair draping like seaweed.

"Lucy, I swam in the ocean!" she cried.

"I *heard*, my duckling! Let me find my big comb!"

Georgie, at her wardrobe, packed a rucksack: dressing gown, change of clothes, then into the bathroom to fetch her toothbrush.

Lark shrugged out of her dressing gown, revealing a pink frock.

"Lark's dress is coloured to look like a rose!" Ruth said.

"A rose by any other name would be a lark," Lucy said.

"Lark is becoming a rose," Georgie said, emerging from the bathroom, as Lark pinkened to the roots of her pale hair. Georgie flashed a jar of Drewe's cold cream at Lucy, to both pre-empt and accept permission for taking it. "See how she blossoms."

"It's just a hand-me-down from one of Mr. Furbert's—"

"Don't you want a bath?" Lucy asked Georgie.

"Archie likes to do the bath." Georgie tucked the cold cream into her bag.

"*Lucy* is becoming a rose!" Ruth exclaimed, as she saw Lucy blush. "I wish I could blush."

"Then everyone would know what you were feeling," Lark said.

"Exactly," Ruth said. "I wouldn't need to explain."

The other three locked eyes for a moment, then Georgie and Lark left.

Now I am alone. Lucy and Matty had argued for stupid weeks whether that was a stage direction in *Hamlet*, in a 16th-century theatre world without curtains or lighting, or a cry from Hamlet's kinless soul: *Now I am alone.*

But she wasn't alone. Ruth crawled down the bed to her. Lucy worked her comb through Ruth's clumped mane. Brushing Ruth's knotted tangles was like raking bracken after a rainstorm. Lucy suggested that Ruth teach her the intricate French braid Ruth had performed on Lucy's hair, but Ruth refused. She couldn't abide the tugging. In turn, she allowed Lucy to plait her hair on the condition that Lucy wouldn't scold her for plucking the plaits apart. It soothed her, she said, to stroke her own hair, although it aggravated her teachers no end. The doctor had agreed that it soothed her, and so her father had halted Aunt Verity's plan to give her a bob.

"Duckling." Lucy picked at one difficult lock of hair. She would massage Ruth's scalp with olive oil, but Lucy couldn't get there until the lower bits were sorted. *Pretend the scalp is Berlin*, she told herself, *pretend the rest of this wet mess is Europe, and you need to get through it to get into Germany.* "What happened to your mother?"

"She died."

"Yes, I'm sorry." Lucy paused in her combing to briefly squeeze Ruth's shoulders. "It's so hard to lose one's mother."

"I didn't lose her." Lucy anticipated another mini-lecture on the literal use of an expression before Ruth went on, "I never knew her. My mother left this world because I came into it, Aunt Verity said."

And blast her for that particular verity, Lucy thought. "She died in childbirth."

"I said that."

"No, not quite. Not quite what you said." Lucy, breathing like Georgie had taught her, to manage to pain of aching muscles, unknotted the whole left side of Ruth's hair until she could glide her comb from scalp to ends. She then sectioned Ruth's hair into rows to braid. "You said your cousins Faith and Charity are 'plain dressers.' What does that mean?"

"They're Friends."

"I'm sure you said they were cousins."

"Society of Friends. Their church is different. Women can be ministers and everyone can speak, but people have to sit quietly and really think about what they want to say. Most people who aren't Friends don't. I'd like to ask Lark, but she's so impatient. I asked Alan. There are a lot of Friends where he's from. They're called Quakers."

"You like Alan. You can talk to him."

"He teaches me things, like you do. He doesn't laugh at me."

"So you *can* talk to people. Alan's big and loud and a Yank, but you get on. Ruth." Lucy paused in her plaiting. "Do you think you could you go back to England? If there was a good job, a job where you know you'd make a difference? I so want to make a difference."

"Aren't you doing that here? You've uncovered Brooklyn Joe."

"But we don't know what he's *up* to. So far it doesn't *matter.* This war destroyed my family. I want what I do to *matter.*"

"Should I want that?"

"I think, duckling, the better question is, what *do* you want?"

"I don't know." Ruth, braided, turned to her. "No one's ever asked me that before. I'd like us to stay together. I've never had a friend, before now."

21.

July 24, 1941

My dear brother,

I realize I am showering you with letters, but I tell myself that if I were in England and had been there when you came home, I would be showering you with kisses, so these billets-doux will have to do. Although I suppose they're not technically billets-doux if they come from a sister. Perhaps the doux bit. The dolce. The sweet. The sweetness of having you to write to again.

I am also writing so many letters as an experiment. It's not like when you were at Cambridge and we could exchange letters daily. Now we must wait weeks if not months for a reply. It has recently come to my attention that my correspondence is sometimes read, both in and out, so I am asking a third party to post this for me, and we will see if and how it gets through.

As you anticipated, I have been approached. That is all I can say.

You were right to surmise that the cream is not stationed here, but it is not quite true that there are no opportunities for romance. The Yanks are here. Part of the Destroyers for Bases agreement. They're building a naval base and an airfield. They have joined our dances on a Saturday night. Our parents never thought much of Yanks, but I tried to welcome them with an open mind.

I agree with Paul that they are uniformly ignorant of matters beyond their own borders. As Tessa said, they are very loud with their opinions. But they are a cheerful lot. I'm afraid in matters of love and the Yanks, I have been a disappointment and been disappointed.

She had gone to the following Saturday dance to call it off with Bill. She'd had another long training day with Georgie, who again departed for what she called a "bunk-in with Archie," as though they cuddled over a campfire, drank tea and swapped ghost stories. Ruth and Lark hurried their own baths, allowing Lucy to soak her aching legs while Lark ironed yet another Furbert-refurbished dress, this one lemon-coloured, dotted with small violets.

Lucy wore her plainest dress, since she did not intend to stay long, and walked down the stairs with Lark. At the dance, Alan stood onstage, playing "How Long Has This Been Going On?" on his trumpet, with only a bare bass line and a sleepy snare beat behind him. Lucy followed Lark, who walked right up to the stage. Seeing them, Alan lingered over the last note and then segued into "Alouette," the French children's song, which stilled the bewildered crowd, since they could neither jitterbug nor two-step to this schoolroom tune.

Inman found Lucy, took her by the hand and led her from the dance floor to the pool behind it, the pool where Lucy now swam laps with her ankles bound to improve the strength in her arms. When he opened the glass doors to the patio, they interrupted a couple spooning in the shadow of one of the changing huts.

"Do you mind?" Inman snapped. "We'd like some privacy."

"So would we, pal!" said a man's voice.

A woman stepped into the light spilling from the open door. She turned to her sweetheart and held out her hand.

"Let's just go, Dan. No point in quarreling with that one, he's such a bossy boots."

The couple had barely passed them before Inman took Lucy's shoulders.

"Listen, Lucy. I may call you 'princess of The Princess' as a joke, but my girl can't act this way. My girl doesn't put me off on a Saturday night, or put her girlfriends first, or think some *job* is more important than me. Do you understand?"

"Yes, Bill, of course." Lucy breathed out in relief. *Well*, this *was turning out to be simple! Sometimes, things just take care of themselves!* "I agree we're not suited. There are *dozens* of girls here who would be *delighted* to be—"

"What?" Inman grabbed her arm. "What the hell are you saying to me?"

His face frightened her into backing up. She stumbled over a poolside chair.

"No, you *change!*" he shouted. "I'm saying you have to *change!*"

"I won't," Lucy said. "Not into what you want, anyway."

"It doesn't matter to you at goddamn *all* that I'm in love with you?"

If he was in love with her, then why did she have to change? He seemed astonished, as though she had encouraged his false vision of her, as though she deliberately failed to fulfill a promise made in intimacy.

"You *can't* be," she said. *Could he be?* Based on what? Some kisses, a stroll under a bomber's moon, his "princess of The Princess" myth? "We hardly *know* each other."

"Hardly *know*?" He shortened the distance between them and grabbed her wrist. "I fell in love with you the moment I saw you! And you're saying I'm not—?"

His hand not holding her flicked back. She jumped away from the blow. She sent the glass-topped table behind her tumbling, and fell down beside it. She hit the ground hard and felt a hum in her hipbone, but was more frightened by the shards of glass and the sudden cessation of the music in the other room.

"*You lying little tease!*"

The courting couple was at their side immediately—*had they even left the patio?*—and then the man was pushing Bill back. Others streamed onto the patio—men for Bill, girls for Lucy. Lark pushed through, took one hard look at Lucy, and dashed away.

"Y'all stay out of this!" Bill shouted. Men grabbed his arms. Tears spilled down his face: "You're a *whore*, Lucy! A goddamned *frigid little whore.*"

"Night's over, Inman," said Alan. Lucy couldn't see him or anything. She was surrounded by skirts and knees. Bill shouted as he was tugged away, the Army and Navy cajoling *knock it off, brother.* The girls cooed concern to Lucy, some genuine, some thrilled by the drama.

"Watch the glass." Her teeth chattered. Her voice, her breath, her hands trembled. "Do be careful, you're wearing sandals."

The gash on her knee dripped blood down her leg and onto the patio.

"Okay, show's over, folks!" Alan returned, with a vocal command he seemed to be born to: volume, authority. "Don't let that hothead spoil this. Go on back inside and pick up the dance. Make it a good evening."

"Yes, do go along." Lark returned with a first aid kit. "I'll take care of her. I have medical training. Gwynne, could you fetch Hector to sweep this up, and bring a glass of water?"

Lark guided Lucy into a chair, then knelt to examine her knee. She took a handkerchief from Alan, wet it, and her hands, in the pool. She attempted to bathe Lucy's knee with the wet handkerchief, but at her touch, Lucy's leg jerked and she kicked Lark.

"Oh Lark! I'm so sorry, I—"

"Bits of glass still in the wound. Alan, are there tweezers in that kit? And could you move out of my light?"

Saltwater, alcohol, analgesic cream, then stitches, five, right there on the terrace, with the Cootie Williams in the background playing on his trumpet. Then a gauze pad, then wrapping. Lark was calm efficiency: Lucy was a wound to be tended, Alan was an attendant to follow orders. When Gwynne brought the glass of water, Lark drank it down in three gulps. Hector arrived with a broom. The glass tinkled as he swept it up. Lark began to shiver so violently she nearly dropped the glass. Alan took it from her, handed it to Gwynne, and pulled Lark into a hug.

"Beck! You did great. Better than a field medic." Alan kissed her hair. "Hey."

Gwynne raised an eyebrow, *So that's the lay of the land?* and returned to the dance.

"Silly of me …" Lark murmured into Alan's shoulder. "My nerves …"

"Your nerves'd hold up the Brooklyn Bridge." Alan rocked her, first humming, then crooning, "*et le bec, et le bec, alouette, alouette* …"

Lucy felt a sneeze of understanding. *Alouette.* French for "lark."

This bond had formed while Lucy ran through the parishes of Bermuda, learning code, learning street German. Alan was the inspiration for the sherbet-coloured frocks Lark wore on Saturdays, floating down the stairs with no trace of shyness while Lucy, *frigid little whore,* fell into a bath and then into bed. She felt happy for Lark, with a dash of disappointment for herself, and a chill of loneliness. It was a bracing emotional cocktail. She left them, refusing their offers of escort, pleading the need for a brandy and rest. Her limping inspired Hector to take her in the lift, back up to the room, and to Ruth.

Now I am alone.

The following Monday, Lucy was informed by Colonel McKay that Clara Frith had been hired by Inks and Papers. The Censorettes were informed that no further dances would be staged at the Princess Hotel, due to their inability to maintain proper conduct. Everyone knew this meant Bill, and most of them blamed Lucy.

22.

London, 1936

Lucy is leaving home.

She is leaving home and she is being taken out to dinner. She is ready for the latter, not the former. At her desk in her bedroom at Mowbray Crescent, she dabs lipstick on her lips and then wipes it away with a tissue so that it will not look like she is wearing lipstick. Even though she triumphed during her summer of exile at Knollborough (wearing lipstick at flower shows, fetes, teas and dinner parties), even though she will dine at Simpson's so that Paul can show off his Cambridge-bound son and daughter, and even though she is, as the dinner indicates, bound for Cambridge the next day,

Paul still objects to his daughter using "paint" on her face. Matty lounges on her bed, plucking at his violin, pushed hither and yon by Tessa, who packs Lucy's trunk. Horatio, at the window sill, chirps at pigeons. Horatio, Lucy and Marcia only returned from Knoll House a week ago, after Paul and Tessa returned from Italy, and Matty from France. A week of reunion, and then, for the first time in her life, leaving home to live alone.

Of course, it doesn't really count, as she will have Matty.

"Matteo, you promise that after an entertainment—a concert, or a lecture—you will walk Lucia home to her door." Tessa shoves him aside to pull open a drawer of Lucy's bureau and select from her supplies of handkerchiefs and gloves. "That is only proper."

"Mama, that's impossible. Girton College is miles from King's. There's a reason they put the skirts on the outskirts! Better she just stays in."

"I won't stay in." Content with her lips, Lucy lotions her hands. "Why should I? I studied twice as hard and I beat you by a year in getting there."

"Leave us, Matteo. Set this trunk down first."

As the door closes behind Matty, Tessa pats the bed. Lucy's stomach storms as she sits beside her mother. This talk will be about Guy Jenner.

"Your grandmama wrote to me," Tessa said. "This Guy Jenner, the one you do not like. She says he pursued you all summer. He was at every dance. He sent flowers. You went riding when you do not ride. But you do not like him. You have always mocked him."

"He's not so bad," Lucy muttered. *Devoted as a dog,* she thought, *with a dog's bright dark eyes. Eager to follow suggestions, his brow never furrowed by the vexing quandaries of intellect.* ("You're awfully clever, Lucy. Cleverer than me.") *(Cleverer than I, Guy.)*

"He wrote notes to you. You offered to let your grandmama read these notes. That was very proper, Lucia. Perhaps too proper? We are not Victorians."

Who on earth was we? Granny was certainly Victorian; she was born in the middle of Victoria's reign and named for her, to boot. Paul

still called makeup "paint"and had girdled her girlhood with tutors
who had proved as effective as a chaperone in curtailing her freedom.

"If you do not like him, do not receive him. It is vulgar to brag about suitors you do not care for. To entertain and disdain. You are cold towards men. You should not be."

"Should *not* be? You always said 'don't encourage'—"

"You should not display his notes and say '*Che seccatura!* How he always talks of love!'"

And how on earth could Tessa know that? Had Granny *written* that *in her letters? Had Granny, after two decades with Tessa, mastered enough Italian to understand it and write it down?*

"I like him, Mama. I don't love him. I was lonely. The whole summer with no one but an old woman and a little girl and—" she gestures at Horatio, who flattens his ears as he growls at the pigeons. "Should I go to parties and speak to no one? I never said I would marry him!"

Tessa rears back as though Lucy has spilled hot tea into her lap. "Who is speaking of marriage?"

"*He* did."

"That is out of the *question!*"

Lucy had threatened Paul with elopement with a sheep farmer when he sent her to Knollborough for the summer, only to be proposed an elopement by Guy Jenner, whose father owned the land the sheep grazed on and cottages their herders rented. Guy didn't love Lucy, any more than she did him. She was pretty, forbidden ("most unsuitable"), and unimpressed.

"You are far too young for marriage and he is far too old for you," Tessa says.

Che ipocrita! Tessa had been seventeen when she met Paul, had waited until eighteen to be married only at Granny and Nonno's insistence. The age difference between Tessa and Paul is exactly the same as that between Lucy and Guy.

"Did you allow him to kiss you?" Tessa asks.

Lucy had *allowed* Matty's friends to kiss her, after ice-skating parties, under the mistletoe at Christmas. Guy Jenner taught her how to kiss. He taught her how to ride a horse, and he taught her how to kiss. They kissed behind the large walnut tree grove at the bottom of the long slope at Knoll House. They kissed on patios, just outside the beam of light spilling on the bricks from the dancing inside. They kissed in the Morris Eight in which Guy drove her home. They kissed until a voice inside of Lucy chattered as Horatio chattered now at the birds across the window, at a primal urge with no real hope of fulfillment. She accepted Guy's caresses along the bottom of her buttocks, his grip of the weight of her breasts. And then she had stopped him. He expected to be made to stop, and she was expected to do it.

When Lucy nods, Tessa sniffs, "Well, good. I am glad."

"Mama?"

"Celestina said, during our visit, Celestina said that giving you so much education would turn you into 'one of those terrible English virgins who moves to Italy for the climate and then deplores that the country is full of Italians.'"

"Aunt Celestina always puts things so nicely."

"You take after her, I think."

Terrible virgin! Lucy thinks, she *can talk*! Living up to her name, Aunt Celestina is the most devoted of the daughters to Nonno's astronomy, the one who had married, just to stay near it, one of Nonno's best students. She spent years as her husband's typist and editor while raising three daughters, before she was widowed and spent more years serving as typist and editor to other impatient scientists in order to support her family, rather than consent to marry again.

I take after her? Lucy thinks. *Heaven forbid.*

23.

Bermuda, 1941

August 22, 1941

Dear Uncle,

I visited our new warehouse in Red Hook. I saw the merchant dice.

    All is well. I hope all of you is well. I hope to see our cousins soon. When they come here, I introduce them to the game of baseball. Mother says it is the key to America. We like the New York Giants. They play at the Polo Grounds. At the Polo Grounds, some have a view of the Hudson River. The Hudson River is the where the piers are, where the ships dock.

    We think of you often, across the great ocean. We wait for a long time. We hope you will come to us soon. The readiness is all.

Joe

"Alright, Barrett," Colonel McKay said. "Alright."

    What had she ever gazed at as intently as that letter? Her mother, when Lucy sat at her bedside after her operation, waiting for her to emerge from anesthesia? The night sky, when she lay on a Florentine hillside with Matty and Nonno, trying and failing to find among brilliant stars the shapes of bear, ram, warrior? The receding shore of England as she fumed on the deck of the trawler that brought her to Bermuda?

    She had walked into McKay's office without knocking, without speaking, and handed him the letter. When McKay finished reading, he set the letter down and tapped his mouth with his finger. She took the letter back and read it again, then pushed it back across the desk to him. He read it again. He gazed elsewhere. They performed this pantomime for a few minutes until she stood up, walked to the door of his office, and called across the rows of bent heads, "Ruth! Can you come in here! Can you go to Inks and Papers and fetch Lark?"

The rows of bent heads looked up. It was not the custom for a Censorette to shout orders. Then the heads bent again to their work, *Dear Uncle, Dearest Sarah, My dear Mama*. Ruth emerged into the Reading Room, paused since she had been given two contradictory orders, chose one, and left the Reading Room for the Inks and Papers lab.

Soon a group gathered in McKay's office: Lark and a colleague from Inks and Papers, another cipher-breaker, Lucy, and Ruth, copying the letter since Lucy knew she would not get it back from Inks and Papers.

"Merchant dice," McKay said. "What's poor English? What's code? Smith, what did he say in the last letter?"

"'Goods.'" Ruth didn't look up from her copying.

"And what's this business about giants?"

"They're a baseball team," Lark informed them. "In New York. My beau Alan talks about them. They play at the Polo Grounds."

"The Polo Grounds overlook the Harlem River," Lucy said. "Not the Hudson River, where the ships dock. And it's nowhere near Red Hook. That's on the East River. I've been *studying!*" she snapped at McKay's raised eyebrow. "I keep *telling* you I think it's about shipyards."

"Yes, your father's in the Admiralty. So you would have a naval frame of mind." Before Lucy could protest, McKay added, "You haven't yet said that the Shakespeare is wrong."

"It isn't. The first was wrong, the second was wrong, the third was a sonnet, and this is right. 'The readiness is all.' They are *ready!* Can they be any plainer? This is the letter with the secret message. 'Where the ships dock.' It's something about shipyards, I *know* it is."

But the Censorship couldn't find the secret message. Inks and Papers tainted the letter with chemicals, held it up to X-Ray and ultraviolet light, and found nothing. After a few days, they were ready to send it on, but Lucy pleaded for a delay. The chemists appealed to the Federal Bureau of Investigation in Washington, D.C. for suggestions. And then they waited.

September 1, 1941

Miss Lucia Barrett
The Princess Hotel
Hamilton, Bermuda

My darling daughter,

It is with such mixed emotions that I write to wish you a happy birthday. Feelings were so high when we parted that I failed to tell you important things: how proud you have made me, how happy I am that you are safe. You have grown into such a fine woman. I wish the one who is entirely responsible for it could see you. You are so like your mother. So beautiful and so clever. I can only thank God that you haven't been beguiled away from me by some fool as Tessa was from her dear father. Your Nonno would say that it is just what I would have deserved.

And now you have come into your majority. And a small legacy. Much of this is moot, of course, as no money can leave the country now. But my father left you a small annual income which will be a welcome supplement to your husband's earnings. Not too soon on the husband, please! Specific details are contingent on so many things that I will not go into them now. I will close with,

> *My profound love and blessings,*
> *Your always loving father*

She had not been beguiled away by "some fool" but she had, she understood, been beguiled away from Paul. Beguiled away by his own actions, by her stubbornness matching his, by her need to make meaning from the hours of study, the hours and times of Paul's desire.

Georgie departed on the Pan Am Clipper for her long-awaited reunion with her husband in New York. He was headed for North Africa, but they had arranged to spend a few weeks together to determine what to do with their marriage. She had promised to bring back Lucy anything that she wanted, but Lucy couldn't think of a thing she wanted, other than to go to New York herself, or better, to go back to London. Even if she were to die in a bombing the day she arrived, her last breath would be of London's briny, sulfurous air.

"Always the poet," Lark had said crisply, scribbling away at Georgie's desk. She tucked a letter into an envelope and sealed it. "Here's the letter for the minister. He's at the Presbyterian church on Fifth Avenue. He's a friend of my father's from seminary. I've asked him to provide counsel to you and your husband, as a favor." Lark continued, as she scribbled on a fresh sheet of paper, "I know you're not much of a believer. But, should you resume this marriage, you need a clear set of expectations. Be honest, and don't be nervous."

"How can you say 'don't be nervous' when there is so much at stake?"

Lark extended her hand. She had done this often with Lucy, but rarely with Georgie. Georgie not only hurried to her and took her hand, but knelt before her, as though Lark had the power to bless her.

"Don't be nervous. What will be, will be. You love each other terribly. But love should not be terrible. He fell in love with a vision. So did you. So do we all, I think. But when you showed him the real you, he lost that vision. So can he love you? *You.* What you are, where you've been, what you've done. My fiancé couldn't forgive me."

Lark continued, "If he can love you as you, wonderful. If he can't, sad. But either way, good. Better to know now before you're trapped in a marriage full of recrimination. My father told me this, when I broke off my engagement. Don't tailor your skirt to a man's vision unless you are willing to wear it all your life. If you ever were that girl in his vision, you're not that girl now. Don't cry. You have nothing to mourn."

Georgie rose from her knees and hugged Lark in her chair. Lark allowed it for a moment, then patted Georgie's back and handed her the second paper. "Here's a list of things I'd like from New York."

"Goodness! It's … rather *long*, Lark."

"It's not for me. Half is jazz records Alan wants. Some are things for Ruth and Lucy."

Lucy said, "I don't need anything."

"I beg to differ. You're very fond of lipstick. And you're running low on gloves and knickers to drop on the floor."

***

Knickers or no, Lucy did not want things. Milestone birthday or no, she did not want gifts. An island was difficult to provision to begin with, let alone with a war on. Only cedar seemed to be indigenous to Bermuda. The onion, the lily and the wild boar had found their way there before its "discovery" by Europeans, and everything else had been brought by them and its development brought its own complications. Ships brought rats; settlers brought slaves.

Be not afeard; the isle is full of noises,
Sounds and sweet airs, that give delight and hurt not.

That was what Lucy wanted for her birthday: *sounds and sweet airs.* She reinforced her *no gifts* policy by adding that if she could not see, hear, eat or drink it, it would go into the charity box at St. Andrew's. Her party was held at a bar on Front Street. Clara presented her with a birthday cake so large and many-layered that Lucy knew before she was told that the flour, sugar, cocoa, eggs and butter had been donated by the unrationed American forces who had all chipped in. Furbert had bartered honey for a neighbor's chickens, which were roasted in the bar's kitchen. Alan, Fleur and Roos performed "Santa Lucia." Gwynne (coached, Lucy suspected, by Clara) had declaimed the "'This blessed plot, this earth, this realm, this England" speech from *Richard II*, which proved surprisingly charming delivered in a Cockney accent. Gwynne inspired a spirit-fortified cheer when she concluded.

Lucy's birthdays in England were marked by a pearl for her add-a-pearl necklace, an additional charm for her silver bracelet, another volume of Shakespeare's works in tooled leather, and an envelope recording a deposit in a savings account. This accumulation throughout her girlhood ought to have seen her bepearled, charmed, Bard-fluent and well-heeled. But of these riches, all she could carry with her was a head full of Shakespeare. Which may or may not prove to be useful in this matter of Brooklyn Joe.

"I realize that everything I've been given for my birthday so far," she announced to the room, standing on a table, "has been in anticipation of some fruition."

"Here's to fruition!" cried one of the Navy, and everyone drank.

"And here I am fruited!" Lucy declaimed. "And I can have none of it, since we're at war. And I'm here, since we're at war. Since we're at war, and my father couldn't stand the sight of me."

"Here's to the sight of you!" called one of the Navy, who was shushed by the others.

At the end of the night, Alan took his trumpet, Lark and the more intoxicated girls in a jeep back up the slope to the Princess Hotel. Lucy, annoyed by the struggle she found in mounting the hill with Ruth, Gwynne, Fleur and Roos, regretted not tumbling into the jeep—*was this a slope or a proper hill? Was she cute-tipsy or sloppy-drunk?* But if she had joined the jeep, who would have looked after Ruth?

"The Giants play at the Polo Grounds." Ruth pranced backward ahead of the rest of them. "Alan told me their names. Babe Young at first base, Burgess Whitehead at second. Alan said the Yankees are the better team. I suppose, Lucy, that you'll want to check the names of the Giants' roster against the names on the Detachment's list? That's what I would do."

"Ruth!" Lucy searched their surroundings: hedges and dusk.

"I say, Lucy," Gwynne said. "Bloody awkward … I wouldn't like to … well, spoil the party, and maybe I shouldn't …"

"Gwynne," Lucy interrupted. They had, one by one, stopped in the road, and then started to walk on, and then halted again, as though they could by such physical demonstrations ease Gwynne's hesitations of speech. "Say it, girl."

"Your Lieutenant Inman. He's asked me out for next Saturday. And I'd like to."

"He's not 'my' Lieutenant. He's not my anything. See him or don't see him."

Lucy realized that the frost in her delivery would do nothing to improve her reputation among the girls of the Detachment. Gwynne would mimic it, plummy accent and all, at the breakfast table at the Bermudiana the next morning. Lucy spent her mornings trotting the soft coral roads to the commandeered golf courses. She ran across golf greens and through sandtraps. Using her breakfast time this way prevented disruption in her work day. Lark brought her a hard-boiled egg and a roll, which Lucy slathered with the dwindling supply of the jam sent by Alice Dodd, then stepped into the shower still chewing. She was late to the work table every day, which caused murmuring ("All right for *some!*"). But Danville had had a word with McKay and all had agreed that fifteen minutes late was better than a prolonged absence in the afternoon.

Since Lucy was not present for breakfast conversation, she was often the topic of it. If Gwynne didn't start it, she furthered it. Ruth reported that Gwynne's impersonation of Lucy was "quite good." Gwynne was not disloyal. Lucy had argued this to Lark after Lark had blistered Gwynne for a mimicry at breakfast. Lucy had been met in the lobby of the Princess by a Gwynne sobbing apologies and a Lark behind her with folded arms and a raised eyebrow, a tableau that inspired in Lucy a pulse of reluctant admiration for her father, who had returned home so often to similar scenes produced by his squabbling children. Lucy, wanting only a shower, a drink and dry clothes, had absolved Gwynne with a haste that outraged Lark.

"You should *never speak to her again!*" Lark had fumed behind her as Lucy pounded up the stairs to their room. "The girl is a *Judas!*"

"How blasphemous," Lucy said.   Lark was behind her and couldn't see her grin. *Which was sweeter, the opportunity to say that to Lark, or the fervor of her loyalty?* Once through the door, Lucy had peeled off her wet shirt and dropped it on the floor. "Surely you knew girls like that at school. Liking me's gone out of fashion, so she doesn't know where she stands."

Gwynne now stood in the road with her fingers on her cheeks. Lucy patted her shoulder. "Do as you like. I feel nothing for Bill. As Mama used to say, '*Con nulla non si fa nulla.*'"

"Nothing makes nothing," Ruth said in the satisfied tone she brought to providing solutions. She explained to the startled semi-circle, "'Null' means 'nothing' in mathematics. When you multiply by a null, you get nothing."

Lucy put her arm around Ruth's shoulder and kissed her hair as they walked on. "*Si, mia cara, è vero.* But here it means, because I feel nothing for him, he cannot be my anything. He is a null."

"Wish he felt the same about you, no lie." Gwynne reluctantly walked on. "Never had a man show me that kind of passion. *Throwing a table!* He's so handsome. I don't pay much mind to what he says. I just like looking while he says it."

24.

The Federal Bureau of Investigation suggested more tests. Those tests revealed nothing. Another week was spent reading letters and eating fish stew. Lucy practiced Greek and Morse code. Another Saturday night found them in the suite while the sounds of the other Censorettes rushing from the hotel for their evening's entertainment floated up to them through their open windows, cresting and abating, like waves.

"Merchant dice. Baseball. The Giants. The readiness is all."

Lucy stared at the letter. Ruth sat poised like a retriever dog, waiting to fetch whatever silly stick Lucy flung. They had checked the name of every player of the New York Giants against the list of ten thousand names the Detachment maintained of suspicious characters. They found three Schumachers and two Hubbells, none of whom appeared to be moonlighting as Nazi spies while playing baseball for the New York Giants. And what of the reference to the Yankees? Did "Yankees" refer to the team or was it code for Americans? Were the "Giants" code for a group of Nazi sympathizers, like the Bund? Or isolationists, like America First?

Lucy ordered Ruth to pick out every other letter in each word, then every third letter, then the first letter, then the first word of each sentence, then the last word, then every other word. But none of these exercises revealed anything.

Lark draped over her dressmaker's dummy another cast-off from the St. Andrew's jumble, a billowing grey garment, which she studied as Lucy studied the letter, trying, as Michelangelo might have, to find the fashionable frock hidden within.

"What?" Lark pinned in the waist, tied a ribbon. Frowning, she pulled it out again. "You're *staring*, Lucy."

"I was thinking of Michelangelo."

"Of course you were."

"'*Non ha l'ottimo artista alcun concetto*,'" Lucy recited. "'*Ch'un marmo solo in sè non circonscriva/Col suo soverchio, e solo a quello arriva/La man che obbedisce all'intelletto*.'"

"What does that mean?" Ruth asked.

"The marble already contains the statue and it is up to the sculptor to find it."

"Why don't you say that, then?"

"Italian is a beautiful language."

Ruth pondered, then asked, "Why say it at all?"

"This letter contains a message. It is *in the marble*, duckling. I just have to find it"

"Or you could leave off." Lark held the dress up to Ruth and tied a ribbon to make an empire waist. "Just forget it, Lucy. The FBI said no … I'm surprised Colonel McKay hasn't asked for it back."

"He did." At Lark's arched eyebrow, Lucy added, "Ruth made a copy. I gave him the copy."

"You kept the original?"

"If I answer that, then you'll be burdened with knowing the answer, hmm?"

"That is such a major violation of protocol I can't begin to articulate it."

"Where in the regulations does it say 'Do not ask your friend with the freakish memory to make an exact duplicate of the letter and pass it off as the original.' It wouldn't do us any good to send on the original if we think of something else to test on it."

"There *is* nothing else! We've tried everything. We went to the FBI for the most innovative techniques. Whatever Brooklyn Joe has used, he's way ahead of us."

"Or way behind us," Ruth said. "Why should he be smarter? Perhaps he's not, what did you call me, 'freakish.' Perhaps he's ordinary and uses ordinary things. Things you could buy at the chemist's."

"Lucy!" Lark clapped her hands. "Give me the letter. Carefully. Put it between two clean sheets of paper."

"Simpler theories are generally better than complex ones," Ruth said, plucking at the apron of the dress Lark left behind. Then she reared back, when Lark kissed her on the forehead.

Lark ran from the room, leaving Lucy to entertain Ruth. Lucy leafed through her book of Bach. Ruth politely offered to continue with Mozart, but Lucy knew she preferred Bach, and started her on a fugue. She had meant to say "exceptional." She had meant to say "incomparable." But she had said "freakish."

They were in their nightgowns, Lucy brushing out Ruth's hair, when Lark plunged into the room, breathless from climbing the stairs.

"Come down to the lab! We've got him!"

She was already running down the stairs, so Lucy and Ruth didn't pause for their dressing gowns but hurried after her as she called, "Ruth was right! It was ordinary! Pyramidon! Sold in pharmacies for headaches! The iodine-vapor test! Simple! Ruth was *right*."

Inside the lab, Joe's letter, slightly damp and tinged with a violet hue, hung like washing on a string pulled taut over a counter, kept in place with small clothespins. The counter held a Bunsen burner, a funnel, cotton wool, and several test tubes. Lark chattered about the iodine-vapor test, but Lucy was examining the lines of handwriting and the drawings revealed by the test, forming a kind of wallpaper behind Joe's handwriting about the merchant dice, the Yankees, the Giants, the Polo Grounds.

Should the Yanks finally join the war, men from all over their country would gather to be loaded onto troop ships at the Brooklyn Navy Yard. Seamen would be sitting ducks for saboteurs or U-boats, eased along in their plans by these directions from Brooklyn Joe.

Lucy turned just in time to fall into the arms of Lark who had been trying, in a rare display of exuberance, to embrace Ruth. But Lucy needed Ruth unmolested, needed her to focus on the writing before the letter was taken away from them and given to the German division of the Censorship. Ruth had found a pad and was copying the writing beneath the typewriting.

"You did it, Lucy!" Lark cried.

"*We* did it. And I don't know what we actually did. I only hope it's of some use."

Lark refused to leave the letter in the lab. The letter wasn't dry, so they left the lab with Lark and Ruth each holding one end of the string to which the letter was pinned, as though they were suffragettes marching behind a banner. *Votes for Women*! They tiptoed across the lobby to the stairs and heard a knocking at the front door.

The knocker was Gwynne. When Lucy opened the door, she was so intent upon redoing the locks properly that she failed to notice anything amiss until Lark asked, "What happened?"

"Walked back," Gwynne whispered. "Took longer than I reckoned."

"Come to our room."

"All those stairs!"

"I can work the lift," Ruth said. She still held one end of the string on which was clipped Joe's damp letter. She handed it to Lucy with a startling confidence. "Hector showed me. Come."

"No," Gwynne said. Ruth, with a clamor that seemed as loud as a Gene Krupa drum solo, shoved aside the ornamental gate to the lift, and then turned a lever which parted the doors. The light in the lift went on and Lark dragged Gwynne into the light and held her chin up so all could see her swollen eyes. Lucy then remembered it was the night of Gwynne's date with Bill.

"What happened?" she asked. "Did he hurt you?"

"I can handle myself," Gwynne snapped. "I know what men are like. I was *married*, remember? I just thought he'd be a bit more —like he was with you. Like you were Waterford bloody *crystal*. Princess of the Princess. No, I don't need your lift, your Highness."

Gwynne shook her head, as though Lucy had vigourously endorsed Inman as a lover, and strode up the stairs.

"That little fool is banished from our breakfast table," Lark remarked in a conversational tone.

"I want a cottage," Lucy blurted. "If I'm to stay here much longer, I want our own cottage. I'll be tidier. I promise. I'll sweep and dust and—I've had just about enough of this."

"Yes." Lark agreed with a speed and a calm which surprised Lucy. She gestured at the letter drying on the string. "I think we have some leverage now."

25.

Several Saturdays later, Lucy joined the stream of Censorettes leaving the Princess for an afternoon out. Instead of heading down the road to Front Street with them, she veered off at the Bermuda Yacht Club. Furbert had written her a note to ask if she would be interested in helping him prepare his "dear old girl" for the winter. *We are discouraged from sailing*, he had written, *because of all the U-boats. But a boat goes to seed without proper tending. You mentioned that you sailed with your father and your cousins. If you would help me tidy her up for her hibernation—a task I used to bestow on one of my daughters—I would be honoured to have you as my guest for dinner at the Yacht Club.*

The cedar gaff cutter yacht *Prosper* sat high in the water. Lucy loved her at once, the way you might immediately befriend another family's faithful dog. Lucy polished the brass and swept the deck, packed into the cabin all that could be secured there, while Furbert fussed with the pump and the anchor. There was no sun that day. The sea was choppy and the wind accelerated through the course of the afternoon from a lively breeze to a strange, slashing affair, a stroke of warm followed by a stroke of cool, as though swift oarsmen propelled the capricious winds. When the breeze grew too high, Furbert advised she should tour the dock to check for boats not well secured. By the time she completed her tour and returned to the *Prosper*, Furbert had climbed the mast halfway up and was scanning the marina. Lucy called out to him.

"Storm coming," he shouted. "Can you finish here? Coil all the stray rope, tie them with a clove-hitch knot! Can you make one? Of course you can," he answered when she nodded. "I'm going to see what she's called," he pointed to a boat parked in an outermost, sea-facing berth. "Her sails aren't tamped secure."

"The ketch? She's the *Alcyone*. I *noticed*!" She said into his wondering stare. "Alcyone is one of the Seven Sisters. Go on, Mr. Furbert! I'll take care of the *Prosper*."

After Lucy had tied off the ropes, she took his binoculars from the cabin, kicked off her sandals and climbed the mast to get a better view of the incoming storm. Perching the arches of her feet on the rungs, and balancing with one hand on a higher rung, she surveyed the incoming storm. All the nuanced blue of sea and sky had been wiped away, as though by a frustrated painter eager to blot out a canvas and start again with a Turner frame of mind—dark grey sea, slate grey sky, and bursts of lightning, flashes of fiery celestial rivers and their tributaries. Through the increasing whistling of the wind, she heard the shouts of men, the horns and klaxons of ships, the brass clangs of the bells and the shrieks of whistles on the smaller craft as they sought the harbour.

The rain gathered in spheres which bounced off the white-cresting ocean in lilac-grey curls. The spheres rolled in like the tumbling coils of wire the farmers trundled out to the fields to bale their hay with, in the farms around Knollborough. Baling seemed fun, like the only daguerreotype which existed of Granny as a child, young Vicky de Guise in long curls, posed with her hoop and stick and an adoring spaniel who leapt alongside her as she guided the hoop around the garden, up and down the lanes. "I could keep the hoop rolling longer than anyone I knew," she had told Lucy. "Of course, I had so few playmates. But I practiced and practiced. I competed with myself, you see. I gave out from fatigue before I ever let that hoop wobble."

When had she told Lucy that? It must have been her 16th summer, the summer of Guy Jenner. Why had she not remembered this before, the warmth in Granny's voice, how she had stroked Lucy's hair while she told her this? Later photographs showed Vicky as a young bridesmaid in a mirthless wedding party, then a debutante, then the bride of Knoll House. Lucy was all too familiar with the later incarnations of Granny. She tried to imagine young Vicky running up and down the lanes, competing with herself, a fierce little girl who lacked a Matty to soften her childhood loneliness, a girl who ran to beat her own record, who would grow up to scold Lucy for "galloping." She felt a swell of kinship, though separated by a ferocious ocean, that she had never felt while sitting in the spotless parlor.

The roiling rain bounced in to the harbour. The lenses of the binoculars blurred. She bent down to wipe them with the skirt of her dress and only then saw Mr. Furbert shouting to her.

"Miss Barrett! Lucy! You come down from there at once!"

She was soaked through, perched on a swaying mast. The boats at dock bobbed and swayed. One, out in the harbour, listed. She tried to lower her foot one rung, but slipped and held on by her hands. Sheets of rainwater slapped her face. *Steady on, Barrett,* she told herself. *Gain purchase. One rung, next rung. Arch of the foot, not*

*the ball. Use your feet for balance; for strength, use your arms. Carry
all your weight in your arms, remember your training. One rung, next
rung, not far now …*

Furbert grabbed her when he could reach her, lifted her at the
waist and set her down on the dock. Then he shoved her towards
the Yacht Club, where the barman found a spare waiter's uniform
for her to change into and a clean tablecloth to dry herself with.
When she emerged from the ladies' room, she found that Furbert,
shivering, had draped a tablecloth over himself, giving him the air
of a weary Senator of ancient Rome.

"Rum, please, straight rum," Furbert shouted at the barman.
"Oh, bring the bottle, Clive! Miss Barrett, what on *earth* were you
thinking, going up the rigging?"

"I don't—I just—I was so—" How to explain it, this revelation
that the youth of passion didn't surrender to duty, but learned to
live alongside it? How the resilience of this little island, battered
by storms, so isolate, so vulnerable, and still so resolutely British,
seemed to her to echo the resilience that ran through her blood? "It
was so *exhilarating*. Watching the storm come in."

Furbert summoned the waiter, ordered their dinner. Other
members of the yacht club who had come to secure their boats
trickled in, soaked, and at their request, the barman turned on the
wireless behind the bar, raising the volume all the way to combat
the shriek of the wind.

Craft at sea shouted through static, calling for refuge in the
port: *Harbourmaster, Hamilton Harbourmaster, the merchant vessel
Cuidad de la Camaguey requests permission to come in. We are registered to the Republic of Cuba. We request shelter from this storm.*
The Harbourmaster sent some craft to St. George's, and told all of
them *you'll need your own water*, which seemed a jocular remark
in the teeth of a hurricane. But there was no water to spare. The
newcomers—the Detachment and the Yanks—had drained the local cisterns dry.

"The *Prosper*." Lucy sipped her rum. "Was she named for Prospero?"

"Prospero?"

"*The Tempest.* Shakespeare." He shook his head at *Shakespeare.* "They say this island inspired it," Lucy added. "The play."

"She was a wedding present from my wife's parents. I'd just started at the bank. And as I was marrying their daughter, well ... they hoped I would prosper."

"Have you always lived in Bermuda?"

"I was born here. The year your hotel opened. The Princess Hotel. Named for the Princess Louise. One of Queen Victoria's daughters. She's why my parents called me Louis. Which I would like you to call me, by the way, Miss Barrett."

"Then of course you should call me Lucy."

"My youngest girl, my Josie, used to help me with the *Prosper.* She loved sailing. Dressed in trousers, climbing the rigging like you just did ... oh, a father's not meant to have favorites, but Josie and me, we did get on. I did hate to lose her."

"I'm so sorry, Louis." Lucy reached for his hand.

"Oh, she's quite well. Lives in Rhode Island. I lost her to a yachtsman. Or perhaps to his yacht. I might've married him myself, for that yacht. I only hoped Josie would be the one to stay. My wife was so restless here. She was a Yank. Here on holiday when we met. To look at me now, you wouldn't think I could sweep a girl off her feet. But it seems I did. Well, marry in haste, repent at leisure. I never claimed to be an exciting man. She never settled. 'Too small a place to live a life in,' she used to say. Restless. She transmitted it to our girls. Like a fever. Then my wife died. She might have lived longer in a bigger place with better doctors, but. Well. And my girls married and sailed off. So I'm in that house alone, that house, which seemed so crowded and *female*, and now seems so big, so empty. Sometimes, Lucy, when you're out sailing with people who don't like the sea—"

"Landlubbers," Lucy supplied.

"Quite." He smiled faintly. "They scout the horizon for the shore. Hold their breath until they see land. And I see that in you."

"*Me*?" Lucy leaned back as the waiter set down their plates. "I'm quite seaworthy."

"Perhaps. But not island-worthy. No, I see that same scouting look in you. You look at the sea as though trying to reckon if you could swim back to England."

"I do miss it. Very much." Lucy blinked several times and cut up her chicken, which was not creamed or tinned but an actual fresh bird, its skin crisply browned, accompanied by a baked potato with pats of real butter, and piles of string beans. No summoning of sad emotion would spoil *this* rare meal, thank you very much. "And I'm doing all—"

"And as a father," Furbert spoke over her. "A father of girls an ocean away, I would ask that you forgive your father."

"I beg your pardon, Mr. Furbert?"

"I know you're angry with him."

"I don't see how you could know that."

"For one thing, you said as much at your birthday party. You were a bit tipsy. Perhaps it's slipped your mind. You said he couldn't stand the sight of you."

Lucy refilled her glass, gulped down the rum, and refilled her glass again.

"Gracious, no one has mentioned that. It must have been delightful for my guests."

"They were dancing. Drinking. Being young and alive. As you ought to be, while you are. I won't defend your father. But if you can't forgive him, then *shed* him. My girls have shed me. Not because I've hurt them. But they're in their own lives now."

Lucy was mortified; she remembered telling Furbert that her father was a tyrant in his grief, but not that she couldn't forgive him. She didn't remember that she had poured out her feelings as she now poured out rum. But Mr. Furbert—Louis—was right. What could Paul do to her now? She had reached her majority and she was free to make her own way in the world. Today her own way seemed to be to shelter from a hurricane in a yacht club with a kindly banker, eating chicken, drinking rum.

The voices on the shortwave radio slowed, stopped. All ships seeking shelter had come in. Other yachtsmen who had entered, soaked, had dried on the outside and lubricated their insides. They joined Furbert and Lucy, drank more rum, and told boating stories, until the rain let up. Furbert had brought his bicycle, but he walked Lucy to the door of the Princess Hotel. She kissed his cheek, and he mounted his bike and rode into the darkness and the mist.

In her room, she hung up her dress to dry, pulled the wet waiter's uniform off, and found a pair of dry pajamas. She fell asleep immediately. In the morning, Lark did not wake her for church, but Ruth woke her to demand her walk, her *dolce far niente*.

"Oh Ruth, must we?" Lucy's tongue felt covered in moss. "I have a terrible headache."

"I was here by myself all day yesterday and all night. I want to go out."

"There'll be so much mud. And storm damage."

"I want to paint the storm damage." Ruth held up her sketch pad. "*En plein air* which literally translates to 'in plain air' but also means a kind of freedom—"

"Ruuuuuuuth." Lucy pulled her pillow over her head. "Please, no. Go without me."

She slept through the brightest part of the day. Unaccustomed to being allowed to sleep until she woke, she devoured sleep, woke briefly from time to time to note the progress of light across the room and then embraced her pillow as she tumbled back to sleep. She was shaken awake. The light in the room told her it was early evening. Gwynne was shaking her.

"Lucy. You've got to wake up. I have bad news. Very bad."

"What?" England had been invaded. There had been a telegram: Matty. Paul. The U-boat the Bermudians had long feared had actually surfaced off the coast of their little island. "*What is it?*"

"It's Ruth. Bloody, bleeding hell, Lucy. *Ruth is dead!*"

Lucy grabbed her dressing gown and followed Gwynne as she ran to McKay's office, where Lark waited, glaring like a cornered animal at the two men wearing the uniform of the Bermuda police. One of them held Ruth's sketch pad. Lucy put her arm around Lark's shoulders and faced McKay.

October 19, 1941

To His Hon. Judge R. Barrington-Smith
6 Tate Street
London

REGRET TO INFORM YOU DAUGHTER KILLED STOP PLAN
LOCAL BURIAL STOP ADVISE PREFERENCES RE FUNERAL
STOP NO FURTHER DETAILS AT THIS TIME STOP CONDO-
LENCES STOP.

Col. McKay
Imperial Censorship Detachment

PART THREE
RUTH

26.

"Strangled." Lark's hand cradled her throat.

"So it would appear," McKay confirmed. "Her body was found in the botanical gardens."

"Her body was found in the botanical gardens." Lark spit every syllable. "Our Ruth. Her *body*. Was she raped?"

Now McKay's hand went to *his* throat, distressed, as Lucy was, that Lark used the blunt term, rather than a euphemism such as "interfered with," or the wanly hopeful "still intact." McKay shook his head forcefully, as if denial could undo what had been done. They stood in the reading room: McKay, two policemen, Lark, Lucy and Gwynne. Sunlight from the ground-level windows pierced the room at severe downward angles, like gangplanks from a ship to a dock. The Censorettes were rarely in the reading room at sunset; they were not accustomed to light in hard shafts.

"Are you sure?" Lark flung off Gwynne's attempt at a sympathetic touch.

"Homicide is rare on the island," a policemen said. "But we know what to do. She was killed earlier today, at the botanical gardens. A groundskeeper found her. Under a banyan tree. Broad daylight. When did you last see her?"

"Just after church. She was going on her walk."

"Robbery?" the policeman asked.

"She had almost nothing," Lucy said. "A sketch pad. Watercolours. We shouldn't have let her go around by herself. One of us should have been with her all the time. But she'd been coming along so nicely. She swam in the ocean. She worked the lift, Hector taught her —" A wince from McKay told Lucy she was babbling.

Lark stepped closer to the police. "Strangulation is usually sexual," she said, demonstrating on the alarmed policeman by cupping his neck with her forefinger and thumb.

"Did you check her fingernails? She'd have scratched. I SCRATCHED!" Lark shouted so suddenly that they all flinched. In a calmer tone, she continued, "There'll be bruising on the thighs, the genitals would be torn ... I want to see the body."

The policemen, accustomed to stolen bicycles and fights among drunken sailors, looked astonished. Gwynne, pouring Lark a glass of water, spilled when Lark shouted and nearly dropped the pitcher at the word "genitals."

"Take me to the morgue," Lark commanded. "I'll speak to the medical examiner."

"Miss Lark, I really can't allow— "

"Colonel *McKay,* this is quite out of your jurisdiction. My father is a minister. I've attended hundreds of funerals. Dozens of deathbeds. The dead hold no terror for me. Furthermore," she stepped forward and they all stepped back. "I am studying to be a doctor."

"What? No." McKay said. "None of you girls are *doctors.* We would have kept them at home—you're a *chemist,* Miss Lark," in the soothing tone he would use to tell a child that there were no monsters under the bed. "Miss Gwynne, could you fetch her file?"

Lark caught Gwynne's arm in a hard grip. "I have no need to see my *file.* My medical studies were interrupted. There is no record of a degree. And as I joined the Detachment to apply my knowledge of chemistry to Inks and Papers, there was no need to mention it."

A farcical series of glances ensued: McKay at Lark and then the police, since Lark had revealed the nature of her work with the Detachment in front of the locals, which was forbidden, a glance of confusion between the police, a common confused look at Lark, Lark's glare at their hesitation.

"Telephone the Ontario Medical College for Women." There was high colour in her cheeks; they seemed almost illuminated, as though she were a Christian soldier, marching off to war, in a stained glass depiction of the Crusades. "Let me see the body. Do you know the rate at which a body decays? You are wasting time."

***

Men who had known Ruth were brought in for questioning: Alan, Hector, Bill, and all the men who had attended the "party" which followed the bombing of London in May. Statements were taken from Lark, Lucy, Gwynne, Clara, and Fleur and Roos. Georgie was still off island. Ruth had no other friends.

Oct. 20, 1941

To Col. McKay
Princess Hamilton Hotel
Hamilton, Bermuda

NO PREFERENCES STOP HANDLE LOCALLY STOP REGARDS.

R.B.S.

Lark organized the funeral like a commander. She handled the transfer of the body from the morgue to the mortuary, the selection of the casket, the location of the cemetery plot, the wording of the obituary in the Bermuda *Royal-Gazette* (*as though anyone in*

Bermuda cared!), the reservation of the church for the service, the drafting of the eulogy. She buried her grief under tasks. Lucy understood. Unfortunately, Commodore Flynn was the officer in charge of Inks and Papers, and he saw fit to hand directly to Lark the terse telegram from Ruth's father, with the offhand request, "Take care of this, would you, Lark."

Lark (reported Clara, who came to fetch Lucy from the Reading Room) held the telegram in one hand, and an Erlenmeyer flask of yellow liquid in the other. When she read the telegram, she dropped the flask. The liquid was a harmless (though noxious) sulphur compound, and a window was opened to air out the room. As one girl swept up the glass and another girl mopped the liquid, Flynn patted Lark's shoulder and said, "Better care next time, Lark." Lark then reached for another beaker on the lab table, held it aloft for a moment, then let it fall to the floor. She did this three more times before Flynn put his arms around her ("in a kind of wrestling hold, I expect," Clara told Lucy as they hurried toward Inks and Papers), and called for help to carry her into the corridor.

She was still in the corridor, sitting in a chair outside Inks and Papers, one leg straight out, the other bent at an outside angle, slumped like an abandoned rag doll. Flynn could be heard within, roaring at everyone to stay calm, although he was the only one shouting. Hector watched them from the top of the corridor, halfway in the Gazebo Bar. He had dragged the chair over. Its track marks were visible in the carpet.

"What should I do, Miss Lucy?"

"Lucy," Lark repeated. She seemed not to have registered Lucy's presence until Hector uttered her name. She raised her head and held out the telegram.

"Frith!" Flynn roared from within the room. "Where the hell did she go? *Frith!* I need to know what was in these beakers!"

Clara bestowed a flat line of a smile and returned to Inks and Papers. Hector stood before them with a glass of water and an enormous dinner napkin. Lucy folded the telegram and tucked it into her skirt pocket as Hector lifted Lark's hand and put the glass of water into it.

"I'm so sorry about your friend," he said. "She spake as a child, like the Good Book says. Understood as a child, thought as a child. She talked to me like I was just another man. Not a coloured man. Only thing ever bothered Miss Ruth about my colour was where my sister could find the right stockings. Some people are too gentle for this world."

Lark, cautiously sipping the water, raised her head when Hector quoted Corinthians. She cried silently but vigourously. She handed Lucy the glass of water and sobbed into the dinner napkin. Hector and Lucy exchanged nods. Hector returned to his duties; Lucy wondered why no one had appeared to order her back to hers. She determined she would let Lark cry for the equivalent of six laps of the pool: the rhythm to swimming was similar to that of Lark's coughing sobs. Lucy listened to six laps of sobbing before she let her hand fall on Lark's bent head. "It's a good thing, if you think about it, that her father has no preferences. We can do what we like. She was ours, after all. She didn't belong to her father. None of us do anymore. Come, Lark. We'll go to the room and you can have a lie down— "

"Not the room. I hate the room," Lark croaked. "I keep thinking she'll come out of her room. Full of her chatter and her questions. But it's so quiet. So damn, damn, *damn* quiet."

Lucy led her to the pool, which, since it was saltwater, was an excellent reservoir for tears. They dangled their feet in the water and listened to the sound of the sea and the sea birds.

"Remember that movie. *To Sin for Love?* That pretty actress. Patience Cobb. The one who died before the film came out. Ruth was so taken with her name. A virtue name, she called it. Like Faith. Charity. Apparently, her cousins have those names, and she was worried that they didn't live up to them. She was glad that Ruth just meant Ruth. A name from the Bible. Like Rebecca."

"Like Lucia," Lucy said. "From Luke."

"She asked me what virtue name I thought would suit me. Because I was so pious. Since I would make a terrible *Patience,* I dismissed her. Snapped at her, most likely. Because I would make a very poor *Charity*."

"Lark, you were kind to her—"

"No, Lucy! *You* were kind to her. I thought her a nuisance, and I let her know it. The people in my father's congregation … we all think we're good people. We follow the teachings of Christ. We're very good, until we're faced with a Ruth or a Hector. Or a woman who's lost her virtue. Not her virtue name. Her actual virtue. The great gift a woman gives her husband on their wedding night."

I scratched.

Lucy picked one of Lark's hands from off her lap, sandwiched it between her hands, and waited. She paddled her feet in the pool.

"When men die in war, it's rarely a clean death on the field," Lark said. "It's not like in the movies." *What,* Lucy wondered, *had she ever done to earn these repeated reminders that life was not a film? Had she displayed some blind devotion to cinematic conventions, that Georgie, Lark and her own brother felt obligated to inform her that life was otherwise?*

"In the last war," Lark said, "some of my father's friends who were badly hurt made it back home. But their wounds festered. The infections persisted. They could have lived, if only they'd been able to treat the infections. At medical college, we were working on a way to produce a form of penicillin in greater quantities. Less expensive. Easy to replicate. Easy to store. I volunteered. I was top of my class at chemistry and here was a perfect study.

"My job was wounding mice. I'd gone into medical school with the notion of developing pharmaceuticals. I knew I wouldn't be good with patients. I'm not good with people. Bit like Ruth. I suppose that's why I lacked patience with her. So I worked with mice. They had to be wounded, so we could see if the treatments worked. So I wounded them. I'd make an incision on their back. The control group always died. The others, we treated with penicillin derivatives. They died, too, most of the time, from licking their wounds. I worked with a lab partner in a lab in the basement near the college. There was a janitor there.

"He was curious about the mice. He asked questions. Questions, all the time. Like Ruth. He wasn't appropriate. Like Ruth. I was in the lab in the evenings. I had classes all day, and then rounds. I had a lab partner, but … well, Saturday afternoons I helped my father. Saturday nights were for Gavin, my fiancé. He was in the first year of his law practice. But I didn't want to let my lab partner down. I'd stop by in the evenings during the week and do the dirty work. Log the dead mice. Dispose of them. Clean the cages. Rinse the tubes. It became harder and harder to keep the janitor out of the lab. He became agitated. Why was I hurting the mice? Didn't I hear the sounds they made? Always the mice squeaked, but the injured ones made a really horrible sound.

"And then one night, he raped me. I'd locked the door to the lab. But he had the keys. Of course he had the keys. He was the janitor. He came in. He tore everything apart. The lab. Me. He hit me. He broke my nose. Threw me on a table—it destroyed months of work, so much work! So much equipment. He held me down by the throat. And all the glass. When you—out here—with that bastard Inman. With the broken glass. That's why I lost control. The sound of it being swept up."

Lark cradled her throat with her hand, as she had when she learned that Ruth died. "His hand was here. The carotid artery. Like Ruth. I found a piece of glass and slashed his wrist—an artery! What a spray! He let go and I got out of the room. Up the stairs. Out into the street.

"Lucy, you can't imagine the scene. Blood running down my legs, *his* blood all over me, *mice* everywhere …! Half the college were out before the police arrived. Not easy to hush that up! Minister's daughter or no. Gavin and my father begged me not to press charges. The reputation of the parish! Of the college! Of … well, everything. My reputation was as dead as the mice. Gavin broke it off with me. He asked why I couldn't have been more discreet. Why did I have to run into the street, he meant. Where everyone could see me."

"The lab *did* press charges. For vandalism. All that smashed equipment. The janitor was sent back to his hospital. And my college suggested I start again. Somewhere else. Hard enough having a women's medical college, but for a woman to be stupid enough to get raped in a lab. What good did *that* serve, except the notion that a woman should be kept safe at home. I was a shame to my father. He wanted me away, the way Ruth's people must have wanted her away. Out of sight. And so I came here."

Lark turned Lucy's hand over and studied it, held out her own palm for comparison, pocked with scars from chemical burns, her fingers sinewy and diagnostic, while Lucy's hands, despite the blisters of her training regiment, were pale and smooth, the result of diligent application of Drewe's hand lotion.

"But I don't belong here," Lark said. "I've been hiding. I need to go back to school, get my degree, work as a doctor. Go where I can do the most good. 'Free a man for the front.' This is too small a place to spend a war in."

27.

October 24, 1941

His Hon. Rupert Barrington-Smith

Dear Judge Barrington-Smith,

Please.

Lucy sat at Georgie's writing desk; she had been sitting there for a nearly a quarter of an hour. She had written the salutation and the word "please." Lark worked on the eulogy. Clara spent the evening bicycling on errands of Lark's devising, then climbing the floors to the honeymoon suite to report on their progress: the lily farmer who donated the flowers for the Easter service would be pleased to donate again for the memorial service. Flyers were distributed advising the Censorship of the funeral service and the reception to be held afterwards in the Gazebo Bar. The honeymoon suite proposed. The Detachment disposed. Clara came and went. Lark scribbled scribbled scribbled and consulted her Bible. Lucy stared at the wall.

"Lucy, just start writing," Lark sighed. "I can't do this and that as well."

"I'm not asking you to," she said.

"My father had to generate fifty-two sermons a year. To say nothing of the christenings and eulogies and marriages. The key is to move the pen. Write what you want to say — 'The world is a wretched place,' for example, and then argue with yourself, on paper. So now you have a dialogue. Underline the bits you want to keep. Write another draft."

"Dear Judge Barrington-Smith," Lucy wrote. *"I would like to think that you are not an evil man. I would like to think there are no evil men. But that is silly, since they are legion in this evil world. But perhaps most of them are, like you, merely weak."*

This was not the desired tone for a condolence letter.

She crumpled it and began again. Several drafts later, she arrived at:

Dear Judge Barrington-Smith:

I write to express my condolences to you upon the death of your daughter.

However, you might consider granting the same courtesy to us, her roommates here in Bermuda. Ruth was not easy to love, but we came to love her. We cannot choose our family. We can choose our friends. We chose Ruth.

Ruth may not have expressed her feelings as you liked, but she felt your rejection keenly. I say I am sorry for your loss because that is expected. What I really want to say is, for shame. You threw a pearl away richer than all your tribe.

It is late and this is the eighth draft of the letter I am meant to write to you, for the sake of propriety. My roommate Rebecca says I should go through my drafts and underline the parts I mean to keep. I will do that in the morning. No, not in the morning, because I will be occupied with the funeral. The funeral about which you wrote 'no preferences.'

Ruth would often say things which we knew were things that had been said to her. Such as 'I'm not the type of girl who can put on a pretty dress and go to dances.' You might be surprised to know that here in Bermuda, she did both. All she needed was a little kindness. We gave her that. I am glad she found it somewhere, in her too-short life.

Now I have said too much and all of it wrong. I have made this letter too long, because I lack the time to make it short. I can't remember who said that. I will look it up tomorrow when I write a better version of this letter.

> *Yours, etc.,*
> *LVGB*

She set down the pen and massaged her writing hand.

Suspicions and traditions were in abundance at the funeral. The cortege walked from the Princess to the church. Ruth, in her coffin, awaited them at the altar at St. Andrew's. They wore their darkest garments. Some wore veils, others kerchiefs on their heads. One shuffling row counted rosaries. Fleur and Roos sang "Jesu, Joy of Man's Desiring," as the procession proceeded. Lark wanted something to make passersby halt, acknowledge, remove their hats (which they all did) but not a group chorus, not "a goddamned gypsy caterwaul" (which she actually said). The "Jesu" was more appropriate to almost any occasion but a funeral, but Ruth had loved it, so they sang it for her. The sisters' voices rose clarion-clear over the susurration of whispered prayers and small gasps of sobbing. Lark and Lucy led the parade. McKay, on horseback, brought up the rear.

Alan waited for them outside the church in his formal Navy dress whites. He walked Lark down the aisle to the pulpit, like a father delivering a daughter to her bridegroom, and then he returned to Lucy to settle into a pew with her.

"We are here," Lark announced at a volume that would have done a thespian proud. "To celebrate the life and to pray for the soul of our friend Ruth Smith. It would be logical, perhaps you assume it would be logical, for me to begin with the famous passage from the Book of Ruth. 'And Ruth said: Entreat me not to leave thee: for whither thou goest, I will go; and where thou lodgest, I will lodge—'"

Her voice broke and she stopped, then cleared her throat twice, first low, then shrill. Then she hummed into a sob. As the concertmaster sets the tuning of an orchestra, Lark's first sound of anguish sent the Censorship into a cascade of weeping. Just behind Lucy, Gwynne wept, no doubt recalling her dead husband. In the pew in front of her, Fleur and Roos remembered some Belgian-born grief. Most were not mourning Ruth at all, but mourning mourning, keen to what they had already lost and frightened by what might lay ahead. *How fresh is any grief during wartime? How many deaths had to occur before all death became nothing more than a kind of tuning fork which evoked the keening of the first grief that set the tone?* Soon, the whole congregation was lowing and snuffling like a herd of cattle, even those blameless Bermudians who had come to the service simply because it was their church, because murder was so rare, because Lark was so popular, only to hear that Lark, who did everything for everyone, was no better than anyone.

Alan placed a clean handkerchief in Lucy's lap, embroidered with his initials, "AMD." All around her, the girls of the Censorship snuffled, lowed, a barnyard of grief, and yet Lucy couldn't find the relief of tears. In Bermuda, Lucy shed tears conceived in England; she couldn't find a release for a grief born here. She held Alan's handkerchief over her shoulder for Gwynne, and then saw a fresh one on her knee.

"No, you'll need it for Lark," Lucy whispered.

"Are you kidding?" Alan whispered. "I brought all I have."

She felt cold and thirsty. Her eyes ached. She grasped Alan's handkerchief as a lifeline of comfort. It seemed to her to be all the comfort she would find today; everyone was depleted by their own sorrow.

Alan had his arm around Lucy by the time Lark finished, but when the congregation rose to sing "Swiftly Pass the Clouds of Glory," he whispered, "I'm deputizing you for all this after-business. I'm taking Beck. She looks all done in and I'm worried about her."

He didn't call her "Lark," like the rest of them. For one thing, he didn't have to. He had no other Rebeccas. And lovers loved to rechristen one another. Her name began, Lark told her, when Alan first kissed her. He kissed her nose as a reward for correctly sorting Benny Goodman from Artie Shaw. *Such a perfect nose*, he said. She had blurted that this perfection was down to science, not nature, as her natural nose had been broken, then repaired. Before she had time to wallow in the horror of what she had related, Alan kissed her nose, *but it suits you so well, your beak*, and kissed it again. Alan called Lark *beck*, from *beckon*, an archaic term meaning to summon or invite. Few would have pulled "inviting" out of a bag of adjectives to describe Lark. And then the *et le bec, et le bec* of "Alouette." *Alouette. Lark.*

Their intimacy sprouted a *patois* of private jokes and pet names. The Barretts had it with their Shakespeare, their *I leali*, their *dolce far niente*. The honeymoon suite had it with Brooklyn Joe, the Swan of Avon, the roses that are peach. Lucy had had nothing of the kind with Bill Inman. Form a private language? They had scarcely been able to agree on a public one. Would she ever know that kind of intimacy?

But what an inappropriate thought to entertain with the tasks that lay before her: laying Ruth to rest, and acting as hostess at the funeral reception while Lark was being guided into a jeep and driven away in a small cyclone of pink dust, hopefully to comfort and solace. *Funny, it had all been set in motion by a jeep.*

No Americans were invited to the reception. None minded. They were over this business of the murdered girl. They'd been brought in for questioning, some several times, to repeat stories and confirm alibis. Where were they on a Sunday morning? At church service. Performing assignments on base. Polishing up for inspection. Writing letters home. Alan and Bill were assessing the storm damage on the golf course they had selected to host the Army-Navy tournament. Which girl was Ruth Smith? Shown a photo, the Yanks shook their heads. *Nope, don't know her*. Did she come to the dances?

The men of the Censorship delivered anodyne tributes ("sharp as a tack," "exceptional memory," "shall be sorely missed") and then drifted on to more entertaining pasttimes for a Saturday afternoon. None of the Censorettes spoke in tribute. They had not been asked to. They left the hall, too disconsolate to comfort one another, too dispirited to gossip. They climbed the stairs to their rooms in small groups.

Lucy went up alone and sat in the empty room, too worn out to cry, too nerve-jangled to sleep, too distracted to read. She sat at the piano and plinked notes from the "Jesu."

You've been crying, Ruth said when they first met, *is someone dead?*

28.

Lucy spent the night alone for the first time since she had come to Bermuda. In the morning, her remaining roommates drifted in like survivors of a shipwreck. Lark drifted in at bird-raucous dawn, with the air of one gratefully recalled to life. She unzipped her dress, draped it over a chair, and, wearing only her slip, slid into their bed. Her hair was damp. She smelled of castile soap, an apothecary-like aroma. Lucy realized that Lark typically smelled of violets. Alan's bed must smell of violets now. Lark had washed with Alan's soap. Lucy pressed her fingertips to the top of Lark's spine. Lark tilted her neck to one side, arched her spine, stretched, settled, a series of movements performed by the cat Horatio. Lark yawned and tried to speak through it: "Alan," and "Ruth," were all that Lucy could make out.

"She saw something." Lark murmured. "Saw it and remembered it. She remembered everything. Brooklyn Joe ..."

"Sleep. Tell me in the morning."

Lark's head drooped. Lucy joined her in sleep. They were breathing in unison when she was called from sleep by a knock at the door. Gwynne entered, carrying a breakfast tray.

"Thought you wouldn't want to see people this morning. The manifest says Georgie's coming in on the Clipper. Colonel wants to know, do you want'im to tell'er about Ruth or do it yourselves?"

"She'll know before she steps in the launch," Lucy said. "It's all over the island."

"It is." Gwynne nodded at the *Royal-Gazette* on the tray. "I'll take your post."

She gathered the pile of letters they had left on top of the piano. Lucy finished half of her breakfast before she remembered that among the letters was her angry draft to Ruth's father. There had been no envelope; the Censorettes had been invited to address their condolences to the His Honour Judge Barrington-Smith, and McKay would bundle them into one package.

She pulled on a dressing gown and ran to the door, hoping to intercept Gwynne. When she opened the door, she faced Georgie, sea-battered and exhausted, a flotilla of suitcases and shopping bags behind her. She bore the swollen lips and eyes of one who had been crying for hours. She had been gone for six weeks without so much as a postcard to her roommates. But they had must have been in her thoughts, if the number of packages she pushed at Lucy was any indication.

"Bring the rest in, will you?"

She dumped a shopping bag on Lark and Lucy's bed. Musical recordings spilled out. Georgie yanked open the door to the long walk-in closet that had served as Ruth's room. Lucy had stayed out of it, except to choose a dress for Ruth to be buried in. Lark avoided it entirely. Georgie lingered in the room so long that Lucy and Lark joined her, found her touching every object, shoes, hairbrush, pajamas, handbag, finally letting her hand come to rest on a discarded watercolour.

"I bought her a new set," Georgie said. "And a set of pencils. A book about Gauguin. She liked him. He didn't get on with others, either, she said, and he lived on an island." She sobbed suddenly. "*Murdered in a park on a Sunday morning? Why was she alone? Don't you go with her on those walks?*"

"Don't blame Lucy," Lark said.

"What is the *point?*" Georgie swept Ruth's tidy desk to the floor. "Reading letters! Bringing girls 'in'! If this is 'in', where the bloody hell is 'out'? Posh idiots sent to France to be caught *immediately*! Posh idiots sent *here* so they can be *murdered* on a Sunday walk! God! What she could have *done*! If her idiot father had kept her in England! What *I* could have been doing, if my idiot husband—"

Lark interrupted her. "Yes. How *is* your marriage?"

"Oh, my marriage? Never better. Second honeymoon, that trip. I don't know when or if I'll see him again. But I know I'll never see Ruth again."

Georgie headed for the wet bar, adding, "Why did God bother to send her here, Lark, only to be *killed*? Why not kill her at home? England's a fine place to be killed!"

"'A fine and private place,'" Lucy said.

Georgie splashed whisky into a tumbler. "Is that Shakespeare, Lucy? Because if it is, I will choke the life out of you."

The realization of what she said washed over Georgie's face. Georgie raised her hand to her mouth, so slowly it seemed almost like a movement from a silent film. In a film, a piano would thunder alarm. Lucy wanted to reassure her: Ruth's life wasn't choked from her; it was snapped. Some hand had cracked her hyoid bone— probably while she was speaking, probably by someone who wanted to silence her. But now was not the time to share that. Now was not the time for words.

The grave's a fine and private place but none, I fear, do there embrace.

***

That line from the poem had been in her head since yesterday afternoon, when she walked away from Ruth's grave. Some girls had thrown dirt on the coffin and Lucy joined them. She wiped the Bermudian soil on her skirt. It left a pink stain. *Terra rossa*, Alan told her they called the soil of the island. *A rose is not always a rose.*

29.

Lucy had a theory. So many messages had passed through the hands of the Detachment. Pleasantries in response to pleasantries. Congratulations, we are pleased to inform you. Condolences, we regret to inform you. Invoices. Bills of lading. Denials in response to pleas, refusals in response to demands. Urgent requests for sponsorship. Help with the papers required for refugee status, denied with demurrals and the "hope and prayers" that there would not "be" a war, when the war was so manifestly, for much of the world, in the state of "is." They read correspondence both commercial and artistic, both mercantile and intimate, both banal and dramatic and rarely, only rarely, simultaneously straightforward and laced with secrets.

And one of these letters or memoranda or bills, Lucy was asking the Detachment to believe (when, after weeks of petitioning, Danville had at last agreed to see her), had proved so incriminating to someone in the Detachment (or on the island, she interrupted) that someone in the Detachment (*or on the island*) had snapped the neck of Ruth Smith to prevent her blurting out what she had read and could not help but memorize—to whom would she blurt this information, sequestered as she was?

"Aside from all those Yanks you girls hare off with," murmured Danville. "They've vouched for one another. They were somewhat at loose ends, they say, as their golf game had been cancelled."

"The Army-Navy golf game," Lucy agreed. "Yes, the grounds were too wet, because of the storm …"

Danville handed a file to Georgie. He quelled Lucy with, "There is a police force on Bermuda? I'm sure they don't rely on visiting girls to solve crimes."

"Maybe it was an America Firster."

Danville paused; Georgie lifted an eyebrow.

"You know. Charles Lindbergh and Ambassador Kennedy and Walt Disney and all those others determined to keep the Yanks out of it."

"I'm aware of America First. *Slightly* more than you, Barrett."

He raised a corner of his mouth. It was the first time his teasing struck her as affectionate. Lucy appraised him. He was Georgie's lover, or had been. Georgie had related that her husband had requested fidelity in this second chapter of their marriage and Georgie had agreed as long as it was mutual. Georgie's return from her marital reunion (which Danville had helped orchestrate) meant her desertion from Danville's bed. Lucy focused on his hands, tried to imagine them caressing. When he raised his eyes abruptly to hers, she blushed. He kept his eyes on hers coolly, while accepting papers from Georgie.

"The first two, secretarial pool," Georgie said. "Third one, maybe intelligence, if we can get her back to England?"

"Maybe Ruth saw, read, witnessed something!" Lucy tried to suppress the parallel conversation. "She remembered *everything* she read. If she read something, proof positive, say, that the Germans intended to attack the United States …"

"If Smith read that," Danville said. "An America Firster would be a fool to quiet her. He'd put America first and notify his commanding officer, not kill her. Much as I would be *delighted* to blame a Yank, it was most likely one of the locals."

"Why?"

"From what I hear, that fellow who works here in the lobby is a little too aware of the comings and goings of the ladies in this hotel. I heard he was seen chatting with her often."

"Are you suggesting *Hector* ... they were *friends*."

Danville picked up his pen again and inclined his head at Georgie to indicate that she should provide the escort from the room that Lucy obviously required.

"Maybe too friendly. Occam's razor, Barrett! Simplest solution and all that. I've no interest in acting out a Dashiell Hammett novel. You girls were warned to give the locals a wide berth but from what I've been told about Smith, she wasn't much of one for subtlety."

"That's silly," Lucy said. "Ruth hardly spoke to anyone. We can't think who she would let get that close to her."

Lark and Lucy enacted the murder out numerous times in their room.

"He was facing her," Lark would say, facing Lucy. "I say *he* because no woman would've had such strength. Strangling is a man's crime. He grabbed her throat. Fractured her hyoid bone. It was quick. Then he dropped her. Like a rag doll. He walked right up to her. As close as I am now. Who would she let so close? We have to figure that."

"He could have just — come at her. Quickly. Some random maniac or — "

As Lucy spoke, Lark paced back to the piano. She pivoted and rushed at Lucy, her clawlike hand outstretched. When her hand clutched Lucy's throat, Lucy grabbed it, her other hand ready to rake Lark's face before she caught a hold of herself.

"Yes." Lark inclined her head toward Lucy's defending hand. "You'd scratch. Anyone would. She didn't. You scratch me— " She picked up Lucy's hand and stroked her own cheek with it. "There'd be my skin under your nails. But with Ruth, no. He grabbed her too hard, too fast. So he was close to her. She knew him. And she knew so few. McKay can't walk. The men were all on base. It was too wet to do anything. That leaves who? Hector— "

"Why would it be Hector?"

"Why would it be anyone?"

On it went, night after night.

Danville closed a file. Lucia Barrett, filed away, as Ruth Smith was filed away. A girl found dead in a soggy garden, strangled under a banyan tree, a notoriously eccentric girl alone on a Sunday morning when the damage from the storm the night before had kept most people at home. Unfortunate business, but we must get on with our paperwork.

"Fetch those biscuits, Taylor? Give one to Barrett here, she's looking a little peaked."

Georgie reached into a crate and pulled out two round tins of Dutch almond butter biscuits, a brand the Barretts favored for tea. Paul liked the biscuits and Lucy and Marcia liked the tins, their blue and white designs depicting tulips and windmills. Was Danville trying to placate her with *cookies?*

"And fetch Lark, Taylor?" Danville consulted a calendar. "It's time."

"Lark agrees with me about Ruth," Lucy said as Georgie left the room. "It was her *idea.*"

"I'm not surprised. The two of you are thick as thieves, Taylor says." Danville glanced up from his file. "We found crates of those biscuits in the cargo of an American Export Lines ship. Three of the tins did not contain butter biscuits. But rather, little Dutch miniatures en route to a New York art dealer. A well-known Nazi sympathizer. That's what we are actually here to do, remember? Uncover this sort of activity? The miniatures are on their way to Canada. Can't be kept here with this humidity. But we had to open every tin. The biscuits won't survive the journey, now we've opened them, so alas. We must cope with all these biscuits. Ah, Miss Lark."

"Lark, he won't listen to me about Ruth! He says it's a matter for the police."

"It *is* a matter for the police. Taylor, would you—" Danville gestured at Lucy, then gave a conductor-like wave to the door and the world beyond it, where Lucy needed to be re-distributed, like a tin of—

"Biscuit, Miss Lark?" she heard Danville ask, as Georgie more or less shoved her out the door. Lucy strode away, made it as far as the Gazebo Bar before Georgie caught up with her.

"I'm leaving. I want to go home."

"You won't find Ruth's killer there. Calm yourself. Sit *down*." Georgie pressed a spot between the bottom of the back of Lucy's hand and the knob of her wrist bone. A hot flash of pain pulsed up Lucy's arm and she felt her hand slacken. In that moment, Georgie pulled her down to one of the plush sofas of the Gazebo Bar. A waiter immediately placed napkins and menus in front of them. The waiter was not Hector. *Had he been sucked?* He said he had seen Ruth talking to an American serviceman, but as they all knew, there were now nearly as many Yanks on the island as there were palmettos.

"Tea for two, please?" Georgie said to the waiter. "Just the tea. We brought our own biscuits."

***

Lark would travel to New York to testify in the trial of Brooklyn Joe, to explain how the pyramidon iodine test had revealed the invisible ink behind Joe's correspondence. Brooklyn Joe was a small but important link of a chain of espionage jointly under investigation by the British Security Coordination and the Federal Bureau of Investigation. Brooklyn Joe and his ring were being charged with treasonable conspiracy and espionage. Lucy had been asked to write out an account of the odd phrasing in certain letters which had aroused Lucy's suspicion: the goods at the 'wear house' in Red Hook, the Giants at the Polo Grounds, *in the words of Romeo, do nothing till you hear from me.* (And *thus I turn me from my country's light,* Lucy remembered, when she was told these plans. That was *proper* Shakespeare as well, but she hadn't developed her theory well enough to manage to hold that letter back. That letter was prime evidence. It was also in Germany.)

Lark would travel by flying boat to New York. Lucy would remain behind. Lark understood and could explain the science, Lucy did and could not, and the prosecution could only afford to bring in one.

Lucy suspected that there was more than science behind this decision. The Yanks could afford to bring both of them. They could afford everything. Lark was a practiced public speaker while Lucy was considered "prone to theatrics." And several of the Censorettes continued to refer to her as 'Miss Airs and Graces.'

Lark, Lucy and Alan stood at the dock where the skiffs arrived from Darrell's Island. Teck was already in the skiff, waiting to ferry Lark over to the Pan Am Clipper. Lark and Alan's parting embrace took full advantage of Alan's trumpet-player's mouth, although Lark, pulling away, gave Lucy the last kiss, one on each cheek, before she hopped into the skiff and waved to them as Teck pulled away.

30.

November 28, 1941

Dearest Lucy,

Yesterday I had my second American Thanksgiving meal in as many weeks. The reverend and his wife offered me a room in their residence but apparently, that arrangement would pose a security threat! So I am billeted at a nice hotel in Gramercy Park. You'll be happy to know I feasted at the meal—there were three varieties of pie—and I felt it would be rude to my hostess not to sample each one! The company, however, with the exception of the reverend, his wife and their spirited (very American!) children, tried their best to put me at ease.

The question of whether the Yanks will come in is a hotly contested one. Our meal was not exempt from political debate. Although I tried to stay out of it, my presence aroused a lot of questions. A Ca-

nadian? Visiting from Bermuda? The Yanks have been shown many Hollywood films showing the plight of Europe. But some grumble that those films are mere propaganda. It's gone as far as a Congressional investigation about the influence of the British and the Jews on the very making of these films. It's a good job Georgie's husband is safely out of Hollywood and back in the war. Just last month, there was a rally by America First. They say it filled Madison Square Garden and spilled out into the street. Charles Lindbergh spoke, so it was very well-attended.

If I am not back in time, could you rehearse Fleur and Roos in 'Adeste Fidelis' for the December 7 service (I have been rehearsing them in the Latin version. Their English is too incomprehensible for 'O Come All Ye Faithful'). 'In the Bleak Midwinter' is for December 14. I hope to be back by then, but who can say?

So, as the song says, "Wish me luck as you wave me goodbye!" I have an interview with Columbia Medical College. Clara Frith did the research. Columbia has been accepting women into their school of medicine for decades. I must finish my degree and "free a man for the front." And I'd rather my diploma say only "medical school" and not "medical school for women," as though my degree were second-rate.

I meant to tell you all this, but I didn't tell anyone, in case it all went pear-shaped. But it hasn't, through some miracle. I suspect one of these FBI men made a call on my behalf. I was told to make a call, and voila! If the interview goes well, I could start in the spring. The trial starts Tuesday.

You are always in my prayers, my dearest friend. It is so strange to be putting my thoughts in a letter instead of just whispering them to you. I look forward to reuniting with you, although I know the time will be so short (if the interview goes well!) At least we will have Christmas! If you could rehearse Fleur and Roos, that is a sufficient gift for me.

Your loving sister,
Rebecca Lark

"But ve vill not, Lucy," Fleur explained the following Sunday, when Lucy tried to guide them through rehearsal of "In the Bleak Midwinter." Their rendition of "Adeste Fidelis" had been remarkably moving, two clarion voices in sororal harmony. "Ve do not vant to sing zat. It hass nussing to do viss Christmas."

"Poem by Christina Rosetti," Clara Frith whispered helpfully, as the floral sisters spat their grievances. "Not sure about the music."

It vas a song about ze cold, and Bermuda vas not cold, her earth vas not hard as iron, her water far from like a stone. *Snow on snow.* Vy would Bermudians wish to hear zis? According to Miss Frith, zere was no snow in Bermuda.

"It doesn't matter," Lucy said. "Sing the hymn you have rehearsed with Lark."

"Ze melody is not in ze canon. Ve vould prefer—"

"Bloody *hell*, Fleur and Roos! Who cares what you *prefer*? Lark has talked of you two doing this hymn since *Easter!* There are *heaps* of things I'd rather be doing today! Could you do this for *Lark* at least? What with the state she's been in, after Ruth!"

Ruth! The name provoked a flurry of Flemish, followed by a torrent of German too swift for Lucy to follow—*Bach? Funeral?*—before they returned to English and expressed their dearest wish, to again sing, "Jesu, Joy of Man's Desiring."

"Fine." Lucy checked her watch. She was due to meet Georgie at the Bermudiana for tennis. "You'll have to do it a capella. As you did at the funeral. I don't have time to rehearse with you. I've a tennis match."

***

Lucy had still not won a match against Georgie. But she had begun to win games. At their most recent match, she had haired a set 6–4, before being crushed like a peasant uprising. On this Sunday, December 7, she won the first set, and the first game of the next set. She shouted *"Forty—love!"* and then saw her serve hit Georgie just above the breast with a meaty *thunk*, as though Lucy had served into a cow grazing in a meadow. Georgie stood still, not even flinching from the impact, which would surely bruise like the devil. She dropped her racquet, staring beyond Lucy. Turning, Lucy saw Danville behind the court, straddling a bicycle, in a beige shirt and Bermuda shorts, more amiably attired than Lucy had ever seen him, yet he might have been Death in a hooded cloak from the terror Lucy saw on Georgie's face. Lucy reflected that she had never seen Danville outdoors, as he opened his arms to receive Georgie, running from the court toward him. She beat at him, when they met, with fists.

Danville embraced her in a protective hug as Georgie released a wail which, Lucy would later write to Lark, raised the hair on the back of her neck.

"No! He's alright—at least, I don't know that he isn't. *Listen*! Are you listening?"

By this time, Lucy had reached them. She took Georgie's hand. Georgie squeezed her hand so hard that Lucy yelped, and reached for Georgie's other hand, trying to return the crush, although Georgie trembled so thoroughly that Lucy could only stroke a portion of the back of Georgie's hand with her thumb. She brought their forehands together and stroked her other hand along the top of Georgie's backbone as she chuffed at the sobs percolating up through her spine. Lucy calmed her cat Horatio this way when horses scared him. After a moment's half-hug, Georgie pushed Lucy away and struck at Danville.

"Bloody tears of *Christ*, Archie! How the *hell* could you scare me like that? What are you doing here? It'd damn well be good!"

"It isn't good. The Japanese have attacked an American naval base in Hawaii."

"What?" Georgie and Lucy said in unison.

"The *Japanese? Hawaii?*" Georgie repeated.

Lucy said. "*Naval base!*"

"It's called Pearl Harbor. All the U.S. military have been ordered to report for duty. Come on. We'll go back to the Princess. Listen to the wireless. Come, darling," Danville added, as Georgie slumped against him like an exhausted child. Danville extended a hand to Lucy. Lucy took his offered hand while registering that this display of affection was the most significant indication of this turn of events. There had indeed been an attack on a vulnerable harbour, not in Brooklyn, but in the South Pacific, and not by the Nazis, but the Japanese.

"Oh, and Barrett," Danville added, as though reading her thoughts. "They said on the NBC radio network that all the active sailors in New York City were ordered to report to their ships. So, well done and all, on catching those would-be saboteurs of the docks. If you hadn't, those sailors might've been reporting to … well, who knows what, eh?"

31.

In the following days, the outside world declared. The United States declared war on Japan. Germany and Italy declared war on the United States, which declared war in return. The residents of the Princess Hotel questioned their futures. Now that the Yanks were in, most of their jobs were unnecessary. Lark would not return from New York. Her things would be shipped to her. Gwynne announced her intention to return to London on whatever boat would take her and assured everyone in earshot that her Ma had "plenty of room" for anyone who needed lodgings. Ships to England were quickly filled, despite the threat of U-boats, with other homesick Censorettes seeking a fresh mission in the war effort. Other boats were bound for North Carolina. The Censorettes would then travel to jobs in Washington, D.C., New York, or Canada.

Fleur and Roos chose England. They sought the advice of Lucy, who was in Danville's office, frowning with him at his maps on the wall. Fleur pointed out on his map the small triangle of land that was Washington, D.C., where they had been invited to take their linguistic talents. They could work for the American war office or they could work for the British one. The four of them regarded the map of Europe, the shoreline of the imperiled British Empire, separated from Occupied France at its narrowest point by a stretch of water scarcely longer than the length of Bermuda, tip to tip.

"So, Fleur, Roos." Lucy wondered how many times in their lives they had been addressed as individual stems and not a bouquet. "What does your heart tell you?" Their responding shrugs and head shakes spoke of hearts long packed away for the duration. Lucy pointed first to England and then to the strange American capital, squeezed between two states named for English queens, "One of these places is the moon that pulls your tide. Which is it?"

"*Engeland*," they said in soft unison.

"*Engeland*. Excellent," Lucy said. "You'll do well in the Admiralty. I'll write to my father."

The wireless played in the Gazebo Bar at all hours. At midnight, after playing a recording of "The Star-Spangled Banner," the American radio networks dissolved into static and Lucy swore she could hear the waves lapping at the shore of their little island. She stood on the porch, it seemed every day, watching a member of her makeshift family disperse, wishing she had capitulated to Granny's nagging and embraced one of the tiresome needlework hobbies pressed upon women to keep them occupied in drawing rooms. Her life held no drawing rooms, but she would have liked something to do with her hands after she hugged her friends goodbye.

Work brought no solace. A few more mailbags came through for them to process, but they needed no longer tread lightly regarding suspicion of Nazi behavior, especially since—

"Especially since we found the Nazis, the whole nest of them," Danville told Lucy, spreading out a series of photographs one Saturday in his office, on the table at which she had drawn maps of Bermuda and Italy. "The ones you knew were there."

It was two Sundays after Pearl Harbor. The Japanese had destroyed twenty American ships, hundreds of airplanes. The Yanks were in. The whole world was at war and she felt ashes rather than fire.

Danville gestured at the table, which held a stack of files and an array of photographs, fanned out. She was right, he told her, as she examined them, one by one. She had been right all along. A warehouse, a dockyard, a photograph of a sketch of the dockyards. The Brooklyn Naval Yard and the piers in the Hudson River where the great ships docked, the Cunard and the White Star liners.

Brooklyn Joe and his group had monitored the shipyards. They had focused initially on the Brooklyn Naval Yard, but then spread out to Philadelphia, and Norfolk. The FBI, issued a warrant to enter Joe's flat, found photographs. They also found drawings, maps, correspondence, and a list of names of potential saboteurs. The FBI went down the list, visiting residence after office after shop affiliated with the names of the Nazi ring. At one office, they found maps of where explosives should be placed. There were photographs of the maps. At a chemist's shop, they found recipes for various explosives, with equations calculating which would do the most damage to ships. There were photographs of the chemist's shop.

"Anything else?" Lucy ran a fingertip down the stack of folders.

"I should think that would be enough, even for you, Barrett." Danville moved from the table to a sideboard, where he was setting out a tea service, laying down the crockery, prying open another tin of the confiscated Dutch almond biscuits. "Safe to say you did well by cracking the case, when was it, end of September, early October? Gave the FBI boys time to run them to ground. There's no telling when the plan was to lay down the bombs. As I said, if they'd managed to do it in December, right after Pearl Harbor, when all the active duty men were told to report to their ships … well, then, an already feeble American military force would have found itself even further depleted."

"Kaboom," Lucy said.

"Kaboom. Quite."

"But was there anything else?"

"What do you mean?"

"Did they *find* anything else?"

"In Joe's apartment? Well, no. Aside from some volumes of Shakespeare. Random volumes. Not the complete works."

"Well, no." Lucy shuffled the files back to read their labels: Correspondence from Bermuda, reports on surveillance, *Brooklyn Naval Yard (I)*, *Brooklyn Naval Yard (II)*. "The complete works aren't easily portable. Quite a chore to get through them all, particularly if English is not your first language. And I suppose being a Nazi saboteur takes up much of one's time."

The Warehouse. Joe Karte.

Lucy opened the file. And there he was. Brooklyn Joe. There was, anyway, his mug shot. A fleshy face, wide pillar of a nose, thick dark hair, swollen pale eyes, thick eyebrows. She'd envisioned a man more dashing, more Aryan, his eyes gleaming within from a private pulse of stirring verse—oh, to be honest, she'd imagined Leslie Howard. A Nazi Scarlet Pimpernel. The real Joe looked like the barman pulling pints at the pub she'd ducked into to escape the air raid that killed Tessa. Such men fed from war, plain men with fervent dreams and fatal agendas. *Maybe he's just ordinary*, Ruth said. He was. He looked stolid, capable. An engineer of some kind, Lucy supposed, a civil engineer, doing the work Bill did, laying down bridges and landing strips and airfields and, when necessary, blowing them to smithereens.

Brooklyn Joe. A man who loved Shakespeare and plotted to drown English-speaking men in the name of the Fatherland. *What noise of water in mine ears!*

Shakespeare. How had they decided on that for their code? She turned the photo over and studied the next one, which depicted what Danville had so generously termed "a flat." It was a dreary bedsit: sink, bed, bureau, chair, desk; three such rooms would have fit inside the honeymoon suite. There was the desk where he had written out his plots, written to a man he called *Uncle* back in Germany. The books on his desk were shabby, their spines broken, all heavily bookmarked with scraps of paper.

"I wish I could see Uncle's Shakespeare."

"Uncle?"

"The man he wrote to. Uncle must have had his own volumes. They didn't use it as a cipher key, but he must have had his own.

Uncle was in Bremerhaven. A port city. Another port city. Perhaps he and Joe maintained the docks together. Or managed the port. Perhaps that's how they got the idea."

"If only we could parachute you in."

"I wouldn't need a *parachute*. It's a port. Bring a fishing boat as close as we dare, launch me in a raft … I could paddle in."

She heard a chuckle and turned to see Danville smiling at her and in his amused appraisal finally understood the consolation Georgie had found with him. He held two amber bottles above the china tea service.

"Whisky or brandy?" he asked.

"Brandy." It wasn't yet lunchtime, but she hadn't slept well in days and there was the matter of her fretful hands. He set the service between them and they sat at his desk, nibbling biscuits.

"If you were a man." Danville pointed his biscuit at her. "We would give you a medal."

Lucy tugged the collar of her blouse to demonstrate she had a place to put a medal.

"What's a medal to a woman?" Danville asked. "You can't display it. You'd have to explain what it was and how you earned it. And since you're only doing clerical work here, and since MI6 isn't quite sure if we're really here at all—well, at best, you'd have a bit of tat to show your grandson in fifty years. That's the time frame of the Official Secrets Act. And in some cases, longer than that."

Lucy sipped her brandy. When men became expansive like this, it was best to let them talk. She and Matty had learned to wait out their father's lectures. Interruption only agitated Paul, whereas rapt attention mollified him and lessened their punishments. When Matty and Lucy had flown to Paris on her sixteenth birthday, for example, they withstood Paul's outrage—*underage! No one knew where you were! No idea of the danger!*—with innocent dismay, which had resulted in what amounted to a suspended sentence: "*I leali* strike again, I suppose. But promise me you'll never do it again."

"… so we thought the best reward for you was a choice," Danville was concluding.

"A choice," Lucy repeated. She had not been listening. She refilled her cup, her immediate choice another brandy.

"Yes, one of those women novelists says something like that. Men have the power to choose, women can only refuse ... Bronte, was it? Eliot? No? Shakespeare only with you, is it? What would you like to do next?"

"What would I *like to do next*?"

"Aside from paddling a raft into Bremerhaven. That's not on. We have ideas. We're not doing at all well in North Africa." *Not doing at all well.* He might have been Granny, discussing a rose hybrid's failure to thrive. "Rommel's quite close to Alexandria. The plan is to drop Taylor in Alex. She's cradle-fluent in German, and German-looking—"

"As she is half-German."

"As you are half-Italian. The plan is for her to fade into the walls should Jerry invade Alex. Should they find her, she is a German officer's widow, desperately grateful for the rescue. Our man on the inside, if you will. And we thought the same for you. Only, the Italian version."

"I see. And in the meantime? Until Rommel marches in?"

"There's plenty to do. Translate intercepts. Help our radio operators understand the Italian pilots—they say those screaming vowels are like listening to opera over the shortwave."

"I quite like opera."

"How very not surprised I am to learn that. Then we need people to teach our boys the lingo ... don't suppose you have any Arabic? "

"Just some Greek. And the other choice?"

"We could chuck you back to England."

"*Engeland.*" Her heart lunged into her ribs, like a captive in a Gothic novel, flinging herself against a locked door. *Let me out!*

"Join the Belgian flowers in the Admiralty? I'm sure your father would welcome you."

That sealed it. "The Admiralty is very deep underground, Archie. And I have have my fill of basements."

32.

Knoll House, Knollborough, 1936

Ich habe Tote und ich ließ sie hin
Und war erstaunt, sie so getrost zu sehen
So rasch zuhaus in Totsein, so gerecht
So anders als ihr Ruf.

Lucy's translation reads:

I have known the dead, and I have forgotten them
and was amazed to see them so confident,
So quickly at home in their dead state, so fair,
So different from their calling.

Her tutor, Karolina Diehl, must have exhausted her supply of red ink marking up this verse. *You translate poetry like a diplomat! Where in the phrase* Ich habe Tote *is the verb* kennen?? *Then why translate it as* "I have known the dead?" *Likewise, where is the verb* vergessen *in* und ich ließ sie hin?? *There is nothing in the line about forgetting!!!"*

Likewise, why is Karolina exploding in punctuation? *We will begin gently, with just one verse, and work our way through Rilke,* Karolina declared at breakfast, while handing her these ungentle corrections. *And my father has sent some simple exercises in modern Greek.*

Wot larks! Matty said, off to help the Ripples with their lambing. Lucy envies him. She would rather be up to her elbows in ewe blood than this reproachful red ink.

The wind argues with the curtain over Lucy's desk. She anchors her papers with books. Marcia has been at her scales for *hours*, first vocal scales with Karolina, who then left for Knollborough, then an hour of practice, then a merciful tea break, and now scales of piano. Granny is in the rose garden, and her parents are God knows where. Lucy has bungled this one verse, the opening of Rilke's *Requiem for a Friend,* which is as long as a play. Paul was delighted to give Karolina Diehl a job to earn walking-around money, and a pleasant stay for the summer holidays while Herr Professor Diehl, in London, toils away translating intercepts for the government.

Ich habe Tote. I have dead. But the noun *ich* indicates the possessive pronoun, so, *I have my dead. Und ich ließ sie hin.* And I have (will? would?) let them go.

I have my dead, and I have let them go.

But she doesn't have her dead. Not really. Grandfather Barrett died when she was a toddler. Her Barrett uncles were killed in the War before she was born. A Barrett aunt died in childbirth, which so alarmed Tessa that she had left the children at home for the funeral.

And was amazed to see them so confident … "confident" must be wrong. Why would the dead need confidence? She consults her dictionary. Marcia thunders at the keyboard. A gust ruffles the pages of her dictionary. A dog barks outside. Through the window, she sees the part-time groundskeeper stride past the barn and summerhouse with his exuberant collie. The collie leaps at Granny, rounding the corner from the rose garden to consult with the groundskeeper. Lucy would rather romp with the collie. Prune roses with Granny. Shop in Knollborough with the peevish Karolina. Instead, she mangles a translation of a sad German poem.

That morning, Karolina told them she was eager to roam a "typical English village." She has now met her previous desire, to stay in a "typical English country manor." Granny, who has allowed Karolina the leniency afforded a houseguest and the patience afforded a refugee from Hitler, can not allow "typical" or "manor" to stand. Knoll House is a Regency-era house of Cotswold honey-coloured limestone, with barn, gardening shed, lambing shed, hen house, smokehouse, summer house. There are two resident maids, and a village girl who chars. There is a gardener/handyman, a groundskeeper (part-time) and a cook. There is an orchard, neglected stables, and farmland, which they rent to tenant farmers. This estate has been self-sufficient and endured centuries of political storms. Karolina winced at "political storms."

Granny's detailing the bustle that makes Knoll House *not* a "stately manor" slumped Karolina into the posture of a spinster hearing a wife decrying the snores of a loving husband. Granny's complaints are centuries old: the stream jumps its banks in the spring, the walnut trees swoon to rot unless they receive constant pruning at the root, the chickens are stalked by foxes Matty is too soft-hearted to shoot, they have to prevail upon that Jenner boy next door … she clucked and sipped her tea.

Karolina inhaled the rosemary breeze of the herb garden. Her eyes spoke of inconsolable yearning. On that morning in June 1936, that vein of sadness is as alien to Lucy as the requiem which begins *I have my dead, and I have let them go.*

Paul shook his head at his mother, took the hand of his wife. Lucy kicked her sister in the shin to signal a change the subject. Marcia exclaimed, "Jolly nice breeze today. Perhaps we can fly a kite later!"

Marcia is a good egg, sometimes. She may be slow at her studies, but then, she will thereby escape all this German, and be allowed music and kites.

She would rather be flying a kite with Marcia.

"*There* you are!" Tessa strolls in, bounces down on Lucy's bed.

"I've been here *tethered* here all morning," Lucy says. "Where have *you* been?"

"Your father and I had a nap." Tessa smiles, as though she and Paul routinely find breakfast so fatiguing that they return to bed. She *does* seem rested, girlish, even, her hair a disheveled braid, exuding talcum powder and Drewe's lotion. She has bathed after this nap … *caressa Tessa?* In the *morning?* At *Granny's?* Lucy firmly shuts the door on this corridor of speculation.

"Your father and I were talking," Tessa continues airily, as though their talks did not bode anything but menace. "It is time Marcia joined the Shakespeare readings. When we go home."

"She's too young."

"She is eight. You were eight. You and Matteo were fairies, I think, in *The Dream of the Midsummer*. No, I mean—"

Lucy double-flicks her wrist; a family gesture forgiving a mid-language switch midsentence, or a blunder in possessives and prepositions. Perhaps she ought to teach it to Karolina.

"She's not a good reader." Lucy frowns. "She's actually a poor reader."

"She is not Lucia Barrett."

"Even at eight, she should—"

"She is *Marcia* Barrett. She does not have your abilities. She has her own." Tessa inclines her head toward the piano scales emanating from downstairs.

"And *that's* been going on for hours! Can't you stop it?"

"Can't you stop *this*?" Tessa waves at Lucy's desk, the Rilke, the dictionaries, the translation bloodied with corrections. The constant study exasperates Tessa, but it is the cost of Lucy's liberty. A slip in her marks will send her away. Paul would not hesitate. He filled out Matty's paperwork for Harrow without so much as a consultation with Tessa who, convent-raised, knew too well the loneliness of boarding school.

"If I am blessed with another child," Tessa strokes her stomach. "He will be ordinary. He will be all mine. Not clever at all. You must be kinder to Marcia. It is not easy to be the less clever sister."

Ignoring the alarming prospect of another sibling, or the activity required to produce one, Lucy asks, "What would you know about that?"

"I know everything! Celestina—"

"You're not less clever than *her*. Why would you want to be? What a dragon! You're wonderful at mathematics, Mama. And music. You're brilliant at Shakespeare, and it's not even your first language."

Tessa displays her palm to ward off her daughter's praise. "Celestina can calculate the distance from the earth to a distant star. I can manage a household budget. *Matematica casalinga, secondo*

Matteo e Marco."

Housewife math, Tessa's brothers called it. Matteo and Marco are engineers, building railroads and bridges in Italy, making the trains run on time for Mussolini.

"We think *As You Like It,*" Tessa adds.

"What? Oh. What role? Not Rosalind! We'll be there all night."

"I hope you have more patience with your own children." Tessa kisses her forehead. "There is a little shepherdess who denies that she's in love. 'Think not I love him, though I ask for him.' Marcia will have that part. You rehearse with her. And now — " She raises the window. The wind scatters Rilke. "Someone spoke of a kite."

They find a kite in the nursery. Tessa, Lucy and Marcia work out a system where Lucy, at the top of the slope, signals to Marcia, at the bottom, to run like mad for the walnut grove, then Lucy releases the kite. Tessa, with her greater height, pulls madly at the string. They fail again and again. The kite dances in the gusts before diving to the ground, like a bird of prey seeking a field vole. Karolina climbs the long hill with her shopping from Knollborough, including a new kite!

They are assembling the kite when Matty returns from the Ripple farm. Tucked into his shirt is a kitten, the runt of the litter which he has saved from drowning, as a study companion for his sister. When Lucy takes him, the kitten shoves his small head under the crescent of her breast, panting in terror. Lucy names him Horatio.

33.

Bermuda, 1941

She wrote to Matty, care of Knoll House. *I'm soon to be stationed elsewhere. I will let you know where I am, when I am allowed to. Do keep yourself safe, my dearest and favorite brother. You are in my every prayer. I am constant as the Northern Star. There is no fellow in the firmament.*

The last two lines were from *Julius Caesar*, which Matty would recognize should he live to see her letter and would discern, she hoped, that she was close to Italy. Georgie wouldn't know the references—Georgie, among others, read all her outgoing mail, openly now since much of the world was at war—and she had cloaked it in prayer, to lead any censors further astray. Nonno, after all, was an astronomer; why shouldn't Lucy discuss stars in correspondence with her brother?

She wrote to Lark, *Well done, my dearest friend, for both the trial of Brooklyn Joe and for your matriculation at Columbia Medical College! I kiss this letter and pretend it is you. I am soon to leave Bermuda and cannot say where I will be next, but I know where you will be. In my heart, always. I will send my address as soon as I have one I can share. You can always write to dear old Clara in the meantime. She has expressed a desire to move to New York City herself.*

"Do tell me you haven't made this choice just because you love me," said Georgie, shoving her satin pajamas under the pillow that had been Lark's.

"Who *loves* you?" Lucy swallowed. A cyclone of pink sand seemed to have whirled into the room, stinging her eyes and clogging her throat. "You're a snoop and a showoff and you never let me win at tennis."

And I will be with you in the danger, Lucy thought. *No one will ever again say to me "I thought you were with her."*

She could not return to England now, not with the war still on and men like her father in charge of it. Her England had vanished

into the mists like the Avalon of the Arthur legend, taking with it
her verdant girlhood: dedicated student (*die Studentin, der Studentin, den Studentin*), dutiful daughter, devoted sister. A girl who had
always done what she should, until, one night, she had failed to.
And so she was sent here. Were she to return to England, she would
only be cloistered in another basement, her obedience assumed.

Georgie moved into Lucy's bed after Pearl Harbor, the larger
room too vast. They huddled together. Georgie's bed held the remains of Ruth's things: blouses and stockings bound for the jumble at St. Andrew's, books headed for the Bermuda Library. Lucy
claimed her sketch pad. And thus, the worldly goods of Ruth Smith
were dispersed.

Georgie talked in her sleep to needy, demanding players: *is there
enough light, here's a lens cloth.* Lark had slept on her back, the top
sheet tucked neatly under her chin, a storybook illustration of a
spellbound maiden awaiting the kiss that would break her enchant-
ment. Lucy tossed in fret. Lark, awakening her for Sunday services,
had often suggested that Lucy might find in church the tranquility
which seemed to elude her in sleep. Through many Sundays, Lucy
prayed for her anger at her father to lift like Bermuda's morning fog.
After a time she couldn't identify, her anger *did* lift. It was replaced
by a rage heavy as an anchor, secured at the top of her ribcage,
which tugged at her whenever she thought about Ruth.

***

Christmas arrived and departed, unsoftened by the harmonies of
Fleur and Roos, who were already in England. A few days into the
new year, Lucy awoke to the sound of drawers opening and closing. Usually, Georgie woke her for her morning run, but she sensed
from the way the light hit the ceiling that the time for the run had
already gone. She half-sat and felt, before her eyes were fully open,
a weight on the bed.

"Wakey, wakey. Eat up," Georgie said. "Heaven knows when
you'll see your next meal."

Lucy rubbed her face and gazed at the tray: toast and a roll, with butter and jam, ham and eggs, coffee and milk, tinned peaches in a bowl, a bud vase containing a single peach rose.

"My goodness! Have we won the war?"

"We've clear skies at last. The Yanks have given us two seats on their plane. Bundle up." Georgie laid clothing across Lucy's legs: trousers, a blouse, a pullover, a woolen scarf, sturdy shoes, and a khaki trench coat. "It's bloody freezing up there."

"We're leaving? We're really leaving?"

"First stop, Morocco."

Lucy shoved the toast into her mouth, sipped the coffee, moved the tray aside, and jumped out of bed. A look in her bureau revealed that Georgie had already packed her smaller garments for her. Lucy fished her bathing suits out of a drawer, only to have her hand slapped by Georgie. "I'll take care of your clothes. You get your personal effects. We'll be in Alex at first, Archie says. So, a bit of social life."

As she said "social life," Georgie pulled out the Schiaparelli gown.

"Nicky's in Africa," Georgie said, explaining her good mood, as Lucy rifled through her desk to find clean stationery. "Or Malta. Hurry! They won't hold the plane for us!"

She scribbled a note to Clara, leaving her the remainder of her things. She put into another envelope all the Bermudian money she had in her purse, for Hector. She tucked Ruth's sketch pad into her satchel and carried it, with her suitcases, down the stairs, for the last time, at the Princess Hotel.

***

Georgie drove them to the airfield-in-progress at St. David's, past a Quonset hut and onto a flattened lot, where the airplane sat. She inclined her head toward the makeshift hangar.

"I have to see the port master," she shouted through the wind. In the distance, a small explosion raised a cloud of pink dust. "Take out our luggage, then drive this there—" she pointed to another Quonset hut, "—leave the keys in. Meet me there."

Georgie pointed to the ladder which led to the open doorway

of the airplane, stepped out of the jeep and ran toward the hangar. Lucy hauled their luggage—four suitcases and two rucksacks—to the bottom of the ladder which led into the plane, then climbed into the driver's seat of the jeep. She paused, studying the gears and the foot pedals, trying to remember what she had witnessed drivers do. She had only been in a jeep a handful of times, and she had never been permitted the driver's seat of any vehicle, neither boat nor motorcar. With a firm nod, she placed her hands on the steering wheel.

"*Allow me!*" a man shouted.

Bill stood by the driver's side of the jeep. She scooted to the passenger seat. The quickest way to get the jeep from here to there was to let him handle it. He hoisted himself into the driver's seat, then stepped on a pedal and pulled a lever and drove them into the hut, into a sudden, cool shade and relative quiet. The metal walls of the shelter shivered in the wind but when Bill next spoke, his voice was conversational. He reached out to tuck an errant lock of her hair back behind her ear.

"Sunlight brings out the red in your hair," he said. "I'd forgotten how pretty it is."

"Yes. I must get on. Thank you for rescuing me." She gestured to the steering wheel.

"Wouldn't call it a rescue. You made it clear I wouldn't ever be allowed to do that."

"Well, I must—" She turned to get out of the jeep. He put his hand on her shoulder.

"I came by to see you, you know. Over and over. That porter wouldn't let me past the door. Then I remembered how you always went on those walks with her. On Sunday. After church. I could never take you to lunch 'cause you were on those walks. I guess you must've felt sorry for her. 'Cause she was retarded."

"Ruth was not *retarded*," Lucy couldn't stop herself from snapping.

"She never gave a thought to what she said to folks. Couldn't she've been more careful? How's I supposed to know she was so fragile? Your duckling. Why'd did you call her that? Did you think she'd turn into a swan if you paid enough attention to her? Me, you wouldn't pay attention to me at all. Your duckling. I was never your anything. I was a null. A *null!*" He slapped the steering wheel. "How do you like that!"

"A null." It hit her like the slap he had once tried to deliver.

When you multiply by a null, you get nothing. That was from the night of her birthday party. When could Ruth have repeated that conversation to him? The following Saturday was the night they had solved the cipher of Brooklyn Joe, and Gwynne had come back from a date with Bill, so Ruth couldn't have been with him then. The Saturday after that was the night of the hurricane, and the next day, Ruth had been murdered. Strangled. On Sunday. After church. The day the Army-Navy golf game had been cancelled.

Her question reflected in his eyes. His eyes gave no answer but a slight misting of tears. The tears were not for her, or Ruth. The tears were for himself. *Poor little null.*

"*Lucy!*" Georgie ran to them and grabbed her arm. "Bloody blazes! They'll leave without us!"

Lucy had not hit anyone since she had hit Matty in the nursery, fighting over the claim to some toy. She thought of Matty and his vengeful talcum powder *Basso Profondo: Repent repent!* But only fleetingly. She had never punched a man.

But she struck Bill with an upraised arm and a closed fist, and all the tennis and the pull-ups of her training had not been in vain. His nose crunched beneath her blow; blood sprouted blood on his face as she shouted, "*You!* You—you—" Words failed her. All her languages failed her.

"Lucy!" Georgie said, as men on the airfield ran toward them.

"You *killed* her! Georgie, he *killed* her! Ruth! She was worth *ten* of you, you stupid, *bloody*— "

"What's going on here?" An American officer arrived, panting. "Look, are they holding that plane for you girls? We've got to clear the airfield. We can't delay for a lover's quarrel—"

"We're not *lovers!*" Lucy sucked at her sore knuckles.

A second American ran to the jeep and spoke to Georgie, since

Lucy, shouting and waving a bloody hand, seemed less receptive: "Miss, the plane's about to take off. We can't hold it, with these winds. Your luggage is already on. Get on the plane now or let it go without you."

"Yes, go now," said the first American. "Go now, and we'll forget about this. If you stay—assaulting an officer is a serious offense—"

"Oh, *bloody tears of Christ*!" Lucy shouted at him. "*Murder* is a serious offense. Your loo-tenant Inman murdered Ruth Smith!"

"What?"

"Lucy, we must go *now*! The plane—"

"You go to the Princess Hotel, Captain Whoever you are, and you ask for Archie Danville, and you tell him what I just told you. Lieutenant William Inman of the U.S. Army Corps of Engineers murdered Imperial Censorship Detachment employee Ruth Barrington-Smith. You do that now, or I will fling myself into the propellors of this plane, which needs to take off right now. And then no one will be able to take off. No!" Lucy added, when one of the Americans laid his hand on her.

"The what? The who? Ma'am. Either get on that plane or come with me."

Georgie laid a hand on her other arm. Lucy had revealed the presence of the Detachment. If she stayed, she would be in the custody of the U.S. military forces, who were less concerned with the murder of a "clerical worker" of the British government (who would no doubt disavow her as anything else) than with the assault of a military officer who was still (Lucy had the fleeting moment to be gratified to note) wiping blood from his nose with the back of his hand. She was with British Intelligence, true, but how long would it take the Yanks to adopt the intelligence needed to process justice, if they ever did? She might wind up in the Military Hospital in St. George's Parish, where they kept the Axis-related women and children.

And in the meantime, Georgie needed her.

Georgie was tugging at her now.

"Lucy. Lucy. Please."

Lucy took Georgie's hand and raced with her across the tarmac. The propellers of the plane were already in motion. Men on the plane seized her arms and hoisted them into the cabin. There were no seats, only benches on each side of the narrow metal pipe which housed them.

Their fellow passengers were not Americans. Although they hadn't spoken, their look was not that of cheerful, well-fed Yanks but of her lean, grim countrymen.

Diplomacy was the continuation of war by other means. No, that was wrong, she had that wrong. War was the continuation of politics ... when had she last entertained that phrase? Just after she arrived in Bermuda, full of grief. And now she was leaving Bermuda, full of grief. But this time, resolve ran through her grief, like blue veins through white marble. Although Georgie hadn't offered her shoulder as a refuge for tears, Lucy took it. She leaned on Georgie and closed her eyes.

PART FOUR
ALEXANDRIA

34.

Alexandria, 1942

Alexandria was another port city, inconstant as the moon, vulnerable on the Mediterranean, resilient for millenia. Italians bombed the port. Germans bombed everything. Alex carried on. Refugees trickled in. Resident Italians were rounded up for internment, although Egypt's King Farouk kept his Italian servants. He also kept the lights burning in the palace during blackouts. The *Deutsche Afrika Corps*, led by General Rommel, encroached from Cyrenaica in the west. The British launched supplies from Alexandria, took wounded in from the Western Desert, and set their watches by the air-raid sirens.

Native Alexandrians carried on like less beleaguered Londoners. They were indeed less beleaguered, their sanguinity borne from the memory of centuries of conquerors. Romans. Ottomans. Brits. Maybe Nazis next? The Nile would flood. The drought would come.

They lived in a Biblical rhythm. The *muezzin* sang the call to prayer. Vendors' calls offered more material sustenance: cheese, fish, olives, oranges and lemons ("say the bells of St. Clements," completed the British, in their heads) delivered by rogue sailors from Greece and Cyprus.

The sea was everywhere, on the swoop of a gull strafing a street for food, on a briny exhalation of breeze. The winds from the desert demanded more attention. Soldiers and supply trucks braved into the Western Desert; the wounded, in ambulances, returned from it. The city teemed with soldiers. British officers frequented the Cecil Hotel, the Union Bar, and the Royal Alexandria Yacht Club. Men of more modest means found plenty of bars, casinos and cinemas. The busy Red Light district along the Rue des Soeurs hosted brothels whose addresses were advertised as boldly as the *mezze* bistros.

If Alexandria failed to entertain, there was Cairo, only a few hours away by train. Cairo had everything: parties, literary societies, and well-stocked department stores. Georgie returned from a weekend trip with a dozen pairs of white gloves for Lucy, to replenish what she had depleted in Bermuda.

Lucy and Georgie initially found rooms in a downtrodden hotel where no one seemed to sleep. Dramatic women performed arias of complaint in the halls, sporting only kimonos. The skittish walls released moans and faint cries of surprise and release. The street below hosted drunken soldiers, crude Romeos who sang a vulgar song about the pretty young wife of Egypt's King Farouk: *Queen Falida, Queen Falida, how the boys'd love to ride her!*

After a few weeks, Georgie and Lucy were invited to a dinner at the Cecil Hotel given for new arrivals to Alexandian English society. Georgie wore her Vionnet and Lucy wore the white dress Lark had sewn for her from a Furbert daughter cast-off, with a headband of seed pearls to save her an elaborate hair dress. English women were a rarity—wives had been evacuated to Palestine or South Africa. Independent young women of curated conversation and Mona Lisa smiles when questioned about their presence in Alex were downright exotic. Georgie and Lucy were the only single women in a party of twelve and so their hostess, Lady Weston, decreed that Georgie should sit at Major Weston's right, and Lucy at the other end of the table at Lady Weston's right.

Lucy was seated next to a Captain Burdock. He interrogated Italian and German prisoners. He stroked his small moustache after he made what he regarded as a witty observation. (*He has obviously been told too many times that he resembles a film star,* Lucy wrote to Lark. *Errol Flynn? Ronald Colman? Although he lacks the fine bone structure which constitutes a movie star. Ruth made such a point about that, do you remember?*) What, he asked, was Lucy up to here in Alex? Signals? Propaganda? Clever girls were usually put to propaganda.

"Nothing at all important, Captain. I just translate what's put before me."

"Translate from what?" When Lucy sipped her soup rather than reply, Burdock offered, "Italian? German? *Both*?" he exclaimed, when Lucy nodded.

She did some work in propaganda, as she could relay from the radio broadcasts from Italy what the citizens of Italy were being told about their men in the desert, but she mainly translated captured documents or intercepted wireless transmissions. On occasion, she was permitted into the radio tower to try to learn the "chatter" of the Italian pilots, but pilots were a jargon-laden bunch. At least the RAF was, if Matty was anything to go by. Fuller duties would come, she understood, once the Eighth Army drove Rommel and the Afrika Corps from the desert, once the Yanks arrived, once the drive into Sicily commenced.

"I say, Miss Barrett," Burdock said as the waiter removed the soup course and placed down the fish. "Who's your C.O.? I'm keen to borrow you. Help us with our Eye-ties. They're a sentimental lot. A woman's presence might loosen their tongues. How fluent are you?"

"Cradle-fluent. My mother was Eye-tie." Lucy sipped her wine, which was also Eye-tie. A Montepulciano. When had she last tasted wine? During her training in Bermuda, the evening she had told

Georgie *Annegret is a German name.* She tried not to gulp it. Burdock was speaking again and she tilted her head at him.

"I asked where you were staying."

"We're at the Hotel Marta."

"The *Marta?* Who in the bloody blazes put you *there?*"

Clinking cutlery stilled. Silence combed down the table. Major Weston looked up from his plate. "Language, Burdock. You'll apologize to Lady Weston. What's the fuss?"

"I beg your pardon, Major, but these girls are billeted at the Hotel Marta."

Major Weston declared this not possible. Georgie confirmed that it was true, that they had been assured that in the housing shortage, this was the best that could be done.

"Nonsense," Lady Weston declared calmly. "You shall be our guests. You'll move to our home tomorrow, if you can cope with sharing a bed and a bath."

"Are either of you nurses?" This came from a tall thin man with eyes far lighter than his his tanned face. He looked up from sorting fish flesh from fish bones.

"Whiting, do they *look* like nurses?" Burdock asked.

"Nurses are not a *species*," the man called Whiting responded. Lucy noticed that his dark hair was cut very close, that he wore no pomade, that he had, like Cassius, *a lean and hungry look.* "They are trained medical staff. That they tend to be women speaks only to the limited educational opportunities of women."

Lucy and Georgie exchanged a look of astonished delight, as children might share if a magician materialized at the dinner table.

"Keep your hair on," Burdock said. "No one's insulting your precious QA's."

"I only ask," Whiting continued, focused on dissecting his fish. "Because kind as the Westons are, the ladies might find the accommodations distressing.

"They'll stay in our daughter's old room," Lady Weston nodded to the waiter to set the next course, "She found it spacious enough. We must all make sacrifices. I'm sure they won't mind sharing breakfast with a few recuperating soldiers."

"We'd be most grateful," Georgie said, and then, to Whiting, "I have First Aid training."

"Excellent," Lady Weston said. "If either of you are readers, that would be *such* a comfort to my husband. He has an enormous library, and almost no one he can discuss it with."

(*It appears, Lark, that Georgie and I were living in a demi-brothel, until Major Sir Hugh and Lady Weston took us in like evacuees. They are set up to house convalescing soldiers at their place. It is like a bed and breakfast for men who need a longer recuperation but can't take up a hospital bed. It's a beautiful villa. The library is beyond description. I wish Clara Frith could see it. I'd sleep in a broom closet to stay here.*)

***

The office into which Lucy's desk was crammed was an actual broom closet, but it was close to the harbour and brought in the sea air when she left her piles of translated documents, walked down the hall, and drank in the view from a window in the corridor. The military jail, where Burdock wished her to try out a job, was a white crenellated fortress further inland. Lucy walked a triangle that day, from her work to the jail offices, where she looked at files of Italian prisoners and chose Lieutenant Eugenio Alessandrini who had been found with a group of soldiers near Bir Hacheim, near-crazy with thirst and blinded by sand. Burdock told her that most of the officers' interrogations were desultory exchanges, the prisoners relieved to be out of the sun and sand and away from the sand fleas, cheerfully answering questions but shrugging off the idea that they were withholding, or had ever possessed, any useful knowledge. They were merely foot soldiers, they insisted. This last part was not true, as the mere foot soldiers were sent into POW camps immediately, and only the officers detained for questioning.

From the jail offices, she went to the American Express office to pick up letters, then to the hairdresser, to have her hair brushed and pinned into a prim *chignon*. She presented herself at the military jail as she had been dressed at the office: in a grey cotton dress, without makeup or jewelry. Burdock sulked at her appearance.

"I thought, Miss Barrett, perhaps a little … glamour …?"

"I'm hardly here to seduce, Captain. If we don't succeed today, you may dress me as you like in the future."

Colouring at her innuendo (*or was it?* she saw in his frown), Burdock brought her into the interrogation room, to the delight of the captured Italian lieutenant handcuffed to the table. He gallantly leapt to his feet when Lucy entered the room, until his chain yanked him still.

"I appreciate the gesture, but do be seated, *tenente*," Lucy said.

She paused, studying the high, barred window, while she summed *la freddezza*. She held the pose to allow the men in the room to summon memories of the vision of a woman in a shaft of light: Renaissance depictions of the Annunciation, for the recalcitrant *tenente*; for Burdock, a Vermeer of a woman reading by a window; perhaps for the sentry, a threadbare Scarlett O'Hara shaking a withered radish against a red sky vowing "*I'll never be hungry again!*" The lieutenant's chain scraped against the table as he shifted his weight. Burdock cleared his throat.

Lucy sat with ceremony, as though her small grey skirt were a ballgown: fuss, smooth, flick. "So. *Tenente Alessandrini*. I understand you have not been of much help."

"I have said all I know, *signorina!* We were in Libya. We were separated from our unit. *Fottuta tempesta di sabbia!*"

"*Si, tenente*. But Libya is large. What is the last place you remember? Before this bastard sandstorm hit? The closest railway station. How many were you. Where was the German Army. Where are their land mines. We're very interested in the land mines."

The lieutenant shrugged. Lucy said, "These ribbons on your jacket, just decoration? I have Italian cousins. They love to brag. Things to show off to a little girl. Killing a rabbit with a knife. Standing down a fierce dog. *Grrrr. Grrrr.*"

Lucy imitated her cousins imitating the dog, which pulled the smirk off the *tenente*. His eyes, red from the blowing sand, showed a flicker of uncertainty.

"I was a girl when I visited my cousins in Cecina. Girls are easily impressed. They showed me medals for themselves. Valour in sailing. Valour in slapping a servant boy. They made medals out of tree bark and bits of ribbon they stole from their sisters. I don't know much about Italian military decorations. But I know I am no longer a girl."

"I will say nothing." Something in the narrowing of his eyes, the pout created by the shift of his jaw, reminded Lucy of Inman's indignation when she had declined him.

"You will say nothing," she replied in the same placating tone she had used on Bill. "That is different from 'I have said all I know.' I *am* sorry. These men—" she darkened her tone, like Marcia shifting from major to minor scales, "they brought me here to convince you to tell all you know. It is no matter to me. I will walk out, and you will be left with—Men are violent. They feed on violence. Women know this. All women know this."

The men stared: Burdock, who had functional Italian, his assistant, who could only bark orders in it, and the lieutenant. She almost allowed a suffusion of compassion, but then thought of Ruth, and of Lear bearing the weight of the dead Cordelia: *Why should a dog, a horse, a rat, have life/and thou no breath at all?*

"Men can break the neck of a woman so easily. Lucy picked up a pencil. "I had a friend And a man grabbed her by the throat." Lucy snapped the pencil in half. "And then she was dead."

She held the business end of the pencil out to the lieutenant. "Before we reach anger, you could draw us a map. How many troops. How many tanks. What railways. What villages. What landmarks."

The lieutenant stared at her, looked to the men in the room for clarification.

"I had hoped you might be of use, but no." She repeated it in English, for the benefit of the room, "A boy of tree bark medals. I am disappointed."

Her disappointment stilled them: Burdock and his assistant, who had gone round-eyed, and the blossom-young sentry at the door who had been braced for rougher stuff than profound dismay. The rhythmic squeal of the overhead fan was the only sound in the room.

Lucy inclined her head and shifted her eyes downward. Paul had delivered the lectures for infractions of manners, but Tessa had been the one to address their moral failings: greed, pride, vanity, sloth: *Is this my daughter? Is this my son? Tell me how I have I failed, to see my efforts reflected in children such as these.*

"A map?" the lieutenant offered. He repeated, in English, "I see a map?"

"No, thank you, Captain." Switching to English, Lucy waved away a commercial map which Burdock leapt up to proffer. "Paper? Anything will do." In Italian, she said, "Brown paper. The stuff we use to wrap the belongings of the dead. Or do we still bother with that? What *do* we send? A telegram?" *No preference,* Ruth's father had telegrammed. Lucy bit next words as carefully as rationed meat. "So. Little. In the end. For a life. A life lived. I think the *tenente* and I might draw a map together. Thank you, Captain."

Lucy sketched quickly. A few strokes evoked Egypt and Libya, the Nile and the desert, the Mediterranean above, with Syria, Turkey. The islands of Greece forming a crescent across the Mediterranean in the north. The men craned in, as rapt as geography students. She raised her eyes to the captured lieutenant's, saw the question in his. What could these *inglesi* be up to, bringing in this crazy, melancholy girl? Lucy sketched triangles of mountains in Italy.

"Where is your home, *tenente?*"

"Genoa."

Lucy drew a tiny star on the northwest coast. "And when did you last see your mother?"

"*Mia mamma?*"

The men flinched. Every man knows *mamma*.

"Does she live in Genoa? Alessandrini must be her name? *Alora,* Alessandrini in Genoa, how many can there be? I'm sure she's safe, as long as the Germans hold Italy. I will see that you get a letter to her. You dictate. I write. After we've made our map. And before you're taken to the work camp where you'll spend the rest of the war, we might arrange a photograph," Lucy repeated, this time in English, "couldn't we, Captain?" Lucy switched back to Italian. "A bath, a shave, a haircut, a proper meal. A photo for Mama. 'Here was my son,' she will say. You're lucky, *tenente*. My Mama was killed in London by the *Luftwaffe*. Your allies. There was no last message for me. Because this message—should we decide to send it—this message may be your last. And as for your wife."

"My wife," Lieutenant Alessandrini echoed dully.

"Oh, a fine man like you must have a wife. What is her name?"

"Francesca," he whispered.

"Francesca would like a last photograph, yes? 'Here was my husband.' So, *tenente*. Can you help me with my map?"

***

She awoke later that night to Georgie stroking her hair as she joined her in bed. At night in their united bed, Georgie tickled her spine to lull her to sleep, stroked her hair to wake her up. "Lucy, love, whatever did you do to Captain Burdock? Aside from refuse his invitation to dinner. Not a wise choice, by the way."

"He's so bloody pompous."

"I filled in for you and we dined at a darling café just up the shore from the Cecil. Fresh fish and *such* nice cheese! A Romanian singer with a guitar. Burdock said you had a POW nearly in sobs today and never batted an eye. I believe the man is frightened of you."

"I'm cold," Lucy said. Georgie pulled her closer and pressed her cheek against Lucy's shoulder, as though they were best mates in boarding school. "No, not that sort of cold. Better not to have attachments, didn't you say? And I'll never see Lark again."

"Never say never. I thought that about Nick."

"Oh, George. Speaking of Nick ...," Lucy said.

Nick was reported to be in the Libyan Desert, filming the war for British Pathé, although Lucy suspected that that was a cover, and a thin one, for intelligence work. He left letters for Georgie at the American Express office in Cairo, and duplicates at the office in Alexandria. Georgie studied them every night. If Lark could be employ pyramidon, she might reveal a hidden message beneath his prose. His straightforward declarations, however, would stir any woman: *If I am killed, at least you will know I never stopped loving you. At least I will die forgiven.*

"What about Nick?" Georgie said. "*What?*"

Lucy nodded at the desk. The letter was addressed to "Miss Georgina Taylor, care of Mrs. Nicholas Lincoln, American Express, Alexandria, Egypt, please hold for pickup." The handwriting was steady (whatever his failings, Georgie's husband had fine handwriting) but the envelope was Red Cross stationery, which had cooled Lucy's enthusiasm, as it must mean Nick was under medical care. Holding it to the light had revealed little, except that the letter was long, longer than it took to write "we regret to inform you," so the news was possibly not dire.

Georgie slid a letter opener very carefully along the glued triangular fold to leave no trace of having opened the letter. *Once a Censorette, always a Censorette.* She scanned the letter hastily, then relaxed and carried it to the window seat.

"'February 14, 1942,'" Georgie read aloud.

My darling,

I am fine. I saw this Red Cross supply truck on its way back east and prevailed upon them to take a letter to you. I hope the stationery didn't alarm you. I am well, aside from the sand and the flies, and the heat and the cold, and the separation from you.

I had hoped I could nip into Alex more often. Rommel's Afrika Corps are—well, I can't say. But we don't want to be caught short. Something big must hit soon. This bloody, bloody war.

We send the shot film back on the trucks who take the wounded in. Fresh film comes to us on supply trucks. If you can find where those trucks are stocked, and get a package to me, I can use half a dozen clean undershirts and handkerchiefs, as many Swiss Army knives as you can get your hands on, any cigarettes—no, I haven't taken up smoking, but they are good to barter with—tape for the tripod if you can find it and felt cloths if you can find them. You know the kind. It's a battle trying to keep the goddamned sand off the lenses."

"Oh, a shopping list!" Georgie raised her head. "I see I *am* a wife again!"

"Can I see?"

Georgie held up the letter. Nick illuminated his letters with sketches, and there it was: a Red Cross supply truck.

"*My darling*," she continued reading. "*I strongly recommend that if Rommel gets any closer to Alex, you and your friend evacuate. If you won't go with the wives to South Africa or Palestine, at least get to Cairo. Don't play the hero. Stay safe. I love you. Nick. P.S. Father Brady saw me writing this. If you could get a bottle or two of wine to him in that package, he'll absolve me of all my sins. Of which I have many, it seems. I am told Jesus, in 40 days and 40 nights, never said 'goddamned sand.' I pointed out that our Lord had no film crew with Him, so we don't know what He got up to. The good Father is stockpiling wine for Easter. I am reminded that Lent has begun, and I am supposed to be repenting for my awful language. Repenting is tiresome, so I must buy indulgences.*"

The second page of the letter contained a sketch of a priest, presumably Father Brady, shaking the last drop from a bottle of wine. Georgie set the letter on the writing desk, fetched a clipboard and stationery, and returned to the window seat. She rested her chin on one raised knee and dangled the other leg. The window seat was her chosen place in the Weston villa. A cushioned ledge along an open arched window, it faced onto the courtyard. Although Lady Weston's description of their accommodations had implied that their quarters would be makeshift, Georgie christened the place her favorite lodgings of the war, even better than the honeymoon suite at the Princess.

Like many Egyptian houses, the Weston's villa turned a white-washed face to the world and hid its beauty inside. The interior courtyard held a fountain from which Lady Weston filled her watering can to quench her bushes of oregano and thyme, her Jerusalem pine and lemon trees, all of which lifted their scent, dawns and dusks, to the second floor bedrooms. When war appeared imminent, Lady Weston had ordered hens from Europe, and added a henhouse to the courtyard.

"The hens have adapted to the heat," Lady Weston said at tea.

Upon accepting the Weston's room and board, Lucy had assumed hen duty, citing her greater experience at Knoll House. Lady Weston, like Granny, chose Russet Blue hens, reknowned for their hardiness and the blue shells of their eggs. Lucy swept up their scat, emptied it at the foot of the Jerusalem pine and lemon trees to fertilize them, then ran the broom lightly over the hens' auburn bodies, to dislodge any loose feathers, while chatting with them, as she might Lady Weston, to settle their fretting. This grooming soothed the hens, and they soon waddled to her, clucking, when she entered the courtyard. Lucy encouraged them into their house at night, fed and watered them, and liberated them in the morning, by which time the Weston's scullery maid had already collected and cooked their eggs.

Lady Weston said, "Hens do *furnish* a courtyard. But a *rooster* seems excessive."

Palm trees shaded the table where the household ate their outdoor breakfast: eggs, fruit, and miraculously strong coffee. "A little spot of England here in Alex," Lady Weston liked to say. Only the crows of the rooster disturbed breakfast. Silence prevailed. The breeze stirred the herbs. Clacking hens waddled to Lucy. Jam and honey was passed, as was goat's milk ("One gets used to it," Major Weston said.) The convalescing soldiers were not permitted to flirt with Georgie and Lucy, or to call them by their Christian names, although Major and Lady Weston, who led all conversation, did. "*In loco parentis,*" Major Weston said over their first gin and tonic. A few days later, he said at breakfast: "Had a chat with your father, Lucy. Well, not a chat, of course," he went on to soothe Lucy's dumbfounded expression. "We exchanged wires. Least I could do for a fellow officer."

Was Major Weston still an active officer? He seemed to command little beyond his thousand-volume library, which he would not allow the convalescing soldiers to browse, although he did from time to time deliver a specific book into a man's hands, with the prescription that he should read it. Lucy was permitted to browse and borrow at will; Georgie had no interest.

"Let him know I had care of his daughter," he added.

"What did he say?" Lucy cleared her throat.

"He said 'See that she continues her Greek.'"

"Her Greek what?" Lady Weston asked.

"I was learning Greek," Lucy said. "Professor Diehl, a friend of my father's, he's a linguist—he studies how people learn languages. He wanted me to learn Greek to see whether it was my ear or my eye that I relied on."

"How extraordinary," Lady Weston said. "But you know so much already!"

"Our girl can barely get by in English." Major Weston flicked his newspaper.

"Now, Hugh. If you would like to continue your Greek, there are certainly enough of them about. Didn't Gregory say a Greek is tutoring little Marina?"

"Cairo, my dear."

"He must know someone in Alex. And what of you, Georgina?"

"Me?" Georgie reluctantly pulled ardent lips away from the rim of her coffee cup. It was extraordinary coffee, raised in Kenya. "My parents died in the flu epidemic. My husband's roaming the desert. There is no one to notify, and I have no desire to learn Greek."

Neither did Lucy, but Georgie told her that night as they prepared for bed that it "wouldn't hurt." Lady Weston found a tutor, and the following Saturday, after breakfast, Lucy had her first session, in the Weston parlor, with the sinewy, sad-eyed Costas, who then walked her to her office by the harbour. For the first time, Lucy was in charge of her own instruction, able to tell her teacher what she needed to learn.

The phrase books distributed to English soldiers to teach them Arabic provided phrases some powers above thought necessary for them to learn, above all other urgent things. They were taught how to address errand boys, how to pick up native girls in nightclubs, how to say "this woman is my harlot." (*El set di khaleelty,* Lucy told one hen while petting another, catching a sharp glare from the cook.)

That morning, Costas taught her, at her request, to say: *My name is Lucy Barrett. I am English. Are the Germans here now? My name is Lucia Gheldini. I am Italian. I am a widow. I work as a translator. Do you have work for me? Are the Americans coming? An American soldier killed my sister.*

On Sunday mornings, Major Hugh shared his newspapers. The soldiers were permitted to make comments on books they had been lent. Sunday morning was also when the nurse made her visits, to check on the soldiers.

Pru was a cheerful Australian nurse at St. Pantaleon's Military Hospital, which was staffed by the Queen Alexandra's Imperial Military Nursing Service, known familiarly as the QAs. The soldiers assumed the ban on flirting did not extend to her. She ignored their saucy remarks as she did the clucks of the roaming hens. The QAs were female military nurses. Pru held the title of Senior Sister, the equivalent of the Army rank of Captain. The soldiers might have remembered this in the hospital but, as Pru pointed out later to Lucy, they had larger concerns, such as coping with life after a rough jitterbug with death. Lady Weston called her "Sister Pru," as though she spoon-fed soup to Christopher Robin at the House at Pooh Corner. The other residents followed suit.

The broken-armed soldier danced the fingers of his good hand across Pru's palm as she took his pulse. The one wounded in the leg tried to dance with her as she walked him toward the fountain. He tripped over a hen and fell. He fell hard. Pru caught him, so that the two of them fell on her rear. She protected his head from hitting the stone patio. Georgie and Lucy rushed to settle him onto the wrought-iron bench. He panted. Sweat beaded his forehead and his upper lip.

"Sister Pru!" Lady Weston called. "Can we help?"

"Bring my bag, please!"

"Clumsy—" the leg wound started to say. Pru pressed a finger to his lips, rolled up his trouser leg and snipped off his gauze bandages. The smell assaulted them as the soldier cried out. Lucy fetched her water glass from the breakfast table.

"Have you heard from your daughter, Lady Weston?" Pru's tone commanded obedience, but her tone reminded Lucy more of Granny steering a dinner party conversation away from awkward lulls than of the bullying nurses in Tessa's ward. "Captain Whiting said she might come for Easter?"

"Captain Whiting's brother ran off with our Felicity," Lady Weston explained to no one. Lucy, handing water to the soldier, wondered that anyone could be charged with absconding with the satisfaction of their hosts. She pressed her hand against the soldier's forehead. It was hot and damp.

"*Ran off?*" Major Weston lowered his newspaper. "If only she *had*. That wedding cost a blessed fortune."

It appeared to be a gunshot wound, Lucy wrote to Lark. *The tissue around it was a dark reddish-brown. When the nurse cleaned the wound, it bubbled like ocean foam. The odor was terrible. The whole time, she chatted about the silliest things, as though we were all at a tea party.*

"One's only daughter," Lady Weston told the lemon tree, as Lucy wiped her hands on a napkin. "We can't be faulted for splashing out. Sister Pru, *do* come for Easter. She'd love to see you. Oh! This *does* look a problem."

She gestured at the soldier's leg, as though it were a dropped serving tray.

"I need your car, Major Weston," Pru said. "Now, please. One of you drive." She spoke to Lucy and Georgie. "Help me carry him." Georgie and Pru hoisted half of the soldier onto Lucy, then they seized his legs. *Thank heaven*, Lucy thought, *for that training on the climbing frame in Bermuda.*

St. Pantaleon's was a hundred-bed hospital which housed rows of soldiers, with a separate ward for officers and a smaller separate ward for prisoners, who were primarily Italian. Pru, Georgie and Lucy carried the leg wound like a lumpy carpet into the reception room, where Captain Whiting met them and lifted the soldier from their arms as though he were a child.

"The Westons called ahead," he said to Pru. "What's happening?"

"You won't like how it's healing, Captain. You," she said to Georgie. "Get back to the car. You can't leave a car unattended in Alex, especially not Major Weston's. Drive it back. I'll come back to finish my check-ups."

"I'll walk you," Lucy said.

"You'll walk *me!*" Pru exclaimed. "You couldn't find the tip of your nose here in Alex. I heard you were living in—"

Captain Whiting, laying the leg wound on a gurney with a gentleness equal to the strength it took to lift him, interrupted, "I need you first, Senior Sister. You," He jerked his chin at Lucy. "Wait here."

They rolled the gurney through swinging doors. Lucy, bookless and agitated, ventured into a ward. QAs scurried past, carrying bedpans, carrying pitchers, rolling carts of medication from bed to bed. Soldiers read, slept, moaned, played cards, sighed at the ceiling.

"Hullo, Miss," a soldier said from his bed. "Are you visiting someone?"

"I could do," Lucy said. "Shall I visit you?"

March 1, 1942

The Hon. Judge Rupert Barrington-Smith
c/o Paul Barrett
Claridge's
London

Dear Judge Barrington-Smith

Please forgive my previous letter. It was a draft posted in error by one of my fellow Censorettes. What I wrote was never intended for your eyes. I was in shock, and am only now coming to terms with the loss of Ruth.

I have asked my father to locate and deliver this to you. I'm sure he would not approve of what I am going to say next. It is this: I believe that Ruth's death came at the hands of a member of the American forces stationed on the island. I believe it was an accident, an impulsive act. But it was still murder. The man in question has a temper and a tendency to violence. His name is Lt. Bill Inman. He all but confessed just moments before I took off in an airplane from Bermuda.

Again, I apologize for my earlier words. I am no one to tell another how to love. But as far as I know how to love, I loved Ruth. She was a tender girl. Tender can mean both kind and easily hurt. She was both. I send you my sincere regards.

Very truly yours,
Lucia Barrett

March 1, 1942

Miss Rebecca Lark
102 W. 96th Street
New York, New York, USA

Dear, dear Lark,

I am sorry this letter is short. I am writing it at the bedside of a patient. I visit the local Army hospital. The head surgeon gives me very fishy looks. Be friendlier to visitors, when you are running a hospital! Visitors mean no harm!

How are your studies? I am sorry to add to your work. But you are there and I am here. We must make Bill answer for what he has done.

I've asked my father for what assistance he can provide in England—mainly by pressing the matter with Ruth's father. But you are in America. Your mail will get to Bermuda more quickly. I think Bill is still in Bermuda. The Yanks will need that airfield. And what Alan was doing (must make it past the censor!) Find out if Bill is still in Bermuda. Write to Archie Danville, your minister at St. Andrew's, Clara Frith and Louis Furbert. Bill's superior officer was Captain Daniel Jackson. It's taken me days to remember that, but I knew it was someone from the Bible, and an American president.

I will write to all of these people myself as well, but your letters will reach them more quickly.

Bill has no real alibi for the morning Ruth was killed. Alan said he met Bill at the golf course to determine whether the course was too wet to proceed with their Army-Navy golf game. But what time was that? How did Bill arrive? By bicycle?

I must close soon to get this letter in the pouch. What else to tell. Georgie and I are finding our rhythm here in Alexandria. Sometimes at night we can hear the guns in the Western Desert. Georgie enjoys a bit of night life. I prefer to be here, or at home. Our host has a vast library, and it does relieve my mind. I hope you, too, are mixing some fun into your studies. Have you taken the "A" train to Harlem to see Duke Ellington? I know Alan would like that!

> Write to me soon,
> Lucy

March 1, 1942

Miss Marcia Barrett
Knoll House
Knollborough, England

My dear little sister,

Here is what I would like you to do until you hear from me again. Sing. Play piano. Cultivate your garden. Climb the walnut trees. Mind Granny. Mind my cat Horatio. Stay strong. Work hard. Remember what Churchill said, 'Victory, in spite of all terror.'

I wish I had been a better sister in idler, peacetime days. But I had my studies, and I suppose I thought we had world enough and time.

For now, on Sundays, I visit the military hospital here. I write letters for the men. Some are not interested in writing letters, so I sit with them and write my own, like this one.

*With much love from,
Your sister Lucia*

The men "not interested in writing letters" at St. Pants shuddered with fever from infections from their wounds or endured agonizing burns from having been "brewed up" in their tanks in the Western Desert. The burn victims, beyond help, were placed on their cots like mummies—heavily bandaged, heavily anesthetized. For the men more able, she transcribed dictated letters, offered water and bedpans. For the latter two activities, she had been roundly scolded by the QAs. *(Do NOT give water to men with stomach wounds! You are NOT qualified to carry bodily fluids about in the corridor!)* When she addressed Pru as "Senior Sister," she was answered, "Don't be daft, Lucy. And mind that bedpan goes in the disposal sink, not the other one, ta."

The QAs considered her underfoot, although they tolerated her performance of the worst tasks. On days when she did not visit the patients, she carried soiled linen to the laundry, and then folded fresh sheets and towels and placed them in neat stacks on the shelves in the rectangular airing cupboard which housed the linen of St. Pantaleon's. She dealt with the flypaper posted at every window, stripped down the ones clotted with struggling insects, and carried them to the incinerator, tacked up new ones, a tedious, Sisyphean chore that the QAs could not carry out because of the risk of carrying the toxins into the operating theater. The hospital employed janitors and maids, but they might as well have been asked to sweep sand off the desert, as to keep the place clean.

When the QAs observed that she flinched at no task, Lucy was graduated to sitting with men while they ate their meals, spoon-feeding the hand-wounded, encouraging them to eat and chat. She noted on their clipboards how much they ate. The Matron conceded that she was "somewhat helpful" in communicating with the hospitalized Italian prisoners.

She sat at the bedside of a lance corporal with a land-mine-shredded lower leg, twitching and moaning his way out of a sedative, when she wrote to Ruth's father and Marcia.

Her patient lurched into a sitting position from his uneasy sleep. He squeezed her hand so hard she had to swallow her cry of pain. (*Do NOT touch the patients!*)

"Do you need a bedpan? Don't be shy. We're all friends here."

He shook his head. "You're an angel, Miss."

"Listen, Corporal. I've tucked two letters into your kit bag. Could you mail them, when you get home. I've left money for the postage."

"Too steamy for the censor, eh?"

"Such a bother, censors. Lie back and think of England, as they used to say to the bride. I'll fetch a Sister."

She hurried from the ward. The lance corporal would return, on the next hospital ship, to the green of England. Whether his festering lower leg would go with him provided a popular topic of debate at the QA office. Amputate here, at the knee, and stop the risk of the infection spreading, or risk shipping him home, if the hospital ship made it through the Mediterranean, if the infection could be stayed at all. In England, should she be reached, the leg might be saved. Or the whole leg might be lost because of the choice to wait. The QAs discussed these factors as calmly as they offered bids during the bridge games they played, in their fluid-stained smocks, when they went off duty but were too agitated to go home. Their debate was the only cool aspect of that sweltering hospital.

Sister Pru slept, slumped over a desk. A radio on a shelf played jazz.

"'allo, Barrett!" a QA sang out. "How's your gangrene?"

"Is it time for his morphine? He's in …" She trailed off. *What was there to say? "In pain"? So were they all.*

Pru raised her head, her eyes crusted with sleep. "Turn that wireless up, will ya? Duke Ellington? Who could be playing *that*?"

The most easily captured radio frequencies came from Italy which, like Germany, had declared jazz "degenerate." When another QA turned up the volume, Lucy heard a tune that Alan Dodd had played at the Princess dances, a trumpet accompanied by a soft drum and a strummed guitar. In this version, after a long instrumental opening, a singer chimed in, "*Do nothing till you hear from me …*"

Lucy demonstrated dance steps to the weary QAs. After she spun Pru, she pulled her back in, and slid her other hand from Pru's shoulder down her spine, to her bottom.

Now the tune was backed by a full orchestra and piano, who played several verses before a singer burst in, "Do nothing 'till you hear from me …"

"Be ready for this, mind." Lucy stroked Pru's bottom. "A Yank won't keep his hands to himself."

They backed into Captain Whiting, blood-stained hands in the air and a bemused expression on his face. The QAs leapt to him.

"Captain Whiting!" Pru replaced his stained smock with a new one, which bore laundered but vivid signs of its exposure to bile and blood, while another Sister ran to fetch a basin for his hands. The QAs were devoted to him. He had a temper. But it was directed at the bloody infection and the goddamned sand, factors which thwarted his progress, his work. His suspicion extended to his patients. If they would only tell the truth, lie still, not scratch, not question his decisions. Lucy liked the sound of his voice and his reasonable tone, but thought she would not like to be his patient because of the way he presented patients to the QAs as a collection of defiance: *This fever hasn't improved. This wound is too slow to heal, how often are you changing the bloody bandages?* But, he gave no false assurances, never said *right as rain in no time.* There was no rain to be right as; if there had been, there would have been less goddamned sand getting into their wounds and bloody infecting them.

She thought of John Whiting at bedtime, one of the few moments she had to herself between the chatter of Weston cocktails and the humming of Georgie in bed. She washed, dabbed her cheeks and neck with Drewe's cold cream, surveyed her face and pictured his: his olive skin, short black hair, wary grey eyes. When he noticed her at all, it was with the startled frown he bestowed on anyone not of the hospital. He was unfriendly to outsiders, the Red Cross, the gin-scented officers who strolled through to "buck up spirits." She thought of him when Captain Burdock tumbled into his clichés: *wrong end of the stick, ship-shape and Bristol fashion, begin as you mean to go on.* John Whiting would never rely on such banal utterances. She found herself thinking of him when her thoughts were needed more urgently elsewhere.

Lucy asked the Westons. He was the brother of their son-in-law Gregory. He was how they had come to host convalescing soldiers, why their chickens had not been confiscated, nor their cranky cook.

"Not sociable," Lady Weston said. "Had a bad time in England, they say."

"Clever," Major Weston said. "Running that hospital at his age."

"Terribly shy," Lady Weston said. "At Felicity's wedding. He only danced with our Fliss and his sisters, do you remember?"

Lucy asked Burdock, after an afternoon on which she had failed to extract any useful intelligence from a clean-shaven Italian prisoner with clipped raven hair, whose superior air, all too familiar, nearly drove her to tears. Burdock, sympathizing with her defeat (*"More shout than shoot, these Eye-ies! Anyroad, plenty more fish in the sea,"*) walked her from the jail to the Cecil Hotel for the drink she had at last consented to have with him. Cecil also happened to be the name of the *paterfamilias* of the Whiting clan. Burdock stroked his mustache as he uttered *paterfamilias,* as though he expected his word of Latin to impress a Cambridge girl. The Whitings were a prominent family of Cairo, the father an English diplomat, the mother an Italian-Egyptian aristocrat. There were six children, three sons. The boys were sent to school at Repton, then Sandhurst. Gregory and his twin Michael were captains in the British Army; John was an Army surgeon. Three daughters: two married, one a child still at home.

John bore the accent of his English education, and the privileges which came with his father's position and his mother's wealth. His aloofness might have been born at Repton—even Matty, who withstood Harrow, thought Repton "rough"—or perhaps in the Army. It might have been that his name was a few hues lighter than his skin. But he carried his solitude with him like the long shadow thrown at midday.

Lucy asked Pru, over a bottle of wine at a café on the Rue des Soeurs. Pru deftly diagnosed the inquiry, despite Lucy's effort to make it sound casual.

"Have a 'pash,' do we? He *is* a bit of a dish. He does see us, know what I mean? The QAs like him. He tells us why as well as what."

Lucy envisioned John meeting Ruth, how patiently he would solicit explanations of her odder pronouncements.

"The gangrene case," John was telling the nurses. "We have to take that leg. Someone prep him. Not you, Pru. Go home. You're dead on your feet."

"The lance corporal?" Lucy asked. She was rewarded with a scoff that she would be so ridiculous as to expect him to recall a *rank* among the severings, sepsis, and fevered deaths. She leapt into his path as he tried to stride away. "How much of the leg? Can you keep his knee?"

"Why are you here?" He glared up and down the height of her.

"If it were my leg, I'd want my knee."

"Sweetheart?"

She smarted at his use of *sweetheart*. He didn't seem the type to dismiss her with demeaning endearments.

"His sweetheart, are you?" he pressed.

"She volunteers here," Pru called out. "Jolly help! Does all sorts of nasty tasks."

"Don't we all." John walked toward the surgery.

"Captain Whiting!" Lucy called. "The knee?"

"Yes, yes," he answered without turning around. "I'll try to save his bloody knee."

March 15, 1942
Mr. Paul Barrett
Claridge's Hotel
London, UK

Dear Father,

Please determine the whereabouts of Lieutenant William Inman, U.S. Army Corps of Engineers. He was stationed at Bermuda while I was there. He might still be there now. They are building an airfield and I imagine that would be of strategic importance. His captain is Daniel Jackson. Shortly before I left, Bill confessed to me that he had murdered one of my roommates, Ruth Smith. She is the daughter of His Honour Judge Barrington-Smith. I have written to him as well but have received no reply. Please contact him. I cannot tell if he hasn't forgiven me for my reproachful letter to him, or if it is only the mail. He will confirm that his daughter was murdered on the island. Please find Inman.

Ruth was my dear friend. I will not give up until the murder of Ruth receives justice. I think you can understand how grief can make one persistent to a task, however misguided, that may appear to remedy it.

With my profound love,
Lucia

Her letter to her grandmother added:

I have written to Daddy and asked him for a favor. I ask that the next time you see him, you remind him of it. It is perhaps less easy to ignore a mother than it is a daughter. I hope to find this out one day.

I trust all of you are well, as am I.
With my love and prayers to you all

She scrolled the letters together, sat back, and rubbed her tired eyes. The lance corporal, leg amputated to the knee, had shipped out with the last batch of the wounded. She sat by the bed of a new patient, a man twitching with malarial fever.

"Doctor," she heard a man say in Greek, several beds down. "If the pretty lady sits with me, I will drink your *something something.*"

"The QAs are not here to be pretty," she heard John respond, also in Greek. "They are here to make you well." A brief silence, then, "Oh. Her. She's not a nurse."

"The men are happy when she *something something something.*" Lucy looked at them. The Greek soldier waved a merry greeting to her. John stood over his bed, holding a glass of cloudy water. She smiled weakly and waved back.

"She is beautiful," the Greek told John. *Eínai ómorfee.*

"Yes." John motioned her over and handed her the glass.

"Get him to drink this," he told her in English. "It's vile. But he needs to be sedated. He keeps scratching at his wounds. Then go home. You look awful. And stop petting the men!" he snapped, as Lucy took the hand of the Greek. "Half of them are contagious."

He strode away. Lucy watched until he was out of earshot. She said to the Greek, in Greek, "Drink."

His face was peppered in scabs. They appeared to be healing shrapnel wounds.

He smiled, drank, grimaced at the taste, and handed the glass back to her.

"Thank you," he said.

"You're welcome," she said in Greek. "Now sleep."

"You have good Greek," he said.

Good Greek? She had spoken six words.

"You come again?" he asked.

"I come again," she said. "If you help me with my Greek."

35.

Georgie was a different woman from the one Lucy had known in Bermuda. (*A different girl*, Lucy wrote to Lark, *you'd hardly recognize her. More like Alice than like the Cheshire cat we knew.*) She was surprisingly freckled and tanned for someone who worked a "tedious translation job" in an office, which was how she claimed she spent her days. Their shared bedroom sprouted headscarves, mainly black ones, and Lucy had spotted her more than once returning from her supposedly dreary office in a long black dress, wearing a black head covering with her head bent, her normally athletic stride reduced to an unfamiliar plodding. She would fool no one up close, but the demi-camouflage blended her into a crowd. When Lucy challenged her, Georgie claimed that she was learning the footpaths of the city, and flourished a copy of E.M. Forster's guidebook of Alexandria to prove it.

Lucy suspected that Georgie was in fact sniffing out fifth columnists. In the meantime, *eat, drink, and be merry, for tomorrow we may die.* At night when she returned from her adventures—chaste, she assured Lucy, but adventurous—she sat on the window seat in white pajamas, her fair hair braided, biting the corner of her lip, as she wrote letters to her husband.

"You're staring." Georgie looked up from her letter. "When you next write to Lark, tell her you're staring again. She always disliked it."

"I've asked Lark to have Bill investigated."

"Does she have that power, as an American medical student?"

"I've asked her to write to Archie Danville."

"Archie considers the matter closed."

"Do you?"

"The matter of bringing a serving American Army officer to justice for a crime he says he didn't commit, I'm afraid I have to agree. The matter you're carrying around like an open wound is another thing entirely."

March 24, 1942

My most cherished Celestina,

You see from the stationery that I have been wounded. I am in the St. Pantaleon Hospital in Alexandria. No one here seems to have heard of St. Pantaleon. Not even the kind lady writing this letter out for me knows him, and she knows so many things. St. Pantaleon is the patron saint of physicians. He was tortured to death. I ought not to mention this to my poor lonely wife, I realize, but at least the sufferings of this saint put mine in perspective. My eyes are not hurt, which is the most important thing. My face, which only you ever found handsome, will heal. Bones are broken, flesh is torn, but my heart is only and eternally yours."

His heart was his own matter, Lucy thought as she wrote out his words. (Just as Dr. Johnson wrote that when a man knows he is to be hanged in a fortnight, it concentrates his mind wonderfully, she wrote to Lark, so does a soldier's prospect of a final letter reveal sentiments he rarely expressed while home.) His heart was his, but his other organs, shredded by a grenade, would soon end him. Pru had nipped by with an IV gurney upon learning that Lucy was in, as the patient's blood type was B positive and so was Lucy's. Lucy gave her left arm to Pru and her right arm to this patient's dying words.

"Men complain of the long days in the desert. They don't understand that the desert comes alive at night. We sleep in the heat of the afternoon and lay awake at night exposed to the sky. I can sometimes see the Pleiades and think of the lectures of Professore Gheldini—' Signorina? Che cosa c'e?"

Lucy had stopped scratching at the spot where Pru had drained her blood, had stopped writing.

"Professore Gheldini? *Matteo* Gheldini? At the University of Padua?"

"*Si si.* I was a student there. This is how I meet my wife."

"But that's my *Nonno!*" Lucy felt light-headed. "*My* Aunt Celestina!

"*Si si,* she is named for her great-aunt Celestina."

"Then, we must be cousins! What is the name of your fa—?" Lucy jumped to her feet in stupid elation, felt an electric surge up her spine, and heard a faint "*Signorina?*" before she tumbled forward.

***

Lucy awoke in a heavenly collar of ice. She sat on a bulging bag of laundry, propped against another bag, surrounded by more lumpy bags of unwashed linens, enshrouded by small tents of flapping curtains of drying sheets hung on clotheslines. She recognized the curtains from her folding. She was in an alley outside the hospital laundry.

John sat on a folding chair, against a lavender sky streaked with fingers of orange as the sun sank behind them in the Western Desert. He straightened when he saw her shift the ice packs behind her head. A bleachy mist wafted over them. She guessed, from the heap of chicken bones near his chair, and the skinny tabby cat butting his head against John's shin, that this was his place of refuge.

"Keep that ice on," he ordered. "Drink this."

He handed her a glass of lemonade, on ice, both tart and oversweet, but as delicious as a longed-awaited kiss. She finished it in four gulps.

"If you're prone to fainting," he said. "You have no business in a hospital."

"That patient—the Italian prisoner—he's married to a woman who's some sort of a cousin to me," Lucy said. "But then I suppose Italy is full of my cousins."

"You collapsed across his bed. If you hadn't had the sense to fall in that direction, you'd've cracked your head on the floor and be taking up a bed and we can't spare a bed."

Italy is full of my cousins, she repeated to herself. Let John prattle on about beds. It was a good line, one she might produce during the next prisoner interrogation. *I am only a woman, tenente. I cannot be expected to understand such things.* Lucy licked at the iced lemon in her drink. *Your war is over. You will lose. Help us.* These short sentences she would deliver like slaps. *This battle must end. How it drags on! When will I see my cousins again? Italy is full of my cousins.*

"Miss Barrett!"

Lucy pulled her attention back to John, who held out a bar of sesame seeds glued together with honey. "Sorry. Miles away."

"I can see that. Eat this." When she shook her head at it, he said, "You need the sugar. Did you eat breakfast?"

Breakfast at the Westons had been mixed that morning. They received the news that the leg wound patient who had brought Lucy to St. Pants in the first place had died from his infections the night before. Georgie fielded the excitement of the Westons' post, in which daughter Felicity revealed that she was in a delicate condition. *Another Whiting for this blighted world*, Lucy thought. She wondered if John knew about the new Whiting and concluded not yet. A daughter would tell a mother before a brother told a brother.

"Pru said you gave blood," the Whiting before her said. "When did you last donate?"

"Erm ... two weeks ago?"

"You *idiot*. You must wait two *months*. I thought you had Red Cross training?"

"No, that's the other one," Lucy said. "Georgie. The blonde."

"Why are you *here* all the time, then? Do you dislike the Westons?"

"Of course not. They're lovely. And that library——"

"That *library*!" John said, the first enthusiasm she had seen from him.

She rattled the ice to hurry its melting. "I come here to be useful."

"Why?"

"Why be *useful*? That's a funny question from a doctor in a war."

"Exactly. I run this hospital. You could be anywhere. But you come here and spend your spare time with wounded men."

All men are wounded, she almost said, and would have, had

John seemed the sort to welcome Noel Coward-type banter. But he wasn't. And it wasn't so much a quip as a truth. All men *were* wounded. All women, too.

"I provide some comfort to them," she said instead. "And the QAs appreciate the help."

"And there was someone, some time ago," he said in the same measured tone with which she pictured him questioning his patients: *chest pain? Shortness of breath?* "Someone you didn't comfort. Didn't help. Is that it? Atonement? But why are you *here?*"

"I've just told you—"

"No, in *Alex.* Most women like you have been evacuated. How did you end up here, if a husband didn't drag you? Propaganda? No. Too earnest."

"I have languages."

"Oh yes?" His look was one of such practiced diagnostic inquiry—*go on*—that she half-expected him to raise her wrist and take her pulse. "Which?"

"Italian. French. German. Some Greek."

He gave a nearly Gallic shrug, an impresario hearing a C major scale, with the expression Lucy's father wore when he said *Reasonably well-informed. For an American.*

She was surprised at her indignation. "What languages do *you* have?"

"Well, *Italian.*" He double-flicked his hand, a brief *shoo* at Italian, which presumably everyone spoke. Even the tabby cat twining his ankles could *miao* on demand. "Arabic. French. Some Greek."

"Yes, I heard you chatting with that Greek."

"I also have ancient Greek. For my degree. But in my day-to-day practice, I seldom see ancient Greeks."

The "seldom" set her off, as though from time to time grouchy Achilles washed in from Troy. Lucy dropped her face onto the back of her hand, with a laugh so out-of-practice that it hurt her stomach. When she calmed, John had re-donned his stiff manner, like a freshly laundered surgeon's mask.

"Hardly *that* funny."

"I made a joke once to my brother. He did Classics at Cambridge. I did Modern Languages. He thought his degree was *so* superior. But when the war started I told him, 'Yes, that'll come in quite handy when the Nazis invade Ancient Greece.'"

"So you were laughing at your own wit."

"Somebody should," she said, which at least drew a smile from him.

"Turkish," he said.

"What?"

"Languages."

"You weren't finished?"

"Some Berber. In those, I can only say doctor things. Like 'How long have you had this pain?' Or, 'I need to listen to your heart.' Or 'You can't save the world.' We learn that quickly, we doctors. I'm sorry you've had to learn it, too."

The tender shift in his tone summoned her tears, which scrimmed her view of him as he stood. He reached for her hand. *A kindness at last*, she thought, before he placed his middle finger on her wrist. He was taking her pulse.

"I had a friend at my last posting—" Lucy began. "I had a friend …"

"Sssh."

He studied his watch. After a moment, he released her, pressed his fingers against the pulse on her neck, pressed her forehead with the back of his hand.

"In my professional opinion, Miss Barrett, you should go out. Half the officers in the Eighth Army must be queueing up. Go dine at the Alex Yacht Club, instead of getting underfoot here. Drink cocktails at the Cecil. Stroll the beach at El-Agami. Go to the cinema, for heaven's sake! I love the cinema. And now I must get back to my actual patients. Keep the ice on until it melts before you even *think* of standing up. And then, go home."

"Why don't you take me?" she blurted.

"What?"

"To the sands of El-Agami. The cinema. Take me."

"'*Had we but world enough and time*,'" he said, one foot on the step to the laundry room, then snapped, when she stood up, "What are you doing? Sit down. And keep that ice on."

Then Lucy remembered the Italian prisoner. *My most dear Celestina ...* When Lucy reached his bed, she saw that his body had been removed. The orderlies peeled back his soaked sheets, and a Red Cross volunteer, collecting his dog tags, made to crumple the letter Lucy had been writing for him. Lucy snatched it away.

"Can you wait while I finish it? It's a letter to his wife."

"She'll be notified through proper channels."

"I'm sure she'd like his last words."

"An Eye-Tie with an Eye-Tie wife. Why should I be bothered with what she'd like?"

The volunteer, too young for her sourness, tried to *shoo* Lucy as Whiting had *shooed* at Italian, but Lucy caught her wrist and barely stopped herself from pressing that pulse point with which Georgie had briefly paralyzed her in the lobby of the Princess Hotel.

"Because it's no skin off your nose to wait five minutes," Lucy hissed. "And when this war is over, we'll all have to answer for how we behaved to one another, bloody friend or bloody foe. Now will you wait or would you prefer to have the use of only one hand for the next eight weeks?"

Patients in the adjoining beds raised their heads. Lucy sat on the wires of the bedframe and used an overturned bedpan as her writing desk, to finish the letter, assuring *Celestina* that her name had been her husband's dying word.

"*Brava, signorina*," one of the patients said.

She heard him translating to the ward what had transpired between Lucy and the volunteer. She heard, as well, a feeble clapping from the patients who were capable of it, but only lifted her head, when she had handed the completed letter to the Red Cross volunteer. They wouldn't be clapping, Lucy told herself, if they knew how Celestina would play a central role in her next interrogation.

36.

The Westons held a traditional Easter drinks and dinner party, allowing their assorted guests and patients to drift in from their various religious services, should they choose to worship, should they, indeed, choose to stay in Alex at all with General Rommel nearly at the city gates. Prior to Easter dinner, they held a Palm Sunday breakfast. So sanguine were the shopkeepers of Alexandria regarding the possibility of the transfer of power from one set of foreigners to another that certain shops were filled with the traditional Italian goods for Easter, in anticipation of their new conquerors, or liberators. Still, Lady Weston's cook, required many things for the feast, and so their Felicity arrived a fortnight early on the train with a peacetime volume of luggage, as well as hampers of tins and jars and cheeses, chatter and kisses and gossip.

"You'll never guess who I came up on the train with." Sir Hugh handed her a gin and tonic and Lady Weston propped her daughter's feet on a footstool. "Little Marina! The youngest Whiting girl. She's been sent here out of Cairo to stay with that *grim* aunt of hers in that *yummy* house where John lives. Some sort of scandal. Apparently, Marina's tutor gave her the most *unsuitable* reading material! The parents wanted to sack him but Marina went on a *hunger strike*. They couldn't bear the drama, so they shipped her here for the Easter hols."

"Marina?" Lady Weston said. "The little flower girl at your wedding? Bit simple?"

"No, she's quite a brainy thing. Bookish. She's excited about coming for Easter. She's mad about your library, Pa. Both of them are coming Sunday for breakfast. And she's awfully eager to meet you two."

It took a moment for Lucy and Georgie to register that Felicity was addressing them. They had been exchanging silent questions, head-tilts toward the door during this "after-dinner drink with our Felicity," to which Lady Weston had invited them and at which they seemed so superfluous. *Should they leave the Westons to family time?* But Felicity beamed directly at them. They met each other's eyes once again, and looked over their shoulders, like actors in a farce, to see if a more compelling pair had materialized in the arched doorway behind them.

"Mummy's written so much about you!" Felicity told them. "A pair of Sphinxes! So *mysterious!* Not like me, eh, Pa? And you're staying in my old room! So nice for the parents. I was afraid they'd be lonely without me. No, no," she waved at them. "I don't want it back. Greg and I can bunk in the parlor. I understand the soldiers have the best guest rooms. Well, there's a war on! We must all make sacrifices!" She shook her head. "Imagine! A *hunger strike* over some naughty poem! We're already *rationed!*"

She sipped her gin and tonic and bit into a lemon cake. Lucy glanced at Georgie, who she knew was calculating the cost of every stitch Felicity wore. Felicity had lost the use of the best guest room, and Lucy had lost Ruth. *We all must make sacrifices!* Would Felicity have lost a Ruth? Of course not, Felicity would never have *had* a Ruth. Ruth would have been cowed by Felicity's capacity to fill a room, but privately pleased, Lucy thought, that she lived up to her virtue name.

John was coming to the house. Later in bed, Lucy would have liked to confide in Georgie, but Georgie was already murmuring down a path into the slumbering world. As Georgie's breathing settled, Lucy punched her pillow, tugged at the covering sheet. She wished she could wake Georgie and ask her about falling in love, if indeed that was what Lucy was experiencing. Maybe she was merely in thrall. Maybe John was merely the first person she'd met who seemed so like her: fed an intense education which bewildered the world. His lips grew tight when infection conquered healing: "You've got to keep them clean! Clean!" she had seen him snap at a QA over the freshly dead body. "These bloody infections! It's the only way we can fight this, the only way we can even hope to—"

"Yes, Captain Whiting. Yes, we know." The QA had guided John away from the lost patient. Another nurse covered the soldier's face with his sheet and drew the curtains around his cot as they wheeled out the body.

And maybe that was what John needed, a calm QA-type, a woman who would soothe, not match, his drive and his frustration. Maybe John, like his brother, needed a Felicity, whose ebullience would butter his daily bread. Maybe he didn't need a Lucy, fueled by her own anger and grief?

Maybe she should avoid the hospital. There was enough translation work for her, in the time between interrogations. There were lessons with Costas, who met her at a café by the harbour where they drink tiny cups of coffee so strong that Lucy had to douse hers in syrup just to get it down. There was Major Weston's library. There was Cairo, which she had yet to visit, just a train ride away. There were the *Pyramids*. The *Nile*. There was no need to keep visiting St. Pant's, if she was such a bother there.

But still, John was coming to the house Sunday.

37.

London, 1940

Marcia weeps over her homework. Chemistry is pointless. Her only consolation is that Lucy was never brilliant at it. Marcia struggles at St. Paul's, where Lucy's matriculation is recent enough that the faculty welcomes the younger Barrett girl with expectations she cannot fulfill. She flounders at all the subjects in which Lucy excelled, does well only in math and music. Lucy tries to create a memory game—perhaps a song?—to aid Marcia in learning the periodic table of the elements. Lucy drilled it into herself, as she drilled the future perfect, the imperfect, the past perfect of her French, Latin and German. But, aside from a fiendish forbearance for scales and exercises on the piano, Marcia has little tolerance for drilling.

She is saved by a call from her father to join him in his study. She never thought she would regard a summons to her father's study as a "save," but she has graduated, she hopes, from lectures on behavior, just as she has graduated from Cambridge. She works with Karolina Diehl finding housing for refugees in London, and has entered an application to join the WRENS. Matty has been missing since Dunkirk. Tessa just that day entered the hospital. As soon as Marcia scrapes through this term, she will be sent to Knoll House (and the village school in Knollborough), for the duration. As Lucy enters Paul's study, he is soothing the bratty cat Charmian into his armchair, covering her with a cashmere shawl. Normally, a fire is lit in his study, but private fires, even if one could find the fuel, are forbidden. Further, most cats and dogs were killed last year, close to a million in just one week, in preparation for food shortages, but Paul forbade this destruction of the Barrett pride.

"Daddy, could you help Marcia with her chemistry? It was never one of my subjects—"

Paul says, "We need to talk about Guy Jenner."

"Oh?"

"He's not for you. The Jenners are fools. Their hopes of merging the estates—positively *feudal*. Say what you will about Mama, but she's got a firm hand on the till. She manages our land like someone, someone—"

"To the manner born?" Lucy suggests. She sits on the love seat.

"I thought they would give up when I didn't marry Veronica."

Professore Gheldini, a visiting lecturer at Cambridge, presented a talk on developments in celestial navigation. Paul Barrett, still in the Navy but not yet immersed in Naval Intelligence, chaperoned a group of undergraduates from Dartmouth to this lecture. The reception afterwards was hosted by Gheldini's youngest daughter, Maria Theresa, called Tessa, newly sprung from her Florentine convent boarding school, to keep his house in Cambridge. She happily stocked his larder, prepared his breakfasts and dinners and feasted, otherwise, on the offerings of the university. As the daughter of faculty, she was permitted to attend lectures—professors were flattered when she chose their class, delighted when she returned—plays, concerts and evensong.

Shakespeare, choirs, stars and Paul. No literal ink stains, no exams, no declension, no late-night cramming, no impossible translations. Tessa's Cambridge was a midsummer night's dream. This is one of many reasons Lucy feels she cannot rely on her mother for advice on love or marriage. *I knew at once, so handsome*, Tessa purred unhelpfully the first time that Lucy asked her about the facts of life. Between Matty's friends and her time at Cambridge, Lucy encountered many handsome boys but had wanted from them only kisses, perhaps a bit of *caressa Tessa*, but certainly not the task of beguiling them into allowing her to commit her life to providing an orderly sanctuary for their return from the clamorous world of business or politics.

"I wasn't meant to fall in love," Paul is saying. "I was meant to make an alliance. But Tessa … I suppose the bloody Jenners are still hoping to merge that land. The cheek! How many acres have they managed to hang on to?"

"How should I know?"

"You had dinner with Guy Jenner last week at his father's club."

"Naval Intelligence has nothing better to do? There is a war on."

"If you wanted it to be kept secret, why go to his father's *club?*"

"Yes, we dined. No, we did not talk about acreage."

They had also made love afterwards, at the Jenners' "place in town." It seemed imperative to make love, with bombs dropping all around, to have that experience of life when life seemed so precarious, to indulge in lovemaking with someone as familiar, as skilled in touching her, as Guy. She represses a shiver when she recalls his long, stroking caresses, down her back and over her flanks.

"Not even half of the 500 they had when I was meant to marry Veronica, I suppose," Paul was saying. "Squandered it. They spend and spend. The Land Girls are working their land now, tilling all that sheep pasture into crops. At least the land's well-fertilized! Well, on their own head be it. George never accepted a word of advice and all this time they've no more fiscal sense than Marcia. How is she, by the way?"

"What?"

Lucy is bewildered. Does he leap from topic to topic this way when he talks to Tessa, during those conferences behind the closed doors of his study? Or does he talk this way this way from nerves, Matty missing, Tessa in the hospital, as the medical staff prepares to remove her womb. What they had hoped was another child turned out instead to be a constellation of tumors. Within a week, the doctors will perform a full hysterectomy.

"Marcia!" Paul repeats. "How is she coping?"

"She's crying over her homework."

"You must help her."

"Well, you called me down here. Also, it's chemistry."

"You must be kind to her."

"I'm not unkind."

"She admires you so. Of course. Tessa and I did such a good job with you."

Paul lifts the whisky decanter from the sideboard and sets a glass on his desk. He lifts another glass, and an eyebrow: an invitation. Lucy is pleased. She has only been permitted wine at dinner or brandy after dinner, and then only in company.

"I like to think," she says, "that *I* had something to do with it."

She accepts her whisky and they clink glasses.

"And don't entertain any thoughts of an elopement with Guy Jenner."

"Elope—Daddy—I was *sixteen*! That was four years ago! The summer you sent me away! I've hardly seen him since!"

Except for that dinner at the club where, come to think of it, Guy had looked dashing in his uniform—all the boys did, clipped and scrubbed, with their veneer of bravado. He had been more subdued and deferential than she remembered. He had paid her compliments, sighed that he had still not found "the right girl," extracted a promise that she would to write to him when he received his orders. In response, she had made appropriate noises, too preoccupied about her mother going under the knife, and her own imminent intimacy with Guy, to spare much worry for Guy's assignment.

"You're to have a proper wedding but *only* when you find the right man and *only* after I have approved it."

"I have no intention of marrying Guy. Nor did he ask me to. Happy?"

"Yes. Thank you. He might still. You know what Dr. Johnson says. The prospect of shipping out concentrates the mind wonderfully. Yes," Paul nods at her startled look. "He ships out soon. George tried to pull strings but the Admiralty is not a marionette. Now, now," he quells the question Lucy is forming, "You know I can't tell you where. Loose lips sink ships, and so on. Just keep your lips away from Jenner."

Too late for that.

"Now," Paul says. "Let's see if we can't help your sister. Chemistry?"

38.

Alexandria, 1942

Lucy tried to exhaust herself on the Saturday before Palm Sunday, lingering after her shift at the translation office, running errands for Lady Weston, staying late at St. Pants where, blessedly, John was absent. She joined Pru and her ambulance driver boyfriend for a drink, and then another, at a taverna. They were both at once exhausted and stimulated, hazards of the trade, Lucy reckoned. As they leaned on one another a moment too long, laughed at private jokes a little too raucously, Lucy saw that they were fellow warriors, finding refuge in one another. They spent their days with bodies and blood, with more defeats than victories, and though spiritually bruised, they were not as haunted as she.

Thou know'st 'tis common. All that lives must die/Passing through nature to eternity ... why seems it so particular with thee?

"*Seems?*'" Lucy read later in Major Weston's study, having left Pru and her boyfriend to their intimacy. Lucy held a copy of *Hamlet* in one hand and a glass of Sir Hugh's grappa in the other. "*Nay, it is. I know not 'seems.*'" She read aloud, trying to summon the coziness of performing Shakespeare in her father's study.

"'Tis not alone my inky cloak, good mother,'" Major Weston said. "'Nor customary suits of solemn black.' Have I got that right?"

He walked across the room and poured a glass of his own grappa, then clicked on a lamp near his bookshelves. "I prefer poetry myself, when I can't sleep. Tennyson. I came down for him. Ought we to have those Shakespeare readings in this study, do you think? Like your family did? Think the soldiers would be up for it? Don't know if our Fliss could get through it. Are you homesick?"

"*Why seems it so particular with thee,*'" Lucy repeated. "I was trying to remember exactly how it went."

"Is there something ... particular ... with thee?"

Major Weston filled his house with people but only spoke to them when he glanced up from his reading. His floor to ceiling bookcases occupied an entire wall, but there were smaller shelves pressed against every other wall in the room, and it was there that he was staring.

"There was something particular with me, you see. I began collecting after the war," he told her. "The Great War. The war to end all wars. Although it wasn't and it didn't. A book is a bit of a life. A man pours himself into it. And the occasional woman." He raised his glass to Lucy, in tribute to Austen or Bronte or Eliot. "Every man ... every friend ... I lost in France ... is a volume."

"I had that thought, that very thought, standing outside the Bermuda Library one evening. With Georgie."

"You two are comrades in arms," Major Weston said. "Like brothers in arms, only sisters. Treasure that."

"I do," Lucy said. "There were four of us. This time, last year, last Palm Sunday. A friend wanted me to go with her to see about the lilies for the church service. But I wanted to get a letter to my father, since the ship was in and I didn't go and ... she was struck by a jeep."

"Killed?"

"No. But I had another friend who was killed. By a former beau of mine."

Major Weston refilled their grappa. "Was he charged?"

She hesitated, fearing another dismissal, but then blurted everything: Bill's flimsy alibi about being at the golf course, his near-confession at the airfield, the diaspora of the women who might have testified to his temper, and concluded, "No one has been charged. No one believes me. There were no witnesses. There is no evidence."

"But there is his reputation."

"What?"

"Your friend, who you loved, will always be known as the murdered girl," Major Weston said. "The manner of her death will outshine the achievements of her life. Why should the man who murdered her have an easy time of it?"

He drained his grappa and stood. Lucy leapt from her chair and embraced him before she had a moment to think about what she was doing. She felt the shock of it in the way he received her, his initial stiffening, then his softening as he allowed his arms to fold her into him. Who knew how long it had been since he had embraced a woman not his wife or daughter, who knew how long, if ever, it had been since he had pressed to himself a woman who wept into his shoulder.

Lucy stepped back from him. They said goodnight. She climbed the stairs to her room, washed and cold-creamed her face and brushed her teeth. She fell into bed beside Georgie, who murmured, "Live in Kent and be content," as she tossed her head on the pillow.

She awoke with a sore head —*oh, grappa!*—already late to the bustle downstairs. Voices floated up from the garden and the parlor. The Westons' cook was shouting at someone who had dared to enter the kitchen. She peered out the window down to the courtyard and was startled to see John at the breakfast table, drinking in tea and Felicity's chatter. She opened the window and leaned out. Felicity waved, calling, "Come meet Greg!" Lucy had mistaken Greg for John. The house was full of Whitings.

Lucy swallowed two aspirin, cupping water in her palm from the tap in the bathroom. A brief wash, a comb-through, an application of lipstick, the old reliable Chanel dress. She walked downstairs and into the library to ensure that she had not made a mess.

She and Major Weston had left their grappa goblets on a side table. As she picked them up, she heard an exasperated sigh and raised her eyes to see a girl perched on the third-highest rung of the library ladder, surveying the highest shelf in the bookcase.

"What are you doing?"

John had entered the room, but he was addressing the girl on the ladder.

"Byron, Coleridge," the girl said. "Oh dear. Major Weston *did* say he'd get Cavafy."

"Come down. At once." John, catching Lucy's eye, nodded a greeting. He wore a handsome white linen shirt, unbuttoned at the neck, and olive trousers. "Slowly. Marina," he added, as the girl complied. "Aren't you in enough bother over Cavafy? What's it to you if Major Weston doesn't want to read a dirty Greek poet?"

"He is *not* dirty, John! That was *one* poem. He mostly writes about antiquity."

"Be grateful he lets you borrow his books at all. Miss Barrett, may I present my youngest sister, Marina," he added, as the girl leapt from the ladder. Her satisfaction in the precision of her landing put her closer to the twelve than the fourteen Lucy had guessed for her age.

The girl twirled toward her. She had John's grey eyes. Her shiny black hair was arranged in swirls at her temples and braids down her back.

"*You're* Miss Barrett!" Marina cried. "John was telling me about you last night!"

"That I'm always underfoot?" Lucy asked

John astonished her by responding with a grin so bright it was as though she just now realized that he had teeth. "Well," he said. "Now we're the ones underfoot."

"So the shoe is on the underfoot," Lucy said.

"Laughing at our own wit again, are we?" John said, but he was still smiling.

"You graduated from *Cambridge!*" Marina said. "You must tell me *all* about it. Come to Cairo and tell my *parents*. Mama can't imagine what kind of parents allow their daughter to become a bluestocking. But John said you were ever so pretty, and look, you *are!* Are you related to Elizabeth Barrett Browning?"

Lucy stepped back, unaccustomed to such enthusiasm. "I don't believe so. I'm sure it would have come up, if we were."

"You never know." John patted Marina on the head; she responded with the expected indignation. "They might've hushed it up. Disreputable, having a poet in the family."

"I'm a poet!" Marina began. "That is, I will be! I work hard at it—"

"Hush, Marina. Miss Barrett has a headache." John nodded at Lucy's glasses: "Hair of the dog, Miss Barrett?"

"Do call me Lucy, it's so silly— and no, we were in here last night. I was reading—" She looked for the volume of *Hamlet* and saw it just as John did.

"So much for Pru's promise to show you a bit of night life," he said.

"Oh, well she did, but—"

"What did you read at Cambridge, did you read Classics?" Marina asked. "I want to read Classics."

"You'll have to get there first," John said. "Run along, Marina. Take your Coleridge and leave us in peace. This is Lucy's home, and we're guests."

"But I want to talk to her!"

"That's as may be, but I want to be quiet with her."

John took the glasses from Lucy and went to the kitchen, where she heard him greeting the cook in Arabic. The cook replied with cheer. John returned with a glass of soda water, shutting the door behind him. He handed Lucy the glass, then crossed the room and shut the other door. She sipped her soda water as John picked up the *Hamlet* and surveyed Major Weston's collection. Eventually, he found its slot and shelved it. He sat on the davenport across from Major Weston's favorite chair and after a while, she sat down beside him.

It was as quiet and companionable as rainy days on Mowbray Crescent when she and Matty took their drawing supplies into Paul's study and created maps from his globe. Men had studies, whether or not they used them to study: her grandfather Barrett, her father, Archie Danville, Major Weston. She would have a study one day, she promised herself, when she had a home of her own, and if her husband insisted on having one, then they would have two.

***

At breakfast were the Westons, Felicity and Greg Whiting, Marina and John Whiting, Lucy and Major Burdock, Georgie and a stray fellow officer of Greg Whiting's, and two of the convalescing soldiers who were well enough to join them.

"They say the *Valiant*'s almost patched up," Burdock told Greg. "Bound for South Africa before the month's out. The *Valiant*," Burdock told the rest of the table, half of whom already knew and the other half of whom were indifferent, "is one of the four ships those Eye-Tie saboteurs got last December. Lost our grip on the Mediterranean for a few weeks there."

The previous December, the Italian submarine *Scirè* had made its way into the commercial harbour of Alexandria. It had released several torpedoes toward Royal Navy ships, including the *Valiant*. They were *maiali*, "human torpedoes," operated by two divers, who guided the bombs into place, then swam away. All the divers had been captured. Most Italian prisoners were sent to build roads or work farms in South Africa. Some were sent as far as England, but those prisoners had expressed little interest in Mussolini. A submariner willing to be a human torpedo would not be deemed amenable enough for farm work in the U.K. As far as she could tell from the files she was permitted to access, the *maiali* were in prison. She knew not where. She would have liked to talk to them.

"It's a clever saboteur who attacks the enemy's ships in the enemy's harbour," Lucy said. "You think of a harbour as a safe place. What's the expression, Captain Burdock?"

"Any port in a storm, I think you mean."

"Yes," Lucy glanced a quick smile at John. "There was a terrible storm in Bermuda, do you remember, Georgie? Oh no, you weren't there. Every ship within fifty miles radioed the harbourmaster for refuge. I was in the Yacht Club. I heard it. But what if they came in from the storm to find no refuge? That's how you really rattle the enemy, don't you think? Strip them of everything that makes them feel safe. Make sure the ship never leaves port."

Burdock said, "You can see why Miss Barrett makes an effective interrogator. She glides in like a ministering angel but then turns rather chilling. How does it go 'The female of the species is more deadly than the male,' eh?"

"Poetic, Burdock," said Greg.

"Do you think so?" asked Marina. "I don't find Kipling poetic. And that's not very flattering to Lucy. I would say that she's enchanting. She ensorcelles."

"Like Circe, turning men into swine," John said.

"Ah, but did Circe turn men into swine?" Marina asked. "Or merely strip their artifice to reveal the swine within?"

Both Whitings pronounced the name with hard K's—*Kir-kee*—not how Lucy had learned it at St. Paul's, but they had grown up with Greece in their back yard rather than Kensington Gardens. *In my day-to-day practice, I seldom see ancient Greeks.*

Lucy didn't bite her tongue, but she did hold it in between her teeth to stop herself from saying that she was not thinking of Homer when she sat in on interrogations, nor of Odysseus and his long voyage home, his encounters with witches and sirens, but of a lonely girl in Bermuda and her encounter with a man's bare hands. A Cassandra, silenced.

"Well, I for one jolly well wish Miss Barrett *could* turn those men to swine!" Burdock said. "Apart from anything else, think of all the bacon and ham!"

"Speaking of bacon and ham," John said. "Lady Weston, Felicity mentioned you need some things from Beccari's? For Easter? Why don't Lucy and I go and pick up those things for you? She looks like she needs a bit of sun."

Once Lady Weston understood that John was indeed offering to do the household shopping, once suggestions of accompanying them from Georgie, Felicity, Pru and Marina had all been declined, and once the Westons' cook had been appeased with not only a written list but a recitation of his requirements, Lucy understood that John was, in fact, undertaking the task of showing her the sights of Alexandria.

Beccari's was a grocer and café popular with the Italian-minded locals, stocked with spaghetti, canned tomatoes, jars of olives, wheels of aged cheese, and freshly baked *Torta Pasqualini.* Lucy handed over the eggs produced that morning by the Weston flock and placed an order for the *Torta.* John ordered the lamb while Lucy selected biscotti and olive oil. Lucy filled out the delivery order while John gave the proprietor a tip to give to the delivery boy. It all felt very domestic, particularly when John ordered two gelati in cups and asked Lucy to "bring lots of napkins."

"I'm a bit leery of walking you to the harbour," he said, as they strolled that way, "now that you've expressed such enthusiasm for blowing it up. In fact, everything about you makes one leery. You show up here in Alex for no real reason. You speak both German and Italian fluently."

"And French," she piped.

"Yes, for French you'd need the other side of the continent. You say you 'translate documents' in some office by the harbour, but you have something to do with prisoners captured in the desert. Burdock's in love with you. And yet instead of spending your evenings at nightclubs with him, you're always at my hospital, bewitching the men into taking their medicine."

"I'm surprised you know so many words, John." Lucy lapped at her gelato like a child denied a year of sweets. "All you usually say is 'go home.'"

"At the hospital, I am a doctor."

It struck Lucy as so similar to a sentence in a language lesson book that she said, "*A l'hôpital, je suis médecin.*"

John smiled—she was still startled by this distortion of his face—and repeated it in Arabic, "*Fi il mustashfa, anadoctour.*"

Lucy said, "*In ospedale, sono un dottore.*"

John answered in Greek. Lucy said, "*Im Krankenhaus, bin ich ein Arzt.*"

John paused his stroll. "Your German's really quite good."

"*Sie sind zu höflich.*"

"It quite makes the hairs on the back of my neck stand up. In another time, I think you might have been burned as a witch."

"I wish I *were* a witch."

"What would you do? Turn men into swine?"

"I'd bring a man to justice." She wiped her mouth with her napkin. "Again, I mean."

She told him about Brooklyn Joe. "They gave me a choice," she concluded. "England, or here."

"And you regret coming here."

"Regret? No, I'm happy here." She surprised herself, but it was true. She seemed to thrum with an unfamiliar contentment. They had arrived at Stanley Bay, with its sunbathers and its splashing bathers and its patrolling soldiers. There were the striped beach umbrellas, there was the white Hotel Rialto. There was the brine of the sea and the cry of the gulls, the modern billboards advertising cigarettes in the foreground, the old crenellated white buildings in the distance. The bay had a festive, marketplace air, despite the fact that the next bay over held warships. It was a satisfactory scene, and there was so much that she looked forward to exploring, as a bride must look forward to exploring the body of her husband.

"Are you? Why? No, don't," he added, as she began to think about it. "Don't retreat into one of your trances. Say it. Say why you're happy."

"The sun. The sea. I'm with Georgie, and I know she's safe. The Westons are so kind, if a little …"

"English?"

"Eccentric. Complacent."

"As I said."

Lucy smiled, "I seem to make a difference. I'm efficient with translation. I get something out of the prisoners. I love this city. The variety of people. All these strivings and saboteurs … " she gestured at the harbour. "Still, the monuments look on. The pyramids, and the Sphinx, if I ever get to see them. It's ancient. It's vast. It's humbling."

"Humbling is good?"

"It's our lot to be humbled. But if it's to be done, let it be done by the Sphinx. Not some bureaucrat who keeps me in a basement reading letters. I'm my own woman here."

"Yes." John searched her face and nodded, as though confirming a diagnosis. "You said 'back' to England. Not 'home' to England."

"I don't know if it is home anymore. My mother—my mother was killed in the Blitz." Her voice trembled, and John took her hand. "I was supposed to be with her."

"What do you mean?"

"The nurses made me leave. They told me visiting hours were over."

"Is *that* how it's done? You merely say 'visiting hours'—oh, hey— "When she started to cry, he fumbled for the gelato napkin in his pocket. "Lucy, I'm sorry."

"I was meant to be watching her. If I'd been *with* her, she'd still *be* here. And I wouldn't be here. I would be there." She hadn't cried about her mother since last Easter. But she felt a fresh sorrow, realizing that John would never meet Tessa, that Tessa would never meet John.

He regarded her with a courteous sympathy, not a doctor in a hospital but not yet the next thing. He tried to smooth his shirt collar against the fluttering of the breeze. Something sank in her when she studied his fingers. They were long, hyper-articulated, as graceful and disciplined as a dancer's pose. *Damn*, she thought. All her languages, all her Shakespeare, had brought her to *damn. Damn, it's him. I wasn't looking, but I've found the one.* She had no right to be falling in love, not with Ruth buried alone in the middle of an ocean, at last in a dark, private place.

"What?" John asked. "What are you thinking? Say it. Don't think."

"*'The grave's a fine and private place/but none, I think, do there embrace.'*"

"*'We would sit down, and think which way/To walk, and pass our long love's day,'*" John responded brightly, as though they were still playing the "at the hospital, I am a doctor" game.

"What?" Lucy said.

"What?" John said.

"What are you talking about?"

"It's from the same poem. *'Had we but world enough and time/This coyness, lady, were no crime ...'*"

"Are you saying I'm coy?"

"I wouldn't dream of it." He did look pleased, though. As pleased with himself as Bill Inman had looked guiding her into a jeep, although with John she had all but declared herself from the rooftops. "Far from it. Woman who dreams of blowing up harbours and saving the world?"

"I couldn't even save my own mother. Or Ruth."

"How would you have made a difference?" John asked. "Was your mother the only one killed in the raid? Did the nurses need help getting her out, or—?"

She hadn't thought of that. *Can't you lot speak English?* Would the nurses have left her? But no—"The whole ward took a direct hit. They were all killed."

"So you'd be dead, too." John pulled to him, placed one hand on her back, the other on the back of her head. His shirt smelled of bracing starch and he smelled of a fragrant soap she had plucked from a basket in a sunny bazaar and held to her face to breathe in its woody scent. Sandalwood? How did she smell, she wondered? Like Drewe's face cream.

"My father blames me," she told his shoulder.

"For the Blitz?"

"He said 'I thought you were with her.'"

"He thought you were *dead*. Come. Walk."

He guided her along the sidewalk along the beach.

"I should have protected her."

"How? You should have known the Nazi's bombing strategy that night? Because the Luftwaffe shares that intelligence with young English girls? Lucy, if you were a witch, if you had some magical ability to save people from the Luftwaffe, I doubt they would have let you out of England. What did I tell you? You can't save everybody."

April 3, 1942

Dear Louis,

Tomorrow is Easter and I am wishing you a very happy one, knowing we will be in 'Ordinary Days,' at best, when you receive this one. I am now stationed in Egypt. Perhaps it is selfish of me to say, but I think you will be pleased to hear, that I am so much happier now than I was in Bermuda. But I wish to thank you for the friendship you extended to me while I was in Bermuda, and for your guidance and counsel regarding bank statements and fathers and daughters. I hope your garden is thriving.

And now I will impose upon you. Haven't I always? You know the matter of the murder of my friend Ruth Smith. I believe she was murdered by my former beau Bill Inman, who is a lieutenant with the Army Corps of Engineers constructing Kindley Field. I believe this because of words he said to me just before I left Bermuda, and because of his behavior while I was there. The construction of Kindley Field required much destruction to the island and its inhabitants, as it was—land was being dynamited, homes were destroyed—that is not Bill Inman's fault. But it may have set in him a pattern of careless disregard for the beauty and fragility of the island and its inhabitants.

What am I asking you to do about this, Louis? I'm not entirely certain. But I am certain that you agree that the women of Bermuda

*should be made aware to exercise caution with the American forces
on the island. At the very least, the constabulary might be made aware
of his behavior should any other woman, heaven forbid, experience
violence at his hands. I wouldn't ask you to take special care* [like fun,
she wouldn't! Lucy thought] *but perhaps if you were perhaps on a
committee with an officer of the law at St. Andrew's, you might put in
a word. Perhaps you might show him this letter.*

*I pray for your safety and health, my dear Louis, and thank you
again for all your counsel (and for all the rum at the Yacht Club!)*

With Louis Furbert, she had emphasized Bill's damage to Furbert's
island and Bill's treatment of women, since Furbert had daughters.
With the minister at St. Andrew's, she emphasized her friendship
with Lark and Louis Furbert, Ruth's love of "Jesu, Joy of Man's Desiring," her innocence, her love of the flora of Bermuda (*strangled
at the agricultural station, sketching a banyan tree!*), the loneliness
of Ruth's untended, unvisited grave on foreign soil, the infamy of
the end of the life. With Captain Daniel Jackson, U.S. Army Corps
of Engineers (whom she had met only once and who she had last
heard chuckling with Bill about how "gentlemanly" he had been in
his goodnight kiss to Lucy), she emphasized her father's position in
the British Admiralty, and Bill's conduct unbecoming an officer and
a gentleman, the violence toward herself and Rebecca Gwynne, that
eyes would be upon them now. With Clara Frith, she wrote what
she suspected, what she knew, what she wanted: *proclaim his infamy
to the world*, and what Lucy (or Clara) might do next.

She wrote and wrote, on Easter Eve, while soldiers coughed in
the courtyard and Georgie hummed in her bed.

***

And then it was Easter. For Lucy, there was a new dress, gaily handed over by Felicity ("it'll never fit me again!"), the *Torta Pasqualina*,
more bloviating by Burdock, John in his formal dress uniform, seated across from Lucy where they exchanged distracted smiles. Afterwards, as evening set in, John and Lucy went into the courtyard,

where Lucy gave the hens their "tea," swept the patio and sang them into their pens to the tune of "Oranges and lemons/say the bells of St. Clement's." John watched her, arms folded, from a breakfast table cast-iron chair, until Marina spilled from the living room into the patio with a book in her hand.

"Marina," John told her. "I believe Lucy has ensorcelled these chickens."

"Miss Barrett! Miss Taylor says you have Cambridge German and might be better at translating this."

"What's Cambridge German?" John laughed.

"German you learn at university rather than in a Berlin kindergarten." Lucy accepted the outstretched book and stepped closer to the French doors to catch the light. "'Sonnets to Orpheus,'" she read. "I did translate some Rilke. You do like your myths, don't you, Marina? The one I know best is 'Requiem for a Friend.' *Ich habe Tote und ich ließ sie hin. I have my dead, and I have let them go, and was surprised to see them so soon at home with being dead, so peaceful, so unlike their reputation …*'"

John took the book from her, handed it back to his sister and motioned her inside.

"Oh, the moon!" Marina cried. "I love the moon from this courtyard. I stood just here at Greg and Felicity's wedding reception. Brilliant, crescent moon. A sun-silver slipper! A smile! A benediction. I wrote a poem about it after."

"That's very nice, Marina. Did you show it to Greg?" Lucy asked.

"No. He'd only laugh. John's the only one who listens to me."

"He doesn't want to listen now," John said. "You run along. Lucy will come to dinner this week. Just us and Aunt Sophia. And you can talk her ear off then."

"I would be happy to." Lucy kissed the top of Marina's head.

"Oh, do you promise, Lucy? I would so like a friend."

"You have one, duckling."

Satisfied, Marina opened the French doors, dousing them with indoor light and several bars of Felicity's piano. When Marina shut the doors, John and Lucy were again shrouded in dusk.

"John," Lucy said. "You might be kinder to her."

"I'm the kindest in our family." John led her to the lemon tree. "You should memorize that poem," he told her. "It has a good message for you."

Except that the friend Rilke eulogizes died in childbirth, Lucy thought. Even in verse, women were imperiled. And you don't want that on my mind, John, not at this moonlit moment.

A light went on in the bedroom she shared with Georgie. A man's silhouette appeared against the curtains. Who could it be? Too fit for Burdock, too short for Gregory (who was, at any rate, playing bridge)—so who did Georgie have in her—*their*—bedroom? She ticked through the men at dinner. Pru's ambulance driver was the odd man out. Why was Pru's ambulance driver in their bedroom?

John had yet to touch her. Bill would have had her in his arms long ago. John left silence between them until he asked, in a pleasant-weather-we're-having tone, "Are the beaches in Bermuda as soft as they say?"

"They are soft. Sand is like face powder. I don't know how well you know face powder—"

"Rather well," John interrupted. Lucy coughed a thin "Oh," surprised at the choke of disappointment she felt and aware of how coy a more accomplished flirt like Georgie could have made such an "Oh" sound.

"When they sent me to school, to Repton, I spent the Christmas holidays with one of the other students. They took turns taking pity on the foreign boy. I saw many quaint English villages. One year, I was in the church pageant. I played one of the three wise men. I was only twelve. Not wise, not a man. The other Magi darkened their faces with cork. But I had no need to. They laughed about it. I covered my face with white powder. To see how I would look a shade lighter. I suppose I was trying to look more English."

"I know what you mean."

"I doubt that."

"I'm only half-English."

"If you mean that your mother was Italian, yes. I know that. But don't kid yourself, Lucy. You're English through and through." This sounded oddly Yank: *don't kid yourself.* And he looked a bit like a Yankee, hands in his pockets, back arched, head back, regarding the moon. The moon was not in its phase of smiling benediction, but a half moon, incomplete. *Swear not by the moon, the inconstant moon/that monthly changes in her circled orb ... oh, pull yourself together, Barrett! Yes, quite romantic, but no need to go to pieces.*

"Through and through," John repeated, as though confirming a diagnosis: anemia, for example, an innately feeble blood. "And yet your father was determined that you learn all these languages. Most English girls, the sisters of my classmates, I mean ..." He shrugged, a summary of their frivolity.

"My father said focusing my thoughts on my studies would keep me from thinking about boys," Lucy said. "Actually, he said declining nouns would teach me to decline men."

"Did it work?"

"Sometimes. But there are so many men."

He looked at her until she looked at him. She was startled by the movement of her heart when she looked at him; it seemed to leap to about in unexpected trills, like a solo by Duke Ellington's trumpet player. She had looked at him so many times, why did this occasion cause such cardiac improvisation? But she knew why. Even in the twilight, she saw the question on his face.

"And so few women of your luster. But I'm only concerned about one man. This one." He pressed his hand to his chest. "Will you decline him?"

She reached for the hand he held against his chest, and braided their fingers.

"Luster," Lucy said. "I've always wanted to have a light."

"Like a lighthouse. There was a lighthouse at Alexandria. Perhaps you've heard? One of the ancient wonders of the world." When Lucy didn't answer, but only pressed their hands together, John added, "And I wonder—"

"Oh, why don't we stop wondering," Lucy said, and kissed him. In his response, there was wonder, but no uncertainty.

39.

May 16, 1942

My dear Lucia,

Although I feel it is premature for us to behave as though I have already reached a state of dotage in which I am directed by orders from my daughter, I have performed the tasks you set out for me and I am writing to you to let you know of their outcome.

First, after sending a note to his chambers, I was invited to pay a call at the home of the His Honour Judge Rupert Barrington-Smith. Even though it was late spring, his rooms were cold and cheerless. I wonder that he, as a widower, had sent away his daughter, as a daughter's touch would have gone a long way toward making that residence a home.

Lucy paused. She was reading the letter aloud while Georgie, on the window seat, sewed. Georgie had just completed an impressive sewing project: modifying a brown *djeballa* purchased at the bazaar into a dressing gown for the convalescing soldier who had burned his hands. His wounds itched. John had all but shrieked at the women of the house to not *touch* his hands unless their own were thoroughly clean. He had allowed Lucy, after she demonstrated competence on the back of John's own hands, to dab ointment at various points on the burn victim's hand, lightly, *lightly,* "light as the fall of an eyelash," no rubbing, in the sitting room only—no risk of a gust of sand, or hen feed or book dust from Major Weston's library. And then John had allowed Lucy to rewrap his hands in fresh gauze (Pru was given this training task.)

The stench of the yellow-brown pus fighting to create a protective crust over the raw pink burnt flesh might have repelled a younger Lucy. But she thought of her mother and Matty, and she thought of Lark, both for her gospel, *as ye do for the least of these, so ye do for me* (or something along that lines) and the way she had stitched up Lucy's knee by the pool.

The burn victim could not manage buttons and found this such an indignity that he refused to appear before Lady Weston at breakfast without a dressing gown. He missed breakfast, vital nutrients and medications, until this was discovered and worked out.

Georgie had cut the *djeballa* down the middle, trimmed a bit from each side, hemmed the opened sides, and used the trimmed bits to fashion a sash. Lucy had delivered it downstairs to the sitting room and draped it across a sofa before returning to their room with the post.

Georgie, humming, now embroidered a white handkerchief, as demure as a niece in a Dickens novel.

"I did not, as you know, attend Cambridge," Georgie said. "But I do recognize the concept of irony."

"Judge Barrington-Smith addressed your conundrum in two parts. For the first part, as a judge. The evidence you have presented as proof of a murder lacks even the shaky merit of a confession by hearsay. This Lieutenant Inman—"

Lucy repeated it in American: *"This loo-tenant Inman did not even confess a crime to you. He used a term you had used in conversation with Ruth and you are purporting that he could only have heard this term within a narrow time frame. I regret to say that this is all a bit too Agatha Christie for the Judge. The lieutenant's eyes 'pooling with tears' and so on—again, not admissible—that is probably down to many other circumstances, primarily, my dear, related to the failure of the romance he had hoped to have with you.*

For the second part, the Judge addressed your petition as a father. He asked me to convey his appreciation of your regard for his daughter, whom he had to raise alone, a 'challenging' young woman of bizarre intellectual skills and peculiar social awkwardness. He told me that, until this opportunity with the Censorship in Bermuda presented itself, his sister was exploring institutions to which Ruth might be committed."

Lucy stopped. Everything within her stopped. She stopped reading, stopped breathing, would have stopped her own heart if it could have been done through force of will.

"Aunt Verity," she said.

"The Nazis started like that, and that's a verity." Georgie looked up from her stitching when Lucy didn't reply. Georgie snapped her fingers as she might at a cat scratching a sofa. "Go on!"

"*The Judge wishes to convey his appreciation for your friendship to his daughter. He believes she might otherwise have never known friendship with and here I quote him, 'such a kind and well-bred young woman.'*

I fail to understand why, when given the opportunity, you did not choose to come home. You argued that your languages would be put to better use closer to where they are spoken, but darling girl, you are far too close. I wanted you to spend the war in a garden. Instead, you have gone into the lion's den. I hope you one day understand, perhaps when you have children of your own, why I sent you to Bermuda.

It was at the same time the most courageous and the most cowardly decision of my life. But after losing my brothers in the first war, and then your mother in this one, I could not stand another loss. I could not stand it. I could not stand to lose you. If all of my loyal children prove to be braver than their father, I will happily live with that cowardice. You have used up all my courage. I bequeath it to you, with the certainty that while you live, you will exercise it.

Judge Barrington-Smith cannot say the same. For this, I pity him. I believe I will call on him again. Perhaps you can write to him again, using kinder words.

Please look after yourself, my precious daughter. Let me hear from you soon. Your devoted father, etc. etc."

***

Georgie folded her completed handkerchief and added it to a stack of others.

"What's all this?" Lucy asked.

"I've embroidered monograms on handkerchiefs for Nicky. Like a good wife. He asked for things. Hankies and lens cloths? Put it on a jeep for him? I asked Pru's ambulance chap. He thinks I can shove in to the jeep myself. He'll put in a word. He says people come and go at the front all the time, if they can get transport. The jeep drivers know where Nicky is. British Pathé is doing a bit on the sappers. For the newsreels. They're taking mail, medical supplies, and me."

"You're going to the *front*?"

"Oh, the front!" Georgie waved a hand at it. "Probably only El-Hamman, where the supply tents are. Pru's chap says people are in and out of the campsites all the time. We're going to a supply depot. Drop off medical supplies. It'll do the boys a bit of good to see a pretty face, don't you think?"

"They'll see two, then," Lucy said. "I'm going with you."

On the day, Lucy sent a note to her office and made a call to Burdock, pleading a headache, adding some alarming symptoms she'd picked up at St. Pants to make her condition seem more critical. Then she squeezed into the back of an overpacked Red Cross truck. Lucy lay flat on her back along the tops of the crates of medical supplies, which left her only six inches of headroom under the canvas ceiling, since the drivers had not known to plan for her. Since Georgie had been expected, she had a job: sitting cross-legged with a three boxes of glass syringes on her lap, her duty to hold them steady.

The jeep was so hot that they had barely made it out of Alex before drops of sweat trickled down Lucy's forehead into her ears. She and Georgie both wore helmets, goggles over their eyes and wet handkerchiefs over their mouths. They looked like Claude Rains in *The Invisible Man*. It was the only way to combat the sand.

After an hour, they stopped at a camp. The driver and his aide unloaded boxes, freeing up some room. Lucy curled into a comma and dozed, her sweat-soaked head in Georgie's lap. Hours later, she woke when the jeep stopped again. Georgie crawled out from under the boxes and lifted the flap.

"Hullo, boys, what's up?"

"You ladies can come out and stretch your legs. But stay by the jeep, please. We don't know if that's the real thing or only for show, for them."

Lucy jumped out. As she stamped her legs into service, she saw a vista of undulating sand and washed-out sky. In the distance, burned-out tanks and an abandoned jeep perched on slopes of sand. Two men holding long wands swept them steadily back and forth as they walked cautiously forward. Sappers, sweeping for mines. Further on, she saw the "them" the driver meant—two men behind a camera on a tripod planted in the sand. One of them was very tall and blond.

"It's *Nick!*" Georgie took off her helmet and waved it above her head. "Nick! *Nicky!*" She dropped her helmet and ran toward the camera crew.

The blond man shaded his eyes, began walking toward her. The sappers leapt and waved their arms, forming huge X's in the air. They looked like windmills, Lucy thought, and remembered the painted tins of confiscated almond biscuits back in Archie Danville's office at the Princess. The decorative tins holding treats for tea had been used to smuggle stolen Dutch miniatures, buried beneath the biscuits, as mines were buried beneath the sand.

The sappers screamed. Their cries dissolved like rain in the hot wind. Georgie was several yards ahead of her. Lucy raced after her, initially slowed by the sand, but then her Bermuda training kicked in and she peddled her legs hard. She grabbed a fistful of Georgie's hair. She yanked it. Georgie spun around, outraged, and Lucy grabbed her by the throat and pushed. *So fragile so fragile.* Bill had killed Ruth and Lark's rapist had subdued Lark at just this place, at this frail pipe that housed a woman's voice. Georgie grabbed at Lucy's blouse as they both fell, Georgie back and Lucy on top of her. Facing the panic in Georgie's eyes, Lucy thought *how stupid she is to be afraid, I'm here and I love her …* Many, many weeks later, she realized that Georgie didn't fear Lucy but her own delay in her long-awaited reunion with her husband.

There was a distant boom like summer thunder. Then, darkness.

40.

Pain capped her head, at a jaunty angle, like a beret. Occasionally, the steady pain which timpanied in her head was joined by one that whined like the metal tuning fork the piano tuner used on the piano at Mowbray Crescent. A meticulous man, the tuner plinked the C above middle C again and again, until the cook protested, until Horatio, ears flattened, galloped to refuge under Lucy's bed, until only Marcia could bear to be in the music room. Marcia leaned on the piano, chin in hand, gazing at the tuner as though he were Leslie Howard, until the wretched man let the wretched girl play with his tuning forks and she mimicked the pitches in her perfect-pitch, bell-clear voice: eeeeeeeeee! Then the drop of half an octave. Aaaaaaaah!

"Will this *end*!" Lucy cried to her mother.

"It can end, if it is time to end." Tessa took Lucy's hand. "So *brown, mia cara*! Why did you not stay out of the sun? Did you use all that lotion? I left you so much lotion."

"Lucy," Matty, taking her other hand, said, "I thought you were *with* her."

"I *was*. I *was* with her this time! I made sure of it."

Everything was wrong. She stood in a dark corridor, a piercing light at the end of the hall and Marcia's fiendish plinking on the other side of the door, playing "Jesu, Joy of Man's Desiring."

The ache in her throat rose in an acidic bile. A hand raised her head (*ow!*). She vomited and spat. When she tried to slip back into the corridor, a hand patted at her face, a patting so vigourous you might call it slapping.

"Awake? Drink. Open up. Swallow."

The smallest peek of a squint smacked her with a dazzling pain that slammed her eyes shut. The darkness hurt as well, but not as keenly.

"Do you know where you are?" a voice asked.

"Home?"

The dream corridor beckoned with its cool dark oblivion.

"Lucy?" a voice said. "Stay here. Stay with us."

A wet cloth was pressed against her mouth, and she sucked the water from the fabric. *For I was thirsty, and you gave me drink.*

In her half-earthly moments, Lucy realized that the presence of the absent meant that she herself was hovering between the states of absence and presence. The absence had a far greater claim on her inclination. In the absence, there was Mama. In the presence, there were questions and tasks. There was also that frightful high-pitched droning, and where, if Lucy had passed into the next realm, was *Ruth?* Here perhaps Ruth would not be so afraid? Because if she was frightened, and she was, she could only imagine what Ruth was feeling.

"Lucy? Drink. It's broth. Another sip. No, no," she felt a hand slapping her cheek. "Stay here. Stay with us."

"Mama! Ruth!" she shouted. Or rather, she didn't shout, as her voice came out a croak, the way a scream in a dream is a gasp upon waking. Her tongue was glued to the roof of her mouth. A cool metal spoon tapped her lips.

"Raise your head. Let me hold it. Drink. Swallow. Good."

Then she was back in the hallway, waking to a minor caw. The pitch *Eeeeeee!* wavered, dipped, rose, warbled. It was not the piano tuner. It was not a dream. It was the call of the *muezzin* to prayer.

She was alive, in Alexandria. Every pulse told her, although she was alone and in darkness, that she was alive, and in a place that a man she loved had pointed out that she loved.

She awoke to another call to prayer, the dawn call, judging by the cautious light in the room. Even this indolent morning light burned her eyes, brought bile to her throat. Squinting, she rolled onto her side. She vomited into a porcelain bedpan on the floor next to the bed.

The desert. The sappers. Georgie wriggling beneath her on the hot sand. The sappers waving X's in the air: *hold, hold.*

She was in a hospital bed, with a visitor's white enamel chair beside it, in a strange small room where three of the four walls around her were composed of built-in shelves. Two of those three shelves were stacked with starched, precisely folded sheets and towels.

The linen airing cupboard, she realized, at St. Panteleon's. She had stacked it often enough. The wall closest to her held a clipboard—her medical chart, she surmised, and a pitcher of water with a glass. There was water in the glass, so she drank it. Above that shelf was one which held a bottle of Drewe's lotion, her framed photo of Matty, a few of her books, some unfamiliar pencil sketches, folded in half and propped up like Christmas cards. A vase of rosemary sprigs scented the room lightly, providing a sweet counterpoint to the hospital smell of disinfectant and bleach. A vent high in the wall threw stripes of weak sunlight against an opposite wall of stacked linen.

Her right arm was bandaged from knuckle to halfway up her elbow. It rested on a damask cushion Lucy recognized from Lady Weston's drawing room. Her other arm, she realized, as she raised it to her face, was scented with Drewe's lotion. Someone had sat in that enamel chair, and rubbed lotion up and down her arm. Over her hospital gown, she wore a satin shawl soft as kitten fur. *Safe in a soft room,* she thought, before darkness embraced her again.

Then she was gently shoved from side to side while Pru and another nurse changed her sheets with her still in the bed.

"Awake, are we?" Pru asked cheerily. "Georgie is fine. That's what you always ask first. You're in the linen cupboard at St. Pants. The British Pathé film crew drove you to the ambulance station in the desert. My lad brought you to St. Pants. Captain Whiting'll tell the rest. I'll fetch him and you," she spoke to the nurse, "fetch some soup and try to get it down her before she falls asleep again. Try to sit up, Lucy. It'll do you good."

She had only one good arm. Her shoulder bellowed when she moved. Her head bleated as she tried to upright herself. At last, she was sitting, Lady Weston's cushion propped behind her. The pain in her head shrieked like an aria from *Gotterdamerung*. She closed her eyes. A finger pressed against her wrist. She smiled before she opened her eyes to see John taking her pulse.

"How do you feel?"

"Like the clapper in a church bell."

"That's new." He widened one of her eyes, then the other, with his fingers. "You haven't said that before. How's your head?"

"Hurts."

"You were hit by the debris of a land mine. The back of your hand," he nodded at her bandaged hand. "And your right scapula. That's where you took the brunt of it."

He put his arm around her, his hand on the bandage over her wound, which leapt at his touch into a bright pain over a deep dull ache.

"Here." He tapped her scapula. The shrapnel went deep here. Where your wing would be, if you were an angel. You'll have a scar. No more strapless evening gowns."

"I've never worn a strapless —!" She stopped when she saw his smile, realizing that "strapless evening gown" was a kind of misdirection, as one would try to startle a victim of hiccups.

"I'd've done a better job, leave less of a scar," John continued, in the tone she had heard him use to instruct the QA's. "But I've never performed surgery in the back of truck speeding through the Sahara, so I suppose one mustn't criticize."

"A scar." Lucy dismissed it with a shrug, then yelped from the pain. "

"Not a pretty scar. A soldier's scar. But you *were* a soldier. You saved her life."

"Who? Georgie! How is she?"

"She's fine," John replied carefully. "Pru said just told you Georgie was fine. Do you remember?"

"Oh … yes."

"It was a good thing you wore goggles. And your helmet."

"Oh, thank God. And how is Archie?" She looked to John for help and found none in his blank expression. "No, not Archie. Archie's in Bermuda. Her husband. The cameraman. He draws pictures."

John reached up for one of the pencil drawings, and handed it to her. It was a pencil sketch of herself sleeping, a fall of dark hair against white pillows. It struck her as oddly intrusive, that she had been thus observed and preserved by a man she hadn't yet met.

"He—?"

"They took you in shifts, all of them. The QAs, the Westons. Marina wanted to, but if Mama found out I'd let her into this place, with all these men … Anyway, there was always someone. Georgie. Her husband. You were never alone. You'd wake up, ask about Georgie, go back to sleep. It's all here." He held up the clipboard.

"*Nick,*" Lucy remembered. "Her husband. Nick is alright? I was the only one hurt?"

"Both the sappers were killed. As for *you*," John continued, bemused. "You've been two weeks in a coma. When you started to rouse—have a bit of consciousness—they wanted to move you to the English hospital. St. Pants isn't set up for women. But the QAs wouldn't have it. We set you up here. I've told you all this before. You wake, you forget. You might forget this. Not unusual with head injuries. But you've a little more colour this time, you're remembering a bit more. So perhaps you'll stay with us. Can you try, Lucy?"

All the while as he spoke, he handled her, pressing her pulse points, tapping her knee to test her reflexes, dragging a pencil along the sole of her foot, which tickled and made her kick.

"I'm hungry," she said.

As if on cue, a QA arrived with a bowl of soup. John patted Lucy's hand and left her. Lucy was disappointed. *A little caressa Tessa would not have gone amiss*, she thought. The QA spooned soup into her mouth, a service which Lucy had not received since the nursery. Lucy took the spoon away from the nurse. Her hand trembled as she brought the soup to her mouth. She slurped it up and scooped another spoonful. *I can understand not kissing me in a hospital, but … two weeks in a coma … a kiss on the hand, even … but I suppose it's not sanitary.*

"Here, let me," the QA snatched the spoon from her and tipped a spoonful of soup into Lucy's mouth. "You've no strength. We can barely keep you fed. You're drifting off again. Careful, you'll get soup all over that beautiful shawl."

"Thank you. I feel like a … " her eyes closed as though weighed down by coins to pay the ferryman, and the last sensation she had was of soup dripping down her chin.

She slept and woke and slept and woke, as the light changed through the single high-slatted window, throwing light on the shelves in the walls.

"How do you feel?" John asked.

"Like a pearl."

John had a habit, both disconcerting and soothing, of running his hands all over her while they spoke, poking, pressing, instructing ("push against my hand"), patting her before he paused to write on her chart, as Guy Jenner used to reassure his horse as he groomed it. The pinky of her injured hand was so weak she couldn't lift it. The scar on her shoulder itched, which John pronounced "good," but then, it wasn't itching *him*.

"That's new."

"These shelves are like the ridges on the inside of an oyster shell," Lucy gestured toward the walls, and winced at the rebuking twinge in her shoulder. "And everyone has tried to make things so soft."

There were satin pillowcases from the Westons, and a peignoir from Felicity which she was wearing now because it was backless to the waist and didn't whisper against her skin. There was fresh rosemary from the Weston's courtyard, sliced lemons to flavor her water.

"And yet I *prickle*," Lucy said. "It's irritating. A pearl is born by irritation, why aren't we?"

"If that were true, every one of us would be a gem. And we are far from that." John set down the clipboard and pulled a jar from his jacket. "I suppose you're referring to the itching. I've brought ointment for it. If you would strip down to your waist and roll over onto your stomach."

"I thought you'd never ask."

She lowered the straps of the peignoir and gave him a moment to look. He wasted it (she felt) by glancing behind him at the door, which was closed but did not lock. No one had thought to put a lock on the inside of a linen cupboard. Then she rolled carefully onto her stomach and felt his fingers skate across her shoulder blade with ointment, bumping across the small mountain range of her scars.

"Can you raise your hands above your head? Put them above the pillow."

So he was going to ruin this rare touching with physical therapy. He was interested in whether a light massage might soon be incorporated into this undignified relief, to stimulate her *teres major*.

"Yes, your *teres major*," Pru confirmed cheerily during a visit. "Georgie asked if it would affect your tennis. When they brought you in. She was in shock. Kept talking about tennis. Your Cortlandt racquet. *Covered* in your blood. Shaking like a leaf. I cleaned her off myself. The sight of her was upsetting the boys."

"Raise your right hand?" John asked. "Higher? Let me know when it hurts."

"It hurts."

A soldier's scar, he called it. He was treating her as a soldier while she was confined to this linen closet. She wondered whether he would find it difficult to see her again as a lover, to stroke the shoulder he was now probing for pain. She would have worried about it, but she couldn't spare the energy.

"A pearl," she repeated. "I told Ruth's father he threw away a pearl richer than all his tribe."

"They say Rommel captured Mersa Matruh," John said. "Took the whole base prisoner. Nearly 6,000 men."

"Matruh," Lucy echoed. "That's less than 200 miles away. They're that close?"

"They're that close." John turned her over, carefully, helped her sit up, pulled up her straps, watched gravely while Lucy tucked her breasts into the cups of the peignoir. She was unaccustomed to wearing anything as caressing and impractical as a peignoir. Her injured *teres major* was unaccustomed to the strain of the tuck, right arm helping left breast into left cup. Guy Jenner would have eagerly helped her breast into its peignoir cup, but John was more interested in the effort it took her, the wincing it provoked. *At the hospital, I am a doctor.*

"And when they come through the city gates," John was saying, "Can I trust you not to run about saving every stray? You've saved someone now. You've saved your friend."

"There is a plan in place," Lucy said. "For what to do if they get through the city gates. Can you hand me — "

John handed her Ruth's sketch book. Georgie had brought it to the hospital, hoping it would comfort her. It still hurt Lucy to read, but she liked to look at the sketches Ruth had made of Lark, of Georgie, of roses, of that banyan tree, over and over, in the agricultural station. She looked at the page where Ruth had practiced Tessa's notations on the Bach. *Lente, lente, luc.* She was able to make out the page where Ruth had practiced Brooklyn Joe's handwriting: *The Hudson River is the where the piers are, where the ships dock. The readiness is all.*

"I'm more concerned with my pearl," John watched her turn the pages. "Than with what you wrote to Ruth's father. She never drew you."

"What?" Lucy looked up from the pages. "No, she never did. She always talked when we were together. Not many had the patience to listen to her. Or I gave her piano lessons. Or—oh, I suppose she thought we had world enough and time."

"Ah, they're playing our poem." He kissed her hand. "I must go to my other patients."

"John. Is there anyone like me in the hospital?"

"Underfoot?"

"A volunteer. I don't want to bother the nurses. They're too busy. But I'd like to dictate a letter."

July 19, 1942

Dear Judge Barrington-Smith,

I am alive. You are dedicated to evidence. Exhibit one, I am alive enough to correspond. Exhibit two, this letter is written on hospital stationery, which indicates recovery. But in argument (I must drop this metaphor now, I did not study law), the handwriting is not mine. I am dictating this letter because I have recently suffered an injury which placed me in this hospital. I incurred this injury saving the life of Georgina Taylor, one of my roommates at the Princess Hotel.

I did not save Ruth. The man who murdered her, Lt. William Inman of the Army Corps of Engineers, told me that he expected to find me with Ruth. He wanted to talk to me, he said. I walked with Ruth often on a Sunday afternoon because she liked to sketch a certain banyan tree at the agricultural station, again and again. I think you might be familiar with the comfort she took in routine. I enclosed a drawing of the tree I have torn from her sketch book.

Regarding Bill Inman, who killed your daughter, I suppose he hoped to "reconcile" with me in what he thought was a great romance. It was not a great romance. It was not love. I am in now in love. It is quite a different feeling. The man I love makes me feel accepted and cared for.

And I hope, Judge Barrington-Smith, that I may have made Ruth feel that way. Calm, and accepted and cared for. I think that is love.

I hope my writing to you again does not offend you. I wanted to let you know that Ruth is no longer my albatross—you know, "and a thousand thousand slimy things lived on, and so did I." I have felt so guilty for living. But she taught me how to love. I hope you discover what she taught you. Forgive me if that is forward. But I can only move forward now.

> *Yours sincerely.*
> *Lucia Barrett*

When the volunteer stopped by the next day to ask if she would like any more letters written, Lucy agreed. She dictated letters to the minister at St. Andrew's Presbyterian church in Hamilton, Bermuda, to Captain Daniel Jackson of the U.S. Army Corps of Engineers, to Clara Frith, and to Archie Danville, saying exactly what she had said—to the extent she could remember it—in her earlier letters.

41.

After a few weeks, she was permitted to return to the Westons, to the room she no longer shared with Georgie, who had decamped to the Hotel Marta for the nights when Nick could make it home from the desert. Lucy became kin with the convalescing soldiers at breakfast. She joined them in the tentative flexing and stretching of their recovery, what physical abilities had still not returned to "normal." For Lucy, that meant reading. She could not read fine print. Her eyes tired easily. Major Weston read her Tennyson. Lady Weston read her the society page of the *Cairo English News*. John came in the evenings and read poetry to her in the back garden. She preferred poetry as she recovered, ephemeral phrases she could savor and not fret over forgetting.

Georgie travelled to Cairo and returned with soft things to wear. After one trip, she returned with letters from the Embassy, only two weeks old. Lady Weston made a tea party of it, with lemonade and biscuits in the courtyard, with the clucking hens.

September 1, 1942

Mia,

In the words of Romeo, "I will omit no opportunity/that may convey my greetings, love, to thee." In my own words—Dad has informed us that we can get letters into the diplomatic pouch to Cairo. He will take them to London for us. I am at Knoll House. Why? Well, as they sang in the Great War, "we're here because we're here because we're here because we're here." In other words, I can't tell you why.

I've barely set pen to paper and Dad is shouting that there is no time, if we're to get our letters into the pouch! Hasn't Dad made a hash of things! He phoned Knoll House—and you can imagine how involved that was, with all the phone connections needing to be made, and in wartime, too—to say 'Lucia is alive.' The telephonist at

Knollborough heard it along with the rest of us, and the news spread through the village and to the Jenner place and to the Ripple Farm and soon all of Knollborough was at our door, like the villagers in a Frankenstein film storming the castle, demanding answers! (I didn't think you had that many friends, sis. You were always studying.)

Dad and Granny are still quarreling. She is foregoing this opportunity to get a swift letter to you in favor of delivering to Dad another bad time. If he hadn't sent you halfway around the world in the first place! etc. etc. (I do quite enjoy hearing all this screaming and crockery banging—I wish you could be here for it. It sounds like she just threw a teakettle at him.)

The man who brings the milk (in a cart and horse, thank you, Hitler) is heading back to town. He's my ride to the train to London. They say you saved someone's life. Write to us immediately. Everyone is frayed with worry.

Your loyal brother,
Basso Profondo

P.S. Marcia wants to add a letter.

Dear Lucy,

Matty is a beast. He only now told me I could write a letter for the pouch! I am running the farm for Granny. I look after the Land Girls, and our last evacuee, Hannah. Her mother was killed in London, and she has no one else, so now she is ours.

I'm so sorry you were hurt. Dad says you will recover. Does that mean you will be coming home? Your friend wired us that you are in good hands. I miss you. It seems so long ago we were all a family at Mowbray Crescent.

In your last letter to me, you asked for a drawing. I think of Granny's garden? Here it is, and a sketch I did of Matty. Matty is saying hurry. I haven't said what I wanted and I know this letter will do *nothing to dispel your notion that I'm poorly educated. I miss you and I pray for you,*

Your sister Marcia

Georgie handed over the sketches, which Lucy examined and shared around the table, pencil sketches of Matty with wearier eyes, and a colourful vegetable garden, which was of great interest to Lady Weston.

"There is one from your father," Georgie said. "And there is one from New York. From an 'R. Lark.' I say, Lucy, do we *know* an 'R. Lark?'"

August 22, 1942,

Dear Lucy,

A kind woman at the British Embassy here has given me the use of a desk, a typewriter, and an hour to get a letter in the pouch to you. An hour! Where do I begin! It is August. AUGUST! I last heard from you in March.

Georgie wrote to tell me that you blame yourself for Ruth's death. You believe Bill killed Ruth and that Bill did so because of you. Let me set you straight on that account.

Bill is an arrogant, violent man. True, he might not have bothered to speak to Ruth, nor she to him, had you not been in both their lives. True, he resented her because your attention to her took attention from him. But how an earth does that make you responsible? Do you believe that Bill's love for you drove him to this desperate act? OF COURSE IT DIDN'T. That desperate act was already within him. I do believe that all acts, both noble and base, are already within us. God, and sometimes certain people, can bring out our better qualities. It is our great struggle in life to turn toward the better qualities, and to eschew the worst. A man in love with you should be glad to be in love with you, and not so bitterly jealous that your love is shared. 'Jealousy is cruel as the grave.' Bill Inman was cruel, and sent our friend to her grave. But the same verse says 'Love is as strong as death.'

Love is as strong as death. You were never anything but loving to Ruth.

But as Ruth is gone, I must ask you to be loving to me.

Yes, I make a blatant appeal to your charity! I endured months of a lonely New York winter, AND my first semester at Columbia Medical College, and I expected—was it wrong for me to expect? —more communication from you. FREQUENT communication! You always had so much to say. I thought we were close. I valued our friendship so dearly, despite your untidy habits.

'Thanks' to the war, I am NOT the only female student at the college. There are a dozen of us. We have formed a study group. It helps, because we study year-round. The urgent need for our services precludes the dictates of the academic calendar.

They are wonderful friends, but they are not you. They are not Georgie. They are not Ruth. They are not even Gwynne!

Georgie sent me a letter notifying me of your whereabouts, the work you were doing, and your melancholy state of mind. How you blamed yourself for Ruth. How you couldn't think of 'what to say' to me. You know now. You will say that you understand that Bill killed Ruth, and not because of you.

You will say that Bill will not silence you. You will say that he destroyed one friendship, but you will not let him destroy another.

You will say you are sorry that the first word I've had from you since last spring was a TELEGRAM! I have it here in my handbag. It says 'Lucy badly hurt. Report to Brit embassy at once.'

Badly hurt? Where? How? I had an exam this morning and had to show my professor your telegram. He asked, as one would, 'Who is Lucy to you?' and I thought YOU MAY WELL ASK for all I've heard from her.

When I got here, I was given Georgie's longer letter, which told me that you saved her life and that you are under the care of a dashing doctor! The kind Embassy woman has given the clock SEVERAL *significant looks, so I must finish. She's just said my name, so I really must stop. WRITE TO ME. You are in my prayers.*

Your loving sister,
Rebecca Lark

42.

Cecina, Italy, 1929

Somewhere in the night sky, there is a hunter. There is a swan, and a dolphin, and seven sisters. There are also two queens, whom Lucy would in particular like to decipher from this dazzle of stars, but she can't even decipher the obvious ones—the hunter, for example, the giant Orion. Or Sirius, the great dog-star who reigns over summer. How does her Nonno, how do sailors, fetch that astral pup out of the night sky, against such a bountiful array which in some places forms frostings so dense they could be smeared across a hot cross bun?

Lucy seeks the two queens. Most of the sky is dominated by men and animals. The queens are Ethiopian: Cassiopeia and Andromeda. Ethiopia is significant to Lucy only because it is among the words which interrupt her contented sleep when she wakes to the arguments drifting up from the patio amongst the adults: *Mussolini, fascisti, totalitario!*

Aunt Celestina types scholarly papers while wearing shopworn cardigans, chain-smoking in front of an open window which looks down on the bay, where she can survey and scold everyone: her own children, her nieces, her nephews young enough to heed her, her sister Tessa, her brothers Matteo and Marco. Celestina has been head of the household since she was eighteen, when Nonna died. She raised baby Tessa along with her own daughters, Seraphina and Aurora. Lucy loves her cousins' heavenly names but fears them as devils who smoke cigarettes at their bedroom window at night, drink more wine at dinner than they are allowed, sneak into town to see local boys and pinch Lucy's arm painfully, as though turning a dial, to ensure her silence.

There are so many cousins, and second cousins, and cousins removed by generations, that the children are grouped in rooms in the villa by age and gender, with the babies, including two-year-old Marcia, sharing the nursery. They spend little time in their rooms. The bay is just outside. There is a tiny beach at the end of a steep staircase of seventy-two steps. Her cousin Santo keeps a small sailboat and takes Lucy out to show her the dolphins. The dolphins leap around the boat like an aquatic *corps de ballet*. Santo imitates their clicking talk, and tells Lucy that the Greeks considered the playful creatures to be the messengers of Neptune. The other bragging boy cousins follow his lead and allow Lucy—*la cugina inglese* — liberties they do not permit their own sisters because Lucy is here only for the summer, until, *che peccato!*, she will turn back into an *inglese*. Aunt Celestina permits the children over the age of eight—so Lucy makes the cut-off—one glass of watered-down wine with dinner. And there are nighttime star lessons with Nonno, who tells of the stars and their stories.

"See, see, Lucia!" Nonno says. "See, see!" She loses track of when he abandons trying to make her see mythical figures in the firmament and returns to Italian to praise the stars. "*Si, si!*" Matty catches on quickly, sorting out the patterns. He is already determined to fly, and has begun to acquaint himself with the heavens. But Lucy struggles even to separate the stars from planets. She cannot connect the dots.

"There," Matty stands back from the telescope and points "Right *there*."

"They're *all* 'right there,'" Lucy complains. "Pointing doesn't *help*. How can I see one star out of millions?"

"It is because there are millions that we must care about one," Nonno tells her. When she turns from the telescope, he takes her hand and pulls her to the grass beside him. This is what she loves, being cradled in his arm, lying on the grass on the hill above the villa. She loves that the grass doesn't fully cool in the evening, embraced as it is during the day by a sun as fierce as the hugs bestowed upon her by her little cousins in the nursery, who cling to her ferociously when she visits to kiss her sister Marcia good night.

The little cousins want kisses, too! They hug her as though their embrace might pull her nine-year-old essence into their four-year-old selves and save them the bother of learning through experience. The cousins are as demonstrative as the English stereotype paints them. They pinch, smack, kiss, hug. Even Seraphina and Aurora pause in their savagery to lavish attention on her. They kiss her cheeks, braid her hair, plop beribboned family photo albums onto her bed to show her sepia images of a stiff, earlier generation, help her sort all these uncles and aunts cousins: *You look exactly like Zia Tessa! Look here! 'The baby, the beauty, the favorite,' they intone dramatically, imitating their sighing mother.*

"It is because there are millions that we must be humble," Nonno says. "We are ourselves one in millions. Yet we each carry a light, no? Millions of stars, millions of people. Ah, your mama says you can say that in French, Can you, *mia cara*?"

"*Des millions d'étoiles, des millions de personnes*. That is not even difficult, Nonno."

"So clever. Your sister is so clever, Matteo."

"She can't see Cassiopeia."

The vacation in Cecina is less easy for Matty. The boy cousins size him up rather than make a pet of him. He is ten, a neither-fish-nor-fowl age, which excludes him from the activities of both the teenagers and the children. He spends his days with kites and atlases and at night, pesters Nonno to take the telescope up the hill. Nonno does so, every night, because Matty is the first born of Tessa, who truly is the favorite.

"I want to see what you see, Nonno."

"That is our tragedy, no, Lucia? We can never see exactly what another sees."

Nonno kisses her temple and Lucy sighs in contentment. She doesn't feel the least bit tragic, nestled in Nonno's arms on this warm hill under a sky full of stories. She can't make out Cassiopeia and Andromeda. But it is enough to know that they are up there, those wise queens, guiding sailors across seas.

43.

Alexandria, 1942

Lucy spent the autumn of 1942 idle, still recovering, unable to read. She sat in on some interrogations. She was able, with the trembling in her damaged arm, to evoke a shared sense of horror in the prisoners. But the captured Italians truly knew nothing, and she was reduced to conversing with them and determining their fates as prisoners of war. She tried to read. But words seemed distant and blurred, like something on the desert horizon.

John took her to the cinema. He took her gleefully to see *I Married a Witch*, with Veronica Lake. He took her to *Casablanca* and *Now, Voyager.* John was rapt at the movies. He noted everything—the disappearance of characters, the mistakes in medical jargon. Afterwards, he and Lucy shared a bottle of wine at a cafe while John picked at plot points. How was shy, chunky Bette Davis in *Now, Voyager* so easily transformed into a suave swan? What sort of psychiatrist was Claude Rains supposed to be—did he provide fashion advice? In *Casablanca*, how was the town so spotless and all the refugees in it supplied with pressed, elegant clothes? Even the grifter played by Peter Lorre wore a pristine suit. (Don't get Lucy started on the wardrobe of Ingrid Bergman, who apparently fled the Nazis with a dozen hatboxes in tow.) Was Claude Rains's change of heart at the end due to a crush on Humphrey Bogart? Was Claude Rains in all movies? Well, no, he was not in *To Sin for Love*, written and directed by Nicholas Lincoln. Leslie Howard was in that.

Although Nick Lincoln bore no resemblance to Leslie Howard beyond a posh blond Englishness, Lucy could easily picture him uttering the damning words from *To Sin for Love*, that his bridge would be "forever tainted" in his eyes.

She tried to like Nick. He was devoted to Georgie. He always kept her anchored to him—his arm around her shoulders, his hand covering hers on the table, as though at the first chance of liberty she would flutter away to sin for love. She saw in him the pomposity he had bestowed upon the Leslie Howard character. He called Georgie "darling," and "my love," as though she didn't have a name. But he had married a woman with a different name. He had married a different woman, and was now reunited with one who Lucy knew better than he did.

Nick photographed them, and made presents of their images. He stayed at the Hotel Marta with Georgie when he came in from the Western Desert, where the battle of El-Alamein raged on. Lucy adorned her now-private room with photographs of Georgie and herself in the garden at the Westons, John and herself at Stanley Beach. When Nick was away for days, Georgie returned to the Westons, hummed herself to sleep at Lucy's side. But most nights, Lucy lay rigid in her now-empty bed, listening to the tutting of the hens and the rustling of the wind and the sirocco of worries that roiled through her head now she was alone.

Then came November, and with it a turning in fortune. Churchill described it in a speech as "the end of the beginning," of the war, when the British won the second battle of El-Alamein. Lucy knew of it almost as soon as it happened. El-Alamein was closer to Alex than Knoll House was to London. Yet her father still thought it necessary to instruct her on the importance of this victory. Despite his sentimental lapse, most letters from her father were bossy, and she took a time in getting through them, batting them back and forth like her cat Horatio with a mouse, before liberating them from their envelopes, reading a sentence or two before huffing and dropping the letter, only to take it up again—

"For *heaven's sake!*" Georgie snatched the letter away. They were in a booth at the bar in the Cecil Hotel, with their men. Nick was sunburned and sand-scratched from his recent sojourn in the desert, filming the German General von Thoma surrendering to Field Marshal Montgomery at the end of the second battle of El-Alamein. Georgie had been flooded with captured German documents to translate and categorize. Lucy's task had turned from interrogating to processing the tens, perhaps hundreds, of thousands of Italian prisoners. She was less the 'Angel of Death' than a beleaguered clerk at passport control, reducing each man to data on a card, deflecting their attempts at flirtation, even connection. No, she could not get word back to a wife. She was not the Red Cross. No, she could not tell them where they were going. She did not know.

And yet her father, thousands of miles away, felt it his job to tell her:

"'Securing North Africa is of vital importance,'" Lucy read. "'Cecil Whiting has a fine reputation in embassy circles. I know nothing of his wife, of course, but I'm told that her father was an archaeologist who made significant contributions to the field. When the war is over, you can ask your Nonno about him.'"

"Or you could ask me," John said. "He was *my* Nonno. We climbed the Pyramids together."

"Why 'of course'?" Georgie asked. "'I know nothing of his wife, *of course*'?"

"A proper lady has a very little public life," Lucy said.

"Oh, Lucy!" Georgie exclaimed. "I shall miss you!"

Lucy understood from the way Nick caught both his breath and her hand that Georgie had gone off-script, that they had arranged this "drinks at the Cecil" in the tumult of El-Alamein, for specific news. They seemed happy. *Sunny*, she would have said, so fair-haired and blue-eyed, a photographic negative of John and herself. The blatant news, that Georgie was expecting a child, was obvious; she was three and half months gone. The other news—that combined Yank and British forces had landed in West Africa, on the shores of Morocco—was also common knowledge. Once again, the

Yanks had arrived.

"*Miss* me," Lucy repeated, suddenly hearing the words, as though they had just emerged from translation. Her stomach performed the same queasy flips she experienced when she fainted across the prisoner at St. Pantaleon's.

"I never thought I'd come to like you this much!" Georgie reached for a cocktail napkin to dry her tears. "I told Archie I didn't think you'd stick it out! But you did. Working out the Brooklyn Joe puzzle. Catching that Vichy witch. So clever. And so kind to Ruth. You blame yourself for Ruth, but it's really my doing."

"*How?*"

"I singled her out. I singled out all of you. Lark and Ruth and you. If I'd just left her in the herd, maybe she wouldn't've—we were a little team, weren't we, the four of us?" Georgie said. "And that's down to you. And now we're all broken up."

"*Why?*" Lucy asked. "Are you ill?"

"My baby."

"Your baby's ill?"

"I'm going to England to have her."

"Of course you're not," Lucy laughed and sipped her wine. "Ridiculous! It's far too dangerous. The trip alone …" She watched Nick and Georgie's eyes meet. "Have the baby here. We have doctors *here*." She gestured to John. When they responded with matching rueful smiles, she repeated, "*No*. How do you think you'll get through the Med? Nick, how can you think of it? *No!*"

John took her hand and nodded at the other patrons, the variations of Major Burdocks whose esteem he both coveted and despised. Even the waiters had turned their heads. Lucy wondered if she could teach John to say *who the hell cares* in all the languages he professed to speak but wondered more acutely if she could teach him to tickle her back when she couldn't sleep, the way Georgie did.

Lark was half a world away, Ruth was buried in foreign soil. Her original family had been reduced to prayers and letters, England to an abstraction of green and tradition, an extravagance of propriety and rain. She had adapted to this parsing of water, both in Bermuda and here in the desert, but she had not expected to have to ration, bit by bit, the hard-won comfort of her friends.

"Why?" she said again. "El-Alamein's won. It's *ours*. It's safer here than in England."

"North Africa isn't won," Nick said. "The war's not won. I have to go back to the field. I won't be here to take care of her."

"Take *care* of her!" Lucy shouted. "Is *that* what you call what you've been doing? All the more reason she should stay here. *I'll* look after her! I saved her *life!*"

Nick asked. "So now you tell her how to live it?"

"Do *you?*" A splash on her hand alerted Lucy to her flow of tears. John nudged her, held out his handkerchief. She snuffled into her knuckles. John pressed it into her hand and she flung it away, as petulantly as she had thrown the red dress Tessa held up as she packed Lucy's trunk for a summer of exile at Knoll House. She had been grieved then by the prospect of only a summer of separation. But *this* separation was surely forever. This was a proper goodbye, and she was flooding it with tears. *What noise of water in mine ears!*

"Look at the state of her," Nick chided Georgie. "How did you ever think she would bear up under torture?"

"What the bloody hell do you think *this* is!" Lucy cried.

Nick offered his handkerchief. This crisply ironed cloth, lovingly embroidered by Georgie, Lucy accepted, knowing she would never return it. Why should he have it when he had everything else.

"*Excusez-moi, messieurs, mesdames.*" A waiter appeared carrying a tray holding four glasses of water, which he set smoothly before each of them. "We provide, if you wish—" he gestured to a corner booth framed by dark curtains. "—a more intimate setting to offer patrons who require privacy."

"Yes," Nick nodded in agreement at the waiter's delicate phrasing of the sentiment *sobbing, cursing women are not the preferred clientele of the long bar at the Cecil Hotel.* "Darling, why don't you two —?"

"No." Lucy gulped her glass of water. "No, I'm alright. When?"

"Quite soon," Nick said. "British Pathé want the films. The battles. The want to see the boys. Monty accepting the surrender of that Jerry general. They want the films in the cinemas as soon as possible. Chuff them up. Pathé will cobble together a documentary about the victory in the desert. Of course, it won't be an *actual* documentary but they'll use the raw footage to augment reconstructed scenes—"

"Nick, will you *shut up about films!* What's that to do with Georgie?"

"She'll be going back with the films," Nick said. "Cargo plane to Lisbon. Leaves tomorrow."

***

Outside the Cecil, Georgie and Lucy embraced and wept, bucked up and fell to again.

"You write to me," Lucy told Georgie. "You write to me as soon as you land, wherever you are. Casablanca, Lisbon. As *soon* as you're in London. If this bolthole where your cad of a husband proposes to shelter you falls through, or if he decides to abandon you again—"

"Oh, Lucy."

"—you go to Knoll House. There are people there. Loads of people. My sister, my Granny. Land Girls. Don't be alone. Promise me. You call my father at the Admiralty. You call him when your water breaks. You call him if you break a nail. You promise me."

"I'll be fine."

"What am I going to do without you."

"Nonsense. You've done it all yourself. The bank statements. Brooklyn Joe. You can manage Burdock. He's wrapped around your finger. And so is Captain Whiting, if you'll have him. I think you should."

Nick and John murmured to each other, eyeing Lucy and Georgie as though they might need to a separate a brawl between them. John wore a greatcoat, Nick, an aviator's flight jacket. The night was chilly but not chilly enough to warrant their stamping their feet and blowing on their hands as they did. When the women turned to them, the men stepped forward hopefully.

"'When the hurly-burly's done,'" Lucy said.

They kissed and fell into one last embrace. Then the men disentangled them and led them on their separate ways.

John draped Lucy under a flap of his greatcoat as he walked her to the courtyard of the Weston's house, where he customarily kissed her goodnight and saw her into the house. This time, he asked her to make him a cup of tea. She led him into the kitchen and put the kettle on. She washed her tear-swollen, snot-laden face in the kitchen sink. On any other night, she would have gone upstairs to reapply powder and lipstick. But she couldn't bring herself to look into a mirror which would never again reflect Georgie. *Now I am alone.* And on any other night, John would have kissed her rather than requesting a cup of tea. She was probably too much of a mess to kiss.

She was drying her face on a kitchen towel when John asked, "I need to ask you something. Are you spies?"

"What?"

"You lot. Nick. Georgie. You."

"What? No. How silly you are." She located the teapot, scooped tea in.

"I am silly." John was so far from silly he could barely form the word. "Like asking a liar 'Are you a liar?' When you two were saying goodbye, Nick said 'I believe Daisy loves that girl more than she loves me.' Is Georgie's real name Daisy?"

"I've never heard her called Daisy." Lucy set two cups on the table. No need to fuss about cream and sugar. There wasn't any. "Maybe it's a pet name?"

"'The kind of German you learn in a Berlin kindergarten,'" John said. "I'm not the jealous sort, not like Nick. My feeling is that if you love other people, huzzah, that shows you're loving. You love Georgie. You loved this Ruth. I never expected anyone's full attention. There are six of us, after all, and the boys all get sent away. If you and I marry, I'd like some attention for awhile. I suppose children will come, although that never seemed to stop my parents. But I would like to know if the woman I hope to marry is a spy. And if so, what side she is on. If you're not a fascist, I think it's only fair to tell me."

"I'm delighted to know you're not the jealous sort." Lucy was too worn out by her grief in losing Georgie (Annegret/Daisy) to experience true delight, but she felt a suffusion of contentment at John's straightforward mention of marriage, without expectation, without entitlement. Guy had presented marriage to her as a wild adventure designed to annoy their parents. Bill had offered it as an honour for which she would be expected to strive daily to prove herself worthy, till death relieved her of the part. "And no, I am not a fascist. But thank you for asking."

She poured boiling water from the kettle into the teapot.

"I was hoping for something a bit more ... robust, I think." John watched the steam rise from his pot. "When I mentioned marriage."

"It's good that we know who we are. What we expect. I work for British Intelligence, you know that. But spy? A spy is in disguise, I think?"

"All women are in disguise, if you ask me."

Lucy sat down and took his hand. "Most of the time, they have to be. I will be whatever I have to be until the war is over."

She heard a stirring upstairs and hoped they had not woken up the Westons. The Westons, she realized, would be kind of in-laws to her. The thought gladdened her more than she expected.

"And then what will you be?" John asked.

"I suppose we'll find out together."

PART FIVE
A WOMAN OF LETTERS

44.

Cairo, 1943

August 11, 1943

Dear Lucy,

I meant to write sooner, first after the birth of my daughter and then after I learned of the death of our dear Leslie Howard. I know you liked him. If you had known him as I did, you would have loved him. That flight he was on, the Ibis, they say it was blown up by the Jerries. It was the same flight that brought me safely home, the KLM Lisbon-to-London route. All the planes in that fleet are named after birds. Ruth would have liked that. I remember thinking of that when I was on the flight, trying to keep my fear at bay, all the logical things Ruth would say. By some gentlemen's agreement, the Jerries never attacked the planes on that route. Until they did. And we lost Leslie

Howard.

Leslie came back from Hollywood. He could have spent a comfortable career there, particularly after 'Gone With the Wind'. But his country was at war. When he was killed, he was in Portugal on a propaganda mission, on his way back to England to make another film.

But we must put that aside. You will want to hear about little Lucia! She is fine and healthy now. I say 'now' because it is all down to your family. You have probably already received letters from them, but I will tell you the story again.

I had a bit of a housing problem when I returned to London. Nick's flat was rented. An actress friend put me up for my confinement but left to make a film shortly after the birth. The birth was not easy. For weeks, I was terribly weak. I was so weak it took all the strength I had to queue up for my rations. Some days I just couldn't. I was too tired and too cold. The hunger only made me weaker. I could not feed Lucia. I didn't have the milk. I never thought that I would not have the milk. But I didn't have food, and so couldn't make food for her. It is strange what we are reduced to. I could not make her settle and to be honest (and if this gets past the censor), I was still bleeding from the birth.

You remember what I told you about my first baby, Rebecca. How she died. One morning, Lucia wouldn't take my milk. She went quiet. I was used to her fussing and screaming and shoving at me. But she just went quiet. I went a little mad. I couldn't lose another child, and I couldn't think who I could call on for help. Then I remembered what you said. I telephoned the Admiralty and asked for your father. Man after man inquired "What is the nature of your call," etc. etc. Finally, I was put through to a WREN with a Scottish burr.

I must have cried myself to sleep because the next thing I knew, the WREN was clucking about in that cold flat. She had fresh linens and napkins and warm milk and bread and tins of food. She made soup. Your father came that night, Lucy, with a hot meal for me. He held your namesake and fed her milk, as did the WREN, drop by drop, from a bottle. They ordered me to bed. For the first time in a month, I really slept. I woke up in the back seat of a car and by nightfall I was *at Knoll House.*

The WREN packed my ration book, toothbrush and towel, nappies, blankets and pots and pans from my friends' flat—this was for the Land Girls little kitchen in their stable. But it's fair to say I arrived with the clothes I stood up in. Your Barretts embraced me like a stray cat. Lucia wears Marcia's baby clothes. Your Granny bosses me about, follows me with cups of broth, takes Lucia from my arms and orders me to sleep. I sleep in your bed.

How I love Knoll House! It thrives with industry. Especially now at harvest time. Your sister and Hannah (she introduced herself as "the evacuee" but was corrected immediately by your sister as an "honourary Barrett"), all of them. The Land Girls, your Granny, and Marcia keep us and the village fed, warm, clothed. The Jenners should by rights feed the Land Girls, since they work mostly his land, but their house holds only Mr. Jenner now, and it is freezing and empty. The girls prefer the stable at Knoll House. It is cozy. They have fixed it up with a stove for cooking, and Marcia chops (!) and hauls in firewood for the chimney. And they have each other. Remember how that felt? Your sister is badgering them into being a choir. At night, after dinner, they gather around the piano and sing, after a long day in the fields.

As for me—well, as Lark would have it, I toil not, neither do I spin. Your Granny would say my job is motherhood now. What do I do? Let's see.

I mind the household linen and clothes, I wash and darn and mend. I walk Lucia into Knollborough in her carriage—your family's baby carriage—with everyone's ration books and I fill the grocery order. Even this is far more than Granny wants me to do. She is vexed by my walking back, up that long hill. But it saves much time for Marcia, who used to do the grocery order and now can attend to her dozens of tasks. I have tiny duties in the garden—it really is the most fantastic garden, Lady Weston would be SICK with envy—but your Granny will let me sit and tell her stories about you and Bermuda, and you and Alex.

I did, as you asked, write to Judge Barrington-Smith and let him know about Lucia. She is Lucia Ruth Lincoln. In return, I received a congratulatory note from his chambers, and a cheque for fifty pounds. Fifty pounds! It is both far too much and far, far too little. I gave it to Granny. She gave it back. So I had a talk with Marcia. She told me to put thirty in the bank. She spent the other twenty. A Land Girl needed new boots and they have to be made by hand, and in London, as it's hard to find boots for women, and even worse in wartime. She had a tractor repaired. She bought curtain fabric (for some reason, curtain fabric is not rationed) and asked me to make additional bedding for the Land Girls. She bought more hens, and a rooster. She went to the Jenners to check if they needed anything. She came back with several useful household items, a great pile of men's clothes, and some very bad news.

I am so sorry to tell you that your old beau Guy Jenner was killed in action on the North Atlantic several months ago. That is why George Jenner is neglecting his house, and it is Guy's clothes he sent home with Marcia. The girls are making use of what they can. I have made a dress for Lucia out of one of Guy's silk shirts. Marcia plans to take the rest to the village. "And not the bloody church jumble, I know who needs what." She certainly does! She is so like you and yet unlike you.

Write to me soon.

Love,
Georgie, honourary Barrett

September 3, 1943

Dear Lucy,

I am now a doctor. I am also probably a fool. Alan was in town on shore leave before he shipped out, to where he could not say. He took me to dinner to celebrate my graduation. We went dancing. He asked me to marry him. He told me that after the war he wanted to study civil engineering at Cooper Union (it is a school here in New York City) and after that we could move anywhere in the country, any-

where that is growing and new, where they need roads and bridges and airfields. He said he thought it would be a fine thing, having a doctor as a mother to his children. He said he would even let me practice medicine, since I had worked so hard for it. He said some other things, but I was still hearing, "Heck, I'll even let you practice medicine."

He thought he was being generous. I was flattered to consider the time he had spent creating this vision, the two of us in Texas or California, him building a community, me healing it, minding our litter of children with scraped knees and fevers. But I have spent our time apart picturing something else.

When we were in Bermuda, I thought that if I could work up the courage to return to medical college, I would focus on becoming a surgeon. I practiced sewing. I have the temperament for it as well. "Very skilled with the knife, and commendable grace under pressure," was the assessment at Columbia. "However," this assessment added, "she is a woman, and no one will hire her once the men come home."

It is obvious that they will let me work while the war is on, but once it is over, I will face a constant uphill climb. I don't have your serenity in the face of scorn. I want to do good work, and not have to fight every day for the privilege to do it. I found myself thinking of what I had been doing before I was attacked in Ontario. The work with the mice and the infection.

There are several pharmaceutical companies in New Jersey who are working to develop a more easily transportable form of penicillin. I told you, I think, that it is imperative that we get the medicine to the men before they succumb to the infections from their wounds. I had begun to picture offering my services there.

So I could not say yes to Alan. The marriage vows say "forsaking all others," and I have always believed that these "others" who must be forsaken are not only people, but also priorities. I would like to be Dr. Lark for awhile, before I am Mrs. Anyone.

But I did not say no, either. I am very fond of him in many ways. I asked him to give me time to think it over while he was away. While he was in Manhattan, we would consider ourselves engaged to be married. With all the privileges that provides. The marriage vows also say 'With my body, I thee worship.' I hope you take my meaning. I am sure the censor does.

Now he is gone, but I like to think I sent him away happy.

And what news of you? Write to me soon,

Your loving sister,
Rebecca Lark

July 1, 1943

My dear Miss Barrett,

I have asked Archie Danville to take this letter with him when he travels to Washington, D.C., and see if it can be transmitted to you via diplomatic pouch. I have written this letter several times, but cannot think of a way to couch it without offending the censors.

As you predicted, Lt. Inman of the U.S. Army Corps of Engineers did indeed indulge in his unfortunate tendencies with another young woman on this island. They were walking out—I don't know what young people call it these days—and one evening, he interfered with her. She confided in her minister, who happens to be my minister, at St. Andrew's. By then, you had already written to him. She was more concerned about the loss of her purity than in seeking justice, but the Reverend persuaded her to file a police report.

Lt. Inman was about to ship out with his unit across the Atlantic. I can't say where because I don't know. Because of these charges, and because of his already damaged reputation (due to the persistence of a certain young lady writing letters), he was detained while the police investigated. His unit left without him. In the end, absent a medical report, and with only her word against his, Lt. Inman was free to go. His unit had already shipped out, however. He was able to secure passage on a merchant marine ship.

That ship was less heavily guarded by convoy than the ship he *would have gone out on earlier. The merchant marine ship on which Lt. Inman booked passage was attacked by a U-boat somewhere in the North Atlantic. There were no survivors.*

I know this is not the outcome you desired. But to paraphrase your friend the Bard, 'Leave him to heaven.' I hope this brings you some peace as fervently as I hope we all find peace very soon. Do stay in touch with me, Lucy. I so enjoy your letters.

Your devoted friend,
Louis Furbert

"Can I read your letters?" Marina asked, refilling Lucy's water glass from a pitcher in which lemon slices floated. Lucy had drained her glass dry when she read about the death of Bill, and its cause. They were seated on the veranda of the Whiting house in the suburbs of Cairo, a bungalow painted white, adorned with sets of chairs and tables large enough to host a tea or a bridge party. Marina had been writing in the notebook she used for her Greek lessons when John passed them on his way into the house to see his mother, bestowed a kiss upon both of them, and handed Lucy her letters. He had come in that morning on the train from Alexandria, stopping by the American Express office to pick up her mail. Lucy had come up a few days earlier. When word reached Alex that the Allied forces had entered Naples, she had gone to Burdock and asked to be transferred to Italy.

"We don't send females into combat," he had said.

"Army nurses go."

"Are you an Army nurse?"

"I can translate."

"We have plenty of men doing that. No, no." Burdock had held up his hand against further argument. "Not this time, Lucy. No. We won't discuss this further. Really. We all have limits, even you."

"Do I have your permission to offer my services elsewhere?"

"You can try. They'll say the same thing," Burdock told her.

They did. The British Embassy, the Special Operations Executive, and the Army had chucklingly hinted at secretarial jobs, duller versions of her current workload. In addition to the translation and map work she did with Burdock, she was teaching Italian to British soldiers. None of the men she spoke with seemed much interested in Italy. They were preparing for a conference with some prestigious visitors, Cecil Whiting told her. These visitors would be discussing a different part of the world at war entirely. There was, after all, the matter of the Pacific to be settled.

The Whitings told her she was welcome to stay with them if she preferred to take work in Cairo. But Lucy considered that out of the question. And further, Lucy was now engaged to John with, as Lark had so primly put it, all of the privileges that provided, and she had no intention of exchanging that sweet freedom for the stifling Whiting household in Cairo.

Her mother-in-law-to-be found her puzzling; so far away from home, so much education. The Whiting girls had been tutored at home, if tutors could be found.

"Too much education makes a woman discontent, and distracts her from her duties as a wife and mother," Piama pronounced at a dinner party to her nodding daughters and daughters-in-law. Piama had performed her duty as a *wife*, Lucy reflected, in producing this brood. But as a mother? She presided over them as though they were a pride, and she a lioness, perched on a cliff in the savannah, flicking her tail as she watched her cubs tussle on the plain below. She certainly hadn't spoiled them with excessive maternal love, if the more sensitive of the brood, John and Marina, were anything to go by.

Lucy would return to Alex, with its Mediterranean ambiability, which she preferred to the Anglo-Arab frippery of Cairo social life, and continue working for Burdock. And if she were not to go into Italy, and her job in Alex was to become merely translation, map-making, and teaching, there was no reason, was there, why she should not marry John sooner rather than later.

"Lucy, please may I read your letters?" Marina asked again.

"Now why do you want to do that?"

"John said one of the reasons he fell in love with you was because of how your friends love you. So I want to read your friends' letters. I never get letters! And if we're going to be sisters, we should share everything."

"Do you read the letters of your other sisters?"

"They're not my *sisters*," Marina said with the chiding gentleness Lucy's Greek tutor employed when she chose the wrong word. "We have the same *parents*. They don't get letters, either. They only receive invitations to boring parties and weddings and christenings."

Sophia and Elena were, after all, much older than Marina, both married by the time Marina was old enough to read. Her eyes were so earnest, like her brother's. Lucy wondered, if she and John had a daughter, if she would look like Marina. She wondered whether naming their daughter Ruth would condemn her to expectations she may not be able to realize. What if Ruth Whiting turned out to be a Felicity, disinclined to intellectual pursuits, burdened with redeeming the tragic fate of a ghost, when she would already be burdened with such serious parents as John and Lucy?

"Very well." Lucy handed her Georgie and Lark's letters, holding back Louis Furbert's. "Georgie had a baby girl and named her for me. This one says an old beau is dead."

"Oh! Are you heartbroken?"

"Well, as the poet said, 'any man's death diminishes me.' But, no."

"Were you in love with him?"

"No."

"Then why was he your beau?"

"He was just ... there. I was lonely. On a lonely island. He expected it. He was handsome, rich. He sent flowers. Paid compliments. Gave me gifts. He was a good dancer. But I could not love him."

"'*But I cannot love him!*'" Marina declaimed. "'*A gracious person, but I cannot love him. He might have took his answer long ago.*'"

The speech was from *Twelfth Night*. Marina had omitted chunks of it, but Lucy was leery of correcting her. Correction only inspired further campaigns for aid in her education.

"If only he *had* took his answer," Lucy said.

"John isn't like that," Marina said. "Flowers and compliments. But you do love him, don't you? And you do want to be my sister?"

"Of course I do, Marina."

"I wish you'd set a date. Once you're in the family, you can *really* help me get a proper education."

The rest of her war would play out in Alex. In the war films churned out by Hollywood and British Gaumont, which John favored as the choice for their cinematic outings (over such melodrama as *To Sin for Love*), handsome soldiers, felled by a single bullet, died with quiet exhalations. John regarded these scenes with the same impassive gaze Lucy wore when Burdock pontificated. But she watched John in profile, saw his jaw muscle twitch as he ground his teeth. In those same films, captured Allied airmen, their sculpted cheekbones smudged with one streak of dirt to convey the ordeal of their plane crash, were told by sneering Nazis, "*For you, zee var ees over.*"

Perhaps her war was over. Or at least, her meaningful contribution to it. Perhaps she had saved what she had been meant to save. If not her mother, if not Ruth, then a million dollars from the hands of the Nazis, then the handsome yachts in Hamilton Harbour, then nameless battalions sent to the Brooklyn Naval Yard who boarded ships unsabotaged, who sailed from New York harbour unscathed. Then she saved Georgie. And so, Georgie's Lucia. And now Marina.

Lucy, temporarily without a family, could summon one with a word. If she told John to set a date, he would kiss her and consult his mother for the family calendar. Yes, she did love him. And Marina needed a champion for her education.

"You can read my letters, if I can see your Greek notebook," Lucy said. "I can't imagine why your progress is so slow. You must have started years before me, and I know twice as many words."

"But I know them more intimately."

She did. While Lucy's notebooks was full of vocabulary, categorized by subject (sailing and the ocean, food and the kitchen, weather and the sky), Marina's notebook paid thorough, splendid homage to one word at a time. Each word was afforded a page, printed neatly in a horizontal oval in the center. From there, spokes of text emanated in her tiny, tutor-trained handwriting, laying out how the Greek word had formed words in other languages, whether it had inspired poetry, how it connected to other words. Harbour in Greek was *limáni* and in the various spokes of text read, "Also: port, seaport, dockside, quay. Greek noun. English noun and verb both: harbour a grudge, harbour a grief. Poem about a harbour: "Epipsychidon" by P.B. Shelley. Shelley = English Romantic poet. (Also, Byron, Keats) Epipsychidon – epi = upon, on. Psychidon – a little soul. Upon a little soul. Opening line of "Epipsychidon": "Emily, a ship is floating in the harbour now/a wind is hovering o'er the mountain's brow." (Poem is very long!)"

For the Greek word for "beauty," *kállos*, Marina had written, "Calligraphy = beautiful handwriting. Calliope, the muse of eloquence and epic poetry. Beauty = eloquence. Poem about Calliope: 'To the True Patroness of All Poetry, Calliope' by Francis Beaumont. Beaumont = English Renaissance dramatist. (Student of Ben Jonson.)"

Ben Jonson, who wrote the eulogy preface to Shakespeare's First Folio: "sweet swan of Avon."

Lucy removed the letters from Marina's hands and set them on the table. Then she embraced her. After her initial startle, Marina hugged her in return, pressing her hands a little too ardently on Lucy's slowly healing wound. *Where your wings would be if you were an angel.*

"I'm going to set a date," Lucy told her. "Would your mother agree to some time around Christmas? I'm thinking that's when most of the family will be home. Then you can come can live with us. I'll see to your education. You have an exceptional mind."

"Do you really think so?"

"Yes, duckling. You would have made a very fine Censorette."

PART SIX
ENGLAND

29.

London, 1948

The solicitor was as grim as her father. All of London, it seemed, was grim, despite playing host to the first Olympics since the one in Berlin, in 1936, presided over by Hitler. Rationing was still on. Some houses were piles of rubble in their lots. People were gaunt and weary; their clothes shopworn, their faces lined. Her father had grown grey and was prone to tears: tears when he saw her again for the first time in seven years, tears when Lucy introduced him to John.

And there was this business with the solicitor settling the estate of Judge Barrington-Smith.

"The Judge asked specifically that you administer the distribution of these funds," the solicitor said. "These other girls, you know their whereabouts? They need to sign these forms. Miss Taylor, Miss Lark?"

"Miss Taylor—Mrs. Lincoln—is staying with my grandmother. Dr. Lark lives in New Jersey. Here is her address. We've all stayed in touch."

Nick Lincoln was filming the Olympics for British Pathé. But when the Games ended, he would take Georgie and their children (Lucia now had a younger brother) to Hollywood, where work and food and money was plentiful.

"The Judge said you were very good about keeping in touch. 'Most persistent,' I think, were the words he used."

"I'll take Georgie's papers to her. One thing. About the sum."

His legacy was five thousand pounds. Among them, the former residents of the honeymoon suite agreed that they would each take fifteen hundred pounds. The remaining five hundred pounds would be devoted to something to honour Ruth. Lark had suggested a memorial pew in the church, but Ruth had rarely attended church. Georgie had suggested a donation to the agricultural station that Ruth had so loved, but Ruth had been murdered there, so Lucy vetoed.

Lucy wrote to Clara Frith to ask her advice. Clara told of the expense she faced in leaving the island for her own education at Smith College. Lucy decided to create a scholarship in Ruth's name. The scholarship would go to a Bermudian schoolgirl who was in some way gifted, or perhaps merely resilient in the pursuit of her education. The recipient would be awarded fifty pounds. Louis Furbert would act as steward for the endowment. Clara would administer the application and selection process. All parties agreed to this.

Lucy explained to the solicitor

"I see," said the solicitor with some frost. "You must do as you see fit. However, the Judge did specifically ask that you not attach the name of Ruth Smith to *anything* which might cause people to remember the manner of her death. It was most indecorous."

"Particularly for her." Lucy presented the smile she bestowed on men who tsked at the behaviour of women. They had, she assured the solicitor, no intention of naming the fund after Ruth Smith. They would to call it the Duckling Fund, in the hope that each of its beneficiaries, in the years to come, would blossom into herself.

"As Ruth did," she added.

"Did she?" the solicitor began gathering papers. "I don't recall Judge Barrington-Smith mentioning that he sent her to university. Quite an eccentric notion, educating girls."

Lucy's mother-in-law, Piama, agreed. Piama had argued for a tutor for Marina; well-bred girls did not attend school. Lucy overruled that swiftly: all was fair in love and war. They were at war, and tutors could not be easily secured. (Marina was also unfamiliar with certain commonplace subjects, primarily the sciences, and hopeless at socializing.) Marina's simple school schedule was supplemented with lessons: Latin, Greek (modern and ancient), Italian and French. Lucy and John lavished attention on Marina as parents would on a sickly newborn.

When the war finally ended, Lucy repaid Piama by moving into the Whiting home in Cairo and teaching part-time at a girls' school for the English. She agreed to move to Cairo because of her other failures to the Whiting clan. She had not produced children. She was not skilled at minding her nieces and nephews. She read too much. She read not only novels but newspapers and discussed the news over the dinner table with her father-in-law. She did not embroider well. She did not sew at all. She disliked cards and gossip, and publicly stated that the former was no more than an excuse for the latter. Piama surrendered, and handed Lucy, like a territory, over to Cecil, the *paterfamilias*, who enjoyed using her hostess and language skills for the diplomatic events this new world had produced.

Throughout their marriage, she and John had never had a home of their own. They were unable, as they often joked, even to adopt a cat, let alone raise a child. When in Alexandria, they lived with Aunt Sophia and Marina. When in Cairo, they lived with his parents. Until the war ended, there had been little point in establishing their own household.

The concept of a family survived the length of a childhood. The current of change flowed always within it. Mothers, careworn from children, sighed into death. Bereft fathers grew tyrannical. Sons left home to pursue their destinies. Daughters remained home to endure theirs. Unless daughters were sent away, to spend a war in paradise.

They moved to England. Piama insisted that Marina could not attend Cambridge unless she had family in England. So John and Lucy sought lives there. John applied for and was offered a position at the London Hospital for Tropical Diseases, and Lucy accepted a position teaching French and Italian at her old school.

John and Lucy intended to use part of the money from Ruth's father to furnish a flat, their first private home together, which they would share only with each other, and a tabby kitten christened Horatio II. The first adornment of their home was Ruth's sketch book, which they placed on the mantelpiece above the fireplace, in the small study that Lucy claimed as her own.

THE END

Notes and Acknowledgments

The case of "Brooklyn Joe" and his Nazi spying activities are loosely based on the case of "Joe K" whose invisible inks were detected by Censorette Nadya Gardner, as detailed in William Stephenson's book *A Man Called Intrepid*. This book also includes details of the duties of the Imperial Censorship and the belief, put forth by Dorothy Hyde, wife of H. Montgomery Hyde (of MI6) that "girls with neat ankles" would prove to be the most suitable for the job of a female censor. The Gardner case is also detailed in the article "How Bermuda's 'Censorettes' Made a Nest of Spies Disappear," in the January 2004 issue of "World War II" magazine. The incident with the Vichy diplomat's wife was also inspired by an anecdote from *A Man Called Intrepid*.

Although the Imperial Censorship Detachment worked from the basement of the Princess Hotel, I have taken great liberties with the layout of the hotel (which no longer looks anything like it did in 1941.) I imagine the canteen dances were far less lively than I have made them. The Bermudiana Hotel was destroyed by fire in the late 1950s.

The incident of the official warning the women of the Censorship to be careful of their attire lest they inflame the sensibilities of the local coloured men of Bermuda is taken from an account written by Gwendolyn Peck describing her wartime career, on file at the Department of Documents at the Imperial War Museum.

Other wartime information
For American attitude toward joining the war, I relied on *Selling War: The British Propaganda Campaign against American "Neutrality"* by Nicholas John Cull and *Those Angry Days* by Lynne Olson.

For life in Egypt during the war, I was greatly helped by Artemis Cooper's *Cairo in the War*, Olivia Manning's *The Levant Trilogy*, Freya Stark's *Dust in the Lion's Paw,* Keith Douglas's *Alamein to Zem Zem*, Roald Dahl's *Going Solo* and Penelope Lively's memoir *Dancing Fish and Ammonites* and novel *Moon Tiger.*

Bermuda
In 1942, scale insects, probably imported with the building material used to construct Kindley Field and the U.S. Naval Base, began to destroy 99% of the cedar trees in Bermuda.

Although there were plans to construct a full community around the Kindley Field air base, including officer housing, a school, a hospital, a theater and other buildings, such plans were abandoned when the United States entered World War II.

Despite the "99-year lease" provision of the Destroyers for Bases Act, the Bermudian government took over the operations of Kindley Field in 1995.

The Duke.
The song "Do Nothing Till You Hear From Me" began life as an instrumental designed to show off the talents of trumpet player Cootie Williams. "Concerto for Cootie" was released in 1940. In 1944, Duke Ellington's version of "Do Nothing Till You Hear From Me," with lyrics by Bob Russell, sung by Al Hibbler, reached number 6 on the pop charts. Here, I cheated, and moved its release up two years. I had to; forgive me.

War and Remembrance
I am indebted to generous research assistance provided by James Cheevers of the U.S. Naval Academy Museum, Dr. Jennifer Bryan, Head of Special Collections & Archives/Archivist at the Nimitz Library, Hannah Westall, archivist at Girton College, Ellen Hollis of the Bermuda National Library, Jessie Moniz of the Bermuda *Royal-Gazette*, Michael Brodhead, historian with the U.S. Army Corps of Engineers, and Terry Charman, James Waitrose, Sarah Botstein

and Katherine Phillips of the Imperial War Museum, all of whom provided valuable assistance.

Languages

Lacking Lucy's language skills, I am indebted to Beatrice Beccari for help with the Italian (and for loaning me her name for my Alexandrian grocery store), along with Linda Fridegotto. If I still write *Torta Pasquelina* and not *Pasqualina*, it is my fault and not theirs! Margaret Whitford assisted with the French. I must say *danke* to Angelika Offenwanger for her help with the German and for her careful read. Any errors are, of course, my own.

Beggar that I am, I am even poor in thanks

Never has one owed so much to so many! I must first of all thank Victoria Guest, who invited me to visit her in Bermuda, where I learned about the Censorettes from a one-sentence description in a guidebook. I must thank my always-early reader, Linda East Brady, and my independently hired editors, the endlessly patient and supportive Julie Miesionczek, the endlessly energetic Allison K. Williams, and the may-she-never-end Simha Stubblefield. Thank you, Alexandra Fletcher. To the Vermont College of Fine Arts crowd, both faculty and hangers-out, thank you for keeping me sane (to the extent that I am), especially Lee Martin, Lee Reilly, JoBeth McDaniel, Margaret Whitford, and Tom Whitford for his repeated reads. Thanks to Dave Barnette, Magin LaSov Gregg, Irene Hoge Smith, Debbie Hagan, and Sue William Silverman and of course and foremost, Ellen Lesser.

Thanks to the Ragdale Foundation, for the residency which allowed me to finesse the Alexandria section. Thanks to my sister, Christine Frank, for general things, like teaching me to read in the first place and listening to me throughout the ten years it took to write this book. Thanks to Netta Johnson, Julie Yerex, Lisa Murphy-Lamb and everyone at Stonehouse.